MW01243125

Web of
Deception
A Story of
Betrayal
Book 1

By J.W. Hill

Web of Deception

A Story of Betrayal

Book 1

Copyright 2022

Jeff Hill

Editing by: L. Montgomery

Dedication

I dedicate this book to my parents, the late James and Deloris M. Hill, who gave us the greatest of upbringings. Not only did they give us a life that was full of great memories, they gave us a love that will remain in our hearts for the rest of our lives.

Special Acknowledgement

I want to acknowledge my brilliant wife, 'Chloe' D who not only designed the cover for the book, but played an instrumental role in me writing it.

Originally, "Web of Deception" was a screen play, titled, "A Cousin's Betrayal". It was Chloe's inspiration that pushed me into changing the format from a screenplay into a novel.

I also want to acknowledge my oldest brother, the late Mr. Vance "Gator Mack" Miles, whose adventures in life, inspired me to create this story.

Most importantly, I want to thank God for his strength, and for being the head of my life.

~J.W. Hill

Chapter 1

What started as a bright sunny morning, had suddenly changed into a stormy and windy afternoon. Tropical storm Albert unexpectedly strengthened, and was wreaking havoc up the east coast; bringing seventy mile per hour wind gusts with it. Torrential downpours and high winds were making Drew's drive home a difficult one, but his quest to get there outweighed the risk of becoming another one of the many casualties broadcasted over the radio.

Experts predicted the storm's path would hover along the Carolina coastlines and through Virginia, before veering back into the Atlantic Ocean, once reaching Maryland.

Disregarding the warnings, Drew left the university minutes before the storm began, and unbeknownst to him, he was traveling directly into its path. It didn't matter that a state of emergency had been put in place, Drew needed to get home before four o'clock.

As he inched his way onto the interstate, Drew quickly realized he hadn't been the only driver to disregard the warnings to stay home. Hundreds of vehicles were crammed on the three-lane highway, trying to reach their destinations before the storm hit.

Driving at a snail's pace, Drew found himself trapped, as he made his way south. His goal to get home and attend Gloria's graduation ceremony was in jeopardy, and by the flow of the traffic, he wasn't going to make it home in time. The thought of not being there, left Drew with an uneasy feeling. Over the years, he'd broken many promises to Gloria, and today was looking to be another. If he didn't make it home in time, the chances of her forgiving him was slim to none.

For years, it had been a dream of Gloria to become a nurse, and now that she had, Drew felt it was his responsibility to be present, as a show of support, but the weather was refusing to cooperate with him.

Cautiously weaving back and forth through traffic, Drew managed to maneuver his way through the maze of mangled vehicles that held traffic at bay. Seeing that he was coming upon an exit, Drew made a last-minute decision to take a secondary route; causing him to veer directly in front of frustrated drivers, who sounded their horns to express their displeasure.

Exiting from the interstate, Drew found himself confronted with the same congestion. Infuriated over his decision to exit, Drew violently struck his steering wheel with an open hand.

"Got Dammit," he screamed, after realizing he'd made the mistake of exiting on another congested intersection.

Seeing he had no other option but to make a U-turn and maneuver back to the interstate. Drew again made a sharp U-turn, cutting off oncoming traffic. He wasn't concerned about the obscenities said to him; his goal was to arrive home in time to attend Gloria's graduation.

Making his way back on the interstate, Drew found the flow of traffic had picked up some, but it was evident, he wasn't going to make it home in time. It was only a matter of time before he would have to make the call to Gloria and give her the bad news. Drew cringed at the thought of having to do so, because he knew the consequences that came with it.

Concentrating on the slow-moving traffic, Drew slid his hand across the front seat of his car, to retrieve his phone. It was time to make that dreaded call to Gloria, and though he wasn't looking forward to delivering the bad news, it was something he had to do.

Frankly, Drew had no one to blame but himself. He'd completed his exams two days earlier, but chose to stay and help his friend Ashlynn (Lynn) study for her finals. If he had left earlier that morning, he would've been home in time. But, being the typical friend he was, he chose to wait to learn the outcome of Lynn's last exam. Now, he faced having to deal with his spoiled, loudmouth girlfriend, who was used to getting her way.

Drew knew the consequences of leaving late, but wanted to stay and support Lynn. Their friendship was like a breath of fresh air, and Drew found himself drawn to her. He wanted more than a friendship, but knew they could never be together. It wasn't that Lynn's feelings weren't mutual, it was because they both were still clinging to a relationship that was heading nowhere.

Drew had been with Gloria since the tenth grade of high school, and within the six years of being with her, he'd experienced more drama and heartbreak, than a bad marriage lasting a lifetime.

Drew wanted to believe, he'd had enough of Gloria and her drama, but he couldn't in good consciousness, make a clean break from her. For one, the thought of reneging on his promise was frightening, but perhaps what was most important, was the commitment he'd made. It had only been less than six months ago that he'd given her an engagement ring, and to break it off now would be devastating. But things had changed since making his commitment, he had found Lynn, and by doing so, he placed his engagement to Gloria in jeopardy.

Before calling Gloria, Drew received a call from Lynn, informing him, she and Ashley had made it home safely. It was a relief to know the girls were home and now, it was his turn to do the same. Lynn's voice had given Drew the perk he needed to fight his urges to pull over and wait out the storm.

Now more than ever, Drew knew his feelings for Lynn were more than an infatuation. His only problem was that he wasn't completely certain how Lynn felt about him.

It was hard for Drew to imagine that he would ever have feelings for anyone other than Gloria, but he found himself feeling just that. He would never have thought that by agreeing to help Ashley with Lynn, he would've fallen in love with her. But as strange as it sounded; it happened.

Thinking back, Drew remembered the day Ashley approached him about helping her with Lynn. She was desperate, and was willing to do anything for his help. Being the kind-hearted person he was, Drew was more than eager to do anything to help alleviate Ashley's pain.

Ashlynn, who went by the nickname Lynn, was the identical twin sister of Ashley, and was recovering from emotional distress, after suffering a debilitating breakup with then boyfriend, and PSU basketball great, Marshall Lathan.

This is where Drew came into play. He was handpicked by Ashley, to help reintroduce Lynn back into the college atmosphere. Drew was far from being qualified to oversee Lynn's emotional recovery, and reluctant to help, but eventually agreed to do so. Why? He couldn't say for certain, but perhaps it was the way Ashley boosted his ego, by saying how impressed she was with his mannerism, as well as his treatment of women. She was confident Drew was the ideal person to help Lynn rebuild her self-confidence. However, there was one stipulation, Drew was forbidden to invade upon Lynn's heart. His job was only to befriend her, and help acclimate her back into society; nothing more.

It didn't take long for Drew to learn the real reason Ashley wanted his help, and it had nothing to do with him being the perfect person to help Lynn adjust back into the college life.

Drew learned he was only a pawn delegated by Ashley, after being assigned the responsibilities by her parents.

You see, by chaperoning Lynn, Ashley had more time to spend with her new love interest. Sure, it was an irresponsible act on her behalf, and it left Drew to entertain the idea of opting out of their agreement, but he'd given his word.

Secretly, Drew had a mad crush on Ashley, and believed that by agreeing to help Lynn, Ashley would see him for the man he was, but Ashley had other ideas. She didn't look at him as anything other than a friend.

Drew accepted his role as being Ashley's friend, and went forward with the idea that he could be of help to Lynn. Ironically, after learning that Ashley wasn't interested in him, Drew looked forward to the challenge of helping Lynn. Though his decision was based around his deep-rooted feelings for Ashley, Drew believed he could make a difference in Lynn's life.

Drew remembered how excited he felt, days before meeting Lynn. Ashley had shown him countless pictures of her, and he was more than impressed. If he had to judge who was the most beautiful of the twins, Lynn would have won hands down. She was a natural beauty, with a smile that could warm the earth. She didn't have to wear makeup, or false lashes to enhance her looks; she was perfect.

Although they were identical, Lynn stood out more to him, because she didn't wear makeup, nor did she wear long nails, or dress as sexy as Ashley. Lynn was naturally beautiful, and Drew couldn't wait to meet her.

In the days leading up to their introduction, Drew remembered how excited he'd been; knowing he was about to meet, what he felt could be the key to his future. Sure, he made a verbal agreement with Ashley not to take advantage of Lynn, but after seeing pictures of her, Drew couldn't help but think differently. Whether he acted upon his impulse remained to be seen, but no one could blame him if he acted upon his instincts.

Before Lynn started the fall semester, Ashley forewarned him that Lynn's appearance had changed drastically from the pictures she'd shown him. But for Drew, it seemed hard to believe. No one could have transformed to look differently from their pictures in less than a year; unless they had been in an accident of some kind.

Drew remembered how anxious he was, as he walked down the hallway leading to their dorm room. As he got closer to the door, he could feel his heart pounding on the outside of his shirt; he could barely contain himself once reaching the room. Behind that door, were two of the most beautiful women on campus, and to think he would be escorting one of them throughout the campus, was a boost to his ego.

Drew stood at the door a few seconds before knocking, then waited impatiently for someone to answer. He remembered feeling queasy in his stomach, as the sound of footsteps approached the door. When the door opened, Ashley emerged from behind it. As always, she greeted him with her customary embrace, and closed mouth kiss, before stepping aside to allow him entrance. Ashley was as ravishing as always, and though it was hard to take his eyes off of her, he wasn't there to see her, he was there to meet her twin sister.

Entering, Drew's eyes scanned the room in search of Lynn, but who he saw bore no resemblance to the pictures he'd seen. Standing by the window, and looking down at the incoming freshmen arriving, was a stranger. Drew stood directly across the room from her, and Lynn never knew he was there. Drew was afraid to approach her, fearing that if he had, he would've startled her. Seeing Lynn in her current condition was as if life had passed her by.

Without interrupting, Drew stole an opportunity to get a full view of Lynn. Shockingly, what Ashley had shared with him regarding her appearance was correct. There was no resemblance to her sister, or her pictures. This once beautiful young woman that proudly posed, while wearing the paraphernalia of her favorite professional teams, was a far cry from what he saw before him.

It was shocking to see the condition Lynn was in. Seeing her left Drew with many questions that only Ashley could answer. Lynn's appearance was far worse than he could have ever imagined, and it scared him. Her zombie like state left Drew with a feeling that he was facing a daunting task far beyond his capabilities.

Drew carefully made his way over to where Lynn was standing. Seeing that she hadn't noticed him in the room, he stopped short of entering her personal space. Softly, Drew called out her name, and waited for a response. Lynn slowly turned to acknowledge his presence, and not wanting to frighten her, Drew extended his hand, and introduced himself.

Lynn paused before responding. She looked at Ashley to get her approval, and once getting it, she reached to shake Drew's hand. Fearing his touch, Lynn lightly gripped the tips of his fingers, then giving Drew a smile, she redirected her attention back outside to the window. Turning to Ashley, Drew looked for instructions on what to do next. Having no idea, Ashley shrugged her shoulders. It was up to Drew to improvise, but he was too stunned to do anything. He could only look at Lynn, and how much she'd deteriorated from the pictures he'd seen of her.

Drew returned to where Ashley was standing. He remained quiet, as he tried to figure out what his next course of action was going to be. "Don't be alarmed, it's the medication she takes to suppress her anxiety," Ashley whispered.

For more than five-minutes, Drew watched from afar, without Lynn ever realizing it. Her multi-colored wife beater t-shirt fell far short of her navel, as did her faded grey sweatpants. It was hard not to stare, but Drew couldn't avoid seeing Lynn's striped cotton panties that fell well below her waistline. Exposed was much of her pubic hairline that was in dire need of a manicure. Lynn made no attempt to hide it, nor did she seem embarrassed by it. It was doubtful that she even realized she was exposed to the world, but it was too early to prejudge her. Drew could only speculate that her behavior was due to her breakdown, and as a gentleman, he shouldn't form an early opinion of her.

Their closeness in proximity enabled Drew to see the psychological damage Lynn had suffered. What was left of her hair had been styled in a ponytail, and pulled away from her face to cover the bald areas that were exposed throughout her scalp. Lynn's eyes were deeply rooted within the confines of her skull, and encased with dark circles. It didn't take a professional to diagnose that she'd gone through a horrific ordeal.

Drew left the room that day with many questions and concerns, but ultimately realized that in order to reach Lynn, he first had to build a rapport with her. Luckily for him, they had early classes on Mondays, Wednesdays and Fridays, and he used it to put his charm to the test. Portraying his astuteness, Drew quickly took advantage of his opportunity. He waited promptly by the doors of Patterson Hall each morning to walk Lynn to class. She resisted at first, but was gradually worn down by his persistence.

It had taken weeks to gain Lynn's trust, and because of his efforts, Drew saw a change in her. It was also thanks to Ashley, who provided him with valuable information regarding Lynn's passion for community service. Drew got Lynn involved with the community outreach programs, that he helped implement on campus, and she immediately fell in love with the after-school program that tutored elementary, and high school students in the surrounding community. With Drew's assistance, Lynn went on to create programs of her own that assisted the homeless, as well as low-income families.

Under Drew's leadership, Lynn was coming into her own. Not only was she falling in love with life again, she was falling in love with him. Drew suspected Lynn had developed feelings for him, but couldn't confirm it. He continued with his obligation to help introduce her back into society. Lynn had come a long way, and he wasn't going to risk doing anything that caused a setback in her mental state.

After spending a large amount of time together, Drew found himself developing strong feelings for Lynn. Like Lynn, love had crept up on him, and was showing its nasty little head. Drew knew he had to fight his feelings, regardless of what his heart was telling him. It was his duty to follow the rules of engagement, and refrain himself from touching the forbidden fruit. His friendship with Ashley was at stake, along with Lynn's fragile heart. He couldn't allow his heart to kneel to his feelings, or his promise to Ashley.

Drew's adventures with Lynn not only opened the pathway for them to become closer; it opened the floodgates to their hearts. It had taken weeks, but Drew could finally see the light at the end of the tunnel. Lynn had turned the corner, and she was ready to take the bull by the horns.

Through his efforts to coach her out of her depressed state, something happened between them. Their feelings for each other had transitioned from a friendship, into romance. They were showing all the signs of falling in love, though they both denied it. It wasn't until Ashley's intervention, that the friends were forced to look closely at what had transpired between them. Needless to say, neither of them was prepared to assume the responsibilities of a relationship. For one, they both had feelings in their hearts for their exes, and secondly, they weren't mentally fit to start a romance.

Drew had all intentions of ending his relationship with Gloria, but wasn't motivated to do so. Gloria had been the only girl he'd ever been with, and to start another relationship was a task he wasn't ready for. Yes, he was in love with Lynn, but his insecurities that she was still in love with Marshall kept him from making a decision, he would regret later. But perhaps, what Drew feared most was Ashley.

As promised, Drew had done what was asked of him. He hadn't crossed the line, but his feelings for Lynn were threatening their agreement. In all actuality, what was he to do? Ignore his heart, and pretend nothing was happening between them, or double cross Ashley, after promising to protect Lynn? Drew was undecided, but ultimately felt running from his feelings weren't the answer. He was stuck between a rock and a hard place, and by early March, the hard place, became even harder.

It started the day Lynn suggested they spend the weekend camping. Like Drew, Lynn was an avid outdoorsman, but as one can imagine, Ashley didn't like the idea. Her anger festered for hours, until she was unable to hold it inside anymore. At two o'clock in the morning, she decided to take her anger to Drew's apartment and remind him, face to face of the agreement they'd made.

Ashley's arrival nearly awakened the entire complex, as she erupted; spewing her anger throughout. She screamed at the top of her voice, airing her displeasure of him taking her sister on a weekend getaway. It went against their agreement, and Ashley wanted it cancelled immediately.

Drew tried explaining their weekend getaway was nothing more than two avid outdoorsmen, spending time and enjoying nature, but Ashley wasn't buying it. She believed a weekend trip together, would increase the probability of Lynn falling deeper in love with him.

In her opinion, Lynn was still vulnerable, and the least disruption could send her spiraling into another depression. Lord knows, Lynn couldn't afford another disruption, especially when Ashley's future depended on Lynn's recovery. Again, Ashley reminded Drew of their agreement, and threatened to expose the truth if he chose to go forward with their trip.

"If you don't cancel this trip, I swear to God, I'm going to tell Lynn about our arrangement," Ashley threatened.

She never flinched, while threatening to expose Drew as a fraud. She was serious, and the thought of Ashley spinning the story to suit her wasn't worth the damage it could cause. Though it wasn't the full truth, Drew couldn't risk losing his friendship with Lynn. Before Drew could regain control of the situation, he needed to calm Ashley down, and to his credit, he tried, but there was no calming Ashley; she was hell bent on destroying his weekend retreat with her sister.

It took nearly an hour before Drew could get a word in to explain his reasons for agreeing to his weekend camping trip with Lynn. He insisted that the trip was for no other reason than to teach Lynn how to trust again, and assured Ashley, he had no other ulterior motives towards Lynn. He would never cross the line, when it came to her mental stability.

Surprisingly, Ashley listened to what he had to say, and though she understood what he was attempting to do, she couldn't risk having him spending a night in a tent with her sister. All it would take is one slip up, and Lynn could be destroyed for life.

Ashley couldn't take the chance of allowing Drew to hold her future in his hand. She was aware of Lynn's weakness when it came to love, and most likely, all it would take was a kiss from Drew, and her future would be destroyed. As it turned out, Ashley didn't give a damn about Lynn, she was only protecting her own self-interest. She wanted to become the front runner in position to head their father's company, after he retires.

"What a pretentious little bitch." Drew thought to himself, as he remembered listening to Ashley's explanation. In spite of her threats, Drew became more determined than ever to spend the weekend with Lynn, but the risk of hurting her was leading him to stand down. By no means did Lynn resemble that bitch sister of hers. Instead, she was warm, honest and beautiful in her own right.

Ashley may have won the battle, but the war was still in question. Satisfied, Ashley placed her arms around Drew's neck; pulling him down to her level. She kissed him, as if to say, she approved of his decision, then left; she'd accomplished what she set out to do. Drew was a push over, just as she anticipated, but Lynn wasn't as accommodating. When Ashley arrived back at the dorm, Lynn found out what happened. As anyone could imagine, she wasn't happy with Ashley. Enraged at what Ashley had done, Lynn ignited a fire within herself, that lasted for the remainder of the night. It wasn't until the rising of the morning sun that Ashley relented, and gave in to Lynn's demands. But before doing so, Lynn had to promise not to cross a line that could lead to something she would later regret.

If all it took was to pledge an oath of celibacy in order to go away with Drew for the weekend, then Lynn was all in. It was a promise she was willing to make without reservation. She had no intentions on sleeping with Drew; they were only friends and nothing more. It wasn't that kind of relationship. There was no talk of intimacy, or their feelings for each other. Before their inner feelings could be discussed, or considered, they both had a lot of baggage to unload.

Two days before Drew and Lynn were to leave on their trip, Ashley had one final meeting with Drew. In doing so, she again expressed her concerns, but validated her support. She apologized for the horrible way she treated him, and wanted to do something to make up to for her actions. So, she unexpectedly kissed him. Kissing Drew was nothing out of the ordinary, because they often greeted each other with a closed mouth kiss, but it was the way Ashley kissed him, that left questions. She didn't give him the closed mouth kiss he was accustomed to receiving. For the first time in their friendship, Ashley had given him a kiss of passion.

Drew and Lynn left early Saturday morning for their weekend camping trip together. They were excited about being in the wild, but they were more excited to be sharing a weekend together. It was early Spring, and the freezing temperatures would have deterred anyone else from wanting to go camping, but not Drew and Lynn; they were ready to face the difficulties the changing weather could bring.

Stopping for gas, Lynn took the initiative to purchase a chicken box, and several other items to eat; just in case they didn't catch any fish. Little did she realize how clever it was for her to err on the side of caution. Once arriving at their destination, Drew quickly constructed the tent, and started a fire for the night. He boasted about how he was going to provide them with fish for dinner to go along with their baked beans, but as the evening came to an end, Lynn became the provider; catching the only fish of the day. Lynn had won bragging rights for the day, and to pay homage to the river, she released her fish to live on. Thanks to Lynn's chicken box from the town's local Zip Mart, they had meat to go along with their beans for the night.

After dinner, Drew and Lynn huddled around the warmth of the huge campfire to keep warm. The cold winds were hovering over the riverbank, and it drew the couple closer together. For hours, they shared their hopes and dreams, and for the first time, they mistakenly looked into each other's eyes. It was nearly impossible to resist falling into each other's arms, but they both managed to do so.

It was important for them to learn more about each other before taking the next step in their friendship. They were both holding on to relationships that was at a standstill, and before they could even consider moving forward, they both needed to resolve what they had.

Before calling it a night, Drew shared never before details, regarding his relationship with Gloria. To Lynn's surprise, Drew made the shocking announcement of his desire to end their engagement. Drew admitted that his frustration with hearing the rumors about Gloria's infidelities had boiled over, and he was tired of having to go through the drama. Gloria had admitted to her indiscretions in the past, but assured Drew it would never happen again. But like the liar she was, Gloria continued to deceive Drew time and time again. Lynn felt Drew's pain, and understood why it was so hard for him to break away. Gloria had been his high school sweetheart, and the only girl to have ever pierced his heart. By all accounts, Gloria's dirty deeds had soiled Drew's love for her, and he was taking another step towards kicking her out of his life forever.

In hindsight, Drew was a good man, who didn't deserve to be treated like he was yesterday's trash. He was honorable, and possessed the purest of hearts. Over the many weeks they'd spent together, he'd become more than a friend to her. Drew was the man she had fallen in love with, and it was no question that he deserved better. Drew was her hero, and the man she was hoping that someday would become hers.

Lying comfortably inside the tent together, with their sleeping bags separated inches apart, Lynn was apprehensive about lying so close to Drew. It wasn't that she thought Drew would make a move on her, she feared she would make the move. Lynn was finding it difficult to resist wanting Drew to join her in bed. It wasn't that she wanted to sleep with him; she just wanted to be held by him, and told that everything between them was going to be fine.

Seeing the tension mounting between the two of them, Drew turned on his transistor radio, to set a relaxing mood. His decision helped combat Lynn's anxiety, and to further calm her, Drew opened up about his childhood, and the tough times his family endured, after the death of his father. Hearing him talk about his family's struggles, made Lynn appreciate Drew even more. His story was not only inspirational, it made her admire him even more. They were a family who refused to give up their dream, and did what it took to get there. Drew was the prime example of what she was looking for.

Drew and Lynn returned to campus late the following afternoon, after spending most of the morning hiking the trails of the park. Arriving back at the dormitory, Ashley was sitting in the courtyard waiting for them. The courtyard was a place Ashley never visited, and by the expression on her face, she wasn't happy. Drew didn't have to ask questions as to why Ashley was pissed at him for returning back later than anticipated. He'd promised to have Lynn back earlier, but had reneged. To avoid a confrontation, Lynn retrieved her bags from the backseat of Drew's car, and walked past Ashley without acknowledging her.

Drew sat calmly in his car as Ashley walked towards him. He was surprised at her tranquil approach, but knew she was about to unleash a can of whip-ass on him, the moment she arrived. It was fair to say, Drew was correct with his assumption. Ashley was quick to voice her displeasure of his handling of Lynn. She warned him about the consequences he would face if he crossed the line with Lynn, and if by chance he had, all hell would break loose. She couldn't say for sure if it had been physical or not, but from her observation, Lynn had fallen deeply in love with him.

Ashley reminded Drew of Gloria, and his plans to marry her. How was Lynn going to accept it, now that she was in love with him? Now, more than ever, Ashley believed Drew had screwed up, and so had she, for allowing this to happen.

"Did you sleep with my sister?" Ashley asked, hoping to God, nothing had happened between the two of them.

"No, nothing happened between us. I would never do anything to hurt Lynn," Drew responded.

Relieved nothing had happened, Ashley reiterated Lynn's vulnerability, and feared the damage her weekend getaway with Drew may have caused. As her big sister, Ashley believed, it was her responsibility to protect Lynn, and the only way she knew how, was to forbid Drew from spending further quality time with her. Refraining himself from engaging in a heated discussion with Ashley, Drew chose not to add fuel to the fire; instead, he remained calm. He knew where Ashley was trying to take him, and he wasn't going there with her.

Recognizing that he was becoming agitated, Ashely leaned inside his car and unexpectedly kissed him. Not stopping there, Ashley said the unthinkable by admitting to having strong feelings for him. Stunned by the lengths Ashley was willing to go, to breakup his friendship with Lynn; Drew drove away, without responding.

Chapter: 2

Speed dialing Gloria, Drew prepared himself for the drama that was surely going to unfold. Without a doubt, his tardiness was going to be the source that sparked an explosion within her. His reluctance to call, stemmed around Gloria's history of being verbally, mentally, and sometimes physically abusive when she didn't get her way. Drew listened as her phone rang. He tried thinking of ways to help ease Gloria's anger that was sure to come. One was to offer her an all-expense trip to St. Croix, while another was to purchase the gift of her choice. Either way, it was going to cost him money, but at least he would have a piece of mind.

Drew blamed most of Gloria's behavior on his inability to take a stronger stance against her. Like a fool, he allowed her to dictate their relationship by taking a step back; believing he could better manage her that way. It didn't work, and by doing nothing to slay the monster he'd created; Gloria became unmanageable. Drew's nonchalant attitude, had coaxed her into venturing outside the boundaries of their relationship, and into the arms of several men; yet he did nothing to rectify her indiscretions.

Like a love sick puppy, Drew swallowed his pride, and hid his embarrassment, while pretending that nothing had happened. Pretending meant Drew could accept Gloria back into his life, without losing whatever self-respect he had left. It was all he could do to maintain his sanity, and though Gloria's infidelities led to many breakups between them, Drew's efforts to break free of her web seemed impossible. Perhaps this time, he'd have the power to break free of the hold she had on him, but if he was a betting man, he wouldn't bet the farm on it. It was as if Gloria knew his weakness, and took advantage of it every time he tried breaking away.

Most who knew and loved Drew, couldn't understand his injudicious decisions which allowed Gloria to continue recycling him back into her life. But unbeknownst to them, it was Gloria's magic wand that gave her the upper hand. She knew how to soothe Drew's aching heart, and by doing so, she could guide him into doing whatever she wanted.

Gloria had robbed Drew of his ability to see the world as a normal man, and as a result, Drew unknowingly had relinquished his will to fight against the powers that be. Somewhere along the way, he'd lost his desire to fight Gloria, and her wicked ways. Gloria had the power, and knew how to use it, but as for Drew, he was too gullible to see what was in front of him. Gloria's control of Drew, went far beyond his ability to interpret morality. She'd broken his will to fight, and though he knew it to be true, he couldn't do a thing to fight it.

To Drew's credit, he made many attempts to break free from within the walls of imprisonment that lay between her legs, but like most inexperienced young men, he didn't have the strength to do so. Perhaps it was her fake tears, and promises of faithfulness that kept luring him back into her web of deceit, but if you were to ask Gloria, she would say, it was the way she made love to Drew that kept his mind perplexed. Gloria not only, etched a picture of herself in Drew's head, she did it in his heart.

It was those same influences that clouded his thoughts during his freshman year of college. It nearly caused him to quit school and return home. As a means of control, Gloria threatened to end their relationship if Drew didn't transfer to a community college closer to home. It was a threat Drew gave serious consideration to, before his mother intervened. Nancy saw the hold Gloria had over Drew, and to counter Gloria's move, she threatened to revoke all financial support, as well as his rightful position as President of Hill Crest Farms Cooperation, if Drew quit WFU.

Needless to say, Nancy's threat presented more of a consequence than Gloria's, and although Drew prepared himself for Gloria to leave him, he knew in his heart, he'd made the right decision by staying. Drew realized, his focus should've been on enhancing his education, and once rededicating himself, he obtained his Bachelor's in Business in three years. He was also one of twenty students selected to participate in the University's Accelerated Master's Program, as a result of him rededicating himself to his studies.

Nancy's intervention, not only helped him make the right decision, it prevented him from pissing away what was rightfully his. Gloria wasn't happy with his decision, but she didn't leave him. She did however, make it difficult for him to go about his day without having to think of what she was planning. But as time went on, Drew's love for her lessened, and after he met and developed feelings for Lynn; the hold Gloria once had on him, had finally ended.

Drew waited impatiently for Gloria to answer her phone. He knew she would be disheartened by the news that he was going to miss her graduation, and as a precaution, he fabricated his story; hoping it would gain him the sympathy he needed.

The obvious story was to use the weather as an excuse, but the Gloria he knew wasn't going to accept the weather as a legitimate excuse. Instead, she was going to complain that he should have left earlier; knowing the conditions he was facing. Waiting for Gloria to answer caused Drew's heart rate to increase. The thought of it going to voicemail, left Drew with a feeling of jubilance. By going to voicemail, Drew could leave a message without having to physically talk to Gloria, but that feeling quickly disappeared, once Gloria answered.

Hearing Gloria's voice, Drew found himself struggling to find words to say. He searched to find the words to explain his tardiness because of the backlash that was sure to come. Lying through his teeth, Drew blamed his tardiness on the weather and the traffic accidents. He braced for the onslaught of profanity and derogatory remarks Gloria was sure to make, but instead, he received an uncharacteristic reaction from her. What was more shocking, was Gloria's concern for his safety and wellbeing. The Gloria he knew, wouldn't have given a shit if he had been run over by a freightliner, as long as he was present for her event.

Gloria's sudden change left Drew puzzled, but it was the suggestion she made, that left him more suspicious. She suggested that he not risk driving home for her graduation, but return to his apartment, and get a fresh start the following morning. Drew was talking to a more mature Gloria, a Gloria that thought about his safety over her wants and needs. Her actions not only left him puzzled, but left him questioning himself. Drew asked himself, was Gloria's feelings for his safety legitimate, or bullshit to cover up what she was really up to.

The rumors of her affair with his cousin Mason had spread across town, like a California wildfire. From what he'd gathered, they were as hot as a whore with the clap, but when he confronted Gloria about it, all she would say was that she and Mason were friends, and nothing more. It was her unwillingness to elaborate further on their relationship, that left him to wonder if she was actually being deceptive.

Though Drew had his suspicions, he didn't have the proof. Sure, there were the rumors, but for him, it wasn't enough to convict her of being a cheater. But even if the rumors were true, he had no reason to be totally upset, because he was feeling something special for another woman. Throughout his on again, off again relationship with Gloria, they struggled to stay afloat. The constant interference from Mason had placed their relationship on the verge of a disaster many times before, but so had many other factors.

Desperate to find anything to preserve what was left of their relationship, Drew made the mistake of placing an engagement ring on Gloria's finger. He'd hoped the promise of marriage was enough to hold their relationship together. But as time passed, and his friendship with Lynn transitioned into something special, Drew realized he'd made a mistake. Things had indeed changed between him and Gloria, and had gotten worse. Like him, Gloria had fallen into the arms of another.

The relationship Drew thought would never grow old, had done so, and now that it had, he found himself looking for a way out. To say it was a poor excuse to use Gloria's affiliation with Mason as a means of ending them was indeed proficient, but to use it without having to place blame on himself was genius.

Drew listened, as Gloria revealed her concerns regarding the weather. She presented reasons why he should wait out the storm, instead of trying to drive home. She was quick to say how the storm's damaging winds had knocked over trees and debris; restricting travel. It was great information to know, but Drew didn't believe Gloria's concerns for him had anything to do with his safety. He believed Gloria had plans to spend the evening with Mason, and was using her safety concerns to hide her true intentions, and to prove his theory he was willing to bet his last dollar.

Out of curiosity, Drew inquired about her graduation. Gloria responded by informing him it had been cancelled. She went on to tell him about the damage the storm was causing, as well as the county wide blackout that was surely going to keep the power off for days. Was it possible that Gloria was telling the truth? Drew couldn't say for certain, but until he could reach his mother, or Karyme, who was running the company, to verify it, he had to take her word for it. It was sad that he couldn't take the word of his girlfriend, because of her history of being a liar, as well as a cheater, and most importantly; a manipulative bitch.

Being told about the power failure caused Drew to focus his attention on the company. He instantly began asking questions regarding the damage to the county, and to his relief, Gloria stated the storm hadn't wreaked havoc in Jefferson County as first predicted. Though they were without power, Gloria said there was little to no damage to her parents' house.

Eager to know the state of Hill Crest, Drew needed to call home and speak to Karyme to verify if the company was running accordingly. Uncertain if Karyme was prepared for the storm, Drew ended his conversation with Gloria to call home, but before doing so, Gloria reiterated the importance of him returning back to his apartment, to wait out the storm. Her suggestion was well received by Drew, and as a means to appease her, Drew agreed to return home, and get an early start the following morning.

Needless to say, he was lying, and continued his trip home. Going home had nothing to do with catching Gloria and Mason together, but all to do with his family, and their company. Anxious to know the state of the farm, Drew first called the office, but only got a voice message. Nervous that something was wrong, he continued calling. Still not getting an answer, Drew called home, only to receive the same results. His failed attempts to contact anyone from his family, or Karyme at the office, caused concern. Finally, after a multitude of calls, Drew made contact with Karyme on her cellular phone. He was relieved to learn the plant was spared of serious damage and was running at full capacity. Thank God Karyme followed her instincts and got the generators fueled and tested before the storm hit. Her quick thinking had saved hundreds of gallons of milk stored in the coolers from spoiling.

Karyme was notorious for being proactive, and for Drew to think otherwise was silly. Out of fear, he panicked, and doubted Karyme after knowing her qualifications. He should have known better than to doubt Karyme, and for doing so, he would gladly admit he was wrong. Like Drew, Karyme was introduced to the business as a teen. Under the tutorage of Drew's mother, Karyme quickly excelled. She implemented ways to better manage the company; expanding the brand up and down the east coast.

Karyme Renee' Rios-Gonzales was the biracial daughter of their housekeeper Sophia. It was by accident they came in contact with the Harrison's, and once they did, the Harrison's household changed for the better. Merging as one, the families worked as a team. Nancy worked countless hours at the office, while Sophia maintained a strong home system.

Working as one unit, Nancy built a successful business, while Sophia raised a successful home. Drew and Karyme both received academic scholarships to respectable universities, and finished at the top of their class.

Chapter: 3

After sitting idle for more than an hour, traffic was finally moving again. Drew wanted to believe his decision to continue his drive home had to do with the welfare of his family, but he couldn't deny he wanted to get home to interrupt Gloria's evening with Mason. The interstate was clear of the multitude of accidents that had kept traffic at bay, and Drew was now free to make up for lost time. He could now relax and revisit the state of his love life; a life that could best be described as being a total wreck.

To support his claim, Drew used his engagement to Gloria as an example. His problems began when he selfishly slipped an engagement ring on Gloria's finger. He had no intention of marrying her, especially after suspecting she was involved with Mason. It was embarrassing to have to admit, but he didn't want to let Gloria go, so he decided to fight for her. Gloria seemed happy when he asked her to marry him, but the novelty wore off weeks later, and she went back to her old ways. It didn't take long for the rumors to begin circulating because she was seen coming out of a hotel with Mason. When she was confronted with the allegation, Gloria denied it ever happened. What should've been an excuse for Drew to escape his bad situation, fell by the wayside when he accepted Gloria's excuse pertaining to the rumors.

Drew knew Gloria was lying, but didn't want to admit to himself that she was about to leave him for Mason. It wasn't that he felt Mason was beneath him, he believed Mason wasn't Gloria's type. Gloria was all about living the cushy life, and from a financial aspect, Mason was far from what she was seeking to have. Still, the fact remained, she was sleeping with his cousin, and Drew didn't want to accept it. To say Drew's problems were based on his own mistakes, was an understatement. In reality, losing Gloria wasn't as devastating as one may be inclined to believe. If the truth be told, Drew wasn't in love with Gloria anymore, he only cared about what the town's people thought of him if he lost Gloria to Mason.

Drew was falling for Lynn, and found himself wanting to devote his life to her, but soon found himself facing a more serious problem. Drew found himself facing a sibling rivalry, that was more devastating than anything he could dream of. From his first day meeting Ashley, Drew had a mad crush on her, and to gain her affection, he was willing to do anything to please her. He went as far as taking on the daunting task of reintroducing Lynn back into society, just to please her. But in doing so, he fell in love with her. Now that his friendship with Lynn had evolved into something special, Ashley suddenly had an interest in him. She'd thrown a monkey wrench into the game by confessing her true feelings for him, but it wasn't enough to pull him away; at least that's what he first believed.

For weeks, Ashley played games with him, while trying to seduce him, but he wouldn't fall for her games. She went as far as to threaten him, and after that didn't work, she displayed her ace card. Ashley made her move the weekend their father drove up to pick up Lynn for her appointment with her therapist. Final exams were approaching and he wanted Lynn to have a clear head before they began.

Things changed after Ashley failed to block his weekend trip with Lynn. You would have thought she'd given up, but she did the absolute opposite, and made her move that Friday evening, after their father picked up Lynn for her scheduled session with her therapist the following morning.

The plan was for Lynn to attend her appointment, and afterwards, she and her father would spend the rest of the weekend together. They even made plans to attend a Ravens game Sunday before returning to campus later that evening. Drew wasn't expecting to see Lynn until late Sunday evening, and he decided to use their time apart to study for his upcoming exams. After staying up for most of the night, Drew fell asleep at his desk. At exactly 6am Saturday morning, his phone rang, and everyone knows that good news rarely comes so early in the morning; this morning was no exception. Reaching for his phone, Drew cleared his throat, before answering.

"Hello," Drew said, expecting to hear Lynn's voice.

"Hey, I need you to come over asap." Ashley demanded, before abruptly ending the call.

As always, Ashley was demanding. She was instructing him to come to her room immediately, without giving a valid reason as to why. Tired from studying for most of the night, Drew dragged himself out of bed, and staggered to the shower. He had no idea what Ashley wanted with him, but speculated it had to do with her father's decision to spend the weekend with only Lynn, and not her.

Ashley often complained about their father showing favoritism towards Lynn, and if you didn't know Lynn's situation, you would be inclined to believe Ashley's allegations. However, from what Drew knew about Mr. Boldmont, he was a man of integrity, and though his treatment of Ashley may have been different, he loved both his daughters equally.

Arriving at Patterson's Hall, Drew parked in a rear lot of the building, and made his way through the back-entrance door, that was left propped opened by Ashley. Drew walked up the back stairs to the seventh floor, before walking down the narrow hallway, that led to Ashley's room. He stood outside the door, undecided on whether to knock, or leave. His intuition was warning him that this was a possible trap, but his inquisitive nature dared him to stay. There was something fishy as to why Ashley requested to see him so early in the morning, but Drew brushed it off. He should've tucked his tail and ran as fast as he could, but instead, he stood by the door as if his feet were glued to the floor.

Nervous, and weighing his options, Drew stood as still as a statue with his hand in a knocking position. Realizing what he was about to do, he lowered his hand, and turned to leave, but before he could, the door opened.

"I thought I heard you, come in." Ashley said, inviting Drew inside.

Like always, Ashley greeted him with an embrace, and a closed mouth kiss to his lips. Unsure as to what to do, Drew went against his better judgment, and accepted Ashley's invitation.

"Why couldn't I resist the temptation of entering the wolf den?" Drew thought to himself, as he followed Ashley inside her room. He tried his damnedest, not to stare at Ashley's ass, as he followed her down the foyer, into the common area of their dorm apartment, but his eyes were glued directly at it. Only the Lord knew what Ashley was thinking, but whatever she had on her mind, Drew didn't want any parts of it. Uncomfortable being in the same room with Ashley, Drew sat on the couch, and waited apprehensively to know why she summoned him to her room so early in the morning.

There was a moment of silence before Ashley began talking, and once doing so, she opened up by asking about his intentions with Lynn. Drew wasn't buying into Ashley's concern regarding her sister. He knew her too well to know that she was up to no good.

Drew assured Ashley, she had nothing to worry about. His intentions were honorable, when it came to making her sister his lady. He advised Ashley, he would end his relationship with Gloria, before moving forward with his plans of making Lynn his lady. From his perspective, Drew understood Ashley's interest in his relationship with Lynn, and though her methods were unorthodox; he wasn't alarmed. However, he remained on alert, expecting the unexpected.

There was something peculiar about the way Ashley kept staring at him, with each question asked. In a weird kind of way, her behavior began to freak him out. Ashley was up to something, but what? He didn't know, and he was hoping not to find out. It wasn't until Ashley sat in the chair and faced him that Drew became alarmed. Maybe it was the way Ashley stared at him, or maybe it was the way she twirled her hair with her finger that triggered his radar. Drew's heart began to beat rapidly, as he anticipated the unexpected. He knew he should have followed his mind to leave, but it was too late now, he was trapped in deep shit.

To help ease his thoughts, Drew focused his attention on the reason for being there. He was there to assure Ashley of his devotion towards Lynn. He wanted to make it known, how much Lynn meant to him, and his plans of making her his lady, but Ashley's constant fidgeting wouldn't allow him to concentrate. It was hard not to believe Ashley had deceptive motives, even after knowing how he felt about Lynn, but what else would cause her unusual behavior. Perhaps, she was just toying with his mind to freak him out, but Ashley was doing things that was causing him to lose control.

To make matters worse, Ashley leaned back slightly to cross her legs, but in doing so, she intentionally exposed herself. It wasn't hard to imagine that she wasn't wearing anything under her robe, and the thought of what was under it was enough to send him into a near frenzy. Drew's worse nightmare was about to happen, and he was well-aware of what would happen if he didn't get the hell out of Dodge.

Feeling confident she'd made an impact on Drew, Ashley went forward with her story as to why she invited him to her room. She began by telling him the fabulous job he did with Lynn's recovery. She acknowledged the pressure he must have been under, and how well he responded, but she didn't need his services anymore. It was Ashley's point of view that Lynn was well enough to lead a normal life without having a chaperone to accompany her. Ashley ended their conversation by relieving Drew of his duties. As she put it, the time had come for her to be a responsible big sister. Ashley went on to tell Drew, it was time to put away his project, and enjoy what they both have been wanting.

What Ashley was suggesting was appalling, but then again, he should have expected as much. Ashley hadn't given a shit about Lynn and what she wanted; as always, it was all about her. What kind of man did she think he was? And why would she believe he would even consider her offer. Yes, he was very much attracted to her, but his loyalty belonged to Lynn.

As tempting as she was, Drew wasn't going to tackle that beast. Instead, he wanted to stay on course with the lady he felt more comfortable around, and to stay on course, he decided to get the hell out of that room, before he would live to regret it. Before getting up to leave, Drew found himself in a stare down with Ashley. It was as if she was daring him to make the first move. Drew couldn't imagine sleeping with Lynn's sister, but Ashley was making it difficult for him to walk away. Standing to leave the room, Drew was met with resistance from Ashley.

"Don't leave." Ashley asked, as she gently grabbed hold of Drew's arm, guiding him beside her. She held Drew's hand, placing it across her legs. Drew could feel his heart beating outside of his shirt. He tried to maintain his sanity, but Ashley was making all the right moves. The mere thought of knowing that all he had to do was tug on the belt of Ashley's robe for full access to her, was making it difficult for him to resist.

Drew tried fighting off his urges, because more than anything, he wanted a relationship with Lynn, but the thought of sleeping with Ashley was too tempting to omit. Seeing what was happening, Drew attempted to hide his most embarrassing moment, by positioning his hands across his groin to camouflage his hard-throbbing cock, but his efforts to do so failed. Ashley could easily see the print of his manhood, pressing outward, against his loose-fitting jeans.

"I see you're happy to be sitting beside me." Ashley joked.

Drew was in trouble, and he knew it. It was time to get the hell out of harm's way, before things got out of hand. Standing, Drew made his way to the door. What they both were thinking was wrong, and Drew needed to leave, before any irreputable damage was done. But Ashley continued to make things difficult, by pressing her will against his resistance. She did so, by confessing her undying love for him, and how great things could be for them if he would forget about being with her sister. Though it hadn't been the first time Ashley expressed her feelings, it was the first time she admitted that she wanted to take things further.

To soften Drew's heart even more, Ashley unexpectedly broke down into tears, as she begged for forgiveness for being in love with him. She apologized for making his life complicated, but reiterated how much it hurt, seeing him with her sister.

In a warped kind of way, it was flattering to hear that Ashley was in love with him, but Drew's obligation was to Lynn. Ashley's admission hadn't erased his determination, or his wishes to be faithful to his pending relationship with Lynn.

Morally, leaving was the best thing to do. So, without giving further consideration to what the hell Ashley was talking about, Drew made the conscious decision to leave.

Once reaching the door, Ashley stopped him by blocking his exit. Grabbing hold of Drew's hand, she led him back to the couch, where she forced him to sit.

"Don't leave." Ashley ordered.

She left the room, then returned seconds later carrying Lynn's laptop computer. Sitting next to him, Ashley opened Lynn's computer. Typing in Lynn's password, Ashley opened her e-mails, to show the communications Lynn had with Marshall.

"I know you're very interested in my sister, but before you walk away from the best thing to ever happen to you, you need to read what's been going on with Lynn and Marshall first," Ashley said, as she passed Lynn's laptop to him.

Holding Lynn's computer, Drew began reading the messages. They were e-mails dating back to Lynn's arrival to WFU onto the most recent. Drew paused before beginning to read them. He hated the idea of infringing on Lynn's privacy, but felt a need to understand the magnitude of Lynn's relationship with Marshall.

There wasn't anything significant in the early e-mails that he didn't already know, but as he continued to read, he learned that Lynn was confused about her feelings for Marshall, and was still in love with him as recent as last week. Lynn had mentioned him in one of the e-mails, but stated he was nothing more than a friend, who was helping her adjust on campus.

Before going forward with reading, Drew looked away to hide his embarrassment. It hurt to know that Lynn was still in love with Marshall, and not falling in love with him as he hoped. Now more than ever, he wanted to leave, but before he could get up for the final time, he felt Ashley's hands on his shoulders. Ashley explained how she struggled with her decision to show him the e-mails, but ultimately believed it was the right thing to do.

Lynn's e-mails had brought to light his suspicions, and even though learning the truth was comforting, it hadn't lessened his pain. Drew logged out of Lynn's laptop, and folded it shut. He passed it back to Ashley, to take back to Lynn's room. It was time not only to leave, but to close the chapter on a possible relationship with Lynn. They were friends, and though nothing would ever materialize from it, at least they could remain friends.

Drew embraced Ashley, and thanked her for looking out for his welfare. It had been a long morning, and it was time for him to go, but Ashley wasn't ready for him to leave. To be honest, he didn't want to, but felt it was necessary. Drew gently moved Ashley aside and made his way to the door; only to be stopped again. Turning him around to face her, Ashley buried her face in his chest and squeezed him tightly. He could feel her warm moist lips press against his chest. It was something he hadn't expected, but it felt good to feel wanted. While in his arms, Ashley began kissing and caressing his body; giving him feelings he hadn't felt in months.

What he was allowing to happen was unethical by anyone's standards, but Drew couldn't resist the feeling of wanting to feel wanted. His intention was to hold Ashley long enough to fill his emptiness, but it quickly got out of hand. Dropping his guard, Drew made the vital mistake of looking into Ashley's eyes. Before he realized what was happening, he was kissing her passionately. Sparks quickly ignited, and began burning out of control. Drew had entered a restricted area; an area that came with consequences.

Aware of the repercussions he was sure to face, Drew chose to go forward. He wanted to explore his inner desires deeper, and did so by opening Ashley's robe to see her completely naked. Lifting Ashley in his arms, Drew carried her down the hallway, into one of the two bedrooms to the left of the common area. He wasn't sure who's bedroom he'd entered, and didn't care at the moment. His desire to make love to Ashley, and the thought of doing so, overpowered every thought he had.

Drew placed Ashley gently on her back across the bed. He again, opened Ashley's robe, and watched as she laid stretched across the bed in a supine position. Drew couldn't help but admire Ashley's flawless body before slowly lowering himself over her. Kissing his way slowly down her neck to her breast, Ashley's faint moan gave Drew the confirmation he needed to continue. He didn't want to rush, or become overly excited, so he relaxed, and slowly made his move, kissing and sucking Ashley's firm breasts. Softly applying pressure to them, Drew used his hand to carefully caress his way up Ashley's legs, making his way, between her inner thighs.

Showing no resistance, Ashley slowly spread her legs, giving Drew full access to her. Deeply kissing Ashley, Drew used his fingers to caressed her clitoris. The moistness from her vagina gave him all the indication that she wanted him just as much as he did her, but he wasn't ready to make his move yet.

Her body shivered from the excitement of his touch, as Drew advanced towards her pelvic area. Drew used his tongue to tease Ashley into surrendering, before he started. She spread her legs, nearly pleading for Drew to satisfy her cravings. Drew's lust for Ashley was stronger than anyone ever before, and even though he was in love with Lynn; he was sexually attracted to her.

The thought of betraying Lynn sickened him, yet he couldn't erase the excitement of sharing an intimate moment with Ashley. Drew questioned himself, before going any further. His conscious was telling him to stop before going any further, but he had gone too far to turn back now. He was about to tread in uncharted territory that was sure to end in disaster, but he didn't care. He wanted Ashley, and nothing else mattered.

Ashley was one of the most beautiful women on campus, and though she could have chosen any man she wanted, she chose him. Why? He couldn't say for certain, but if he had to guess, he would argue it had to do with envy towards her sister. Like a deer in headlights, Drew stood admiring the flawlessness of Ashley's body, and the more he stared, the more he wanted her. Drew couldn't believe his luck, he was seconds away from a world of ecstasy and yet, he was afraid to take the final step.

Drew made his way from between Ashley's legs. He hadn't tasted the kitty, but it was not because he didn't want to, but because he was afraid to. He was afraid of what it would do to their relationship, as well as his relationship with her sister. Sure, Lynn may have been in love with Marshall, but Drew felt the tide turning in his favor.

"We can't do this." Drew said, as he raised up to hold Ashley in his arms.

"I know you're into my sister, but I can tell you, choosing to have a relationship with her won't work," Ashley said.

She couldn't give Drew a comprehensive answer as to why, but insisted it had to do with Marshall's treatment of her before their breakup. Ashley confided to Drew the facts regarding Lynn's fears of becoming involved with another man. She teased that Drew wouldn't get to first base with her, and warned that if he tried, Lynn would shut down without giving an explanation. In retrospect, Ashley had been correct because it wasn't that long ago that he attempted to kiss Lynn, only to be turned away. Lynn refused to give him a clear explanation as to why, but from her actions, and e-mails, it was obvious she was still in love with Marshall.

Feeling hopeless that a relationship with Lynn would never be; Drew refocused his attention back to Ashley. He was fixated at the sight of seeing Ashley lying naked in front of him, and though she was candy to his eyes, he struggled to make sense of what he was about to do. He salivated at the thought of making love to her, and weighing his options, Drew was willing, and ready to cross the bridge into fulfillment.

"Are you sure you're ready for this?" Ashley questioned, as she sat up in bed to free herself from her robe.

Seeing Ashley completely naked left Drew visually shaken. Seeing her fully exposed left him in awe; so much so, it made it impossible for him to resist her.

Today, he was yielding to temptation, and even though the waters were filled with boulders, Drew was diving in head first. He didn't care about the red flags, or the consequences that came with making love to Ashley. Drew wanted her, and nothing was going to stop him from having her. Only God could save him now, but to be honest; Drew didn't want to be saved. He wanted Ashley and he was going to have her.

This wasn't the way it was supposed to be. Drew wasn't supposed to allow his lust for Ashley to overshadow the love he felt for Lynn. What he was doing was wrong, but Drew couldn't help himself. The burning desire to make love to Ashley had overpowered his morals and values. He was in a face-off with his inner demons, and it was a fight he couldn't win.

As Ashley made her move, Drew could feel the perspiration run rapidly from his forehead to the pillow he was lying on. They were seconds away from ecstasy, yet he was despondent at what was about to happen. It didn't take being a rocket scientist to know that it wasn't ethical to sleep with the sister of the woman you were interested in, but what was the meaning of ethical, when you are about to live the fantasy you've dreamed of for months.

Drew raised his arms, allowing Ashley to rip the shirt from his body. Ashley was on a mission to get the man she wanted, and she wasn't stopping until she got him. Drew melted from her touch, as she kissed his neck. She rubbed her hands across his chest, and made her way down to his waist, until she reached his waist. There, she unbuttoned his jeans, pulling them to his knees.

Drew was putty in her hands, and she was molding him the way she wanted to. Ashley meticulously used her tongue to stimulate Drew's nipples, as she kissed her way down to his waist. Once there, she violently pulled his boxer briefs to meet where his jeans were.

Ashley was startled to see Drew's erected penis. It was far larger than what she was accustomed to seeing, and the sight of it intrigued her.

Using her hands, Ashley gripped the shaft of Drew's penis and placed it in her mouth. Drew released a sigh of relief, as Ashley began working her magic. Drew's heart rate increased, far beyond that of a man experiencing a heart attack.

"God help me," Drew said to himself, as he pleaded for the strength to hold on to his sanity.

He was helpless, and his mind was too cloudy, to think clearly. He wanted to push Ashley away, but couldn't. In more ways than one, Drew was where he wanted to be, and he could hardly wait for what was to follow.

Whether Ashley was his destiny, remained to be seen, but for the moment, he was living out his fantasy. For a split second, Drew encountered thoughts and visions of Lynn, but those visions quickly dissipated once Ashley unexpectedly engulfed half of his penis down her throat. Her technique caused Drew's toes to lock; leaving him to fight to control his emotions. Ashley had Drew wanting to scream her name, but instead of doing so, he bit down of his hand to prevent screaming out. Ashley's performance had him too weak to open his eyes, and as his body lay helpless in a state of confusion, he could only think of how skilled Ashley was.

The first thought that came to Drew's mind was Gloria. For years he believed no one could measure anywhere near what Gloria was capable of doing, but how wrong he was. Gloria was an amateur compared to Ashley. Not only was Ashley gorgeous, she had skills.

Eager to reciprocate, Drew turned Ashley onto her back. It was time she felt the pleasure she'd given him, and he didn't disappoint. Squirming from the gyration of Drew's tongue, Ashley's low moans emerged into episodes of ecstasy that could be heard throughout the floor. Her chants, forbidding him not to stop, gave indication she was nearing an orgasm. Not wanting to disappoint, Drew obliged Ashley's wishes, and allowed her to experience the outer body experience she was seeking.

For a second, Ashley's body went limp. She reached for Drew; pulling him up to kiss him, and to thank him for taking her to the land of enchantment. By doing all the right things, Drew had guaranteed himself an invitation to enter where only a few select men had gone before him. While advancing towards his prize, Drew's progress was rudely interrupted by Ashley, who fought for the right to regain the advantage she once had. She did so, by rotating her hips, and turning Drew onto his back.

Straddling Drew, Ashley positioned herself to give him the ride of his life, but before doing so, she removed the pins from her hair, and allowed it to fall freely. Things began to happen in slow motion after that. With her hair covering his face, Ashley leaned forward to kiss him. In doing so, she placed her hand behind his head, and guided his mouth to her breast.

Believing the time had come to take their final step, Ashley raised her body to allow Drew to insert his penis inside of her. At the point of entry, they both released a sigh of relief, as they took a moment to enjoy the pleasures they were providing for each other.

Drew placed his hands on Ashley's hips, and slowly penetrated her, intensifying her pleasure, even more. Once comfortable, Ashley began encouraging Drew to thrust deeper inside of her. Drew hesitated at Ashley's request, but eventually chose to oblige her wishes. Ashley was already screaming at the top of her voice. The likelihood of them being heard throughout the hallway was very high.

It didn't take long for Ashley to reach her second orgasm, and when she did, all hell broke loose. Ashley's screams intensified, as she grinded faster and harder. The perspiration from her face covered Drew, as she rode him. Their lovemaking became so intense, it could easily have been mistaken that Ashley was being attacked. The noise Ashley made, was enough to cause Drew to bring their morning lovemaking session to a sudden halt. Drew couldn't afford to get caught in Ashley's room. Most of the girls on the floor knew Lynn was away for the weekend, and to be seen in Ashley's room after hearing what was happening would be devastating if Lynn ever found out. Ashley rolled from on top of Drew and onto her back in the bed. Drew had given her the fuck of a lifetime, and she was in dire need of a break.

"Oh my God, you were amazing." Ashley said, as she attempted to catch her breath.

Staring at the ceiling, Drew wondered if he had done the right thing by sleeping with Ashley. He should've talked to Lynn before jumping in to bed with her sister, but it was too late, he'd crossed the line. Sitting up in bed, thinking their morning had come to an end, Drew reached for his underwear to get dressed, only to have Ashley bear hug him from his rear.

"Where do you think you're going?" Ashley asked.

"It's getting late, everybody is waking up for the day." Drew replied, hoping it was enough for Ashley to scrub any plans she may have had for him.

Ashley wasted no time pulling Drew back in bed. She had recovered, and was ready for another round of lovemaking, and it didn't take much to change Drew's mind. Just as she had done earlier, Ashley's screams were heard throughout the hallway of the seventh floor. She was like a ball of fire, and wanted to be made love to rough; pleading for Drew to do so. Anxious to change positions, Ashley got into the doggy position and demanded that Drew pull her hair, while maximizing every inch of his penis inside of her.

"Awe baby, give it to me just like that." Ashley screamed out, as she felt another orgasm on the horizon.

She wanted Drew to know how fulfilled she was by his effort to please her. Falling face first on her pillow, Ashley screamed into it, to muff the sounds from her orgasm. Her body shook, as she reached the pinnacle of her expectation. It was now time for Drew to complete his mission. His desire to have Ashley burned inside of him, like a raging fire, and in an effort to release her inner feelings, Drew longed for Ashley to stare into his eyes, as he made love to her the way he wanted to.

Enjoying the pleasure Drew was giving her, Ashley began sucking on neck, like a blood thirsty vampire. She implanted her nails deeper into Drew's back, with each thrust of his penis inside of her. Drew grimaced from the pain, but welcomed the pleasure of being inside of her. He could feel himself building, for an all-out explosion with each thrust he generated. The pressure was becoming unbearable, and Drew knew he couldn't control it anymore. He had met his goal by giving Ashley, several orgasms, and now, it was his turn.

This morning had been a morning neither of them would ever forget, but like the old saying goes; all good things must come to an end. Giving Ashley the green light that he was about to bring it home, Drew began penetrating deeper inside of her. The sheer pleasure of knowing what was about to happen was becoming overwhelming. Turning the corner for home, Drew sprinted towards the finish line, in a blaze of glory. His actions were a sure sign of what was about to happen. But unfortunately for him, he wasn't ready for the bomb Ashley was about to drop on him.

Without notice, Ashley blindsided him; reneging on her promise to allow him to reach his pinnacle. Demanding that he stop, Ashley pushed Drew, from on top of her.

"Stop, this isn't right, I can't do this to my sister." Ashley said, turning her back on Drew.

Just like that, it was over. It took a few seconds for it to sink in, but it was now making sense. Ashley had set him up, and most likely, she was going to hold what happened between them over his head.

Drew's theory was proven correct, as Ashley preceded to say how disgusted she was with him for sleeping with her while pursuing a relationship with Lynn. She demanded that he sever all ties with Lynn, or she would reveal their affair. Never in his wildest dreams did Drew ever believe Ashley would have stooped so low to break them up, but she did just that.

It was hard to believe how things quickly plummeted after going so well. Ashley had capitalized on his infatuation of her, and used it to her advantage. She was now threatening to destroy his relationship with her sister, a relationship he wanted more than anything. How could he have been so stupid to fall in her trap? She'd played him like a fiddle, and for his mistake, he was going to have to pay the piper.

Fastening the button to his denims, Drew searched for his t-shirt; only to find it thrown across the room; ripped into pieces in their moment of passion. After dressing, Drew slipped his feet into his shoes, and made his way to the door. Once at the door, he opened it to survey the hallway for the presence of anyone. After finding the hallway empty, Drew began making his way out the room, but before leaving, Ashley left him with a parting request.

"Hey Drew, once you end this charade with my sister, we'll finish what we started."

Too stunned to respond, Drew stood dumbfounded. Only seconds ago, Ashley threatened to reveal their affair, now she wanted them to finish what they started, but at the expense of her sister. Ashley made no secret about how she felt about his relationship with Lynn. She hated the idea, and was willing to do what it took to break them up. But for Drew, Lynn's happiness meant everything to him. Sadly, she was going to be hurt either way; there wasn't a damn thing he could do about it. He'd done the one thing he promised himself he would never do; he deceived the woman he was in love with.

Making this mistake would most likely cause a setback in Lynn's recovery, and he only had himself to blame if it did. Although Drew hadn't been a lone participant, he assumed responsibility for his actions, and was adamant about accepting the consequences if Lynn ever learned what he'd done. As a man, he was going to accept whatever fate he was given. He made an unpopular decision by being unfaithful to the woman he loved, and by doing so; he was inclined to make things right.

With his head hung in shame, Drew turned to exit the room. Once again, Ashley volunteered additional news involving Lynn. Again, she warned him of Lynn's lack luster approach when it came to sleeping with any man other than Marshall. She laughed, as she urged him to do what was right. Her smirk nearly triggered Drew to say what he was thinking, but instead of making a scene, he quietly left the room. It was clear as to what she was insinuating, and it caused him to rethink his position. If he was to continue his relationship with Lynn, he had to get his house in order.

Closing the door behind him, Drew made his way down the long hallway; exiting the floor by the stairway. He'd left without being detected, and couldn't have been more relieved. It was over, he had escaped the lion's den, and was about to return home safely. Drew's drive home seemed longer than usual, but it gave him the opportunity to reflect upon his mistakes. The guilt he was feeling had returned with a vengeance. It was a repulsive feeling to relive what he had done, but he knew, in order to reverse what was wrong, he first had to change his mindset.

Drew made a vow, never to allow himself to go against his morals and values again, but most importantly, he vowed to concentrate harder on his relationship with Lynn.

Chapter 4

After being on the road for more than six hours, Drew was less than eight miles from home. Reminiscing about his past had made his trip seem shorter, but more importantly, it gave him time to reflect upon the path he wanted to take. Both Lynn and Gloria had played important roles in his life, and the thought of breaking either one of their hearts haunted him. But he had to make a decision before returning to WFU for the first summer session, and sadly, he had only two weeks to do so.

Since middle school, Gloria had been his girl, and for years they always believed they would someday be married, but like most high school relationships, it often ends in disappointment. The time Drew spent away from home made him realize that his relationship with Gloria had run its course, but letting go had become difficult. Drew wanted more than anything to go on with his life without Gloria, but he'd made a promise to marry her, and to give her the life she deserved.

Having an affair with Mason should have disqualified Gloria from the life he'd promised to give her, but Drew found it difficult to release the hold Gloria had on his heart. It was hard to explain, because he strongly believed he was in love with Lynn, and though his feelings were strong for Lynn, they hadn't been strong enough to make a clean break from Gloria. The thought of Gloria meaning more to him than first anticipated scared Drew. He was planning to end his relationship with her on his short break home, before leaving back for school in two-weeks. Whether he had the balls to stand up to Gloria and tell her how he felt remained to be seen, but if he was going to pave a future with Lynn, he had to do the unthinkable, which meant ending his engagement with Gloria.

Finally, after what seemed like the drive of a lifetime, Drew could finally relax; he was home. It had been a long, tense trip, one which he wouldn't soon forget, but it gave him the opportunity to review his life, and what he needed to do to change it for the better. The rain was still falling, but not at the blinding rate it once had. Even the winds had calmed down, but the havoc it left kept Drew on alert.

Several tree limbs had fallen across the highway; forcing Drew to maneuver around them. Drew arrived at his driveway, only to be faced with another problem. A large tree limb had fallen across the driveway. When he attempted to maneuver his way around it, he got stuck in the ditch. Damn, he was going to have to foot it the remaining way home.

It wasn't like his house was fifty yards away, he had at least a quarter mile to walk before reaching his house. Putting on his hat and jacket, he had in the back seat of his car, Drew cringed from the roar of the thunder, as he got out to walk the remaining way home. He ducked from the streaks of lightning that stretched across the night skies, while tackling the onslaught of mother nature. Lightning continued to stretch across the sky; giving Drew the light he needed to see, but the rain was cold and hard; pounding Drew's body savagely, as he walked home.

Once arriving home, Drew found himself soaked from head to toe. He entered the house, and was greeted by burning candles that led into the family room. He heard the soft voice of his mother calling to verify if it was him, and was relieved after learning he had made it home.

Hanging his wet jacket and ball cap on the coat rack, Drew followed the candlelight down the foyer into the family room, where his mother and sister were awaiting his arrival. He saw the relief in his mother's face, as she praised God for guiding him home safely. It had only been minutes earlier, that Nancy had arrived from City Hall. She had stayed until the county report was submitted, and by the grace of God, no county resident was injured or killed during the storm.

Chapter 5

Standing at his window, Mason looked out into the darkness. His thoughts were of his mother, who bravely faced the storm to travel to work. Dolly Mae was the owner of four assisted living facilities that specialized in caring for the elderly. Although considered a retirement retreat, it could also be compared to a rehabilitation center. Unfortunately for Dolly Mae, two members of her team failed to report for duty; forcing her to have to cover in their absence. She'd gone to work against Mason's advice; leaving him to worry if she had arrived safely. Before leaving, Dolly Mae promised him she would call once she arrived, but hadn't done so as of yet. It had been more than an hour since she'd left the house, and by Mason's estimation, she should've reached her destination thirty minutes ago.

As Mason waited nervously, he felt the comfort of Gloria's arms wrap around his waist. Though it wasn't enough to help ease his worries, it served as a consolation. Gloria placed her lips firmly against the back of his neck and began kissing it before whispering in his ear.

"Penny for your thoughts?" Gloria whispered, while rubbing his chest.

Mason smiled, but didn't respond right away. He wanted to say the right thing, but chose to say what was on his mind.

"When are you planning to tell Drew about us?" Mason asked.

In a calm and confident manner, Gloria responded by promising she would talk to Drew before the weekend was completed. She was aware that Drew would be home for two weeks, and was hoping to talk to him about it sooner than later. Fearing the worse, Mason asked if she'd had a change of heart. He had a right to feel this way, because Drew had given Gloria a ring; a ring which she was still in possession of, and even wore on occasion. Gloria assured him, the moment she got the chance, her plans were to return Drew's ring, and end their engagement. Gloria went on to explain that she needed more time before she could completely sever ties. It was a decision Mason was totally against, but nonetheless; he agreed.

It was no denying that Gloria was lying through her teeth, but it was all she could do to keep Drew in her life a little longer. By prematurely ending their relationship, Gloria would forfeit her graduation gift; something she wasn't willing to do. She was sure Drew was going to give her something special, and to piss it away by ending their relationship would be foolish. Gloria wanted to receive her present before she split with Drew, and believed Mason owed her that much, and why not? Chances were, he hadn't brought her jack shit for graduation, nor had he any intentions of doing so. If she had to guess, Mason's idea of a graduation gift was taking her out to dinner at some cheap restaurant, followed by a night's stay at a local Super 8 motel. Some would argue that Mason had done enough by paying her tuition for the final two years of her college, but Gloria didn't see it that way.

You see, Gloria believed it was Mason's responsibility to take care of her. After all, she was furnishing the goods he so desperately wanted. What was so funny about Mason was the poor bastard had never been with a real woman before. His idea of wining and dining her was eating at an all you can eat restaurant, followed by a short stay of fucking at some rinky dink motel, before falling asleep.

Maybe, that's what attracted her to him. He was green, and could be easily misguided into doing anything she wanted. Mason was more than someone she could boss around, or mold into the fool she wanted him to be. He made her laugh, but most importantly, he was there when she needed him most. Listening to the smooth silky sounds of Angela Bofill playing in the background, Gloria began singing into Mason's ear, as he closed his eyes to imagine what it would be like to have a future together. Gloria was everything he'd ever wanted, but waiting patiently for her to live up to her promise was becoming more than a virtue. More than anything, Mason wanted to make it official, and inform the world of their affair, but in his opinion; Gloria was stalling. It was as if she wanted to protect Drew's feelings from the humiliation he was sure to experience. By Gloria's own admission, she was searching for the right way to tell Drew.

Perhaps it was a bullshit reason to hold on to Drew, but Mason had no other choice but to wait for Gloria to do the right thing. He wanted a future with her, and to do so out right, he needed to have a little more patience. Gloria often accused him of wanting to rub salt in Drew's wounds, and in a lot of ways, she was correct. He wanted Drew to suffer the same pain and humiliation he felt after Gloria was stolen from him. Drew knew about his feelings for Gloria, and like the little bitch he was, he turned Benedict Arnold, and stabbed him in his back. Now it was his turn to get even, and he was going to get his get back on that crooked motherfucker if it killed him.

It wasn't hard to articulate Mason's hatred towards Drew. It's fair to say, it went deeper than stealing Gloria from him. Mason's jealousy surrounded the Harrison family's stature, and what they'd created over the years. He didn't understand the hard work, and sacrifices the Harrison family made to get where they were. In his mind, he believed Drew's success had come from his late father, but Mason's beliefs were far from the truth.

To tease Mason, Gloria began gently sucking on his lower ear lobe, as she sang softly into his ear. Her actions were causing his hormones to run rapidly; overshadowing the dark cloud of not hearing from his mother. Turning to face Gloria, Mason held her tightly in his arms. He stared directly into her eyes to show how much he loved her; ready to commit his heart with promises of a forever love. Kissing Gloria passionately, he began to unbutton her blouse. Gloria excited him unlike any woman before, and he wanted her permanently in his life. To have that, Mason needed to convince Gloria, not to have any doubts about his love for her. She needed to know; he was willing to do anything for her to make her his. Gloria had played a vital role in his life, and since being with her, he'd changed from being a thoughtless, and unsympathetic person, into a more sincere man, who was willing to assume responsibilities for his shortcomings. Thanks to Gloria, Mason had the love he was searching for. But until Gloria could sever ties with Drew, he couldn't have the security their relationship needed.

With Gloria's arms wrapped around him, while singing in his ear, Mason felt her hand slide down the front of his pants. Grabbing hold of Mason's penis, Gloria slowly began stroking it, intensifying Mason's desire to make love to her.

Turning to face her, Mason unbuttoned Gloria's shorts and began using his finger to explore inside of her panties. The feeling of having Mason's fingers inside of her was overwhelming, causing Gloria's head to collapse on Mason shoulder. Gloria felt herself wanting Mason, but now wasn't the time to give in. Before doing so, she had to be sure Drew wasn't coming home. If her calculations were right, Drew should have been back at his apartment by now, but for some odd reason, he hadn't called her. Gloria was on fire, and she wanted Mason to extinguish the flame, but until she was absolutely sure, nothing was going to jump off. Unable to take the pressure any longer, Gloria pushed Mason away. She buttoned her shorts, as she made her way to sit on the couch and take out her phone.

Mason was astounded at what Gloria was about to do, and had thoughts of stopping her, but opted not to. Frustrated, he made his way over to the makeshift pallet that was spread across the floor, and laid on the floor. Staring into the ceiling, he tried to decide how he was going to handle his relationship with Gloria. It was obvious she was still hung up on Drew, and calling him verified it.

Mason listened as Gloria called and talked to Drew. It was tough having to hear her tell Drew how worried she was about him, as well as how relieved she was to know that he had made it back to his apartment safely. What was most disturbing to Mason, was to hear Gloria tell Drew how she was looking forward to spending time with him, when he came home. It was chilling to think of what could happen once the two of them were alone together. It wasn't that he didn't trust Gloria, but Mason knew the influence Drew had over her, and the likelihood of Drew convincing her to stay with him. He had agreed to give Gloria the time she wanted to break things off with Drew, but now, he wasn't so sure it was a good idea.

Mason waited until Gloria finished her conversation with Drew before voicing his concerns. He should have kicked himself for allowing her to carry on a conversation with her ex-boyfriend in his presence, but it was too late to do anything about it now. To save face, Mason shared his feelings with Gloria regarding her disrespect towards him; warning her not to make it a habit.

"You got some nerve, calling another motherfucker, while you with me." Mason stated.

There was anger in his voice; Gloria heard it loud and clear. She was well aware of Mason's temper, and didn't want to be a victim of his wrath.

"I wanted to be sure Drew was staying at his apartment tonight." Gloria responded. "I didn't mean no disrespect."

"Why was it so important to know if Drew was staying in Maryland tonight?" Mason asked.

"Because I didn't want us to be disturbed." Gloria answered.

"Meaning what?" Mason asked.

"Meaning, I'm spending the night with you." Gloria responded.

Gloria joined Mason on the pallet, and greeted him with a kiss; hoping it was enough to forgive her. Mason wished he was in a better situation, but felt lucky just to be lying next to Gloria. Soon things were going to be different; once Gloria broke things off with Drew. But for now, he had to maintain his patience. Turning Gloria on her back, Mason was amazed how her yellow complexion reflected from the light of the burning candles. The sight of seeing Gloria glow captivated Mason. It helped ease the tension that was built up inside of him.

"You enjoy messing with me, don't you?" Mason asked.

"Of course not, I love you." Gloria responded.

Gloria's decision to refrain from intimacy had Mason's body in an uproar. It was confusing that she'd confessed to have been intimate with Drew many times, but for some unknown reasons, she felt the need to rob him of the pleasures she was capable of giving him. Though there were many rumors of her being seen coming out of the motel with Mason, none of them were true. Yes, she'd slept with several interns at the hospital while she was a nursing student, but she hadn't done so with Mason. She promised Drew she would never sleep with anyone else if he gave her another chance, and after receiving that chance, she'd kept that promise. But the winds were blowing in another direction, and Gloria was ending her engagement with Drew, which meant she was free to do whatever she wanted.

Gloria was about to tread on shallow waters by giving in to Mason's wishes and sleep with him. To make things more compelling, Gloria chose to share her past sexual encounters with Drew. It was hard to imagine Mason being interested in hearing about Gloria's sexual encounters with his cousin, but his curiosity peeked after he was informed that Gloria and Drew had always used a condom when being intimate.

Gloria confessed, that she wanted him to be the first to make love to her without using a condom. Just the thought alone, nearly sent Mason into a frenzy. From Mason's perspective, Gloria was still a virgin because Drew hadn't officially per say, made her a woman.

God knows Gloria was lying her ass off, and Mason fell for it, hook, line and sinker. Hearing how he would be the first to raw dog Gloria was like music to his ears. Somehow Gloria had amazingly, tricked him into believing her bullshit, but it didn't stop there. Gloria also said she'd never traveled south on Drew, but admitted, she wanted him to be her first. Gloria's confession left Mason speechless. His eyes grew hungry for her even more. He was going to be her first in all aspects of making love. Overwhelmed at what Gloria had told him, Mason needed clarification as to what Gloria was communicating to him.

"So, you're telling me, you've never polished old boy's knob?" Mason questioned, to clear up any misconception.

"No, never." Gloria responded.

"And he never raw dogged you?" Mason asked.

"Never." Gloria again responded.

Mason couldn't believe his good fortune. It was rare to find a virgin mouth, and if you were lucky to do so, she was a sure keeper. "Hot damn;" Mason said to himself, after realizing the gem he had. Gloria was damn near perfect, and he was going to be the first to spoil her. The idea of him being Gloria's first was causing Mason to consider pressing his luck. He was circling Gloria like a hungry lion, and with Drew returning home for a two week stay, he had only hours to make his move. Knowing all of Gloria's hot spots, Mason capitalized on his opportunity by kissing Gloria, while lowering her to the floor without resistance. He began kissing her neck, before unbuttoning the remaining buttons to her blouse. Removing her bra, Mason kissed his way to her breast. His hands shook from nervousness as he struggled to maintain his sanity. He'd slept with many women before, but none that measured up to the caliber of Gloria. She was perfect, his dream girl, and the woman he wanted to spend the rest of his life with.

Mason fumbled over himself before getting his act together. With Gloria's bra removed, he could now focus his attention on removing the booty shorts she was wearing. In a surprise move, Gloria raised her body, and allowed Mason to freely remove her shorts.

Gloria followed, by rolling onto her stomach; giving Mason a full view of how perfectly rounded her ass was. The sight of it, caused Mason to salivate at what he was in for. He watched in disbelief, as Gloria arched her ass to give him a better view of what he was about to have. Mason lightly caressed Gloria's body with his lips, as he spread his body across Gloria's and began kissing his way down her back. Mason's actions alone, was enough to persuade Gloria to raise her body and allow him to remove her panties, but Mason was determined to take his time. He carefully turned Gloria over onto her back, and preceded with his pursuit to make love to her.

Skillfully, he slithered his tongue and the movement of his tongue sent shock waves through Gloria's body; leaving her to squirm from the pleasure he was giving her. Although her intentions weren't to become intimate, Gloria found herself wanting more. To further enhance sensitivity, Mason used his tongue to caress the outside of Gloria's silk panties gently touching the outer layers of her vagina. Mason had Gloria exactly where he wanted her to be, he was seconds away from heaven, and though he tried to maintain a clear mind, the thought of making love to Gloria was driving him mad. Inches in front of him was perhaps, the most beautiful, and neatly shaven vagina he'd ever seen. It was perfect, and it was about to be his.

Without blowing his top, Mason returned to what had been working for him, and resumed his plan, by kissing Gloria from her feet to her inner thighs. His methods were relaxing, and it prompted Gloria's legs to widen; giving him the greenlight to continue without interruption. For his patience, Mason was about to be rewarded, and he could hardly contain himself.

Lying helpless on her back, with her eyes tightly closed, Gloria was enjoying the moment. Although they weren't in the king-sized bed located on the twenty-first floor of some expensive penthouse overlooking the city, she welcomed the pleasure being given to her. She was with the man she wanted to be with, and he was providing her with all the love and romance she needed. It was time to do what was most important for her man, and that was to satisfy him fully. Mason had earned the right to be with her. He'd covered her tuition during the last two years of her college education, without expecting anything in return. Within those years, he had become her protector, as well as her provider. Mason had been there for her financially, and thanks to him, she earned her degree. He stepped up to the plate when Drew refused to do so. So just maybe, it was time for her to leave Drew in her rear-view mirror.

Gloria remembered going to Drew for help after her father lost his job at the mill. She understood Drew wasn't in a position to support her financially, but his mother had the means to do so.

All she requested, was that he speak to Nancy on her behalf, and the cowardly little bastard refused. His excuse was that his mother was supporting Karyme, and couldn't afford to take on another responsibility. It was all bullshit, because Karyme had gotten a full scholarship from the UVA. The most that little burrito eating wetback would have needed, was gas money for the car Nancy bought her for her graduation.

What mostly pissed her off, was the fact that she was supposed to have been Drew's girl, and for him to refuse to talk to his mother about securing a simple loan on her behalf, was the straw that broke the camel's back. It was the moment she decided to open the door and allow Mason into her life. She'd been with the wrong man, and making a change became her mission. It was no secret that Mason had a crush on her. He'd been in love with her since their early teen years, and though she knew it, she never found him attractive in any way. But somehow, fate had put them together.

Using his fingers to massage Gloria's clitoris, Mason delicately inserted his index inside of Gloria's vagina; using his finger to symbolize his penis. His methods excited Gloria, and her body reacted to his movements naturally. The nervousness she believed would happen wasn't there; she was ready for whatever he wanted. It wasn't until Mason made his move to please Gloria further, that she began having second thoughts. Maybe the way Mason was licking the kitty, reminded her of what she was about to give up. By no means could Mason's performance be summed up as being horrible, but it reminded Gloria of what she had to lose. If she chose to go all the way with Mason, things would change dramatically for her. For one, she wouldn't be able to hide her affair anymore, and she would lose Drew forever. Her previous affairs were different because Drew had forgiven her, with a promise not to betray him anymore. But if she chose to go all the way with Mason, she was walking away from Drew for good.

It was true that Drew had been a total dick to her by not lifting a finger to help her with her tuition, but he was the only person capable of giving her the lifestyle she wanted to have. Sleeping with Mason meant losing the opportunity of a lifetime, and she wasn't sure if she wanted to risk it. Time was running out, and Gloria was faced with the decision to satisfy her new man, or risk losing him by being faithful to her soon to be ex-boyfriend. It should have been an easy decision to make, but needless to say, it wasn't, and after serious consideration, Gloria chose to go forward with satisfying Mason.

"Don't stop," Gloria pleaded; encouraging Mason to continue. She was seeking a much-anticipated orgasm, and couldn't have denied Mason, even if she wanted to. Gloria did however, have second thoughts about penile penetration. Feeling her orgasm on the horizon, Gloria held Mason's head tightly between her legs. Her outcries from her upcoming orgasm excited Mason, but left him struggling to breathe. Not wanting to stop, Mason continued his pursuit to please her. It didn't matter that he had to take a quick breath each time Gloria's body spasmed from his tongue, it was the outcome of his masterful performance that was most important.

Mason held on for the ride, as Gloria's legs tightened around his head, and her body shook uncontrollably. He felt justified in having accomplished his goal of leading Gloria to an orgasm, but thanked his lucky stars the ride was over. Taking a second to catch his breath, Mason kissed his way up towards Gloria's lips. He'd taken her to the promise land, now it was his turn to join her, but Gloria was hesitating. Once again, she was playing games, and it frustrated him.

Mason removed himself from the pallet and walked over to the window. He didn't have to take this crap from her, he could've been with any woman he wanted tonight, but he chose to be with her. Maybe it was time he took her home. Better yet, maybe it was time to cut his losses and walk away before someone got hurt. Before announcing his decision to take Gloria home, she joined him at the window. She saw his frustration, and felt the urgent need to do something about it. She didn't want to take the risk of losing the man who had been willing to do anything to make her happy so, without saying a word, Gloria took Mason's hand and led him back to the pallet.

In a pornographic kind of way, she ordered him to lay on his back, and crawled to him. Next, Gloria ordered him to remove his clothing, and after doing so, she performed perhaps the best head he'd ever had. Gloria's performance was one Mason wouldn't soon forget. He didn't have to direct her on what to do, she knew exactly what made him tick. Her skills weren't by far, that of a novice, she was a pro, but now wasn't the time to question her. Gloria had him trying to imprint himself into the floor. Her performance was masterful, and though she had just begun, he felt himself on the verge of exploding.

Fighting his urges, Mason thought of any and everything to keep his mind focused, but couldn't. Gloria was too good, and her skills had Mason calling out her name. In a move to prevent a shortened lovemaking session, Mason attempted to push Gloria away but couldn't, she wanted to taste him, and urged him not to fight his feelings. Screaming, "I love you" at the top of his voice, Mason released his hot magma, that exploded recklessly inside of Gloria's mouth, and like the superstar she was, Gloria didn't lose a drop. It was the moment Mason knew he would do any and everything to keep her.

Chapter: 6

Mason stood with the sun at his back, and stared at his reflection that sparkled against his 1969 Mach 1 Mustang. He was amazed by its Grabber blue finish, but most importantly, he was anxious to show it off. Ready to showboat, he and his best friend Gator, headed for the local convenience store at the speed of light. Mason salivated as the roar of its 428 Cobra jet big-block engine, gave notice to everyone in his vicinity. Driving at speeds surpassing one-hundred-ten miles per hour, Mason arrived at the small country store within minutes.

Scared shitless, Gator was still shaking like a leaf on a windy day when Mason drove into the store yard. He was thankful that he could put his feet on the ground, and thanked God for hearing his prayer. Getting out of the car, Gator's legs felt like spaghetti, as he made his way inside the store. He'd had enough of Mason driving fast, and was going to insist that Mason drove like a normal driver on their way home, or he was willing to walk.

Inside the store, the friends brought a case of beer and two bags of ice for their cooler. Tonight, Mason was planning to celebrate the announcement of his relationship with Gloria; that's if everything went according to plan. Gloria was scheduled to meet with Drew later in the afternoon to break things off. Still, Mason remained uncertain if Gloria had the nerve to tell Drew it was over between them. From what she had told him, Drew could make things difficult by refusing to let her go. To make their transition go smoother, Mason suggested that he be present, in support of her and their future together, but Gloria insisted that she do it alone. She wanted to handle Drew on her own, and made Mason promise to stay away until she did.

From the rear of the store, Dusty and his friend Jasper watched Gator pack his cooler with beer; covering it with ice. They joked about strong arming him, and taking the entire cooler, but knew with Mason present, they wouldn't have a chance at pulling it off. Jasper and Dusty were aware of Mason's qualifications when it came to hand-to-hand combat. Mason was proficient at fighting, and he was willing to do whatever it took to protect his friends. It was something Jasper and Dusty learned firsthand when they challenged Mason and Gator to a fight at Club Funky's a couple of years ago. They tried to double team Gator, after hearing he was sleeping with Jasper's girl, and seeing that Gator was too drunk to function properly, Jasper and Dusty decided to jump him, but what they hadn't factored in, was that Mason would take them both on. I guess it was fair to say, Mason made quick work of them, by knocking Jasper out with one punch, and as for Dusty, he gave up after being knocked to the floor.

"I hate them motherfuckers." Jasper said, while secretly harboring his animosity towards Mason for knocking him the fuck out, and for Gator, because of his on-going affair with his girlfriend. For a second, Jasper entertained the idea of confronting them, but that idea was quickly squashed by Dusty, who wanted no parts of them. Dusty had felt Mason's wrath, and wanted no further involvement with him. Besides, he was hanging out with his uncle Pistol, who stopped to talk to him about something important. Dusty drank the remainder of his warm 40-ounce Colt 45 beer, and he watched with envy as the young men spread the remainder of their ice in their cooler.

"Hey, it's hot as fuck today, I know y'all broke motherfuckers are dying of thirst over there? Y'all want a cold beer?" Mason teased.

"Man, fuck y'all. We don't want shit from you." Dusty responded.

In actuality, Dusty was lying to himself. The temperature was hovering close to ninety degrees, and a cold beer would have hit the spot, but he was willing to die of thirst before accepting beer from a man that had kicked his ass. Besides, he had some spare change in his pocket, and could more than likely buy his own beer. Dusty reached inside his front pocket and felt four quarters roaming loosely. He realized he didn't have enough money to buy another cold 40 ounce from the store, and leaned back on the picnic table. He was broke, and seeing Gator and Mason dressed to impress, with money in their pockets, left him infuriated.

Feeling the urgency to focus their attention back to reality, Dusty ripped up the volume to his old boom box that was zipped tied against the handlebars of his refurbished scooter. Singing along, Dusty challenged Jasper to a sing off. Dueling to see who was the best, the young men took turns singing an old Isley Brothers tune. They were seemingly dueling well, until they rudely interrupted old man Monkey Carson's afternoon nap. It was a mistake they'd soon regret, because Monkey stormed from his shack to confront the guilty parties. From his facial expression, Monkey wasn't in a pleasant mood. Anyone would have guessed that Monkey would've focused his rage at the owner of the boom box, but he didn't. Instead, he targeted Jasper; who he had a dislike for. Standing nose to nose with Jasper, Monkey screamed at him, at the top of his voice.

"Why da fuck you playing that got damn music so loud. Didn't you know I was getting my evening nap?" Monkey screamed.

It was no secret that the old man disliked Jasper. No one knew exactly why, but Monkey hated Jasper's guts. He seemed to lose his temper every time Jasper was in his presence, and today was no exception. Like always, Monkey was condescending when it came to Jasper. He often used his skin complexion as a means of superiority. But on this day, Jasper stood firm. Without so much as a flinch, Jasper stood nose to nose to the old man; refusing to show any weakness. From the stance both men had taken, it was obvious what was about to occur. Seeing the potential problem, Pistol took matters into his hands by stepping between Monkey and Jasper; eliminating any chance of further escalation.

"It was me Mr. Carson, I turned the music up, and I apologize," Dusty admitted, as he hung his head in shame.

Taking Pistol's advice, Monkey stepped away, returning back to the picnic table to sit. Thanks to Pistol, an altercation between the old man and Jasper was prevented. It wasn't unusual for Monkey to show aggression, he often did, but his bark was always louder than his bite. To many, Monkey was just a grouchy old man with a short fuse, but those who knew him, knew that he didn't play when it came to being disrespected. There were rumors that Monkey had a number of shotguns hidden around the grounds where his old shack stood, but no one had actually seen more than one of them. As for Jasper, he believed Monkey was all talk and no action, but he soon learned the rumors of Monkey's many shot guns weren't rumors at all; they were for real.

Just as Pistol had calmed Monkey down from his altercation with Jasper, Jasper reignited Monkey's fire, by sparking another argument. He referred to Monkey as being Mr. Goodwyn's nigger boy. Well, as you could imagine, the reference didn't sit well with the old man, who in turn revisited the subject of Jasper being a bastard child of a white man, who refused to acknowledge him.

It was a sensitive subject to Jasper, and the old man knew it. By unearthing the skeletons hidden in Jasper's family's closet, Monkey brought back all the hurt and pain Jasper tried burying. Monkey didn't hold back on Jasper, and by depicting his mother as being a whore who gave birth to a bastard son; Jasper was stunned and furious. The mere mention of his mother being compared to as a whore, enraged Jasper, and he took their joking to another level. Without considering the consequences, Jasper challenged the old man to a fight. It was a challenge no one expected Monkey to take seriously, but like a game of chess, Jasper made the first move; drawing first blood.

"You're nothing but Mr. Goodwyn's little nigger boy who jumps through hoops when asked," Jasper teased. "He got you living in a shack, and sleeping on a strawbale, just like a nigger of old." Jasper laughed. "Look at cha; a foot shuffling, Bojangling ass house Nigger."

Disturbed by the allegations, Jasper played right into the old man's hands. The time had come for Monkey to tell the never heard of before story of Jasper's family. It wasn't going to be the outcome Jasper wanted but "Fuck it," he asked for it." the old man thought to himself. Jasper had opened the door for Monkey to enter and reveal his dirty laundry for everyone to hear. Monkey's decision to broadcast the facts leading up to Jasper's mother's death was something Jasper wanted to keep buried.

For years, he wondered if anyone knew the truth of his mother's death, and from the look in the old man's eyes, it was no doubt he knew the facts. Monkey's response was just as Jasper had anticipated. He began by questioning Jasper's black heritage, and followed up by questioning his mother's indiscretions.

"Who are you? What are you?" Monkey questioned. "You ain't black, and you sure as hell not white; not with all that nigger blood running through your veins. "You're the son of a wench, and a whore, who was used by that white man, and after he got your momma pregnant, he threw her back to the pig pin where she came from. Distraught after getting dumped, the stupid bitch used your grand pappy's gun to blow her fucking head off."

The old man had taken his comical teasing to another level. Monkey Carson had sunk and dug to a new low; a hole Jasper was unable to crawl out of. Unable to endure the shocking allegations, Jasper lost control of his emotions and punched the old man in his chest; knocking him to the ground. Pistol and Dusty quickly intervened, before further harm could be inflicted upon Monkey.

"Get him the hell out of here." Pistol ordered. It was a must that Jasper be removed from the premises before the old man could get up and retrieve one of three shotguns he had hidden.

Removing Jasper wasn't as difficult as Dusty anticipated. Jasper realized what he'd done, and displayed immediate remorse, but now wasn't the time to apologize. He had to leave as quickly as he could, so Pistol threw Dusty the keys to his truck.

Sprinting to the truck, the boys fled the scene as quickly as a hit and run driver leaves the scene. Once on the road, Dusty released a sigh of relief; knowing he was out of the range of Monkey's shotgun. It was over for now, but the boys knew another confrontation with Monkey was sure to follow.

Chapter: 7

Monkey remained high strung after being knocked to the ground, and remained a ticking time bomb; ready to explode at any second. Needless to say, Mason and Gator's plan to drink a few beers behind the store wasn't going to go as they anticipated. At the sight of seeing them walking to the back of the store, Monkey began verbally attacking them. Without paying much attention to what he was saying, the friends proceeded to walk towards the back; carrying a six-pack of Schlitz's beer tucked under his arm. Mason was the first to sit at the picnic table to enjoy a beer or two; with Gator following.

The friends hadn't taken heed to Monkey's warnings, nor had they seen the shotgun he had tucked under his arm. They had no qualms with the old man, and didn't want to create any, but Monkey was making it impossible for them. At first, they thought he was kidding around, due to his comical nature, but after seeing that Monkey was carrying a shotgun under his arm, they realized he was for real.

"Hey man, what the fuck you doing with that shotgun?" Mason asked.

"I'm bout to put some holes in your punk ass if you don't get the fuck away from round my store." Monkey warned.

Mason didn't fully understand why Monkey's behavior was so hostile. Just yesterday, they were laughing and drinking a beer together at the table.

"What we do?" Gator questioned.

Monkey responded, "Nothing, I just want y'all little bastards to get cha punk asses in that piece of shit blue car, and scat on back where you came from."

Standing with his double barrel shotgun pointed to the ground, Monkey held it with a firm grip. He had no intention of discharging it, but reserved the right to do so, if needed. Seeing what they were confronted with, Mason hesitated. He felt somewhat comfortable after Pistol intervened, and convinced Monkey to secure his weapon, but Mason remained cautious as he witnessed Monkey hesitating. To ease his tension, Mason popped the top on a beer and began drinking it. To further aggravate Monkey, Mason drank his beer, and tossed the can across the yard.

Feeling disrespected, Monkey pointed his weapon at Mason; demanding that he leave the premises immediately. Again, Pistol intervened; demanding that Monkey put away his weapon before someone got hurt. Though Pistol's influence didn't convince Monkey to put away his weapon, it did cause him to consider it, but before he would do that, he wanted Mason and Gator gone.

"You think I'm playing, don't cha boy?" Monkey ranted.

He had no qualms with Gator, in actuality, he liked Gator and his family, but he despised Mason. It was Mason's lack of respect that Monkey hated most.

"What is wrong with you old man?" Mason asked, while trying to determine what he had done to provoke Monkey. Lord knows, Mason wanted a peaceful ending to their situation, but the old bastard was making things difficult.

Resolved to the fact that the old man wasn't going to compromise, Mason became defiant. Monkey's threats irritated him, and his patience began wearing thin. To further aggravate Monkey, Mason opened a second can of beer and guzzled it, before tossing it across the yard.

"Hey Toby, you can go fetch that can as well," Mason said, while laughing at Monkey. "Well go head boy. What'cha waiting on? Go fetch, I tell you." Mason teased.

 Mason's taunts infuriated Monkey, who became even more determined than ever to run he and Gator away from the store yard. Disregarding Gator's advice to leave, Mason drank a third beer, and just as he did to the previous two cans; Mason threw the can across the yard.

"I guess you motherfuckers think I'm bullshitting," Monkey responded.

He stood over Mason, who was seated. "Hey, hey you, I'm talking to you motherfucker."

Fearing the worst, and not wanting to be caught in the middle of a pissing contest between Mason and Monkey, Gator made the decision to leave before any one got hurt. Positioning his arm under Mason's, Gator began to escort Mason from the table towards his car. Together they walked, as they engaged in a private conversation. Gator was doing what no one else was successful at doing; he was peacefully removing Mason from the scene, without incident.

Things were seemingly coming to an end, until Monkey opened his mouth. His statements antagonized Mason; adding fuel to the fire that was nearly extinguished.

Pushing Gator away, Mason was determined to show, he wasn't intimidated by Monkey, and stood firm, while staring down the barrel of the devil's gun.

"I ain't scared of you because you got a gun in my face." Mason said.

Mason was lying, he was afraid. His heart was hiding in the pit of his stomach, but his pride wouldn't allow him to show weakness. Monkey was holding him at bay with the barrel of his shot gun pointed straight at his face, but Mason stood firm. He wasn't by any means, going to be marked as a punk bitch. He was willing to die for his belief. Maybe it was the unorthodox way Mason stood up to Monkey that gained the old man's respect, but Monkey's abrasiveness seemed to lessen after the stare down.

Realizing it wasn't worth it, the old man took a step backwards, and lowered his weapon. It was over as far as Monkey was concerned, but for Mason, it was all he needed to substantiate his claim that the old man was all bark and no bite. Monkey's indecisiveness, not only disclaimed his account of being the meanest motherfucker on the east coast, it destroyed what little reputation he had left. Monkey often bragged about whipping up on boxing greats like Archie Moore and Bob Foster during sparring sessions in the ring, but that was nearly seventy years ago. Monkey was only a shell of what he was back in the day. His bite now, could barely penetrate an over ripened banana. Feeling he'd made his point, Mason tucked the three remaining beers under his arm and began his walk to his car.

"Come on Gator, let's get the fuck out of here. I knew this old pussy won't nothing but mouth."

Relieved the ordeal was finally over, Gator winked at Pistol; thanking him for his assistance and made a b-line in front of Mason towards his car. It wasn't until they'd reached the car that he heard the racking of a shot gun shell in Monkey's gun. The old man was in the shooting position, and was aiming directly at the back on Mason's head.

"So, I'm a pussy huh?" Monkey responded, standing in a shooting position, ready to pull the trigger. "I see you one of them motherfucker's that's gotta be shown."

Hearing the sound of the shell being racked in the chamber of the shot gun, Pistol's approach was vital. He was the only one in position to stop Monkey, but the likelihood of him doing so was nearly impossible. By the grace of God, Pistol was able to reach around Monkey in time to engage the safety switch before he could pull the trigger.

Seeing Pistol and Monkey fighting to gain control of the shot gun, Mason joined in. He was able to overpower the two older men, and gain control of the gun. After doing so, he pushed Pistol aside, while using the stock of the gun to strike Monkey across the face; knocking him to the ground. Seeing the old man on the ground, Mason stood over him, and placed his foot on his chest.

"Move as much as a flinch and I swear to God, I'ma blow your fucking head off," Mason said with a stern voice.

The seriousness in Mason's voice, combined with the blank stare in his eyes, alerted Gator, he was about to do something he would later regret. Seeing what was about to happen, Gator went into action again. Along with Pistol, Gator began lobbying for Mason not to do anything stupid. He tried to convince Mason that Monkey was nothing more than a useless old man, that craved attention.

Gator knew he had to talk quickly, if he was going to help the old man. Mason had a history of uncontrollable anger, it had gotten him into trouble countless times, and Gator felt that if he didn't do something fast, the penalty could result in the old man's life being taken. He approached Mason with caution, and didn't want to provoke him, nor eliminate any chances he had in negotiating with him. Gator looked down at Monkey lying helpless on his back; silently pleading for his life. The old fool had placed himself in a bad situation, and it was going to take a near miracle to get out of it.

Standing at an ears distance, Gator began talking, reminding Mason of the repercussions he would face, if he inflicted any bodily harm to Monkey. Realizing his advice wasn't going to work, Gator had to create another plan of action, or the old man was going to lose his life. Standing out of the line of fire, Pistol spoke briefly, in an effort to convince Mason not to pull the trigger.

"He's just an old man son, he ain't worth going to jail over," Pistol repeated. "Think about the life you have. You don't want to do something you'll regret for the rest of your life."

Pistol's advice seemed to have triggered Mason's thought process, but it was what Gator said that triggered his attention back to reality. Gator reminded him that he was hours away from officially being introduced as Gloria's man. If he chose to pull the trigger to end Monkey's life, Gloria would be lost to him forever. Closing his eyes, Mason visualized Gloria's hazel eyes, sparkling from the rays of the sun. She'd been his dream his entire life, and after years of praying, she was going to be his by the end of the day. It didn't take long for him to realize that no one, not even this old grungy, rotten scoundrel lying beneath his foot, was going to deny him of the happiness he deserved.

Lying on his back, Monkey struggled to breathe with Mason's size twelve and a half shoe pressed firmly across his chest. Monkey was sweating profusely, and with the feeling of a heart attack vastly approaching; he began to feel his time had come. Monkey's fear of dying suddenly abandoned him, and he wasn't afraid anymore. His only concern was having to see the flash from the blast of his shotgun as his final vision. The thought of having to see it, wreaked havoc on his bowels; causing them to escape, followed by a sudden urge to urinate on himself; soiling the overalls he was wearing. Mason stood in silence, as he tried to figure out his best option. If by chance he returned the weapon into the old man's possession, Monkey would undoubtedly use it against him. His only option was to keep it.

Raising the barrel of the shotgun was a signal the ordeal was finally over. Without speaking a word, Mason removed his foot from Monkey's chest and walked to his car. Releasing a sigh of relief, Pistol continued to lean forward with his hands resting against his knees as he watched Mason and Gator drive away.

He'd just witnessed a miracle, and he had God to thank for there being no bloodshed. Pistol rushed over to assist Monkey, who was struggling to stand. Helping him to his feet, Pistol's anger got the best of him, and he began chastising the old man for his poor judgment in challenging a man sixty-years his junior.

"You should be ashamed of yourself, out here fighting like you a young man. You may have sparred against the likes of Bob Foster and Archie Moore, but that time done passed you over. You ain't twenty no more."

Pistol continued to chastise Monkey, while brushing the dirt from what was left of Monkey's matted gray hair, and the back of his overalls.

"Just look at you, dirt all in the back of your head, and you done shit yourself." Pistol said, while helping brush the dirt from Monkey's back.

Embarrassed by what occurred, Monkey went on the defensive, lashing out at Pistol, by releasing the secret he'd been keeping.

"You telling me what I should da done, you need to tell that pretty yellow gal of yours to stop fucking that weasel." Monkey boasted.

Pistol had no idea what Monkey was talking about, and chalked it up to him trying to save face for soiling himself.

"Shut up ole man, you don't know what you talking about."
Pistol responded.

"The hell I don't. That nigger's been lying up, under your roof,
with that pretty ass gal of yours for months now." Monkey
teased.

"I know that's a damn lie. Kelly's only sixteen, and Gloria is
engaged to Nancy Harrison's boy, Drew." Pistol responded.

"Bullshit." Monkey screamed out. "The weasel's been tearing
that oldest girl of yours up for almost a year now. That
motherfucker's been sneaking in your house damn near every
night. Matter fact, rumor has it, you nearly caught him crawling
out of her window last week." Monkey replied.

Stunned by Monkey's accusations, Pistol questioned his
knowledge about Gloria's audacious behavior. He wasn't sure if
Monkey was lying to get even for being chastised, or if he was
serious, but from the look in his face, the old man seemed to be
enjoying the fact that he had evened the score. His allegations
had caught Pistol off guard, but more than that, it had pissed
him off.

"You don't know what the fuck you talking about?" Pistol
responded. "My Gloria is engaged to Nancy Harrison's boy."

Laughing at Pistol's response, Monkey began making his way
back across the store yard to clean himself. He'd struck a nerve,
but unfortunately, he felt remorse for the way he told his good
friend. Before entering his shack, Monkey turned to Pistol.

"Look, I'm sorry for the way I told you, but in all seriousness,
you need to nip it in the bud before that boy sinks his fangs in
her."

Still finding it hard to believe, Pistol couldn't fathom the thought that his beautiful daughter would make the mistake of walking away from a successful future with a wealthy family. Especially to be with a man who held a stop and go sign for a paving company. Was it possible the old man had blabbered out something he knew nothing about? Pistol wanted to know more as he pushed on for answers.

Approaching Monkey at his shack, Pistol tried to secure more answers to his many questions. He needed to know more about what the old man knew. Monkey's answers were short and inconclusive, so Pistol knew the only way to learn the truth was to confront Gloria. He waited anxiously for Lester to return with his truck. Once he did, Pistol nearly pulled him from behind the steering wheel, before jumping inside and speeding away with the front door still open.

Chapter: 8

Driving as fast as his old pickup would carry him, Pistol made his way down his long driveway, with a trail of dust following him. He couldn't wait to confront Gloria about the rumors that she was sleeping with Mason.

Entering the house, Pistol made his way through the kitchen, screaming for Gloria's immediate response. Hearing his screams, and thinking something was wrong, Gloria rushed from her bedroom to meet her father.

"What's wrong daddy?" Gloria asked, having no idea what she was about to be confronted with. Seeing the furiousness in his eyes, Gloria instantly realized that her father had heard the rumors about her and Mason. His mild-mannered temperament had gyrated into an erratic behavior that sent chills down her spine. She had never seen him lose his composure before, and from his reaction, she knew she was in for a long afternoon.

"Is it true, are you screwing around with that black motherfucker?" Pistol screamed, demanding to know the truth.

Before answering her father's question, Gloria paused. Her first response was to lie, but after thinking more clearly, she felt it was in her best interest to tell the truth. It was no surprise that he found out so quickly; rumors had surfaced weeks ago regarding their relationship. In a way, she was relieved that the cat was out of the bag and she didn't have to hide anymore. Now they could walk hand and hand, without having to sneak around like a cheating married couple.

Although relieved that the truth was out, Gloria's heart sobbed from having to see the disappointment in her father's eyes. In Pistol's mind, Drew was her ideal man. But in Gloria's defense,

Drew wasn't the man she wanted to be with, Mason was. Hesitating, Gloria confirmed her father's suspicions by acknowledging it was true. The confirmation was a blow that jarred Pistol into doubling over from the pain of having to hear what he feared most. He refused to accept Gloria's relationship with Mason, and demanded that she end her association with him immediately, or risk being disowned by the family.

Pistol's demands drew an immediate spark that brought on an argument between them. Out of respect to her father, Gloria spoke her mind without being belligerent or disrespectful. She reminded her father, that it was her life, and she was living it the way she wanted to. Hearing Gloria's response, Pistol could feel his blood pressure rising. He'd lost his composure and tried getting it back, but it was too late. The echoes from Gloria's rants, ravaged his mind, and sent throbbing pains to his head. His daughter had just stabbed him in the heart with a dagger, and he was slowly bleeding to death.

Disheartened by the news, Pistol stormed towards the kitchen door, needing to escape the nightmare he was experiencing. He was met by his wife Mattie who was entering the house after hearing the commotion from outside.

"What is going on in here?" Mattie asked. "I could hear y'all clear outside."

Seeing that she had intervened in the nick of time, Mattie saw the hurt, and frustration in her husband's face; and saw that he was visually shaken. Not wanting to take sides immediately, Mattie gave Pistol the opportunity to speak first.

"It's that damn daughter of yours. She's messing with that good for nothing boy of Dolly Mae Tyler. I heard they're having sex and everything." Pistol ranted.

Interrupting her father, Gloria denied the accusations of having a sexual affair with Mason. However, she confirmed their relationship was true. Gloria's admission sparked another confrontation; resulting in them screaming at each other, each eager to get their point across. Having to separate them, Mattie found herself playing peacemaker. She ordered Gloria to leave the room; choosing to discuss the matter with her at a more appropriate time. She was more concerned about her husband, and trying to deescalate him before he had a stroke.

"That boy is trouble I tell you. He damn near shot and killed Monkey Carson today," Pistol went on to explain. "I had to beg for the man's life. I'm telling you, before she least expects it, that black bastard is going to be beating her ass."

Eager to stand up for her man, Gloria began fighting for his honor. No one, who didn't know Mason was going to tell her about him. More than anyone, she knew what Mason was capable of. He'd never been abusive to her, and never would, because he was madly in love with her.

"Daddy, you know Monkey is always pulling that gun out on people. If anything had happened to him, he would have brought it on himself."

Seeing his daughter stand up for a man without morals brought tears to Pistol's eyes. He pleaded for Gloria to sever ties with Mason while she still had the chance, but he could see his pleas weren't going to be considered. Gloria had fallen for that snake in the grass, and there was nothing he could do about it. Pistol had witnessed how unstable Mason had become, and was convinced he wasn't worthy of his daughter's love, but unfortunately, Gloria refused to see it.

Pistol knew it was up to him to save Gloria from making the biggest mistake of her life. He strongly believed Mason was going to destroy her, and everything she worked hard to accomplish. Pistol felt Gloria's only option was to correct whatever wrongs she'd made with Drew, and work at building a future with him. It wasn't that he didn't want his daughter to be happy, he only wanted what was best for her. In Pistol's heart, he knew Drew was best for her, and wished that Gloria would reconsider her decision. But it was too late, Gloria's mind was made up. She knew exactly what, and who she wanted to be with, and sadly, it wasn't Drew.

Entering her room, Gloria closed and locked the door behind her. She was relieved that their secret was out, because now the town didn't have anything to gossip about. Lying across the bed, Gloria heard what she thought was someone at her bedroom window. Believing it to be her sister, Gloria got up with all intentions of releasing her frustrations upon her. She forcefully opened her curtains, and to her surprise, Mason was standing there with a smile.

"What are you doing here?" Gloria asked.

"I wanted to see your beautiful face, so I took a chance that you were in your room." Mason replied.

"And now that you have seen my beautiful face. What now?" Gloria asked.

"I can go home knowing you've made my day." Mason responded.

Mason's presence had erased the tears and sadness Gloria felt earlier. He was a sight for her sore eyes and left her relishing the moment they'd be together again. Mason's boldness left Gloria impressed by the way he risked being caught by her father after knowing how he felt about him. It was Mason's daring ways that attracted her to him. Even though he was far from being the romantic that Drew was, it was his unpredictable ways that attracted her the most. Only Mason could send her into a frenzy that could satisfy her until they could physically be together.

By no means was he the man who brought her flowers, or opened doors for her on a date, but the way he stimulated her, generated a feeling inside that was equal to nothing. Drew was in a position to give her any and everything she wanted, but it wasn't enough to keep her happy; only Mason could do that. From her window, Gloria inquired about the incident that occurred at Goodwyn's store. She listened as Mason explained, and was left even more convinced that he was protecting himself while trying to scare the old fool.

Gloria believed Mason. She had heard about Monkey's temper, and though she never observed him pull out his shot gun on anyone, it was common knowledge to everyone who frequented the store. The couple talked a few minutes before being interrupted by a knock at Gloria's bedroom door. It was her sister Kelly, who'd come to inform her that Drew was waiting for her in the living room. Before having to say goodbye, Gloria assured Mason that she would get rid of Drew and meet him at his house later that afternoon. She reiterated her plans to end their relationship before the day was complete; which excited Mason even more.

Before leaving, Gloria leaned out of her window to kiss Mason goodbye. Closing the curtains, she opened her dresser drawer, and removed the engagement ring, and placed it on her finger. She stood in front of the mirror to view her appearance, then brushed her hair, and freshened her makeup. Once she was satisfied, she left the room to make her way down the hallway towards their living room, where Drew was waiting. She entered the living room, to find Drew sitting. Seeing her enter, Drew stood and greeted her with a kiss.

Drew's six foot four-inch frame towered over Gloria, as she melted in his arms. She had nearly forgotten how great it felt being in Drew's arms, but was quickly reminded of what she promised to do. Seeing Drew again left Gloria with second thoughts, about wanting to end their relationship. There were no questions regarding her feelings about Mason, but she still loved Drew, and until she could determine who she wanted to be with, she remained at a stalemate.

Gloria gazed into Drew's eyes after he released her. His stare hypnotized her; reminding her of how important their past once was. Feelings for Drew echoed with each beat of her heart, but she was obligated to her relationship with Mason. Drew still meant a hell of a lot to her, and she wished she could have them both, but knew it was a fantasy she could never have. Sitting on the couch, Drew reached inside his jacket pocket, and removed a rectangular box. He smiled, before presenting it to Gloria. It was her graduation gift, and it was a gift she'd been expecting.

Unsure as to what was inside, Gloria assumed it was expensive. Like a child on Christmas, she ripped open the wrapping to uncover the blue velvet rectangular box. The sight of the box, gave all indication that jewelry was inside. Gloria's only questions now was what kind of jewelry, and how much did it cost?

Opening the lid, Gloria's eyes widened at the sight of seeing a diamond bracelet. She hadn't expected such an elaborate gift, but accepted it just the same. It was what she requested the Christmas before, but received the engagement ring instead.

"I wanted to give this to you last night, but the weather wouldn't permit it. Congratulations." Drew said, as he removed the bracelet, to place around Gloria's wrist.

The two-thousand-dollar bracelet had temporarily derailed Gloria's plan to dump Drew; leaving her to have to come up with a lie to tell Mason. Sitting with her arm extended, Gloria watched as Drew placed the bracelet around her wrist. He followed it with a kiss on Gloria's cheek. Seeing her instantly reminded Drew why she'd been so special to him. For a moment, he forgot about their ups and downs, and entertained thoughts of attempting to rekindle what was lost, but ultimately realized, as a couple, their time had run its course. They'd given it a good fight but they both knew their hearts belonged to someone else.

Chapter: 9

A week passed, and Gloria's promise to end her relationship with Drew still hadn't taken place. Her lack of communication with Drew incited Mason's frustration; impelling him to take matters into his own hands. He threatened to blow the doors off Gloria's scheme and reveal the truth to Drew about them if Gloria hadn't done it by the end of the week. Mason knew Drew was scheduled to leave for WFU by weeks end, and relented to Gloria's promises to do so before Drew left.

The fact that Mason had reached his limit was taking a toll on their relationship. Mason strongly believed they had come to a standstill, and he was tired of waiting. Gloria made several excuses for procrastinating, and though she wasn't convincing, Mason gave her the benefit of the doubt. He knew she didn't want to let go of her gold mine. He'd seen the bracelet, and felt less of a man because he was not in a position to afford a gift so lavish.

To ease his guilt, Gloria persuaded Mason that his contribution of paying her tuition was more valuable than any gift Drew could have given her. In a way she was right, he had given her the gift of all gifts, but it hadn't erased the sight of having to see his girl wear the diamond bracelet her ex-boyfriend had given her. Holding on to Gloria's promise to inform Drew about their relationship, Mason again, was looking forward to a weekend out of town. He'd made reservations for dinner at an upscale restaurant, and reserved tickets to attend a concert at the Altria Theater in Richmond for Saturday evening.

Gloria was excited about their upcoming weekend get away, but Mason let it be known that if Gloria hadn't informed Drew about them by Thursday afternoon, it was over between them.

Sure, he was lying, Mason wouldn't dream of walking away from the only woman he'd ever loved, but Gloria didn't know that, and it left her faced with a decision she hoped she wouldn't later regret. Wanting to be with Mason wasn't the problem. Gloria loved him enough to have a future with him. Her problem was having to admit to Drew that she was cheating on him with his cousin. It was something she wasn't prepared to do, or wanted to.

Gloria wasn't sure if she could walk away from the life of luxury Drew could provide for her. With Drew, she could have nearly anything she wanted, but with Mason, she would be stuck with a life of uncertainty. By all accounts, Drew and his family were millionaires, though you wouldn't have known it by the 1970 Ford Woody station wagon he drove. Being wealthy didn't mean jack to Drew, but it meant the world to Gloria.

If there was some way, she could have them both, her life would be perfect, but it was silly to think she could get away with having her cake and eating it too. Gloria continued to toy with the idea of balancing Mason and Drew. She wanted to enjoy the fruits from their labor, but ultimately knew it would be impossible to do. Within a week, Drew was leaving to receive his Master's Degree. She undoubtedly had to end their relationship; whether she wanted to or not.

She wanted to believe she could be happier with Mason, but deep within, she knew living the life she wanted would be a struggle with Mason. Only Drew could give her the life she wanted, but he was way too boring for her. Yes, she was still in love with Drew, but he wasn't the same guy she fell in love with. He had spent most of his time at the university, and when he was home, he spent most of his time with his little "wetback," and so-called best friend Karyme Rios-Gonzalez; better known as the daughter of the help.

Gloria hated the idea that he spent so much time with Karyme. She addressed her concerns to Drew many times, but like the typical dumbass, he laughed it off, saying, it was only work. She could never prove her theory, but Gloria chose not to wait around to find out. She had to find her own way, and she chose the path that led her to Mason.

Chapter: 10

At 6am Thursday morning, Drew arrived at the office earlier than usual to find Karyme already present. She greeted him with a hot cup of his favorite fresh brewed coffee, and a smile to match. Karyme was perky, and in a playful mood. She had already made the rounds, and completed the inspection of the coolers, logging the date and time of each of them. With the paperwork in order, Karyme was anxious to catch up with Drew, and what was going on in his love life. Rearing back in his chair, Drew began to share his experiences, by introducing the new lady in his life. Karyme couldn't have been happier for him. Drew was finally putting Gloria in his rear-view mirror; leaving her skank ass on the side of the road where she belonged. Karyme's only hope was that it was for good this time. For years, Gloria put him through so many changes, but thank God, Drew had found the courage to walk away.

So many times, she wanted to tell him how Gloria was making a fool out of him, but was advised not to by his mother. Ms. Harrison wanted Drew to see Gloria for the slut she was, and though it was an unorthodox way, she understood her method. Ms. Harrison wanted Drew to concentrate on the family business, as well as his dreams of becoming a track and field champion in the Olympics. She also believed Drew was too young to get married; especially to a woman with a shitty past, present and future. Nancy was old school, she didn't want to get involved with her children's affairs, but she had no problem getting into Drew's affair with Gloria. She couldn't allow Gloria to destroy what Drew had worked so hard to achieve.

Karyme listened as Drew spoke about attending Gloria's graduation. She was surprised that Gloria had given him a ticket, but then again, Drew had dug deep into his bank account to buy her the diamond bracelet, she so proudly was wearing. Although it felt great knowing Drew was finished with Gloria, it was disappointing to learn he was interested in someone else. Karyme had hoped after Gloria, Drew would somehow see her as a love interest, but her wishes were dashed once again. As sad as it was, there was a bright side; at least he was getting out of his toxic relationship from Gloria. Karyme didn't know much about Lynn, except that she and Drew had become close. She wanted to learn more about her, but unfortunately, it wasn't meant to be. Drew was in a rush to attend Gloria's graduation. Pressed for time, Drew kissed Karyme on her forehead and left the office. Though it felt like old times, Karyme wished it could be more between them. She had been in love with Drew since learning how to love, but Drew only looked at her as his best friend, and nothing more.

Arriving minutes before the ceremony was to begin, Drew found a seat on the front row, beside Pistol. He applauded and stood, as the nursing class of 2022 entered the auditorium. Seeing Gloria march in, gave Drew an exhilarating feeling. It was touching to see what she had accomplished. Becoming a nurse had been her dream, and now she was about to live it; he couldn't have been happier for her.

Drew found himself questioning what happened to them, and why they strayed so far away from each other. He didn't have all the answers, but he couldn't place all the blame on Gloria. In a lot of ways, he wanted to end things and to begin his relationship with Lynn. Knowing Gloria was having an affair with Mason, made things better for him. Gloria's inability to control her wild side, had ruined his dreams of wanting to have a future with her; he'd forgiven her so many times for her indiscretions and affairs with other men.

Drew couldn't deny he still loved Gloria, but it wasn't enough to encourage him to want to make it work between them. His dream of them being together was over, and all he could wish for now, was for them to part as friends.

Drew sat on an outside bench in front of the town's Multi-Center Building, and watched Gloria take pictures with her classmates. Seeing her interact with her classmates, reminded him of the power she possessed; she could warm the coldest days, just with her smile. Love her or hate her, Gloria was Gloria, and once you met her, she left an everlasting impact on your soul. Gloria was special in every sense of the word, but for Drew to be truly happy, he had to follow his heart, and his heart was leading him to Lynn. Never in a million years, would he have believed that he would ever want to call it quits. But like Gloria, he had done the unthinkable, and fell in love with someone else.

Seeing Drew sitting alone, Pistol joined him. By attending the ceremony, Pistol held on to the hope that Gloria had a change of heart, and was coming to her senses. Drew had been his choice for Gloria and after they became engaged, his prayers were answered. By marrying Drew, Gloria's future was financially secured. He wouldn't have to worry if she was being mistreated, because Drew was the perfect gentleman.

Like all parents, Pistol was ecstatic that his daughter had found the perfect guy to live out the rest of her life with. Drew was not only rich, he was level headed, and he loved Gloria. God had answered his dreams, and he couldn't have been more grateful, but then came the devil. Under his radar, appeared the snake of all snakes, the man that the devil had sent to interfere with his Garden of Eden. Mason Tyler was the worst of the worst. He was the spoiled, hard headed, disrespectful son of Dolly Mae and the late Paul Tyler; he was carrying her down a path of destruction.

"Isn't she the most beautiful young woman you've ever seen?" Pistol asked, while waiting for Drew to respond.

"Yes, she is?" Drew responded. His eyes temporarily lit up, before realizing it was about to be over between the two of them.

Drew's sudden change in demeaner scared Pistol. Drew wasn't his happy go lucky self, and possessed a look, that was puzzling. He displayed a serious persona about himself that left Pistol wondering, if he had already learned the truth. Pistol was left with questions that needed answering. He was desperate to know what was happening between Gloria and Drew, and began probing for answers.

"I guess you and Gloria will be setting a date, now that you both have graduated." Pistol asked.

"Yeah." Drew responded.

Pistol was fishing for answers, but Drew wasn't giving him anything to go on. Feeling the need to deviate the attention away from him, Drew refocused Pistol's attention by announcing their wedding plans were on hold because of his pursuit to achieve his master's degree.

"How long is it going to take?" Pistol asked.

"If all goes well, it'll be in a month, but I've been training to make the upcoming world's track and field team, and if I make the team, we'll have to look at a later date," Drew responded.

Drew's answer left Pistol optimistic about Gloria's future. There was still a chance for them, and if Pistol had anything to do with it, they would be married by late autumn.

Gloria became paranoid after seeing her father talking to Drew, and felt an urgent need to join them. She was hoping to run her father off, because she believed he was going to spill the beans about her affair with Mason. Gloria wanted to be the one to tell Drew, so she quickly left her classmates to join her father and Drew. Gloria embraced Drew and kissed him on his cheek. She thanked him for coming, before telling him that she would be joining her friends to celebrate their graduation; it was her way of telling Drew their day had ended. Gloria felt no remorse in the way she told Drew, but in her defense, she extended him an invitation to come along; even though it wasn't sincere.

Feeling Gloria was more interested in celebrating with her friends than him, Drew declined her offer. He was disappointed at her decision not to include him, but hid his feelings with a smile. He gave Gloria a final embrace before leaving. Withstanding further embarrassment, Drew walked away; knowing his day and life with Gloria was over. His intentions weren't to break up with Gloria on her graduation day, but to do it before he left for school.

Chapter: 11

Things had quieted down since Monkey's altercation with Mason and Gator. He was back to being his old self; but he was alone. So much had changed in the past week, and Monkey found himself missing the loud sound of Dusty's old refurbished scooter, riding to the rear of the store and waking him up from his afternoon nap. He even missed the noise from his old 1980's boombox that was duct taped to the front of his handlebars, not to mention jawing with Jasper about his dirty red skin tone. But what Monkey missed most, was talking to Pistol. It was fair to say, he genuinely loved Pistol like a son, and hated the way things went between them. He had no right to say what he said to Pistol, and he hated himself for doing so. Although Pistol had the right to know the truth, Monkey shouldn't have smeared it in his face, out of anger. He'd been a complete asshole, and he wanted to apologize, but Pistol was nowhere around.

No one could argue the old man wasn't a pain in the ass, because in actuality he was, but overall, he was a good person. He didn't have a family of his own, and loved the company from the patrons who frequented the store. Desperate to repair the collateral damage he caused, Monkey took the first step by sending an olive branch to Pistol, Dusty, Jasper, Gator and Mason; requesting them to come by the store and talk over a beer or two. Dusty and Jasper were the first to respond. Monkey wasn't sure if they came because of the free cold beer, or because they missed being around him. Whatever the answer, he didn't care, he just wanted them there to talk to. As for Gator and Mason, Monkey did get the opportunity to talk to Gator, and made a formal apology, which was accepted. But as for Mason, well, he had no interest in meeting with Monkey. However, he did send a message for him to go fuck himself.

By clearing the way for everyone to return, Monkey couldn't have been happier. All he needed now was for his best friend to come, so he could apologize to him. It was disheartening, because Monkey sent several messages for Pistol to meet with him, but hadn't gotten a response. With the thought looming over his head that he'd lost the son he never had; Monkey spent the remainder of the afternoon sitting on the bench daydreaming. It wasn't until he heard Pistol's truck coming around the rear of the store yard that he perked up. He became excited; nearly jumping from the picnic table to run to the truck.

It was shocking to see Pistol struggle to stand erect as he slid from the front seat of his old pickup. Pistol was in bad shape, and as he made his way over to the bench where Monkey was sitting, his face told the story of his broken heart. Pistol flopped beside Monkey, and leaned backwards against the table to stretch his sore back.

"Damn, man, what's wrong with you?" Monkey questioned.

"Man, my back is killing me." Pistol answered, with a painful expression on his face.

The news of Gloria's rendezvous with the black mamba had taken all the steam out of him. It was obvious that Pistol was struggling to accept his daughter's decision to throw her future away by associating with Mason. Worse than that, Gloria was too head strong to realize what she was doing. It was hard to stand idly by and allow Gloria to ruin her life, but he hadn't a clue of what to do. Gloria was her own woman, determined to do things her way. Pistol had always been an advocate for allowing his children to follow their dreams, but when it came to Gloria wanting a future with Mason, he couldn't allow her to ruin what she'd worked so hard for.

To ease his friend's tension, Monkey reached inside of his bib overalls, and removed a bottle of his best spirit. Opening it, he passed it to Pistol, who took a stiff drink. It burned as it passed through his esophagus, but it left a smooth minty sensation in its path. Nodding while giving his approval, Pistol passed the bottle back to Monkey.

"Good shit, ain't it?" Monkey asked.

"Yup, where you get that from?" Pistol asked.

Monkey smiled, before turning the bottle to his mouth. He was correct in assuming Pistol was going to need something to take the edge off of what he was experiencing. It was a shame how his beautiful Gloria had stooped to feed off the bottom of the swamp. The men continued to drink as the afternoon progressed, and after finishing the last of Monkey's private stash, Pistol remained on the bench, while Monkey called it a day. He had gotten drunk, and decided to return to his shack.

Sitting alone, Pistol removed his pocket knife and began cleaning the dirt from under his fingernails. His mind continued to reflect upon Gloria, and how she was destroying her life. Though it wasn't anything to laugh at, Pistol found himself doing just that. Since the announcement of Gloria and Drew's engagement, he had fantasized about walking Gloria down the aisle to take Drew's hand in marriage. But thanks to that no good, black ass Mason Tyler, that wasn't going to happen now. It was the ideal dream for any man to have his favorite daughter experience such a wedding, but his dream was now a nightmare. He was left feeling helpless, and desperate to do anything to free his daughter from a life of uncertainty. The mere thought of not being able to protect Gloria frustrated him. If only he could see Mason right now, he would do what Monkey couldn't, and blow his fucking head off his shoulders.

Pistol's thoughts were rudely interrupted by the noise of his nephew's refurbished scooter coming around to the rear of the store. Before Dusty arrived, he shut off his music box. God knows, he didn't want another replay of Monkey losing his marbles again. Joining Pistol at the table, Dusty was immediately confronted by allegations of knowing about Gloria and Mason's affair, and not telling him about it. Fearing retaliation, Dusty denied any knowledge of knowing about Gloria and Mason. He stated he only found out about it a few days ago. He did admit to hearing the rumors, and said he confronted Gloria with them, but she denied the allegations.

Dusty felt awful about having to lie to his uncle, but it was all he could do to hide the truth from him. He didn't have the heart to ruin Pistol's hopes that Gloria was the angel he'd made her out to be. God knows, she was far from it. If the rumors were true, Gloria was fucking Mason, to pay for her college tuition. Whether it was true or not, Dusty couldn't say for certain, but it all made sense. Why else would she want to be with Mason? He resembled the creature from the black lagoon, but more than that, he was just as dumb as he was. Still in conversation with Pistol, Dusty's attention suddenly focused on a young lady, who was driving a 1966 red ragtop Pontiac GTO, and signaling to turn into the store yard. With his attention now focused on her, Dusty tuned out Pistol, and began contemplating on how he was going to meet her.

Dusty's eyes followed her, as she slowly got out of her car; she was mesmerizing. He followed her with his eyes, as she made her way inside of the store. Pressing his luck, Dusty waved, and out of courtesy, she returned the gesture. Dusty couldn't believe his luck, he instantly believed she wanted him to personally introduce himself to her, and abruptly ended his conversation with Pistol. He began making his way towards the front of the store, before realizing Mr. Goodwyn's unwritten rule which was, not to enter his store without purchasing merchandise. Dusty's pockets were empty, which meant he wasn't allowed inside the store. He was desperate to meet the young lady, so much so, he swallowed his pride, and did the unthinkable; asking his uncle Pistol for a five-dollar loan. Pistol was old school, and frowned upon any capable adult male begging for money. He was a firm believer in the American way, and believed a man should accept any job to support himself and his family until he was capable of doing better, and his nephew was no exception. Dusty was the same age as Gloria, and at twenty-one, it was his responsibility to get off his lazy ass, and find some kind of work; no matter what it was. Feeling somewhat regrettable for denying his nephew's request, Pistol went against his better judgment, and reached into his wallet and gave Dusty a five-dollar bill. Thrilled to have received the money, Dusty promised to repay the loan within a week. He quickly made his way inside the store with his crisp five-dollar bill in hand.

Once inside, Dusty searched the aisles, looking for the young beauty he'd seen enter the store. His search extended through the first two aisles, but there was no sign of her. Continuing his search, Dusty located her in the rear of the store. She was staring at a display of lighthouse candles that were stored on the upper shelf, and man was she ever beautiful. He stood from afar admiring her beauty, and watched her reach for a candle high above her head. His heart began beating like a drum, as her dress rose; exposing the bikini stretch panties she was wearing. The sight of seeing her cheeks, caused Dusty to quiver. He couldn't believe his luck, as he slowly made his way over towards her. As he approached, Dusty could feel his heart beating outside of his body. He could only imagine what was hiding underneath her panties, and with any luck, he was going to find out.

Standing frozen in time, Dusty fantasized about smashing her in the rear of the store after what he saw. Slowly, he began making his way closer. Feeling she was being watched, Lynn turned to find Dusty invading her personal space. His cold stare, gave her chills, and realizing she was alone in the rear of the store with him; Lynn began looking for an exit.

"I see you need some help with that wax candle?" Dusty said; reaching and retrieving the candle for Lynn. "Here you are."

"Thank you." Lynn replied.

"You're most certainly welcome baby cakes." Dusty responded; referring to Lynn's small perfectly rounded buttocks.

Dusty now had Lynn where he wanted her, he had gotten her attention, and was aggressively moving in on her private space. Feeling uncomfortable by Dusty's aggressive behavior, Lynn took a step backwards; creating space between them. Dusty gave her the creeps, and her instincts were telling her to remove herself from the rear of the store, as soon as possible. Extending his hand, Dusty introduced himself, as he attempted to talk with a debonair voice.

"By the way, I'm Dusty Collins, people call me D.C. So, what's your name?" Dusty asked.

"Ashlynn;" Lynn responded.

Avoiding eye contact, Lynn extended her hands just enough for Dusty to touch the tips of her fingers. Her mission was to get to safety as soon as possible, but Dusty was preventing her by blocking her paths of escape.

"Ashlynn, that's a pretty name for such a pretty lady. So, do you have a last name Ms. Ashlynn?"

"Boldmont." Lynn answered.

"Ashlynn Boldmont. Wow, that got a nice ring to it. Ashlynn, I haven't seen you around before. Where are you from?" Dusty asked, leaning against the stock on the shelf.

"Actually, I'm on my way to see my boyfriend, so would you excuse me please?" Lynn said, as she made her way around Dusty.

Following Lynn, Dusty grabbed a bag of chips from the rack and treaded close behind her. Scared to death, Lynn walked as fast as her legs could carry her. When she made it safely to the front counter of the store, she released a sigh of relief. Lynn soon realized she wasn't completely out of danger. No one was at the counter and she would have to wait until Mr. Goodwyn returned from the cooler. Now at the counter, Dusty positioned himself close behind Lynn. He stood literally inches from touching her, and the scent from the cheap malt liquor he'd been drinking, nearly caused her to vomit in the open box of candy that was on display.

To escape from being groped, Lynn nearly walked behind the register. Her body shivered, as Dusty brushed against her. He seemed to not care about her safe space, nor did he respect her. Finally, after what seemed like forever, Mr. Goodwyn returned from the cooler. He quickly took notice of Dusty's unusual behavior. He saw that Lynn was visibly shaken, and wasted no time intervening.

"Ma'am, is this man harassing you?" Mr. Goodwyn asked.

Nodding her head yes, Lynn gave Mr. Goodwyn the proof he needed to banish Dusty from his store. Embarrassed, Dusty denied any wrongdoing, other than trying to be neighborly. He tried arguing his case, but Mr. Goodwyn didn't want to hear his explanation. Dusty had been found guilty on the word of a stranger who was driving through town. Dusty's quick exit was only a temporary sense of security for Lynn. She feared the likelihood of him waiting outside to seek revenge for being kicked out of the store. Mr. Goodwyn saw that Lynn had been shaken up by the ordeal and to ease her tension, he attempted to poke fun at the situation, by comparing Dusty's behavior to that of a retard. But regardless, if he was mentally challenged, Dusty's presence was very intimidating.

Mr. Goodwyn offered to escort her to her car, but she declined his invitation. Though afraid, Lynn believed the ordeal was over, and left the store. Highly motivated, and knowing she was only minutes away from surprising Drew, she made her way to her car, only to spot Dusty standing at the passenger's side door of her car. Her first thought was to return inside the store, but she chose to continue walking to her car instead. She wasn't in the mood for any more of Dusty's shenanigans, and hoped he would move aside, to allow her to go on her way.

Seeing Lynn approaching, Dusty leaned against her driver's side door. Hesitant, Lynn hid her fears and continued walking towards her car. Once arriving, Lynn politely asked Dusty to step aside, but her request was ignored. Dusty felt Lynn's fear, and opted to capitalize on it, as he continued to block the driver's side door with his arms crossed. He stared at Lynn for more than a minute, before demanding an apology. But before getting it, he had a few choice words to say.

"Just who in da fuck you think you are Bitch?" Dusty said with hostility. "You think you can disrespect me, like I'm some pile of shit, and I'm supposed to just let you get away without speaking my piece?"

Afraid to respond, Lynn could only stare at the husky dark complexion man. She didn't want an altercation, all she wanted to do was to leave and surprise Drew. Seeing that Dusty wasn't going to allow her to come past him, Lynn made her way to the passenger's side of the car. The idea was to slide across the passenger's side, onto the driver side, and quickly start the car and leave, but Dusty was one step ahead of her. He opened her car, and sat at the steering wheel.

"Give me the keys, and I'll give you the drive of your life." Dusty boasted; ending Lynn's escape plan. Dusty was proving to be the freaking retard, Mr. Goodwyn said he was, and it was getting old quickly. She was powerless to him, and from the look in his eyes, Lynn had no doubt, he wanted to harm her. Putting space between them, Lynn stood by the front of her car. She was considering making a mad sprint back to the store, but didn't think she could beat him in a foot race.

"Look at cha, walking your little stinking ass around here, wearing all that sexy see-through shit. I should da fucked your little ass back there in the store when you were showing all your ass; reaching for that got damn box candle. I tried showing you some fucking respect, and how you repay me? You go and tell the white man I was harassing you." Fresh out of ideas, Lynn felt the need to reason with Dusty. She thought if she apologized, he may accept it, and she could go on her way.

"Dusty, I apologize if I disrespected you in anyway. Believe me, it wasn't my intention. I'm just in a rush to see my friend, so please step aside and allow me to go on my way."

Hoping her apology was enough, Lynn quickly learned it hadn't been. As expected, Dusty continued criticizing her, for the harsh treatment of him. His anger was becoming increasingly hostile, as he began walking towards her.

"You rich bitches are all the same. You think you can come in these parts, and treat us good country folk like we some stupid motherfuckers. And it always got to be you mixed bitches. I hate you half black bitches. Y'all all the same, always thinking you better than the chocolate brothers and sisters. Yellow bitches like you, won't give a nigger like me a chance, but I bet you'll lick the white boy's ass. Fucking bitch! I tell you, you black bitches gonna learn one of these days. Sooner or later, you gonna learn, you ain't nothing but a nigger in the white man's eyes."

Before Lynn could react, Dusty had narrowed the gap between them. He had shut off her point of escape to the store, but wasn't far enough away from the car, for her to escape. Now on full alert, Lynn opened her clutch bag and removed her pepper spray. She dropped her purse, and her small bag that contained the gift she'd purchased for Drew, and stood guard. She most likely was only going to get one chance to render Dusty helpless, and she wanted to be accurate.

Shaking the can of chemicals; Lynn aimed directly towards Dusty's face, and prepared herself for deployment. Lynn understood, she needed to render Dusty helpless to get away, and looked for an avenue of escape, before activating the can.

As a courtesy warning to Dusty, Lynn gave her final warning, before dispersing the chemicals. She reminded Dusty of the consequences he would face if he chose not to stand down.

"Dusty, DC or whatever your name is; I haven't done anything to you, so I suggest you move your ass, before we both do something we'll regret later." Lynn warned.

Lynn had had enough, and was prepared to do what she had to do to end their standoff.

"Aw, so you gonna spray me?" Dusty asked; "Well bitch, you're going to have to do it."

Hiding his fear, Dusty slowly began walking towards Lynn, causing her to retreat to maintain a safe distance. Her first instinct was to return inside the store, but she felt he would catch her before she made it inside. Her only option was to stand firm and fight. She had to let him know she meant business, and was prepared once and for all to do what she needed to do.

"If you take one more step, I swear to God, I'm going to spray your country ass." Lynn warned, with a stern voice.

Her stern approach was enough to intimidate Dusty. He now realized she was serious, and was ready to go to war. He had been sprayed before, and remembered the unpleasant feeling it presented. But still, he wasn't ready to back down.

"I ain't scared of you Bitch, I eat that shit for breakfast." Dusty boasted, while trying to control his buckling knees.

The truth was, Dusty was afraid. The thought of feeling the burning sensation, and having his breath temporarily stolen, by the effects of the chemicals, scared him shitless. He wanted to take a step forward, but ultimately chose to stand fast. By keeping things at a standstill, Dusty was doing what he set out to do, and that was to prevent Lynn from leaving. He wanted to make a statement, and felt he had done so without having to go hands on. No matter how many threats he made, or the intimidation he tried showing, it wasn't in his nature to put his hands on a woman, but Lynn had disrespected him; it was too much for him to ignore.

Wishing she was holding more than a can of pepper spray; Lynn was thankful she had it in her possession. She remained in position, waiting to disperse the chemicals at any sudden movements by Dusty. Her hands shook uncontrollably, as she decided the time had come to escape her would-be abductor. She felt it was time to take control of the situation and Lynn took the offensive, by walking slowly towards Dusty, moving him away from her car.

Seeing what was about to happen, Dusty instinctively took a step backwards; exposing a crack in his armor. Lynn now knew he was afraid, and she was eager to take advantage of it. Though convinced the momentum had switched in her favor, Lynn remained cautious. She blindly searched the ground for her purse and merchandise, while still holding the nozzle pointed directly at Dusty's face. Seeing himself being pushed away from the car, Dusty removed his pocket knife, and placed it against the hood of Lynn's car.

"Bitch, if you take one mo step, I'ma scratch a jigsaw puzzle in this motherfucker." Dusty said calmly.

Dusty had executed a bitch move, but it was an effective one. He was going after Lynn's prize possession, by threatening to disfigure it. Lynn's heart stopped at the sight of seeing Dusty's knife resting against the hood of her car. Again, she dropped her bags to the ground and raised her hands in surrender. Dusty was about to inflict serious damage to her classic 1966 GTO, and she wanted no parts of it. Her GTO was her baby, and a special gift from her mother.

"Dusty, please, don't." Lynn pleaded.

"What you gonna do for me?" Dusty asked.

Dusty had regained momentum, and laughed now that Lynn was at his mercy.

"I art to make you suck my dick." Dusty teased.

"Why are you doing this to me? I haven't done anything to you." Lynn said out of frustration.

"I'm doing this because you're a disrespectful little bitch." Dusty answered.

Lynn didn't have a clue as to what to do next, but knew she had to do something, if she was going to leave the store yard unscathed. Having no idea what Dusty's motives were, Lynn thought money would motivate him, but learned that trying to bribe Dusty only infuriated him more. Again, she was forced to apologize for any misunderstanding. Refusing her apology, Dusty continued to make things difficult by refusing to comply to her wishes. His threats of damaging her $20,000.00 paint job had Lynn so discombobulated, she was willing to do just about anything to save her car from being vandalized.

It took a minute or two, before she could regain her senses, and once doing so, she realized, she could repair the damage, but she couldn't repair the possible damage she could sustain by an attack from him. With her focus back to Dusty, Lynn made the decision to disperse the chemicals. Applying her index finger to the trigger of the can, Lynn again aimed at his face, and was milliseconds from dispersing the chemicals, when she heard a loud voice, commanding Dusty to stand down.

Not sure if what she was hearing pertained to her, Lynn kept her finger on the trigger. Again, the loud commanding voice, instructed Dusty to leave the scene immediately.

"Thank you God," Lynn thought to herself, as she released a deep breath, and dropped her hands from a defensive position. She had just dodged a bullet that was aimed directly at her, but the threat remained, as Dusty was hesitating to leave as instructed. He wasn't ready to give up so easily, and stood firm against his orders to vacate the premises.

As the stranger got closer, Dusty's resistance lessened. He stared at Lynn with hatred in his eyes. It was as if he was wishing for another chance at her, a chance to dismantle her into a million bits and pieces.

Lynn remained baffled, as to why he had such dislike for her. She hadn't done anything that warranted the treatment he inflicted upon her. She watched carefully as Dusty reluctantly surrendered his hard stance. He slowly folded his knife, and placed it back into his pocket. Before walking away, Dusty chose to leave Lynn with a few parting words.

"I better not see you again, you hear me bitch, because if I do, you can bet your sweet little ass, I'm fucking the shit out of you."

Dusty's statements weren't taken lightly, Lynn believed him, but for the first time, she felt confident. His threats didn't deter her from responding to his comments and saying what she wanted; knowing her security guard was standing at the corner of the store observing what was happening.

"Fuck you." Lynn responded. "Now take your country ass home and fuck your sister." Lynn knew it was a horrible thing to say, but Dusty had pissed her off, and she wanted pay back.

Lynn's comments momentarily stopped Dusty in his tracks. Thank God, he didn't return to finish what he wanted. His cold stare alone, sent chills throughout her body. Lynn watched as Dusty walked towards the stranger standing at the corner of the store. She wasn't certain what relation he was to him, but when Dusty approached him, he seemed to have dropped his head in shame, before disappearing behind the store.

After Dusty was gone, that the older gentleman walked over to her. His intervention had rescued her from a sure beat down, and she was thankful for his assistance. Once the middle-aged man approached, Lynn greeted him with an embrace. She was thankful for his assistance, so much so, she offered to reward him for his heroics. Of course, Pistol declined her offer; he was relieved she hadn't been hurt.

Retrieving her bags from the ground, Pistol used the front of his shirt to wipe the dirt away. He smiled, while passing her bag to her.

"Are you ok?" Pistol asked.

Lynn smiled and nodded yes. His concern for her safety was genuine, and after being assured that Lynn hadn't been physically harmed, Pistol opened the door to her car, so she could enter.

"I apologize for Dusty's stupidity, he's a borderline retard." Pistol said.

"So, I've been told." Lynn responded, as she started her car to leave. Her ordeal was finally over, but Lynn remained concerned that Dusty could follow her to retaliate for what he believed she had done to him. She hadn't seen a car, and was uncertain if he had access to one. Minutes later, she got her answer, after hearing a deafening noise coming from the rear of the store. Followed by a purple haze of smoke, rode Dusty. He was traveling in the opposite direction, but didn't miss his opportunity to give Lynn one final stare, and the middle finger.

Chapter: 12

The thought of seeing Drew's face when she arrived, overcame any anger Lynn had from her altercation with Dusty. It had been more than two weeks since she'd seen Drew, and she was anxious to see him. With any luck, Drew had ended his relationship with Gloria, and was ready to begin one with her. Though she didn't want to rush Drew into doing anything he wasn't completely on board with, she hoped he was open to them being together. Lynn never imagined she would ever have feelings for anyone other than Marshall, but somehow, Drew had stolen her heart. He had come into her life unexpectedly, with only a promise of a friendship, but as the months passed, she found herself wanting to spend every spare second with him.

Never once, did he judge her as far as her mental status, or her inability to completely shut Marshall out of her life. Instead, he continued to support her, and cheered for the efforts she was making. Drew's support not only made him the perfect gentleman, it impressed her to the point that she felt herself falling for him. By discussing his intentions to end his engagement with Gloria, Drew not only opened the idea for her to become a part of his life, he gave her a reason to close the door on Marshall. But until he broke off his engagement, Lynn was left to wonder what could be.

Drew had all intentions of ending his engagement with Gloria. Lord knows, he'd had enough of her wheeling and dealing, as well as the mind games she was playing. It was fair to say that he was just waiting for the most appropriate time to end things. But as for Lynn, well, she hadn't been able to wipe clean her slate of Marshall either. Maybe it was the lies Marshall was feeding her that kept her from ending all contact with him.

What was so unbelievable, was the fact that she knew he was lying, but like a woman lost in a fog, she resisted not believing him. Marshall never told her that he loved her during their time together, but once he suspected another man had taken his place, he suddenly realized, he couldn't live without her. Sadly, Lynn's heart continued to cling to Marshall. Their history together should have been warning enough for her to run like hell away from him, but something was keeping her connected to him, and she didn't know why?

It was impossible to understand why she couldn't sever ties with Marshall. Lord knows, he not only was one of the biggest liars she'd ever known; he was a cheater that showed no remorse. But most importantly, Marshall was an abuser, who mentally and physically controlled her mind. What should have been a slam dunk in kicking Marshall's ass to the curb, was an opportunity lost. Lynn wanted to blame Ashley for placing her in harm's way, but Ashley didn't force her to do anything against her wishes, it was a decision she chose to make. Like a fool, Lynn agreed to help Ashley cater an NBA draft party for Marshall; placing herself in the middle of an inferno. The problem was, Lynn didn't know how to tell Drew that she was driving down to her parent's beach house to meet Marshall, after she left him. She had no idea how she was going to tell Drew, but knew it was in her best interest to do so.

Lynn cautiously rounded the curve, nearing the Harrison estate. For the first time since driving the narrow road, she was seeing signs of civilization. It was a totally different scene from where she lived, but it seemed serene. Sure, she would have to get used to the scent of the cows, but the exuberance of knowing she was going to be in the presence of the man she loved, overpowered the cows. Lynn imagined herself living in the country, and from the picture she drew, she would be happy. It could be a challenge, isolated so far from the rest of the world, but she envisioned her life, a happy one. All she needed was for Drew to say yes. Parking in front of the family's Victorian styled house, Lynn's adrenaline was pumping. She was seconds away from giving Drew the surprise of his life, and wasn't sure how he was going to react once she saw him.

Getting out her car, Lynn made her way towards the front door. Before reaching it, she heard music emanating from behind the house. Following the sound, she came upon, whom she believed was Drew; working under his car. Lynn laughed to herself, while seeing Drew's legs moving to the sound of Billy Ocean, playing on his music box. Anxious to get Drew's attention, Lynn knocked on the hood of his car. When that didn't work, she turned off the power to his music box. Believing it was Joanna playing a trick on him, Drew crawled from under his car to confront her, but instead, was confronted by Lynn. Just as Lynn had suspected, Drew was surprised to see her, but embarrassed by his appearance. Filled with emotions, Drew attempted to embrace her, but realized he was too filthy to do so. Lynn didn't seem to care if her white sun dress got soiled or not, she was where she wanted to be, and that was in his arms.

"I've missed you so much." Lynn said, while pressing her body tightly against Drew.

Feeling secure, she closed her eyes, and buried her face into Drew's chest. She wanted to enjoy the moment of being held in his arms, before having to tell him about the upcoming event that was literally just hours away from beginning. Knowing what was about to happen after her embrace, Lynn prepared herself for what she hoped was a kiss on her lips, opposed to the customary kiss on her forehead. She was disappointed that she didn't get the kiss she was expecting, but focused her attention on enjoying the time she had with Drew before having to leave. Clutching Lynn's hand, Drew led her behind the house to where his mother was relaxing on her patio with a glass of wine, after surviving a rough day at city hall. Nancy was surprised to see they had a guest, but more than that, she was surprised that it was the friend Drew had spoken so highly of.

Nancy was finally meeting the girl who'd seemingly stolen her son's heart, and after being formerly introduced, she understood why. Lynn was not only stunningly beautiful; she possessed an aura about her that radiated brightly. She was articulate, and displayed a personality that anyone could fall in love with. She was the girl every mother wanted their son to bring home. Without a doubt, Ashlynn Boldmont was a keeper. Finally, after years of punishment, the time had arrived for Drew to rid himself of that alley cat, who had attached herself to him for his entire teen life. For eight years, Drew gave his all to a doomed relationship, only to see no results. Now, there was a light at the end of the tunnel, and that light was Lynn.

Drew watched from afar as his two favorite girls were getting to know each other. From his prospective, Nancy was seeing what he saw in Lynn, and like him, she was overly impressed. They talked for nearly an hour, before going inside the house. Drew followed at a close distance, as the women entered the main house, by way of the kitchen. He was astonished at the sight of them bonding so quickly, and as he sat at the kitchen table, he watched Lynn help prepare dinner. Amazed at what he was watching, Drew could only laugh to himself and wonder if Lynn had a clue as to what she was doing. He'd hoped his mother would become attached to Lynn as he had, and from the looks of it, his wish had come true. Only Karyme had received the amount of attention his mother was giving Lynn, which was proving to be a sure sign, she was intrigued with Lynn. To further support his theory, Nancy's decision to share her sweet potato, and apple pie recipes with Lynn was not only astounding, it was downright crazy. The Nancy Harrison he knew, would have never done such a thing. But that was the effect Lynn seemed to have on her.

Although it was late-afternoon, time was becoming a factor. Lynn needed to leave, if she was to be at her family's beach house to meet Ashley before 9pm. She hated the idea of having to leave Drew and his mother, but Ashley was expecting her. Lynn would have rather spent the evening with the Harrisons, but felt obligated to her sister. Marshall was scheduled to fly into town later that night, and Ashley was expecting her to be there to greet him. Looking at her watch, Lynn made the announcement that she needed to leave, if she was going to arrive in Virginia Beach by nine o'clock. Wanting to learn more about Lynn, Nancy invited her to stay for dinner. As Nancy would explain, she didn't want Lynn to get on the road with an empty stomach, and plus, she wanted her to meet her daughter Joanna, who was due home later that evening.

Nancy was intrigued by Lynn's charm, and sensed that Lynn was perhaps the ideal girl for Drew. If she would've had her way, her choice would have been Karyme, but ultimately, it was Drew's decision, and by the looks of things, he had chosen someone other than Gloria. Not wanting to disrespect Nancy, Lynn accepted her invitation with a smile. She had no idea how she was going to explain her tardiness to Ashley, but was happy Ms. Harrison had saved her from having to meet Marshall at the airport. Lynn had answered Nancy's prayers, and for the first time in years, Drew seemed complete. He was smiling now, more than ever before, and from the looks of things, she had Lynn to thank for it. If her wishes went according to plan, "The High Yellow, Hazel Eyed Devil" would disappear from Drew's life, as quickly as she appeared. But before Nancy could completely place all of her eggs in one basket, she first needed to know more about Lynn, and her intentions for Drew.

Nancy hadn't been the mother who shielded her children from the world. She'd always encouraged them to be independent, and if they made a mistake, she left it to them to find the solution. But in the case of Gloria, she was a mistake that kept reoccurring. Drew's relationship with her was a long and difficult one, and to refrain herself from interfering was a task that proved to be impossible. As luck would have it, Gloria began cheating on Drew with Mason, and though Drew was away at college, he was aware of her infidelities. Nancy couldn't say for certain, as to why Gloria chose to date Mason, but suspected it was because she had slept with all of the eligible men in the county. But there was a storm on the horizon, and her name was Ashlynn Boldmont, and if things went as she suspected, Gloria's reign was coming to a crashing end, and she couldn't be happier.

Needing to push the envelope further, Nancy again pressed her luck, and invited Lynn to stay the night. It was a decision she believed was vital to Drew's relationship with Lynn. As Nancy looked at it, this could be the final push to get Gloria out of his life permanently. To support her decision, Nancy gave a rational explanation as to why Lynn should stay the night. For one, it was dangerous for her to be traveling so late. As a mother, Nancy advised, she wasn't comfortable allowing her to travel alone at night. But what Nancy wanted more than anything, was to get to know the girl her son wanted a future with. Faced with the decision that could kick start her relationship with Drew and his family; Lynn accepted Nancy's invitation. She explained that she needed to contact her sister to not expect her tonight. It was a decision Lynn knew wasn't going to be popular with Ashley, but she felt compelled to stay with the Harrison family after being invited for dinner, as well as to spend the night.

Excusing herself, Lynn stepped into the dining room for privacy. She was overwhelmed that Nancy felt comfortable enough to have invited her to spend the night, but remained uncertain if it was the appropriate thing for her to do. After all, this was her first time meeting Drew's family, and she wanted to make a good impression, but she had to consider Ashley, and the promise she made to her. It wasn't fair that she was standing Ashley up, knowing what was at stake. By being a no-show, she was placing Ashley in harm's way. Leaving Ashley alone with Marshall was like throwing gasoline on a burning fire. Marshall was by far the most charming guy she had ever known, but there was a dark side of him that only she knew. It was too dangerous for Ashley to be left alone with Marshall. If given the chance, he would use her, and after doing so, he would discard her like a bag of trash. Marshall's plane was due to fly out of the University Park Airport later that evening. Needing to delay Marshall's flight, Lynn called   him to reschedule his flight for the following evening, but got no answer.

Desperate to get her message across, Lynn followed with a text. It was uncertain if Marshall would respond to her text in time, so she opted to err on caution, and called Ashley. It was important for her to tell Ashley about her change in plans, and how detrimental it could be if she allowed Marshall to spend the night. Needless to say, Ashley didn't answer her phone, and just as she'd done with Marshall, Lynn left a message; instructing her to return her call asap.

As Drew followed Lynn upstairs to her bedroom, she was excited about spending the night, but more than that, she was happy to be surrounded by a loving family. This was the first time she was spending the night at another man's house, and it was exciting. Lynn had heard many stories from her friends about how their boyfriends sneaked into their rooms at night and made love to them, while their parents were sleeping in the adjoining room. Lynn was sure she and Drew wouldn't have an experience such as that. As exciting as it sounded, Drew wasn't going to be sneaking into her room for a night of passionate lovemaking. She was going to be respectful, and so was he.

Once the layout and tour of upstairs was complete, Drew left to allow Lynn to freshen up and change into something more comfortable. He was planning a tour of the farm, which consisted of an office visit, followed by a short visit to the lake. Before meeting Drew downstairs, Lynn called Ashley again. She wasn't looking forward to telling Ashley about her change of plans, but felt she had no other choice. Answering on the first ring, Ashley was in a near state of panic after listening to Lynn's voicemail; explaining that she wasn't coming until the following morning. Ashley was interested to know why the sudden change.

"What do you mean you're not coming?" Ashley said, when answering her phone.

Hesitating, Lynn began to explain. "Well, that's what I'm calling about," Lynn responded. She was undecided whether to tell Ashley where she was, or why she decided to accept Ms. Harrison's invitation, but ultimately knew she had to deliver the disappointing news.

"Please tell me you changed your mind?" Ashley said, hoping to hear good news.

"I am coming, but just not tonight." Lynn clarified. She was delaying her arrival until the following afternoon without saying why, because it was going to be a hard pill for Ashley to swallow. Lynn knew about Ashley's infatuation for Drew. She hadn't been altogether sure how Drew felt about her, but expected it to be nothing more than a friendship.

"I may as well tell you the truth." Lynn said. "Drew's mother invited me to stay the night, and I accepted."

Lynn held her head down to the floor, with her eyes closed. She was prepared to hear feedback from Ashley, and she didn't disappoint.

"You did what?" Ashley responded in disbelief. "Have you lost your rabbit ass mind?" Ashley followed.

Ashley was bewildered by the news, but more than that, her temperament transformed from one of near panic, into that of infuriation. Ashley hadn't expected Lynn to deviate from their plan by spending the night with Drew, and accepting an invitation to shack up with him for the night. Lynn's poor decision, was not only unexpected, it was damning to Ashley's plan to reunite her with Marshall, who was scheduled to fly in later that night. Lynn's unconscious decision had brought Ashley's blood to a boil, and she showed it by lashing out at her sister.

"I knew it, I knew you were going to somehow fuck me with this. God, I can't believe you're doing this to me. Like always, you find a way to stab me in my fucking back. After everything I've done for you, you find a way to dry fuck me."

Disappointing Ashley was the last thing Lynn wanted to do, but spending the evening with the Harrison family was something she couldn't turn away from. Closing her eyes, Lynn rested her head against the headboard of her bed. She listened, without interruption, while Ashley bitched about the sacrifices she made for her, and how selfish Lynn had been in return. Ashley had no idea of the sacrifice she was making for her. Just to be in the presence of Marshall was more than she could stomach, and though she couldn't deny her feelings for him, Lynn knew it was in her best interest, to keep her distance from him. Spending the remainder of the week with Marshall wasn't something she was looking forward to, but it was a promise she'd made to Ashley. Lynn's promise to arrive the following afternoon didn't make Ashley feel any better, but it gave her the answer she hadn't expected. Drew wasn't as interested in her, as he was with Lynn. Learning the truth, cut like a knife, but it hadn't completely left Ashley without hope. She had one thing Lynn didn't, she had a sound mind, and knew what she wanted. Lynn on the other hand, still had feelings for Marshall, and after spending time with him, Ashley was willing to bet Lynn would go back to the man she wanted more than anything.

It was disheartening for Ashley to know her sister was staying under the same roof with the man she was expecting to be hers. Ashley tried convincing herself that nothing was going to happen between them, but couldn't say for certain. She was aware of Lynn's fears of becoming close to another man, but Lynn had gone ape shit crazy over Drew, and based on her history, she would most likely be willing to do whatever it took to get the man she wanted. It was her responsibility to make sure that didn't happen.

Somehow, she was going to convince Lynn to give Marshall another chance. Sure, Marshall had fucked up by getting caught fucking Lynn's best friend, but it shouldn't have been severe enough, for her to lose her freaking mind. There was no way his penis could've been that good, but then again, Marshall was the only man Lynn had ever been with.

If you ask Ashley, she would agree that Lynn was living in a fantasy world. Lynn's fairy tale beliefs that true love exists, was as factual as saying the tooth fairy left money under your pillow after losing a tooth. If Lynn thought she had true love with Drew, she was sadly mistaken. Drew was as weak as they came. All it took for her was to lay her arm across his crotch; making his dick become so hard, it nearly ripped open the jeans he was wearing. The thought of revealing what happened between her and Drew crossed Ashley's mind, but she wasn't ready to reveal that yet. Ashley hoped once Lynn was alone with Marshall things would fall into place. But first Ashley needed to secure her plan, and to do that, she needed Lynn to show up. Marshall was arriving in town later that evening, and though Lynn had thrown a monkey wrench in her plans, it hadn't derailed them completely.

Worried that Ashley would have to spend the night with Marshall, Lynn voiced her concerns. It wasn't that she was jealous; she was afraid for her sister's safety. With an unseen smirk, Ashley put Lynn's concerns at ease after announcing that she would be in the company of her ex-boyfriend, who had driven down to spend the week with her. It was a lie, but Ashley felt the need to put Lynn's concerns to rest.

Although the afternoon hadn't gone as expected, it hadn't been a total disaster. Lynn was coming, but it wasn't until tomorrow. This gave Ashley the time she needed to put her plan into motion. Marshall was coming, and he was going to be accompanied by his parents. Lynn had no idea what she was about to face, and when doing so, it was going to be too late for her to back out.

Chapter: 13

Drew's decision to give Lynn a tour of the farm came about at his mother's suggestion. Nancy knew Karyme was out of town; exempting her from having to endure seeing Drew with another woman. Nancy made no secret about her feelings for Karyme, she was like a daughter to her and loved her very much. Her only wish was that Drew could find it in his heart to love Karyme as much as she loved her. But if there was such a thing as a bright side, or a silver lining; having Lynn to play spoiler was it. Nancy had placed Drew in position to start the future he wanted with Lynn. She had pulled it off by inviting Lynn to stay the night, now it was up to Drew to do the rest, but if by chance he needed more ammunition; she carried extra in her pocket.

While touring the temporary office Drew shared with Karyme, Lynn noticed how close in proximity their desks were to each other. It went without saying, the office was small, but self-consciously Lynn felt the office was large enough to separate the desks further apart. To make things worse, there was an 8.5 X 11-inch picture of Drew and Karyme together on Drew's desk. It was the second picture Lynn had seen of them cuddled together, and from her prospective, they resembled a couple more than friends. Seeing the pictures, Lynn began having negative thoughts, which led to a host of questions concerning Drew's relationship with Karyme. Her problem revolved around her past, and what she experienced with Marshall. Before she could take the next step towards a relationship, Lynn needed clarification regarding Drew's true feelings for Karyme.

Having nothing to hide, Drew answered most of Lynn's questions, but quickly became evasive once Lynn inquired about his true feelings for Karyme. Drew's behavior triggered Lynn's overly suspicious nature. Drew seemed to dance around her questions, without clarifying how he truly felt for Karyme. He would only say, they shared a brother/sister relationship, and nothing more. Drew understood Lynn's pain. He knew what she experienced with Marshall, and no woman should ever be subjected to it, but his relationship with Karyme was complex. His love for Karyme was far greater than even he could describe. They grew up together and lived under the same roof, until Karyme's senior year of high school. Within that span, their love had taken on a new meaning. What, he wasn't sure, but what he was sure of, was his love for Karyme went deeper than that of a sister.

Scarred after having seen another picture of Drew and Karyme together, Lynn left the office quietly; keeping her feelings inside. It was a feeling she knew all too well; a risk she couldn't afford to take. She worked hard to rebuild her life and knew if she risked it, the walls would come tumbling down. It wasn't that she didn't trust Drew, because she did to a certain extent. She just wanted to play it safe, and not have her heart destroyed again. Seeing Lynn's expression, Drew tried clearing any misunderstanding that could have evolved from her seeing what she misconstrued as being something more than it actually was. So, before they left the office, Drew did what he thought was the right thing and removed his picture with Karyme from his desk; placing it into his file cabinet. He was closing the drawer on any thoughts of him being with Karyme; promising Lynn to never display it again. It was important to their relationship that they have a smooth take-off, and by taking the first step, he was displaying what he was willing to do, to have a future with her.

Lynn remained quiet during the remainder of their office tour, as well as their tour of the new state of the art plant that was still under construction. Seeing pictures of Drew and Karyme had impacted her into a state of reclusion. Although Drew explained the significance of his relationship with Karyme, Lynn wasn't buying it. In her opinion, it was hard to believe Drew could sit across from Karyme for twelve hours or more each day, without having some kind of a reaction. To say he didn't recognize Karyme's beauty was absurd. Karyme was drop dead gorgeous, and most likely the envy of all women who knew her. She would be a fool to think Karyme wouldn't pose a threat, especially after having seen the signs of affection being shown in their picture together. Lynn wanted to believe Drew's love for her outranked his feelings for the beautiful Karyme Rios-Gonzales. She needed to trust Drew, and to refrain herself from comparing him to Marshall. There shouldn't have been any comparison when it came to Drew. He'd proven not only his love, but his loyalty to her. He was more than Lynn could have ever asked for. Lynn needed to understand, Drew and Marshall were totally opposite, and if she was to make it work between them, she had to learn to fully trust him.

At the completion of their tour of Hill Crest Farms corporate office, the couple got into a golf cart and took a short drive to one of the company's underground storage facilities. Hill Crest Farm's underground facilities stored some of the company's most sort after cheeses across the nation, and after hearing the story, Lynn was excited to sample some of their domestic brands, as well as those slated to be exported to other countries. Drew forewarned her about exotic brands; advising her against sampling them, but Lynn's curiosity got the best of her. After being accosted by the pungent taste and smell from an exported brand, they burst into laughter; it was more than enough for Lynn. She declined further sampling, and was ready to continue her tour.

The tour continued, with the couple settling by the lake. It was now less than an hour before dinner was scheduled to take place, but it hadn't stopped them from wanting to enjoy what little quality time they had left. Lynn took time to apologize for her earlier reactions to Karyme's picture. It was the first time since knowing Lynn, that she had shown any hint of jealousy. In Lynn's opinion, Karyme wasn't just another woman. She was not only smart, but gorgeous, and she was working beside Drew on a daily basis. More than anything, Lynn wanted Drew to be her man, but sharing him with Karyme, or Gloria was out of the question. In order to move forward with their relationship, Lynn had to establish trust. Drew hadn't given her a reason not to trust him, nor had he ever lied to her that she knew of. As far as she knew, he was the most honest man she'd ever met. Drew had proven himself, and had been consistent with his care involving her. Still, she found it hard to let go of her past. Marshall's departure had left her badly bruised, and getting over it was going to take time. Her only hope was, Drew could extend her the time she needed.

Dangling her feet in the warm water of the lake, Lynn took a deep breath, before throwing caution to the wind. It was time to tell Drew how she felt about him. Her only hope was that he felt the same for her.

"I don't know how to say this, so, I'm just going to say it. I know we've been knowing each other for less than a year, but I'm in love with you." Lynn confessed.

Finally, she had the gumption to say what she'd been wanting to say for weeks. Hopefully, Drew would respond positively. Drew reached for Lynn's hand, and scooted closer to her. He wanted to assure her that his feelings for her were mutual, and he verified it, by kissing her. It wasn't his customary kiss to her forehead, but a kiss on her lips. Drew had finally did it, he'd crossed the threshold of friendship, onto the path leading towards a possible relationship. He wanted the same thing, but first had to sever ties with Gloria.

"You don't know how long I've waited to hear you say that." Drew confessed. "I love you, and have felt this way about you a while now. But I have to be honest with you, I haven't taken care of my situation with Gloria yet." Drew announced.

It was not because he didn't want to, the actual fact was, Gloria had been busy; preventing him from doing so. Drew's admission promoted Lynn's theory; Drew was in love with her. It also answered questions pertaining to Ashley's warning concerning Drew's faithfulness. Drew never hid the fact that he was engaged, nor did he omit considering to end his relationship. Drew had been honest with his intentions, and never once crossed the line. He was the ideal gentleman, that placed her needs first. It was his unselfish ways that attracted her to him, and as time passed, she found herself falling in love with him.

Lynn didn't have to second guess Drew anymore. She felt his sincerity, and from this moment on, she wouldn't have to question his integrity. She had faith in Drew, and believed he would make it happen. But before she took the next step in their relationship, it was essential that he end his relationship with Gloria. Lynn didn't give Drew a timeline, nor did she make it an issue to force him to sever ties with Gloria immediately, but until he did, they could be no more than friends.

Excited to have broken the ice, Drew was ready to move forward with his future with Lynn. There were no second thoughts, Lynn was who he wanted to be with. But before he could make it official, he had to be honest with her. His belief that honesty was the key in laying the foundation to a great relationship was being challenged by his past mistakes. It was imperative that he reveal the truth of his sexual affair with Ashley before it came to light. He knew if his secret should ever be revealed, it would undoubtedly destroy any chance of a future they could have together. Drew was remorseful for his mistake, and though he made several attempts to reveal the truth, he couldn't. He couldn't risk the chance of losing Lynn. Maybe in the near future he would have the strength to admit his indiscretions, but today wasn't the time. Today was their moment to enjoy the feelings of being in love.

Returning home, the couple cuddled on the front porch in Nancy's favorite swing bench. Dinner was running behind, and it gave Drew and Lynn time to recap their future together. In doing so, they found themselves gazing into each other's eyes, and for a second, they nearly lost their composure; giving in to the passion that burned within them, but at the last second, Lynn pulled away. She urged Drew to concentrate on their future and not the present. She reiterated her feelings about his unresolved relationship with Gloria, while refusing to go any further than they had already gone. Lynn was determined not to play the fool again, and stressed the importance of honesty and fidelity. She didn't want to suffer through another nervous breakdown; she didn't believe her heart could take another blow.

Lynn's confession had put Drew on the spot, leading him to contemplate, whether to reveal what happened between he and Ashley. He didn't believe Ashley would air their dirty laundry, because if she was going to, she would have done so already. Maybe in time, he would build the nerves to confess what happened between them, but now wasn't the time. After dinner, Drew joined his mother in the kitchen, to help with packing away leftovers, as well as helping with dishes. Their time alone presented them with the opportunity to discuss his relationship with Lynn, and where it was expected to go. Across the hallway, Lynn played the piano to the delight of Joanna, who was high on Drew's choice. Like her mother, Joanna disagreed with Drew's decision to give Gloria an engagement ring, but she kept her opinion to herself. Everyone but Drew was aware of Gloria's indiscretions with Mason, and though they hated what she was doing, the decision was made to stay out of his affair. But a new day was on the horizon. Drew had taken the step to search for a woman who cared for him, and not for what he could do for her. It was the first time Drew had ever been so eager to introduce another girl to the family. It was obvious that Drew was in love with Lynn. His constant stares at her, and his bubbly personality was all the proof his family needed to substantiate their analysis. Tonight, there was going to be an intervention, whether it was Joanna, or Nancy, Drew was going to be told the truth about his so-called fiancé. The decision was made, and as Drew's mother, it was Nancy's decision to tell Drew the truth. While washing and drying the dishes, Nancy had taken the opportunity to explore Drew's mindset. She contemplated which angle to approach, and after reviewing all of them, she decided to go straight ahead at him.

Though Nancy's heart went out to him, there was no other way to tell him but to lay the truth on the table, and let it rest as it may. Having to tell Drew the truth was going to be difficult, especially knowing of his plan to marry Gloria, but she was the town's slut, and Nancy wanted Drew to have no parts of her. Without wavering her feelings any further, Nancy shared her knowledge of Gloria's indiscretions. Drew needed to know the full truth to gain his freedom from a loveless engagement he was imprisoned in. It was fair to say, Nancy deputized herself as the one to break the news to him. She saw how happy Drew was, now that Lynn had become a part of his life, and though Nancy didn't know much about Lynn, she was sure, she could make a better girlfriend than Gloria ever had.

Nancy saw this as Drew's opportunity to get out of the mess he had gotten himself into. She was about to throw him a lifeline, and hoped he had the good sense to grab hold of it. Nancy wanted to make what she had to say, short but firm. She wanted it to sink into Drew's clouded mind to clear up the lies, and excuses Gloria had told him. Nancy didn't have to think about what she was going to say; she knew exactly what to say.

"Honey, I need to tell you something." Nancy said. "There's no easy way to say this, but Gloria and Mason are in a serious relationship, and have been for some months now. From what I've been told, she's supposed to break up with you before you leave for summer school." Nancy said.

Drew wasn't totally oblivious to the news. For a long time, he suspected Gloria's involvement with Mason went beyond what she was saying. Now that the truth had finally come to light, he was ready to make his move. Things had played out the way Drew had hoped, but he still found the news hurtful. As funny as it sounded, Drew was hurt by Gloria's decision to seek comfort in another man's arms while he was away at college. For more than three years, he pondered about what he had done wrong, and what caused Gloria to be so unhappy. He now realized, it wasn't anything on his part, Gloria was being Gloria. She thrived on attention, and when he wasn't around to give it to her, she found it in the arms of someone else.

Without giving his decision a second thought, Drew grabbed his car keys hanging on a hook by the kitchen door, and left for his car. Nancy followed him, and pleaded that tonight wasn't the time to confront Mason or Gloria, but her pleads went unheard. Drew left to take care of the business he should have taken care of years ago. It was something he knew he had to do, and felt strongly that Lynn would support him on it.

Chapter: 14

Still hyped from her phone conversation with Marshall, Ashley could barely wait for his arrival. He was the key to getting Drew back into her life and bed. Marshall's pending reconnection with Lynn was a win/win situation for both of them, but it could only work if Lynn chose to give him another chance. Though Lynn denied her feelings for Marshall, Ashley strongly believed Lynn's love for him remained deeply embedded within her heart, but something drastic had happened, which affected Lynn's mental status; causing her breakdown. Desperate to know the cause as to why Marshall and Lynn called it quits, Ashley tried prying, but got very little information. Marshall would only say that it was his fault, but was adamant that he didn't do anything to physically harm Lynn.

Ashley's envy of Lynn went back to their childhood, and though she was proclaimed the most beautiful of the two, it wasn't enough to hide Ashley's pain. Lynn was everything she wanted to be. Lynn had the love and respect of their father, she was super intelligent, and what perhaps was Lynn's greatest accolade, was how well she adapted to the family business at such a young age. You see, everything came naturally to Lynn. It was as if she had the Midas touch, and everything she touched, turned to gold; at least in Ashley's eyes. Lynn excelled in everything she attempted; from her grades in school, to the way she intermingled with people. The only thing she failed at, was her relationship with Marshall, but then again, Lynn could argue it that wasn't worth saving. Lord knows, Marshall wasn't worth a wooden nickel, but he was Lynn's first and only love, until Drew came along and stole her heart. Now, Ashley found herself the odd one out.

Ashley was betting on Marshall, and his manly charm to reconnect with Lynn. Marshall had a plan to get back the woman he deemed to be his everything, and if he could work his magic, Ashley would be grateful. But in order for him to pull off what Ashley deemed as impossible, his dumb ass had to learn how to keep his penis in his boxers, and prove to Lynn how serious he was in wanting her back in his life. It was obvious by their letters that Lynn was still in love with him. After all, she did say she was looking forward to spending the week with him. In Ashley's mind that meant Lynn wanted to be with Marshall, and these comments left Ashley hoping for a reconciliation between the two of them. If the week proved to be as successful as she predicted, Lynn would fall back in love with Marshall; leaving Drew available for her. But it would only work, if Lynn brought her little narrow ass to the beach house as promised.

To further hype Ashley's hopes and dreams, Marshall assured her that he intended to reconnect with Lynn, and make her his wife. Ashley was impressed by his intentions, and was quick to jump on his bandwagon. She was ecstatic to be presented with what she felt was a sure avenue that would lead Drew back into her arms. Ashley knew how deeply in love Lynn was with Marshall, and the devastation he caused her, but she hoped it wasn't too late for her to give it another go. What she didn't know was what attributed to their breakup, but again, she was assured by Marshall that it had nothing to do with allegations that he physically abused her.

Ashley heard many versions of what happened, but couldn't say for certain if any of them were true. She wanted to believe Marshall truly loved Lynn, and hadn't physically harmed her in any way, but remained unsure if his intentions for Lynn were in her best interest. Most of what she heard was from a third party

and not her sister. Lynn refused to speak on it, and so had
Marshall.

Without wanting to speculate any further, Ashley chose to
remain neutral; without favoring support to either Lynn or
Marshall. Her only concern was to get Drew back into her life.
However, Ashley reserved the right to protect her sister, if need
be. If Marshall was the crazed monster Lynn made him out to
be, she wouldn't hesitate to get involved, and would quickly
abolish her plans to unite the two. To believe Marshall was a
monster, without having adequate proof, could be bias on her
behalf, but he showed no signs of being a monster, yet there
was something fishy about their breakup. Neither of them
would discuss details that caused their breakup; it was as if they
had been placed under a gag order.

Ashley knew it was more to the story than either of them were
saying, and the fact that Marshall never tried hiding his cheating
ways, while Lynn continued to stay with him was a red flag. But
why now? Why had Lynn finally called it quits, after enduring so
much embarrassment? Something happened, but what? What
made the two decide to call it quits, after being together for so
long? And what happened to cause Lynn's mental breakdown?

Perhaps the most telling question, was why was Marshall so
interested in wanting to have a future with Lynn, when he was
about to go pro. He was sure to be drafted in the first round,
with an assurance he would be the top pick in the draft. He
didn't need Lynn; he was days away from becoming a
multimillionaire. Why did he all of a sudden want to marry
Lynn? Ashley couldn't put her finger on what Marshall had in
mind, but was sure this weekend was going to tell the entire
story.

For Ashley's sake, her hopes depended upon what Marshall was
willing to do to get Lynn back. If he was sincere about making

Lynn his wife, nothing was going to stop her from gaining Drew's love. Ashley saw this weekend as Lynn's chance to not only reunite with the man she truly loved, but to become his wife. Marshall had only four days to work his magic, and Ashley warned him against creating any distractions that could ruin his chances. She had a lot at stake, and she was risking it all for a man she was suspicious of. There was no doubt, it was going to be a hard pitch to sell to Lynn, but Ashley was obligated to bring forth the effort. Though many questions arose regarding the validity of Marshall's motives, Ashley made the decision to go forward with their plan. She remained leery of what could happen if their plan backfired, but felt it was worth the risk.

Chapter: 15

Ashley waited impatiently for Marshall's plane to land. She paced back and forth, while trying to decide what she was going to tell the Lathan family regarding Lynn's absence. Lynn's unscheduled cancellation had placed her in an uncomfortable position, and to pull it off, she had to have a convincing reason for Lynn not being there. As Ashley contemplated on what to say, she created the story that Lynn was on a business trip with their father, and wouldn't be joining them until the following morning. It wasn't a great lie, but it was the only believable thing she could come up with. Standing by the baggage department, Ashley saw Marshall and his parents come into view.

Rushing to greet them, she did so with an embrace. Marshall and his parents hadn't seen her in two years, and were stunned by her beauty. After seeing Ashley, Marshall could only imagine how Lynn looked in comparison. He was anxious to see her, and scanned the airport in search of her. Her tomboyish image, remained vivid in his mind, and he couldn't wait to hold her in his arms. Where is that beautiful woman with the heart of gold, who was once my biggest cheerleader, and why isn't she here to greet me? Marshall thought to himself. Marshall smiled to himself, as he reminisced seeing Lynn with her face painted, as she cheered for him; wearing his Nittany Lion jersey.

Lynn was all he ever wanted, and like a fool he destroyed it by getting caught up in the fame of being a star basketball player. Now, he had only the memories of what they once shared, and he wanted her back. It haunted him to know the pain he put Lynn through, but this weekend, he had a chance to make it right. God knows, if he could relive that part of his life, he would do things differently. For one, he wouldn't have ever cheated on her, nor would he have put his hands on her. Marshall could only pray that this weekend would be the start of a new chapter in their lives. However, Lynn's absence made it obvious that she was hesitant about seeing him. After greeting the family, Ashley announced that Lynn was on a business trip with their father, and wouldn't be joining them until the following afternoon.

Discouraged, Marshall tried keeping an open mind, but had second thoughts about inviting his parents. He felt it was a strong possibility that Lynn was going to be a no show; ruining the surprise he had planned. Chances were that Lynn was still broken by what happened between them. He couldn't blame her if she didn't show; he was a pure ass during those times.

For months he'd beaten himself up, after denying what actually happened between them. He hid behind the coattails of his parents, as well as the university, while Lynn was forced to take the full brunt of the rage from everyone who was familiar with the case. Marshall was fortunate to have a stable of well-wishers protecting him, but the crime he committed didn't warrant the protection he received. He should have gone to prison for what he did to Lynn, but instead, he got only a slap on the wrist.

He carefully followed the advice of his lawyer, and denied all claims that was brought up against him. It was by the grace of God, and Lynn's decision not to pursue charges, that he was exonerated. Lynn's decision to drop all charges, was the key to him continuing his education, and collegiate career. To further help his case, Lynn left the university and transferred to WFU after a brief visit to a hospital's mental facility. Meanwhile, he continued with his life as if nothing ever happened, and it wasn't until the end of the season, that things began to unravel.

Several women came forward; charging him with physical abuse. The allegations, not only damaged his draft status, it nearly destroyed his reputation.

That's where Lynn came into play. Marshall needed her to accept his proposal of marriage in order to save him from being overlooked in the draft. As he viewed it, Lynn was the pigeon he needed to save his professional career.

The family left the airport for the beach house, with questions lingering. Mrs. Lathan remained concerned about Lynn's absence, and believed it was more to her not being there than Ashley was admitting. She knew the truth, her battles with Constance to save her son from going to prison could be considered legendary, but she did what she felt was right at the time.

At the time, Mrs. Lathan was more than convinced that Marshall was innocent, and Lynn was only pressing charges against him because of his decision to end their relationship. It wasn't until she got a dose of reality that she believed what happened to Lynn was true.

Mrs. Lathan got that dose of reality, when she arrived home and found Marshall in a drunken state with his father's loaded 9mm handgun pressed against his temple. Engulfed in tears, Marshall confessed his involvement in what happened to Lynn. He was the monster she'd labeled him as, and he didn't want to live with the guilt.

Though the situation was tense and downright scary, Mrs. Lathan talked him out of wanting to end his life that day, and entered him in therapy to help deal with his guilt. After months of therapy, Marshall seemed to have recovered, at least that's what she thought. She couldn't say for certain when, but Marshall resorted back to his old ways.

It was after the season ended that more allegations resurfaced, accusing Marshall of physical abuse against several women. It was at that moment that the university turned their backs on him. It wasn't surprising, because it was at the end of his collegiate career, and the university didn't need him anymore. Now, Marshall was on his own and needed help desperately. He believed Lynn was the only person that could help him, and he was willing to do anything to save what reputation he had left.

Chapter: 16

Carrying a dishcloth across her shoulder, Dolly Mae entered her family room to confront Mason, who was sitting and polishing his shoes. Her mind was heavy with thoughts of what Mason was doing to Drew and the family. She wanted to try and convince Mason to talk to Drew about his relationship with Gloria, before it came back to bite him in the ass. Dolly Mae argued that it was wrong what Mason and Gloria was doing behind Drew's back, and as soon as he got wind of it, there was going to be trouble.

Dolly Mae feared Mason's reckless behavior would do further damage to an already strained relationship with her sister-in-law. But more than that, she worried it could spark a war between the families. It hurt her to know Mason was parading around town with Gloria, without even trying as much as to conceal it. Gloria was Drew's fiancé, which meant she should've been off limits to everyone, but Mason didn't seem to care.

It was as if he wanted Drew to find out about them. He, nor Gloria, was showing any respect to Drew, and sadly, the news regarding them had spread across town like a California wildfire. It wouldn't have been surprising, if Drew had already got wind of it. If this was the case, it would be just a matter of time before Mason and Drew would come face to face.

There was still time for Mason and Gloria to sit down with Drew to iron out their differences, but Mason refused to believe he was doing anything wrong. His decision not to do the right thing, ticked Dolly Mae's last nerve. Mason had crossed the line, and it was time he heard from her. Without as much as giving Mason a second to think, Dolly Mae attacked him verbally, and released her frustrations upon him.

"What are you thinking?" Dolly Mae screamed. "Don't you know Gloria and Drew are engaged to be married? Where are your morals, or don't you give a damn?"

Offended that his mother had chosen her nephew's position over his, Mason became defensive. He was appalled by Dolly Mae favoring Drew's happiness over his own, and he let his feelings be known.

"So, I'm automatically the bad guy, because Gloria chose me over him." Mason asked.

"No, Gloria is just as responsible, if not more. But you know better, Drew's your cousin. When it's all said and done, you're going to be the one that's going to get burned." Dolly responded.

"Me get burned? I don't think so." Mason responded. "The only cocksucker getting burned out of this deal, is going to be that dumb ass Drew. My only regret, is that I won't be there to see him cry like the bitch he is." Mason replied.

Dolly Mae was appalled at Mason's nonchalant attitude towards something so serious. He had no idea what he'd gotten himself into, and the thought of him being in the middle of a troubling dilemma was frightening. Mason argued that it was unfair to blame him for what had happened between he and Gloria. It was Gloria who came after him. He tried ignoring her flirtatious advances, but she wouldn't take no for an answer.

"I told her that I didn't want to fool with her because she was Drew's girl, but she told me, she won't interested in Drew no mo. She said she wanted me to be her nigger, so I asked, why me? She said because she wanted a real man, not some pussy who can't stand up to his momma." Mason chuckled, as he explained. Mason knew talking about Drew negatively in the presence of his mother always got under her skin. She loved

Drew, and often talked about him, as if he was the second coming. As far as Mason was concerned, faith had intervened and brought he and Gloria together, and now that it had, he had no intentions of stepping away. Gloria was the best thing that ever happened to him, and he couldn't walk away, even if he wanted to. He was in love, and leaving or quitting the woman he loved was impossible.

The thought that his mother chose Drew's happiness over his was upsetting, but not surprising. It hadn't been the first time his mother chose Drew's interest over his. It started with their childhood, when Dolly Mae began following Drew's successes, while turning a blind eye to his. Not once did she attend an after-school program he took part in, but found the time, and energy to follow Drew to all of his football and basketball games. She feared flying, but took a plane to Tallahassee Florida to watch Drew participate in a fucking track and field meet, but somehow couldn't come to his high school Spring Concert to see him play in the band. His mother's excuse was that she couldn't find a replacement to work for her at the group home; a group home she owned.

The truth remained, that his mother loved her brother's child more than her own. Maybe it was because of Drew's resemblance to her deceased brother, but whatever it was, she wasn't ashamed of it. In Mason's opinion, Drew had everything he didn't. Drew had the looks, the intelligence, and the personality that seemed to attract some of the most beautiful women he could only dream of. After years of fantasizing, God had answered his prayers, and sent him the only woman, he'd ever loved. Maybe that was why it hurt so much to know that after years of waiting, he'd finally captured Gloria's heart, only to be encouraged to stop seeing her.

His mother's demands to quit seeing Gloria only benefited Drew. It had nothing to do with him doing the right thing. Dolly

Mae knew Gloria wouldn't agree to a sit down and tell all meeting with Drew. For one, she didn't want to put him out like that, and secondly, she didn't want a confrontation between the two of them. Gloria wanted to work things out on her own, and though he agreed with her, his mother thought differently. She would rather protect Drew's feelings, than to see him happy.

Sadly, Dolly Mae's support of Drew only heightened Mason's animosity towards him. Mason became motivated to dig his feet into the ground even deeper; preparing for the showdown that was destined to come. There was no way he was going to step aside, and allow Drew to marry the woman he was in love with. As far as Mason was concerned, Drew could go fuck himself, because Gloria was his girl, and he was going to protect his interest if it killed him. Dolly Mae listened, as Mason confessed his love for Gloria. Ever since learning how to love; Gloria was it. She was the only girl he'd ever loved, and he wasn't going to turn her over so easily. Mason also confessed to his mother how he'd told Drew to talk to Gloria for him, but Drew only talked for himself.

If what Mason was saying is true, Dolly Mae felt he had a legitimate claim to Gloria. Drew had stolen the love of Mason's life, and it was only right he reclaimed what rightfully should have been his. However, Dolly Mae continued to disagree with what Mason and Gloria were doing. Mason didn't have to be a snake, because Drew had been one. If he and Gloria loved each other as much as they professed, it wouldn't be hard leveling with Drew. Somehow, Dolly Mae couldn't overlook the idea that Gloria was playing Mason for a fool. For one, she hadn't removed the engagement ring Drew had given her; giving all indications that she intended to marry Drew. Dolly worried about her only child getting his heart broken. It was going to be tough having to stand by, while that yellow whore changed her son from being a man, into a wuss, who would need permission from her to fart. This wasn't the Mason she raised. The Mason she raised, would have been man enough to tell Drew about his involvement with his fiancé. Her son would have proudly stood eye to eye to Drew, and admitted his feelings for Gloria. He wouldn't take a back door to anyone, but he was doing it now, and it was sad to see.

Gloria was dictating his life, and Mason hadn't even married her yet. The image Mason was displaying, was a man who had lost the confidence, along with his ability to think for himself. He was allowing Gloria to think for him, and man was she ever doing a number on him. As a favor to her, Dolly asked that Mason respect his cousin and sit down with him as men, and discuss his intentions with Gloria. Dolly was sure Drew would handle it well, but warned Mason, if he chose not to, he would regret it. Saying all she had to say, Dolly Mae made her way back into the kitchen. She hoped Mason would take heed to what she had said to him, but had a feeling he hadn't. He was so madly in love; he was willing to say and do anything that yellow bitch wanted him to do.

It was nearing six o'clock when Drew arrived unannounced at Gloria's house. Gloria was in the process of packing, when she was told that Drew was waiting for her in the living room. Drew's unexpected arrival was shocking nonetheless, but Gloria was curious to know why he was there to see her. Entering the living room, she greeted him with a smile.

"Hey, what brings you by?" Gloria asked nervously.

Expecting the worst, she sat beside Drew, and prepared herself for the onslaught that was bound to follow, but Drew remained cool as an underground stream, and calmly began asking questions pertaining to her association with Mason. Drew knew it was a touchy situation, and tried to be as gentle as he could, but he needed to hear the truth. It was the chance Gloria was looking for, but she was either too selfish, or too afraid to confess her indiscretions. So, she did what she was accustomed to doing; she lied. This was supposed to be the moment she was waiting for, but instead of being truthful, Gloria choked, and lied, while denying the allegations, before following suit of bursting into tears.

Drew had rehearsed what he was going to say on his drive over, but forgot everything he was going to say. Gloria's crying had caused his mind to go blank. He should've expected Gloria to cry, because she always faked crying when she wanted to get out of a sticky situation. But on this day, Drew was determined not to allow her to cry her way out of this. Wanting to know the truth, Drew again demanded that she speak the truth, and again, Gloria refused to change her story. She would only say, that they were friends and nothing more.

"For once in your life, just be honest with me, as well as yourself. I know Mason paid your tuition, I also know he allowed you to use his car to go back and forth to school. People have seen you together many times. You were seen kissing at the town festival, and there was even talk that you're going to give back my ring, before I leave to go back to college. Believe me, I'm not upset, I understand why you did what you did. I wasn't here for you, and you got lonely. I just need to know the truth." Drew pleaded.

He was hoping it was enough to cause Gloria to break, but like the master liar she was, she stuck to her story. However, Drew had backed her into a corner, and Gloria came out fighting like a honey badger. Instead of trying to deflect the question, Gloria became irate, causing a scene inside her home.

"Ain't nobody told you a got damn thing. That shit came from your nosey ass momma. She hates me, and always has." Gloria paused, before continuing to lash out at Drew. "Your momma only thought she saw me kissing Mason, but what she saw, was me giving him a kiss on his cheek for being a good friend. Mason was there for me when you were too much of a chicken shit to go to your momma to secure a loan for me."

"Gloria, I explained to you, mother couldn't afford to pay your tuition." Drew responded.

"But she could pay that illegal "Wetback's" tuition, and even brought her a fucking car. Gloria said.

"The car was a gift, for helping run the company, but honestly, mother didn't have the money." Drew explained.

Man, don't come to me with that bullshit. I know you and your mother are fucking millionaires. You're just a cheap ass." Gloria replied.

"You need to calm down." Drew said, while reminding Gloria, they weren't the only people there.

"Aw, fuck you man. If you would have protected me like you do your little senorita, I would be planning our wedding."

Suddenly, Gloria realized she'd messed up, and immediately began backpaddling to cover her lies.

"Drew, I love you." Gloria cried out. "We're supposed to be getting married, but it feels as if you want to break up with me.

"Please Gloria, just tell me the truth, so I can be out of your life for good." Drew asked.

Desperate to convince Drew how much she loved him; Gloria went into defensive mode.

"Why would I throw away the best thing to ever happen to me?" Gloria questioned. "They're lies, they are all lies. Mason and I are just friends, and nothing more. I swear to you, there's nothing going on between us."

Frantic at what was about to happen, Gloria locked her arms high, around Drew's left arm, and placed her face against his shoulder. She tried to cry, but was unable to shed a tear. She had accidently let the cat out the bag, and was fearing the worst. Turning to Gloria, Drew placed his forehead against hers; it was time to say goodbye. Drew had no idea what he was going to say, but knew he had to say something. Lynn was at home waiting for him, and it was time to go home to her. Drew slowly began to say what was on his mind. It may not have been what he'd scripted, but he was going to get his point across.

"Gloria, I'm sorry, but I don't believe you. You've cheated on me enough to know, and I've had enough. To be frank, I'm fed up with you and all of your drama and allegations, regarding you and Mason. I'm to the point that I can't take it anymore. I'm sorry, it's over between us."

It was the first time Drew had the courage to stand up for something he believed in, and though his relationship with Lynn was never discussed; as a man, he did what he thought was the right thing.

Hearing that Drew had broken things off with her, sent Gloria into a frenzy. Her plans of tricking him into staying with her had failed. He wanted nothing else to do with her, and it was frustrating for her to convince him to give her one final chance. Never in a million years, did Gloria ever believe that Drew would leave her. He'd promised her, he would always be there for her, whenever she needed him. What happened? Why was he going back on his word? There was only one other answer, he had another girl.

"Be honest, you're fucking some other bitch at your college, aren't you?" Gloria asked.

"There is no one else." Drew responded.

If there wasn't another girl, why didn't Drew want her anymore? What happened to cause him to give up on her? Had he finally had enough of her cheating? These are questions Gloria asked herself, as she pondered how she was going to keep Drew in her web.

"I beg you, please give us another chance." Gloria pleaded.

"I'm sorry, I can't do this anymore?" Drew responded.

Drew had taken all he could handle from Gloria, he was exhausted, and had lost his desire to fight for their engagement anymore. For years, he loved her unconditionally, but her inability to maintain a stable relationship, prompted him to call it quits. He wanted a stable relationship, as well as someone he could trust. It was hard going to sleep at night; wondering who she was sleeping with, or what scheme she was masterminding to deceive him. It was over, and now, more than ever, the time had come to walk away while he still had his sanity.

"Where you going? Gloria asked.

"I don't want this. I think it'll be better if we end this before it gets out of hand." Drew said, making his way to the door.

"You're not going anywhere, until you tell me why you want to break off our engagement." Gloria said, while grabbing Drew by his arm.

It was at that moment, Gloria attempted to strike Drew, but fortunately for him, he caught her hand. Drew warned that her violent behavior was another reason he was ending their engagement. He wasn't going into a marriage in which they couldn't argue, without going hands on. Gloria followed Drew as he went to the door. She tried reasoning with him, but Drew didn't want to hear what she had to say. His determination to leave, irritated Gloria even more. Once outside, Gloria began expressing what was on her mind.

"You're a bitch, you would rather believe that bullshit that I'm fucking Mason, than to hear the truth. I have never slept with Mason, we're only friends. But you don't have to worry about who I fuck now, because it's over between us. Is that how you feel?" Gloria asked.

Drew turned to her, and didn't know whether to respond to her, or to let things go as they were.

"Regardless of what you think, I'll always love you. I just can't be with you." Drew responded.

He opened the door and left the house. His goal was to have a peaceful exit, without getting into a brawl. He didn't want to have to explain the bruises to Lynn, and how he got them. Making his way to his car, Drew could hear Gloria only steps behind him. She needed an explanation as to why Drew chose to end their engagement, but Drew was refusing to talk to her.

"Drew please, listen before you leave." Gloria pleaded.

She didn't want to lose Drew, not until she knew for sure Mason was who she wanted to be with. Yes, Mason was exciting, and he was willing to do anything to please her, but he wasn't Drew. Drew could afford to give her the lifestyle she wanted. He was boring as they came, but he and his family were rich.

Gloria wanted it both ways, and was willing to swing back and forth with them, until she was satisfied with the cousin who passed her test.

"Are you going to talk to me, so we can work this out?" Gloria asked.

"No, I'm done with you. You have been an embarrassment not only to me but to my family." Drew responded.

"You motherfucker. Now, I get it. This is not about you and I. It's all about your precious momma. Well, you know what, take your little bitch ass home to your momma. I don't give a fuck anymore." Gloria responded by picking up a hand full of gravel from her driveway and threw it at Drew; hitting him and his car.

"Being that I'm supposed to be fucking Mason, I may as well go over to his house and fuck him." Gloria yelled out, as Drew drove away.

Hearing the doorbell, Dolly Mae rushed to answer the door. To her surprise, Drew was standing with a smile, as bright as the noon skies. Seeing Drew standing at her front door, reminded her of her baby brother. She tightly embraced Drew, before inviting him inside. Drew had grown up to look exactly like his father. Dolly Mae was excited to see him, but felt his visit was personal. To lighten the mood, Dolly Mae relayed how proud she was of him, and was anxious to know of his accomplishments. Though she was delighted that Drew had come to visit, she knew why he was there. It was obvious Drew had come to confront Mason regarding his association with his fiancé. That yellow, hazel eyed devil, not only had torn the cousins apart for life with her whoring ways. She may have brought on a war between them.

As a mother, it was her responsibility to protect Mason, even though he was dead ass wrong for what he was doing to Drew. He and Gloria deserved the karma they were facing, but not at the expense of Drew. In many ways Mason had been correct by accusing her of loving Drew more than him. But it wasn't Drew that she loved, it was the memory of her baby brother she was in love with. Drew had grown up to resemble the spitting image of Andrew, and it was all she could do to honor him.

After greeting Dolly, Drew asked if Mason was home, which nearly sent Dolly Mae into a panic. Her nightmare was about to come true. Drew knew the truth, and was there to confront Mason. She'd warned Mason it would come down to this, but like the hard headed bastard he was, he disregarded her warnings. Now, it was too late, the shit was about to hit the fan, and she was going to have to play peacemaker. Dolly Mae's knees shook uncontrollably, as she led Drew through a long hallway and into the den where Mason was watching television.

"Mason, look who's here to see you." Dolly Mae announced.

Shocked to see Drew standing in front of him, Mason nearly shitted himself. He tried remaining calm, but his inner voice was telling him, Drew was there to kick his ass.

Unsure of what to say, Mason began asking questions pertaining to college. Like his mother, Mason suspected Drew had found out about his affair with Gloria, and was there to challenge him to a fight. Nervous, and realizing Drew had an advantage by standing over him, Mason stood to shake his hand. He invited Drew to sit, and remained standing, until he did. Drew was first to open the conversation, and did so, by talking about Mason's Mustang; inquiring about the work he had put into it. Somewhat relieved, Mason was more than happy to talk about his car instead of Gloria, but he knew it was only small talk which was going to lead into a conversation regarding Gloria.

"So, what brings you by?" Mason asked; trying to get a better idea as to how Drew had taken the news.

Leaning back in his chair, Drew became comfortable enough to begin discussing the rumors about Mason's affair with Gloria. Drew was uncertain how to begin, but knew he had to start someplace. Now knowing Drew's reason for being there, Mason's hair stood on the back of his neck. Got dammit, I'm going to have to fight this motherfucker. Mason thought to himself. He had to think quickly, but nothing would come to mind. He needed to say something to ward off any possible confrontation that could happen, but again, nothing would come to mind.

"So, have you talked to Gloria?" Mason asked, before placing the lid on his can of polish, and placing it on the arm of his chair.

"No, not yet." Drew answered. "I thought I'd come to you as a man first."

Drew had lied, but to see the beads of sweat streaming from Mason's face was electrifying. Drew had gotten the satisfaction he wanted; Mason was as guilty as a kid getting caught with his hand in the cookie jar. It was only right that Drew stood down, and allowed Mason to be with the woman he'd wanted his entire life. Standing to leave, Drew extended his hand; giving Mason a stern shake before leaving for the front door. As Mason cautiously followed him, he continued to engaged in conversation with Drew.

"I'm not sure what you heard, but I can assure you, your fiancé and I, are just friends, and nothing more." Mason added.

"So I've heard." Drew responded.

Drew's first thought was to bitch-slap him for the liar he was, but he thought about what his mother and Aunt Dolly would think of him, if he did. As Drew approached the front door, he turned to Mason to shake his hand good bye.

"You know how this town is man, they like to keep shit going. You should know, I wouldn't do that to you Cuz." Mason said, with a smile of assurance.

Drew explained, it wasn't his intention to create any misgivings between them, and he hoped they could eradicate any animosity that may have generated during their discussion. With a sense of relief, Mason assured him it wouldn't be any, and shook Drew's hand goodbye. Closing the door, Mason turned to find his mother standing behind him. She was dissatisfied with the way he chose to handle the situation. By not admitting the truth, her son was a coward, and she was ashamed of him.

"That was your opportunity to make things right, and you failed miserably," Dolly Mae shouted, as she followed Mason down the hallway.

Frustrated, Mason sat in his chair, and resumed polishing his shoes. He tried ignoring his mother, but she continued badgering him regarding his cowardly act. Her antics were irritating him, but he kept his composure, and withheld his feelings to prevent disrespecting his mother, but her actions were tempting fate. Seeing his frustration, Dolly Mae realized she had been too hard on him, and tried a softer approach. She convinced herself that it wasn't Mason's responsibility to reveal the truth, but Gloria's. After all, it was Gloria, who came after her son.

Seeing that she was running late for work, Dolly Mae quickly got dressed to leave. Before leaving, she wanted to make sure she had cleared the air with Mason. Embracing him, she kissed him, and told him she loved him. Mason wasn't perfect by any means, but he was all she had left, and she wanted him to know, that she loved him.

Dolly Mae got as far as the back door, before realizing, she'd misplaced her house keys. Fearing she was going to be locked out of her house, she told Mason to leave the rear door unlocked, when he left for the evening. Pressed for time, she left the house; electing to drive the interstate instead of the secondary road, to get to work on time. Her decision to take the interstate was bad news for Drew, because his car stalled on the way home.

After locating the potential problem, Drew maneuvered himself from underneath his car. There was no way he was going to make it home with the defective water hose not being repaired. Another problem Drew was facing, was the inability to receive cellular reception in the area where he had broken down. There was only one thing to do, and that was to return to his aunt Dolly Mae's house to get the proper tools he needed, and make the necessary repairs.

Chapter: 17

Wearing only a towel, Mason paraded through the house, dancing to the sounds of a hip hop song over the radio. He was excited about his evening plans with Gloria, and was rushing to get into the shower to get an early start on their drive to Richmond. This was going to be their first night spent together at a hotel, and the excitement of it nearly caused him to hyperventilate. His bags were packed, and so was his heart. It was official, Gloria was his girl, and he couldn't wait for the world to know.

In preparation for the night, Mason had reserved a table for two at a sushi restaurant. Eating raw fish wasn't his cup of tea, but it was something Gloria was accustomed to eating. After dinner, he and Gloria were going to attend a comedy show at the Altria Theater, and once the show ended, his plans were to walk with her hand in hand by the canal; hoping it would lead to a long night of lovemaking.

By no means was he a romantic, nor did he claim to be, but he was willing to do what it took to get the job done. Hearing a knock on the door, Mason covered himself with his robe before answering it. To his surprise Gloria was early. She was dressed in a short mini skirt that hugged every inch of her body with a sleeveless blouse to match. Gloria was two hours early, which meant, she was there to deliver bad news. Mason's first thought, was that Drew had somehow caused the cancellation of his night, and it pissed him off.

"That punk motherfucker, did it to me again." Mason said to himself.

Stepping aside, he allowed Gloria to enter the house, and watched as she walked past him, and made her way to the couch, where she performed a free fall.

"Where's your mother?" Gloria asked

"At work," Mason replied with a sound of disappointment in his voice.

It was frustrating for Mason to have to compete against Drew. It was proving to be difficult; living up to his legend. Mason had done everything humanly possible to show Gloria how much he loved her, and had gone to great lengths, just to satisfy her, but she hadn't seen it. Maybe this was a sign for him to quit, before someone got hurt. It was demoralizing to have lost to Drew again, but Mason should've expected as much. Dejected, he made his way over to the couch where Gloria was sitting.

Looking into Gloria's eyes, Mason wanted to tell her, how much she meant to him, but it was useless. By canceling their date for the night, it was obvious who she was planning to spend the evening with.

"We got a little problem." Gloria said to Mason.

"I figured as much. What is it now, Drew?" Mason asked, expecting to hear the worst.

"No, the hospital called. They want me to report for duty at 7am tomorrow morning. So, I guess tonight is off. You still love me?" Gloria asked.

"For life." Mason answered.

It was a relief to know, Drew had no association with the cancellation of their plans for tonight. Not only was Mason happy for himself, he was happy for their relationship. Sure, the hospital had fucked up his plans, but it hadn't totally ruined his evening.

Mason pulled Gloria to him, and began kissing her. Damn, he loved that woman, and though their plans to spend the night in Richmond fell through, he was happy just being with her.

"Was you about to get into the shower?" Gloria asked.

"Yeah, you want to join me?" Drew jokingly responded.

"Yes, but first we need to get our sweat on." Gloria countered.

Mason stood, and reached for Gloria's hand. Before giving it to him, Gloria opened his robe, exposing his naked body. She reached, and grabbed hold of his penis. Stroking it, she watched, as it transformed from a flaccid state, to becoming rock-hard.

"Are you going to pump me up, to let me down again?" Mason asked.

"No, I got something special in store for you." Gloria responded.

Gloria indeed had something special in store for Mason, and willingly gave it to him, beginning with kissing the shaft of his penis, before placing the head of it in her mouth. Without question, Gloria was proficient at her craft, and it showed, as Mason began sucking in air, from the gratification he was receiving.

Feeling the sensation of Gloria's warm, and moist mouth; Mason's knees began to buckle, leading him to wrap his mind around what was happening.

"Oh, my goodness." Mason thought to himself, as he fought back the pleasure Gloria was giving to him.

She was guiding him towards a sure explosion, and Mason knew he had to do something, before it was over, before it even started. He tried pushing Gloria away, but she was refusing to let go, so he was forced to try to concentrate his attention to something else. Any other time, Mason would have taken it like a man, but he found it difficult to concentrate on anything, because Gloria was too damn good not to resist losing his load.

Mason tried his damndest to fight his urge not to lose it, but seeing how beautiful Gloria was, made it impossible. Lucky for him, Gloria stopped in the nick of time. He was only seconds away from blowing up, and ruining their afternoon together. Gloria stood and removed Mason's robe, allowing it to fall freely to the floor. Gloria followed, by stripping down to her bra and panties, before grabbing Mason by the hand, and leading him down the hallway, to his bedroom.

Like a scene in a movie, Mason lifted Gloria in his arms, and carried her the remaining way down the hallway to his bedroom. Not wanting to get overly excited, Mason remained calm. That soon changed once entering his bedroom. There, Gloria became the aggressor, pushing Mason on his bed, to resume pleasuring him orally.

So many thoughts raced through Mason's mind. He was convinced that today was going to be the day he would finally engage in intercourse with Gloria. Maybe it was the way she was responding to him, that made him believe the bond between them was broken. Why else would she be so aggressive towards him? Her actions were showing him that she wanted him, just as much as he wanted her.

Pushing Gloria over on her back, it was Mason's turn to pleasure her, the way she had done for him. With only a sheer mesh thong standing in his way, Mason kissed his way south of the border. It didn't take long for him to reach his destination, and once there, he pulled Gloria's thong aside, and dove in face first.

From the sounds Gloria was making, Mason wanted to pat himself on the back. He was doing things to her she probably had never experienced before, and that alone was going to kick Drew out of her stable permanently. Mason never considered himself, what was called a bona fide pussy eater, but it was a job he took seriously.

In a surprisingly move, Gloria had Mason to sit on the edge of his bed. She began dancing provocatively, unfastening her bra; placing it across Mason's face to smell. Throwing her bra across the room, Gloria began her lap dance; placing her size 36D breasts in Mason's face. Her actions had Mason craving for more, but he wasn't allowed to touch, only do what she instructed. She was getting pleasure by teasing him and it showed by how she was grinding her body against him while doing her lap dance.

Mason didn't want to play the game anymore. He was ready to take things to the next phase, but Gloria felt differently. Gloria stood in front of Mason, with her back to him, then leaned forward, touching the floor with her hands; giving Mason a bird's eye view of her vagina from the rear. Her attempts to arouse him had worked, and he was ready to end the charade, and commence to some serious fucking, but he had to remain calm, if he was going to make the afternoon special.

But it was proving to be nearly an impossible task to withhold the excitement Gloria was generating inside of him. Her body was like that of an hour glass, and as she rubbed it against his face to the beat of the music Mason became temporarily lost in the moment. He felt the heat emanating from Gloria's vagina, as she became comfortable with what she was doing.

Mason fought his urge to toss Gloria onto bed with him, as his overly erected penis ached to be inside of her. Gloria had him where she wanted him, and to have her, he was willing to fight the devil.

"What do you want to do to this?" Gloria teased.

 Mason was stunned by Gloria's actions, but it didn't deter him from giving her what she was seeking. His quest to satisfy her was forthcoming, but she was delaying it, by teasing him. He had never performed oral sex on a woman from the rear before, but welcomed the opportunity he was presented with.

Spreading Gloria's cheeks, Mason began exploring the unknown. His performance became so intense, Gloria nearly fell forward on her face from the rush of her orgasm. Mason was doing everything right and Gloria was more convinced than ever, that he was going to be a better lover than Drew was. It seemed strange to envision Drew being the one performing oral sex on her, instead of Mason. She came only because she convinced herself it was Drew who was making love to her.

Seeing his lady react from his performance, Mason nearly lost control of his emotions, narrowly avoiding an automatic discharge. He couldn't take the pressure of being teased anymore, and lifted Gloria in his arms, placing her in his bed. Once on his bed, Gloria raised her body, to allow Mason to remove her panties. She spread her legs wider for his tongue to slither up and down her inner thighs, like a snake crossing a body of water. The sensation sent chills throughout her body; causing her to scream from the pleasure she was receiving.

From there, Mason slowly caressed her clitoris with his tongue, while inserting his finger inside of her; simulating the motion of his penis. Mason further sent chills throughout Gloria's body, by spreading her outer vaginal lips with his fingers; and used his tongue to stimulate her already sensitive snatch. His goal was simple, he wanted to give Gloria another orgasm before putting the finishing touches on her.

Mason's efforts didn't disappoint. Gloria quickly came stronger, and louder. Her screams of ecstasy could be heard throughout the house, as she reached another outer body experience. Mason had gone out on a limb to satisfy Gloria. He'd licked her up and down, and all around; giving her the greatest of orgasms. It was now Gloria's turn to give him what he wanted, and what he wanted, was to have intercourse, without having to wear a condom.

Mason slowly moved his way on top of Gloria. He was nervous, and his heartbeat could be felt beating against Gloria's naked body. Kissing Gloria, Mason tried relaxing, but was unable to do so. He felt Gloria gradually spreading her legs, allowing him to fall between them. Carefully, Mason guided his penis inside of her. Gloria gasped, as Mason slowly penetrated her. It was happening, Gloria had finally given in to his persistence after months of being a couple.

Running for more than two-miles, Drew arrived at his aunt's house within minutes after leaving his stalled vehicle. He was covered with perspiration, and used his t-shirt to wipe the sweat from his eyes. Making his way to the front door, Drew knocked but there was no answer. He waited a few seconds, and knocked a second time, but still, there was no answer. Drew made his way to the rear of the house, and was encouraged after seeing Mason's car parked. Perhaps, Mason was in the shower. After all, it was late in the afternoon, and he was getting ready for the night.

Racing up the back deck, Drew knocked on the rear door, but again got no response. Out of curiosity, he turned the knob, and found the door unlocked. He cautiously made his way inside; announcing himself as he walked through the kitchen. The house was quiet, and Drew didn't hear the shower running, which led to believe, Mason was in his room.

Walking through the kitchen, Drew remained on alert. He didn't want to be mistaken as an intruder, so he announced his presence again. Entering the family room, Drew found it empty, but saw a telltale sign of a female presence. Scattered across the room were female clothing, and from Mason's bedroom, Drew heard moaning. Not wanting to interrupt Mason's groove, Drew turned to leave, but before doing so, he recognized Gloria's voice. Stunned by what he had stumbled upon, Drew couldn't believe his luck. He was inches away from busting the both of them, but questioned if it was worth it.

His first instincts were to leave, and give them the privacy they were enjoying, but his resentment of what they had done to him, got the best of him. Drew wanted them to see his face, as well as, to hear what excuses they had to say. The thought of catching them red handed, over took any concerns of the hurt and pain that was sure to come their way.

Drew made his way down the hallway, to Mason's bedroom. He could feel his heart pounding through his shirt, as he became closer to the opened door. The sun was setting for the day, and its rays temporarily blinded Drew, as he reached the end of the hallway.

Once there, Drew stood outside of the threshold of the door, waiting for the moment to make his grand entrance, but before doing so, he began having second thoughts. He wasn't sure, if he needed to disturb them. God knows, he'd found out what he'd wanted to know. The rumors were true, Gloria was sleeping with Mason.

Though reluctant to interrupt, Drew made the decision to enter the room. It was heart-wrenching having to see Gloria lying on her back with her legs tightly wrapped around her lover's waist, but it was time to announce his arrival.

Fighting to maintain his composure, Drew channeled his anger towards Gloria, rather than Mason.

"So, there's nothing going on between the two of you huh? Well, what the hell is this?" Drew shouted.

Hearing Drew's voice, Gloria froze. What seemed like a nightmare, was actually for real. Drew had caught her in the act, and there wasn't a damn thing she could do about it.

"Aw fuck." Mason said out loud, after realizing he'd been caught. "I can explain."

With his back turned to Drew, Mason didn't know if Drew was pointing a weapon of some kind at him, but assumed he had come prepared to confront him.

"You can't explain jack to me." Drew replied. "You looked me in my eyes, and said nothing was going on between you and Gloria. Your cowardly ass, didn't have the balls to tell me, you and Gloria were a couple.

Now, more than ever, Mason was convinced, Drew was packing. Why else would he be so confident to talk shit to him. In Mason's opinion, Drew was a bitch ass nigger, who never could fight, and had always looked to his mother to fight his battles for him. But today his mother wasn't with him, Drew was alone, and the fact that he had caught him red handed smashing Gloria, meant he was pointing something at them. What? Mason couldn't say for certain, but he was convinced, it had to be something.

The thought of being shot, nearly caused Mason to throw up his hands in surrender. Thanks to his mother, he was about to be killed. It was Dolly Mae who'd lost her key, and wanted him to leave the kitchen door unlocked. Knowing he had to get up, Mason carefully, stood up from off Gloria, and slowly turned to face Drew. His penis had reverted back to being flaccid, for what he suspected was the final time. Embarrassed, after being caught with Mason in an uncompromising position, Gloria turned away to face the wall. To further conceal her identity, she used a pillow to cover her head.

It was a relief to know that Drew wasn't in possession of a weapon of any kind; releasing a load from Mason's shoulders. Mason did however, feel the need to address being disrespected by Drew in his own home. His first thought was to dust mop Drew's ass across the floor, but thought about what it would do to Gloria. She was already distraught by getting caught, but Mason felt he had to do something to feed his ego. Sitting on the edge of his bed, Mason began to speak.

"Yo man, what the fuck you doing coming in my house, uninvited? Mason asked.

"I came to borrow your tools to fix my car, but I see you borrowed mine." Drew answered.

"Son, I ain't borrowed shit, I strong arm robbed her from you. Now get your stupid ass out of here, so me and Gloria can finish what we're doing. Mason rudely shouted.

Drew nodded in agreement, and left the room. Although Mason was being overly confident, he was right, Drew had no business there, nor did he have the right to disturb their intimate moment together. Hearing Drew leave the room, Gloria's closed eyes, suddenly opened. She had been lying for months about her relationship with Mason, and her lies had finally caught up with her. This wasn't how Gloria envisioned Drew finding out about Mason, but now that he had, the only thing to do was to stand up, and face the music.

Getting out of bed, Gloria ran after Drew. She was naked, but for some reason, it wasn't as important as catching up with Drew. Running through the family room, Gloria saw Mason's robe lying on the floor. In stride, she grabbed it from the floor, and covered her body, while opening the front door in time to catch up to Drew, before he could get away. Gloria needed to explain, and pleaded for Drew to listen.

Her confession wasn't a total surprise, Drew was aware of her intentions. He understood that by being away at school, Gloria would become lonely, and find comfort in the company of someone else. But he never expected her to fall into bed with Mason. Not because he believed he was far superior than Mason, but because Mason was his first cousin.

For the first time, Gloria apologized for something she was found guilty of doing. She admitted to being embarrassed by what she'd done, and pleaded for his forgiveness.

"I am so sorry for all the hurt, I brought to you. You didn't deserve it, and I don't deserve you." Gloria said. It was the most honest thing she had ever said to Drew, and she meant every word of it.

Approaching Drew, Gloria removed the small diamond engagement ring from her finger, and placed it in the palm of his hand. With teary eyes, she closed Drew's hand, and squeezed it tightly. It was her way of saying, it was over.

"I've never been worthy of this. Gloria said. "You deserve a lot better than me."

She could see Drew's disappointment in her, and wished there was something she could do to erase the hurt and pain she'd caused him. It wasn't supposed to end like this. Drew was supposed to be the one waiting for her at the altar. Instead, she had given up on them; choosing to go in another direction.

For perhaps the final time, Gloria embraced Drew, before turning to walk away. She continued tearing up, as she made her way back to the rear deck, where Mason was waiting for her. She was going to miss Drew immensely, and whether she wanted to or not, she was with Mason now, at least until she could do better.

Seeing Drew turning to leave, Mason couldn't resist bad-mouthing him.

"Hey Cuz, now that you know the truth about me and Gloria, stay the fuck away from her." Mason laughed.

Mason expected an immediate response from Drew, but got no response. Mason knew what he was doing was wrong, but he felt no guilt. Feeling guilty was a show of weakness, and Drew needed to respect his authority, as well as his relationship with Gloria.

"I hope you got it through that thick ass head of yours, Gloria don't want you anymore. She's with a real nigger now; not some momma's boy." Mason yelled out, while beating his chest.

There was triumph in Mason's voice, as he stood proudly; holding the woman he loved. For the first time ever, he'd gotten the upper hand on Drew, and man did it feel good. Disregarding Mason's taunts, Drew continued walking without looking back.

It was a bitter sweet moment, now that he had gotten the answers he'd been seeking. Drew could now move forward with his life, and concentrate on his relationship with Lynn. But this thought remained, he wasted nearly seven years of his life, in pursuit of something that wasn't to be.

Mason and Gloria watched on, until Drew disappeared from their view. Arm and arm they returned inside the house to finish what they'd started, before being interrupted. Finishing with a strong orgasm, Mason rolled off of Gloria, and onto his back. He looked to the ceiling and released a sigh of relief.

"Damn baby, you're everything I dreamed you would be." Mason said.

Gloria thought to herself how embarrassing their first real experience ended. But what she thought mostly about was Drew. She hated having to see him walk away the way he had, and began to worry about his welfare.

"Babe, I need to ask a favor." Gloria asked.

"Anything," Mason replied.

"I need to borrow your car. I want to go check on Drew. I know what it sounds like, but I didn't like the way things ended. I just want to make things right." Gloria said.

As you may have imagined, Mason wasn't at all happy with Gloria, but went against his better judgment, and passed her his keys.

"Go on, do what you have to do, but hurry up and bring your ass on back to your man." Mason instructed.

Leaving, Gloria tried thinking of what she was going to say, once she caught up to Drew. On her drive, she questioned herself, as to whether she had made the right decision to leave Drew for Mason. But it was too late to change her mind now, the truth was out.

Seeing Drew's car stalled on the side of the road, Gloria slowly pulled up behind it. Before getting out, she turned on her flashers, and walked to the front of Drew's car, only to find his hood was up.

Leaning over the engine, she announced her presence. Seeing that Drew was attempting to make the necessary repairs to his car, Gloria took the opportunity to explain her version of what happened. Needless to say, Drew wasn't in the mood to hear what she had to say, and instantly stopped her, before she began.

"Stop it, I don't want to hear your bullshit excuses." Drew screamed out. "I gave you every chance to come clean, and yet, you continued to lie to me."

After making the necessary repairs, Drew crawled from underneath his car and reached inside to turn on the ignition. Once starting his car, he rechecked the repaired hoses for any additional leaks, and after finding none, he got inside his car to leave.

"Please, could you listen to what I have to say." Gloria pleaded.

She wanted Drew to know how hard of a decision it was for her to make. She also wanted him to know that she still loved him, even though she chose to be with Mason.

Drew had heard more than he wanted to, and found it difficult to stay quiet; knowing what Gloria was facing, by being involved with Mason. It didn't matter that she'd chosen Mason over him, she had to know the truth about Mason, and what he was capable of.

"Mason is going to hurt you." Drew warned.

"Mason loves me, he would never break my heart." Gloria replied.

"You don't understand, I don't mean hurt you, as in break your heart. I'm referring to him putting hands on you when things don't go his way. He has a history of violence." Drew explained.

Refusing to take heed to what Mason was physically capable of, Gloria went into protection mode. She quickly shut Drew down, and accused him of badmouthing Mason because he was upset with him. She knew, without a shadow of a doubt that Mason loved her, and would never do anything to hurt her.

Chapter: 18

Nervously, Nancy continued to walk back and forth to the window, glancing out, with hopes of seeing Drew's car driving down the driveway, but each time, her hopes were dashed. She worried that something had gone wrong, and was now regretting her decision to tell Drew about Gloria. Her fears were beginning to show, and it was making it difficult for her to entertain Lynn the way she wanted.

Seeing Nancy pace back and forth left Lynn to form her own opinion. Drew's so-called errand was taking longer than expected, and she suspected it had to do with him going to see Gloria. Lynn believed Drew was living up to his promise to end his relationship with Gloria, but it was taking longer than expected.

It was nearly 9 pm before Drew arrived home, and when he entered the house, he was covered with dead grass and grease. Seeing Drew's condition left everyone with suspicions that he had gotten into a scuffle with Mason. It wasn't until he announced his car had broken down that everyone was relieved. Nancy released a sigh of relief after Drew made his announcement. Lord knows, Gloria wasn't worth fighting over. Then again, why would he want to fight over an oversexed slut, who was willing to sell out to the highest bidder? Thank God, he'd finally seen Gloria for the trash she was, and was ready to move on in life with Lynn.

In a soft-spoken tone, Drew apologized for his tardiness, before excusing himself to go upstairs to shower. Concerned, Lynn asked if she could go upstairs to talk to Drew. Without hesitation, Nancy granted her permission. Immediately, Lynn followed Drew upstairs to his bedroom.

She stood outside of his door, contemplating if she should wait, but chose to lightly knock on his door.

"Yes," Drew said.

"Is it ok for me to come in?" Lynn asked.

"Sure, come in." Drew answered.

Slowly, the door opened. Lynn placed her head inside the room, and found Drew sitting at the foot of his bed. His head was resting in his hands. He was covered in sweat, but it hadn't deterred Lynn from lying her head on his shoulder after sitting beside him. It was obvious something had happened. What, Lynn wasn't sure, but Drew's face was showing all the signs of a man who had just experienced a breakup.

Lynn didn't have to ask what happened; Drew was quick to open up. He began his story with his visit to see Gloria, who continued to lie about her affair with Mason. Drew went on to say, how he visited Mason, and was met with the same story of denial. On his way home, Drew stated his car had stalled, and that he had to jog to Mason's house for help; only to find him in bed with Gloria.

Drew tried selling the feeling of happiness that it was over between him and Gloria, but he failed miserably. In all honesty, seeing Gloria in bed with Mason, nearly ripped his heart out. No matter how badly he wanted to end things with Gloria, no man should ever have to witness seeing their so-called girlfriend, being made love to by another man; especially a first cousin.

"How does it feel, now that you know the truth?" Lynn asked.

Drew didn't know the answer to her question. He didn't know whether to fall into Lynn's arms, and break out into tears, or jump for joy. He was relieved his suspicions weren't a figment of his imagination, but it still hurt. To be frank, Drew knew his relationship with Gloria was over a long time ago, he just didn't want to accept it. For months, he prayed that by some miracle, they could somehow reignite the magic they once shared, but unfortunately, it wasn't meant to be. Instead of rekindling the love they once shared, they fell for someone else.

When looking over the past year, Drew could argue, that it wasn't a total lost. Out of the ruins of his broken relationship with Gloria, he'd found Lynn. He wanted to believe Lynn was ready for another serious relationship, but couldn't say for certain. He never doubted her capabilities of loving someone other than Marshall, nor did he doubt her love for him. His biggest concern was if she was mentally strong enough for another serious relationship. Lynn had done her best to stand strong, but there were tell-tale signs of weaknesses. Though concerning, Drew was convinced within time, the both of them could walk away from their previous failed relationships, and come together as one.

Having seen Mason and Gloria in bed together was the damaging blow Drew needed in order to walk away without reluctance. If that wasn't enough, knowing Gloria only accepted his ring because she didn't want to hurt him, should have been. But the straw that broke the camel's back was when Gloria returned his ring, ending any chance of a reconciliation.

Removing his shirt, Drew began preparing for his shower. He gathered his belongings and kissed Lynn on her forehead, before leaving for the hallway bathroom, he shared with his sister. He was a free man now, and there was nothing holding him back from entering into a relationship with Lynn. The ball was in Lynn's court, and it was up to her if she wanted to play.

Chapter: 19

While Mr. and Mrs. Lathan were enjoying an evening out at one of the local restaurants in town, Marshall and Ashley were home enjoying an intimate moment together at the beach house. Ashley and Marshall had sealed their deal to work together and help reunite Lynn back with him. Marshall wanted another chance to be with Lynn, but in order to get that chance, he needed Ashley's help. Needless to say, it was something Ashley was all too happy to do; being that she was going to benefit from their arrangement. Reuniting Lynn and Marshall presented her the perfect opportunity to have an open road into Drew's heart. It was an evil plan that could have a disastrous outcome, but Ashley was all too willing to do her part in the scheme to reunite Marshall with the only woman he'd ever truly loved.

In retrospect, Ashley saw their plan as being beneficial to all parties; Marshall could get back the love of his life, and she of course, could be with Drew. It was a brilliant plan, at least in Ashley's mind. This was partly because she wanted Drew more than she wanted to see her sister happy. The way Ashley viewed it, Lynn would be happier with her first love, than a man she hardly knew. In the meantime, as Ashley waited for Lynn to arrive, she decided to explore what had driven Lynn to the nut house. Her desire to sleep with Marshall was based on curiosity, rather than being attracted to him, but after doing so, she understood why. Marshall had answered her question as to why Lynn was forced to take a pit stop to the loony bin. Lying on her back, Ashley stared into the ceiling, as she made a surprising admission.

"I now understand why my sister went ape shit crazy over you." Ashley confessed.

"Why is that?" Marshall responded.

"You have me paralyzed from my waist down." Ashley joked.

Suspecting he had fulfilled Ashley's sexual desires to its fullest, Marshall began to open up; speaking freely regarding his past lovers. He showed no respect for Lynn while doing so, but sadly, nor did Ashley for sleeping with him. Instead of refraining from her desires, Ashley chose to explore what drove Lynn to a nervous breakdown. The excitement of reuniting Lynn and Marshall left Ashley with an overwhelmingly jubilant feeling. To know she was doing this in the name of love, made it that much more special. As Lynn's big sister by twenty-two minutes, Ashley felt the need to protect her, and this time was no exception.

There was no denying, Ashley was looking out for Lynn's happiness, but in this case, she was looking out for herself as well. As she saw it, it was a win/win situation for everyone involved. Ashley laughed, as Marshall described the gory details of his illicit affairs with women he'd slept with, while being Lynn's boyfriend.

He bragged like he was the world's greatest lover that ever graced the face of the earth, but in reality, and in all honesty, Marshall sucked ass when it came to making love. He possessed the smallest penis ever to have ever been attached to a body as sculptured as his. By no means was he Lexington Steele, Rico Strong, or the great Shawn Michaels.

As a virgin, Lynn probably had no difficulty accepting his manhood. Truth be told, Ashley had to pretend she could even feel him inside of her. However, there was one thing that sky rocketed Marshall far above the rest, and that was his ability to taste the kitty. Without prejudice, Ashley would be the first to attest to Marshall's ability to taste the cat. Traveling south was his calling, and it was something he performed with excellence.

Marshall had given her several intense orgasms that evening, but perhaps, it was her last orgasm that she remembered most vividly. While experiencing her first outer body experience; Ashley felt, what she believed was her head exploding. She was so convinced her head exploded, she found herself searching for her own brain matter, that may have splattered against the walls. Yes, Marshall was that good. What he lacked in penis size, he made up for with his tongue.

Chapter: 20

Waving goodbye to the Harrison family, Lynn took a final look in her rearview mirror before reaching the main road. She couldn't refrain from reflecting upon her visit, or the memories of spending the night with the Harrison family. She enjoyed her visit, and learned that the country wasn't like she first imagined. Yes, it was dark and quiet, and the scent of cows would take some getting used to, but Lynn could see herself living in Jefferson County. Her heart melted as she relived the moment Drew put his arms around her and kissed her. What followed were promises to love, respect, and honor their relationship; something she hadn't gotten from Marshall. It was a moment Lynn had dreamed of since falling in love, and after going to hell and back with Marshall, she had finally found someone she could trust.

Using her GPS, Lynn chose to take a longer route to the interstate, instead of having to drive by Goodwyn's store. She didn't want to risk running into Dusty again, especially after being threatened by him. Selecting the longer route mapped out by her GPS took her through a winding secondary road that was full of pot holes. Her car was taking a beating as she traveled the secondary road. She'd gone less than five-miles, before she began experiencing difficulties with steering her car. Maintaining control, Lynn pulled over to the side of the road, and got out to investigate. Once out, she found her front passenger tire flat. She wasn't a stranger to changing a tire, but she'd never used the old-style jack, and had no idea how it worked. To make matters worse, she didn't have a manual to go by.

Needing to call for help, Lynn found herself faced with another problem. She didn't have cellular reception, and she was in the middle of nowhere. She was at the mercy of the first person to drive by, and prayed that Dusty wouldn't come riding through on his scooter. Anyone else in Lynn's situation would have panicked, but not Lynn. She was confident in her ability to take care of herself, and didn't fear anything. She was however, frustrated by the condition of the road that caused her flat, and took it out on her tire by kicking it. Fortunately for her, she had broken down in a shaded area, and could enjoy her top being down, while reading a book.

Lynn was undoubtedly going to be late arriving to meet Marshall, but it didn't dampen her spirits any. In a lot of ways, she felt fortunate to have gotten a flat. She hadn't been receptive to the idea of having to stay under the same roof with Marshall; especially after being traumatized by him. She wanted nothing to do with him, but out of respect for Ashley, she agreed to help with throwing him a draft party in his honor. It was a decision she was now regretting, but unfortunately, it was too late to back out now. Still, Lynn worried about the potential problem that being around Marshall could cause, as well as the impact if she made a mistake.

✶✶✶✶✶✶✶✶✶✶✶✶✶✶✶

Driving up to the house, Mason blew his horn and waited patiently for Gloria to come out. He agreed to drive her to work after scheduling an appointment to have his car serviced at the city garage. Though he wanted more than anything to knock on Gloria's door and greet her and her family good morning, he knew it was for the best that he didn't. Pistol hated his guts, and the idea that he and Gloria was a couple enraged him even more. But not even Pistol wasn't going to dampen his spirits this morning. This was his moment to rejoice and celebrate the official announcement of he and Gloria being a couple. For Mason, it didn't matter that Pistol believed he wasn't the man for his precious daughter; what mattered was what Gloria

173

wanted. Finally, after a most anticipated wait, Gloria came out of the house, and closed the door behind her. Mason had to wait ten minutes, but the wait was well worth it. Gloria was professionally dressed in her uniform, and she was as beautiful as he had ever seen her. He could barely wait for her to get into his car; just to touch her to see if she was real.

As Gloria made her way to the car, Mason saw, who he believed was Pistol, looking through the blinds of one of the front rooms. He didn't give a damn that Pistol was looking, he didn't have to hide his relationship with Gloria anymore. Everyone was going to know that Gloria was his girl, and he didn't give a shit if they liked it or not. Mason chuckled to himself, as he visualized seeing Drew's face, after catching him and Gloria in bed together. It had taken years, but he had gotten his revenge against Drew for stealing Gloria from him. To say Mason felt guilty for the way it ended between Gloria and Drew would be like comparing apples and oranges. After months of wanting to stand on the mountain top and tell the world about them; starting today, he could finally do so.

Opening the door, Gloria got in and kissed Mason good morning. She thanked him for a perfect night, and was looking forward to spending the evening with him after work. Her upbeat spirits had brightened Mason's morning. They were still on a high, and it seemed as if nothing was going to bring them down, at least that's what Mason thought. From the corner of his eye, he saw Gloria's head hang at the mention of Drew's name.

"You alright?" Mason asked.

Gloria nodded yes, but continued to daydream. She barely slept during the night, and continued seeing Drew's reaction, after catching them together. It was over between them, and Gloria knew it, but what she didn't know, was how she truly felt about it. She celebrated with Mason, because it was what he wanted to do, but she couldn't help but think of Drew. She was always going to love Drew, but his inability to strengthen what was weak in their relationship ruined what could have been. So many times, she'd forewarned him about his close friendship with Karyme, and the damage it was causing, but he disregarded her concerns.

Whatever they did, Drew somehow found a way to include Karyme. She even came on dates with them, whether it was to the movies, or to dinner; the little "Wetback" always rode shotgun. The only time Karyme wasn't around, was when she and Drew were intimate, and sometimes, she believed Drew wanted Karyme to be lying between them. But now, she didn't have to worry anymore, Drew was free to be with his little Senorita without having any interference from her. For the first time in her life, she had a man who worshipped the ground she walked on. Mason loved her unconditionally, and would move the world to make her happy. He'd proven himself, and she was lucky to have him.

On their way into town, Mason continued to glance over at Gloria. He could see the guilt on her face, and wished she had told Drew about them before being caught red handed. By feeling a sense of guilt, Gloria wasn't being fair to him. She should be enjoying the freedom to be able to walk with him hand and hand, without having to look over her shoulder. Mason was thrilled their secret was finally out, but Gloria wasn't. He suspected she still had feelings for Drew, and rightfully so, they'd been together for a long time, but it was time for Gloria to let go, and enjoy the love he was offering.

Fixated on how sexy Gloria looked in her vintage nurse's uniform, Mason placed his hand on her knee. She was showing just enough of her thighs, to cause him to want to see more. Unlike the nurses of old, Gloria wasn't wearing thick pantyhose.

Instead, she wore no hosiery at all, only bobby socks. The sight of seeing her was enough to urge him to press his luck. He slowly moved his hand towards Gloria's crotch; stopping short of entering Gloria's restricted area. His playful behavior was on the verge of getting him in trouble, so he decided to stop while he was ahead. In a comical way, Mason explained his juvenile behavior, as expressing his desire to make love to her, while she was in uniform. It was an idea Gloria fully embraced. She was down with role playing, and was excited by the idea of making plans to satisfy her man, but she was going to work.

Changing the subject, Gloria confirmed Mason's suspicions that she had been thinking about Drew. She admitted to being embarrassed by being caught in bed, and wished things would have ended differently. Gloria regretted her decision not to end her engagement sooner, but it was too late to harp on it now. The damage was done, and though it may not have ended the way she expected it, the fact remained; it was over between them. Expecting to hear the "I told you so's," Gloria was instead confronted with positive support. For the first time she saw a caring side of Mason she hadn't seen before. He had become a gentler, and more understanding person. His awareness and affections towards her were indicative to the type of man he'd become.

While holding her hand, Mason added how he wished he would have taken more responsibility towards leveling with Drew. He believed if he had, things would have transitioned easier. His acknowledgements were astonishing, so much so, it prompted Gloria to lean over the console to kiss him.

"What was that for?" Mason asked

"For being so understanding." Gloria responded.

Mason discovered his sensitivity response had scored more points than expected, and in a surprise move, Gloria did the unthinkable by unzipping his pants and removing his penis. Leaning over the console, she began performing oral sex on Mason as he drove. It was her way of showing her appreciation for exposing his softer side. Mason couldn't get over his good fortune. It was just as he'd seen in movies, and like the movies; it was exciting as well as fulfilling.

Things took a sudden turn for the worse, once Mason drove into a small neighborhood that was located just on the outskirts of town. He found himself faced with a decision no one should have to make. Seeing what he thought was a small dog walk in front of him, Mason thought about applying his breaks, but realized he had a decision to make. He was faced with three options, and none of them were good. The first option was to attempt to swerve around the small dog, but that may cause an accident. His second option was to slam on his breaks, and that too could present a potential lifelong problem, with his penis in Gloria's mouth. The only logical thing to do, was to continue forward, and run over the animal.

Hearing a loud thump, Gloria jumped. She raised her head to witness the gruesome sight of having to see a defenseless dog, struggling to stand. "Oh my God, you just ran over a dog." Gloria screamed. She was horrified at the sight of having to see the small dog struggling to breathe in the final seconds of its life. Traumatized, Gloria was too upset to continue satisfying Mason, and abandoned his rock-hard penis; leaving it exposed.

"So, you're going to leave me like this?" Mason asked.

"You should at least stop?" Gloria argued.

"For what? The fucking dog is going to die anyway."

Upset by Mason's comments, Gloria leaned back in the passenger's seat. She buckled herself in for safety, and reached for her purse to retrieve a stick of gum. It was a quick fix, until she got to work to brush her teeth. Mason's early morning surprise had ended in controversy, and so had their conversation. Gloria had made a mistake in believing Mason had changed. He had proven himself to be the same selfish bastard he'd always been, and she was done talking to him for the morning. It wasn't until Mason drove up on a stranded driver that Gloria showed interest in talking. Seeing that it was a beautiful young female, Gloria was quick to take notice. Stopping beside the car, Mason rolled down his window.

"Hey, is everything ok?" Mason asked.

"I got a flat tire, and I don't know how to change it." Lynn responded.

Backing up, Mason parked in the rear of Lynn's car. His intentions were to shield her car from being struck, but as expected, Gloria wasn't receptive to the idea. She was appalled at the thought of being placed in harm's way, while protecting a stranger.

"You couldn't stop for the dog, but I see you're stopping to help this bitch." Gloria said.

She was worried about being late, but Mason assured her, they had time.

"Chill out, we got plenty of time." Mason advised. "Besides, this won't take but five minutes or so."

Approaching Lynn, Mason saw how attractive she was, and was anxious to introduce himself. Relieved help had finally come, Lynn greeted him with excitement. Her bubbly persona instantly captivated him, leaving him eager to offer his services. He greeted Lynn with a handshake, as he impatiently began displaying his southern hospitality.

"How long you been stranded?" Mason asked.

"About thirty minutes." Lynn responded.

Unlike Dusty, Lynn felt comfortable in Mason's presence. Maybe, it was because of Gloria being with him, but she couldn't overlook the idea and thought that stranger things had happened in the company of another female. Seeing that out of state tags were on Lynn's car, Mason used the excuse to strike up a conversation. Lynn was as beautiful as Gloria, but more elegant, and even though she was attractive to the eye; it wasn't her beauty that Mason was drooling over, it was her 1967 Pontiac GTO convertible.

"Are you lost? Mason asked.

"No, I was visiting my boyfriend, and I was on my way to the interstate." Lynn responded.

"Damn, what a lucky man," Mason thought to himself.

He followed Lynn to the front passenger side of her car. The tire was damaged beyond repair, but the rim was intact. From there, Mason followed Lynn to the rear of her car, and stood by, as Lynn began removing her luggage, to create space for Mason to remove her spare. It was impossible for Mason not to stare, as Lynn's dress rose; nearly exposing her panties, as she bent over to remove the last of her luggage. Her ass was much smaller than Gloria's, but sexy nonetheless. She was much too beautiful not to admire, and though Gloria was watching from his car, he couldn't hide the fact that Lynn was stunning. Taking advantage of the situation, Mason used his knowledge of muscle cars to engage in a deeper conversation. He was impressed by Lynn's love of muscle cars, and continued to question her.

Not wanting to disrespect Mason in any way, Lynn answered his questions, but her attention remained on finding a signal to call her sister. Ashley needed to know where she was, and how late she was going to be; now that she had experienced car trouble. Calling Ashley wasn't something she was looking forward to doing, but out of respect, it was something she had to do.

Tightening the last of the lug nuts, Mason expressed his desire to someday purchase a GTO. Lynn countered, by showing her interest in his Mustang. Her interest peaked Mason's curiosity; prompting him to offer her the chance to drive his car.

"Think you can handle all my horses?" Mason asked jokingly.

Stunned by his unexpected proposal, Lynn countered.

"Without any difficulty. I can also handle a stick like a professional." Lynn responded with a smirk.

Her counter left Mason speechless. He couldn't match her response, and chose to chalk it up as a loss. Parting with a wink, he carried the damaged spare to the rear of the car and secured it. He hoped Lynn hadn't taken his flirtation seriously, but entertained the thought of what it would be like to fuck a rich bitch. In Lynn's defense, she felt obligated to flirt with Mason. After all, he had been the good Samaritan who rescued her by changing her tire. She found their flirtation hadn't posed a threat, especially after seeing Gloria inside of his car.

However, Mason had proven to be no different than the rest of the assholes who spit a weak game with hopes of getting lucky. Lynn was turned off by his lack of respect for his lady, who was just yards away. Standing with her bags in hand, Lynn waited for Mason to secure her tire before repacking her trunk. She was ready to hit the interstate to make up for the time she'd lost. With any luck, she would arrive in an acceptable time.

Seeing that things were about to wrap up, Gloria joined Lynn and Mason at the rear of Lynn's car. From the facial expression Gloria displayed, she wasn't happy with Mason, but remained quiet. To speed up the process, Gloria grabbed a loose bag and tossed it in the trunk. It was her way of informing Lynn, it was time that she moved on, and to notify Mason that she was ready to leave. In a momentary stare down, Gloria continued gawking at Lynn. In some weird sort of way, Lynn looked familiar, but Gloria couldn't put her finger on why. It was something about her that left Gloria feeling as if she'd seen her before.

"Excuse me, but do I know you?" Gloria asked.

Not recognizing Gloria, Lynn responded by saying no. It wasn't until she saw Gloria's hazel eyes, sparkling in the morning sun that Lynn realized, who she was talking to. It was hard to believe she was standing face to face, with Gloria and Mason, and they had no idea, who she was.

Seeing the out-of-state plates on Lynn's car, Gloria began asking a series of questions. She was curious to know who Lynn was and what she was doing in Jefferson County?

"You sure I don't know you?" Gloria asked.

Seeing that Gloria was digging for answers, Lynn didn't hesitate to give her the answers she was searching for.

"No, this is my first time here. I came down yesterday to surprise my boyfriend." Lynn answered.

"Who's your boyfriend?" Gloria questioned.

"Andrew Harrison." Lynn answered.

"Drew!" Gloria shockingly responded, after hearing that Drew had another girlfriend.

"Yeah, you know him?" Lynn asked.

It was an overwhelming feeling to know, she had gotten payback for Drew, and once doing so, Lynn went forward with her plan to continue rubbing salt in Gloria's wounds. The news broadsided Gloria; leaving her at a loss for words. She stood dumbfounded; having no idea of what to say.

"That motherfucker!" Gloria said to herself. She tried picking her bottom lip up from the ground, but it was too heavy. She'd barely slept a wink, after feeling guilty for cheating on Drew, and he was cheating on her all the while.

Gloria's first instinct was to slap the smile from Lynn's face, but she couldn't show her jealousy in Mason's presence. Instead, she pretended not to be bothered by the news, even though she was as hot as a ghost pepper. Having to watch Lynn drive off after saying the last word, pissed Gloria off to the max. It was at that moment, she vowed to get even with Lynn, and she was going to do so by sleeping with Drew.

Chapter: 21

Ashley silently prayed to herself that Lynn hadn't reconsidered her decision to come down for the weekend. She had a lot riding on Lynn coming, but her inability to get in contact with Lynn was causing concern. Marshall was also nervous. Although he displayed a look of confidence, he had an eerie feeling that his plans were about to blow up in smoke. He needed Lynn, she was the key to his future and without her, the likelihood of him being drafted was in jeopardy.

The rumors of him physically abusing five women were running rampant throughout the news. He'd been warned by his agent that the league was weighing whether to even draft him. It didn't matter how great he was on the basketball court; he was seen as a problem for the league. As a last-ditch effort to keep his draft status alive, Marshall's lawyers met secretly with the women who accused him of physical abuse, and promised to pay them if they recanted their stories. All that was left for Marshall to do now, was to con Lynn into recanting her story, but he had something else in mind for Lynn.

For months, he'd been engaging in conversations with Lynn, which convinced him she was on board with becoming his lady. If his instincts were correct, he would have Lynn eating out of his hand by the end of the week. But before he could work his magic, she first had to show up.

There was so much Marshall had to do, and there was only a small window to do it in. In four days, he was going to have to convince Lynn to drop her guard and give their relationship another chance. Not only that, he somehow had to get Lynn to accept his marriage proposal. If he was lucky enough to accomplish that, they would fly to Las Vegas to get married.

It was going to be a hard task to complete, but if he was to salvage his career, he had to make it work. By the grace of God, Marshall had hurdled the first of his many obstacles; beginning with his lawyers working out a deal to pay each of his five accusers one-hundred thousand dollars to recant their stories. Like clockwork, each of the women changed their stories, and though his alleged victims had changed their testimonies; he hadn't been completely exonerated. He needed Lynn's help, and he was taking it to the extreme to get it.

It was hard for Marshall to believe that he would have to kiss Lynn's ass, after treating her like shit for most of their relationship. It's true what they say; "Karma is a bitch." But if he was to get his career back on track, he was going to have to do what it took, to get what he wanted. It seemed funny that he would need Lynn, after doing everything in his power to discredit her allegations of physical, and sexual abuse. Marshall went as far as calling Lynn a liar to her face in front of everyone that was on the university's panel. His lies to save face had annihilated Lynn mentally; leaving a scar too large to ignore.

Privately, Marshall could never deny what he did to Lynn, and because of it, he felt a sense of remorse from the pain he inflicted upon her. To his credit, he wanted to be a better man, but in order to be a better person, he had to sweep his past under the rug forever. Marshall hoped this weekend could jump start his friendship with Lynn, as well as jump start his NBA draft status. It was fair to say, Marshall still cared a hell of a lot for Lynn, but not enough to marry her. Unfortunately for Lynn, when he got what he needed from her, he was going to dump her like before.

Yes, Marshall's intentions were fraudulent, but it was all he could do to protect himself. He hated the thought of having to take advantage of Lynn again, but ultimately felt there was no other way. He knew Lynn's biggest hang up, was that she was too honest when it came to her feelings. Sadly for Lynn, she made a mistake by confessing that she was still in love with him. As much as he hated to, Marshall had to exploit her love, not only to have his way with her, but to convince her to deny the allegations she made against him. Marshall was sitting on the front porch when Lynn arrived. He was relieved she hadn't reneged on her promise to spend the remainder of the week with him.

He watched as Lynn got out of her car to make her way up the stairs. He was amazed at her beauty, and could barely wait for his turn to greet her. Lynn had become the lady he expected, and with a little luck, she was going to be his again, even though it was only going to be temporary. Marshall believed that once he placed his two-carat diamond engagement ring on Lynn's finger, she would clear him of all wrong doings.

With outstretched arms, Marshall awaited, as he anticipated Lynn's embrace. As she made her way to the front porch, his excitement heightened. It had been a long time since their bodies touched, and the thought of holding Lynn again, captivated him. As he held Lynn in his arms, a part of him wanted to believe his feelings went deeper than he imagined, but he had to stay on course and execute his plan to perfection. Marshall's embrace triggered an eerie feeling inside of Lynn; causing her to revert back in time.

 She immediately broke free of his grasp; placing distance between them. Lynn had no desire to be in the presence of a man she deemed a monster, but for Ashley's sake, she had to remain calm. Anticipating her inability to cope with Marshall's presence, Lynn prematurely had taken a double dose of her anxiety medication. She hoped it would be enough to carry her through the day, but in case it wasn't, she was prepared to take as many as she needed.

"Look at you, my God you're more beautiful than ever." Marshall said, staring with lustful eyes.

"I've always looked this way. You were too busy chasing skirts to notice." Lynn responded.

Lynn was rude, but deservedly so. She hated Marshall for what he'd done to her, and although she said she had forgiven him; in actuality, she hadn't. Whispering into Ashley's ear, Lynn voiced her feelings by questioning her sister's reasons for wanting to host a celebration party for Marshall. She had an uneasy feeling about his intention, and let it be known that she didn't want to be left alone with him. Ashley's support of Marshall hadn't changed Lynn's opinion of him. In Lynn's opinion, Marshall was a snake in the grass just waiting for the chance to strike. She had no doubt that he was up to something, but what? She wasn't sure.

From the porch, Marshall watched as the sisters returned to the car and began removing Lynn's luggage. He couldn't get over how beautiful Lynn was, as well as, how sexy she looked in her short dress. Seeing her in person not only spearheaded him into pursuing his plans for her to be his temporary fiancé, but it motivated him to do so within the three days he needed.

"I want to know one thing." Ashley asked. "What inspired you to want to spend the night with Drew?"

"His mother invited me to stay. She didn't want me to be on the road alone at night, and good thing she did, because I had a flat on the way here." Lynn said.

Dying to know what happened, Ashley inquired about the events leading up to Lynn accepting Nancy's invitation. She was afraid what the night had led to, but was dying to know what happened, for her peace of mind.

"Did you guys sleep together?" Ashley asked, fearing the worse.

"Heaven's no, I'm not screwing my boyfriend in his mother's house." Lynn responded. "Besides, my room was across from his mother's."

Relieved Lynn hadn't slept with the man she was hoping to be with, Ashley released a sigh of relief. She could now relax, knowing Lynn hadn't tainted her pending relationship with Drew, but it had placed a possible strain on Nancy's judgment of her, once she and Drew got together.

"Just one more question." Ashley asked.

"What?" Lynn responded

"Drew's mom. Did she approve of you? After all, Drew is engaged." Ashley inquired.

"Most definitely, Ms. Harrison is rooting for us. Oh, I failed to mention, that engagement is over." Lynn responded with a high five.

Ashley was disappointed to learn how favorable Lynn had become to Nancy. The fact that Lynn had been introduced to Nancy was a mark against her, and the chance of Nancy approving her relationship with Drew was now in doubt. Before approaching the steps to the house, Ashley delivered more unexpected news to Lynn regarding their unexpected guests that was staying the week with them.

"Sis, there's something I need to tell you, but first you have to promise me you won't get mad." Ashley asked.

Lynn knew Ashley was about to drop another bomb on her, without giving her ample time to prepare. This weekend was looking to be a bust, and Lynn was having second thoughts about agreeing to help Ashley. She wanted to support Ashley, but doing so meant having to overcome whatever ailments she was about to be faced with.

"What did you do?" Lynn asked.

"Nothing, I forgot to tell you that Mr. and Mrs. Lathan are here. They'll be spending the weekend with us," Ashley confessed, as she looked to the ground.

"What! You can't be serious?" Lynn asked. "They're going to be here the entire week?"

"I'm afraid so;" Ashley answered.

"What did I do to you to deserve this?" Lynn questioned.

"I'm sorry sis, but they wanted to come. What was I to do?" Ashley asked.

"Tell them no." Lynn answered.

Pissed that Ashley had gone behind her back and invited Marshall's parents, Lynn walked away and up the stairs to the cottage. There was a time when her friendship with Mrs. Lathan was in good standards. However, it quickly diminished after the demise of her relationship with Marshall. It was Mrs. Lathan who notified her mother; falsely accusing her of being scorned and unable to accept the realization that Marshall had moved on. It was a claim Lynn adamantly denied, and despite the evidence detailing Marshall's abusive behavior, Mrs. Lathan refused to believe he could have committed such a heinous crime.

Lynn's allegations of abuse not only infuriated Mrs. Lathan, but ignited her attempt to destroy Lynn's character, as well as her family's. It was a move that ultimately worked in her favor. Fearing public ridicule, Lynn's mother convinced her to drop all charges against Marshall and his accomplice. It was at that moment things went south for Lynn. She elapsed into a depression that led to being hospitalized. The pressures from losing the only man she'd ever loved, along with the backlash from his family was too much for her to absorb. Over time, Lynn was able to accept Marshall's apologies and somewhat mended their differences, but she hadn't done so with Mrs. Lathan. Maybe it was time she did, and maybe after doing so, she could fully heal.

Entering the house, Lynn was embraced by Mrs. Lathan, who pretended to be delighted to see her. Lynn felt chills rushing through her body, and politely pushed away. She presented Mrs. Lathan a fake smile, while pretending to be excited to see her. Lynn couldn't erase the coldness Mrs. Lathan displayed towards her, nor had she forgotten her treatment towards her. As far as Mr. Lathan, Lynn had no animosity towards him; his treatment of her never changed. He was more than understanding when it came to the way his son treated her.

Without showing her displeasure towards the Lathan family, Lynn used the excuse of wanting to freshen up after her drive. Her short meeting with them wasn't as bad as she anticipated, but then again, it wasn't good either. Excusing herself, Lynn left the room for the bedroom she was sharing with Ashley. She was feeling the pressure of having to keep from Drew that she was staying under the same roof with Marshall for more than four days. Lynn had made a foolish decision by not confiding in Drew about her plans, and could only pray that it wouldn't come back to haunt her.

She already regretted agreeing to help Ashley with Marshall's party, and though she hadn't fully given in to speaking at a press conference the following afternoon, Lynn knew the likelihood of her doing so was high. More than anything, she wanted to put Marshall behind her, and if it took lying about what he did to her, then she was willing to do so. Before undressing to shower, Lynn heard a knock on her door.

"Who is it?" Lynn asked.

"It's Mother Lathan dear. May I come in?" Mrs. Lathan asked.

Taking a deep breath, Lynn answered the door with a smile. She wanted to show Mrs. Lathan respect, even though she felt she didn't deserve any. Entering, Mrs. Lathan sat at the foot of the bed. It was obvious what she was feeling, and she needed to get it off of her chest. Before announcing the reason for her visit, Mrs. Lathan embraced Lynn. She needed a boost of confidence, before going forward with what she wanted to say. Mrs. Lathan, started by conveying her deepest apologies for her past indiscretion regarding her treatment of Lynn. By her own admission, she made a mistake by prejudging her, and also admitted that Marshall confessed his role in what he'd done to her.

Mother Lathan's apology was long overdue, but her heart wrenching apology sent chills throughout Lynn's body. They both cried, and as they held each other, Lynn's pain softened. She felt Mother Lathan's remorse, as well as her tears. Mrs. Lathan was truly sorry for how she treated her, and now she was asking for forgiveness.

Chapter: 22

Later that afternoon, the sisters were treated to dinner at the Pelican Bay Restaurant. The Pelican was a quiet intimate place that was known for its good food and great hospitality. The dimly lit table set the mood for an enjoyable evening. Dinner began on a high note, but quickly fizzled after Marshall took it upon himself to hold Lynn's hand to impress his parents. His antics didn't stop there. He led his parents to believe that he and Lynn were still in love. It was a tactic Lynn was dead set against, and she found herself fighting Marshall every step of the way.

Lynn wanted to end the shenanigans of them being a couple, but her promise to Ashley prevented her from doing so. She was supposed to be on her best behavior, but so far, she was acting like an ass. To combat her anxiety, Lynn had taken an extra pill, with hopes of it keeping her calm, but it wasn't working. Barely in control of her emotions, Lynn played the game Marshall and Ashley wanted her to, but it soon began to unravel, after Marshall leaned over and kissed her on the cheek.

For Marshall, it was his way of showing his parents how solid their relationship was, but for Lynn, it unleashed the monster that was caged inside of her. Marshall's efforts to sell their love to his parents had placed everything in jeopardy. Lynn was resisting his every move, and it was painting a different picture to his parents.

As the evening progressed, Lynn's behavior became more erratic. Her medication wasn't working, and her anxiety was quickly taking over. Nervous and sweating profusely, Lynn began experiencing difficulty breathing. Her hands began trembling, and her heart rate increased. At one moment, Lynn felt as if she was having a heart attack, but was quickly calmed down by her sister. Aware of what was occurring, Lynn excused herself and rushed to the ladies' room.

Concerned, Ashley followed and found Lynn on her hands and knees with her face in the toilet. Needing privacy, she locked the door, and rushed to help Lynn to her feet. Ashley voiced her concerns, and questioned Lynn about the number of pills she'd taken.

"What in the world is going on with you?" Ashley asked.

"I don't know, it must be the medication." Lynn responded.

"How many pills did you take?" Ashley asked.

"I'm not sure, maybe three or four, but it's not the medication, it's Marshall." Lynn explained.

Rinsing her mouth, Lynn stared into the mirror at herself. "Ashley, you don't understand, there's so much you don't know. Marshall isn't the person you think he is."

"Then who is he?" Ashley asked.

"He's a monster." Lynn replied.

Lynn's refusal to elaborate further, left Ashley frustrated. If something happened between them, Ashley needed to know, but Lynn was refusing to elaborate.

"What did Marshall do to you? Ashley asked.

"I'm sorry sis, I can't do this, I want to go home." Lynn said.

Hearing that Lynn was about to abandon her, sent Ashley on a rampage. She couldn't allow Lynn to ruin her plans, and knew she had to do something to stop her. The only method Ashley knew was rage, and she let Lynn hear what she was thinking.

"So, you're going to fuck me." Ashley screamed, striking the wall with an open hand. She turned to Lynn and cupped her face. "You promised you would do this for me, now you're backing out. I shouldn't be surprised, you're always, finding a way to fuck me. I stood by you and supported you after you were released from that nut house, and this is how you repay me. Well, fuck you."

Reaching the door of the rest room, Ashley turned towards Lynn, who was shocked by Ashley's antics.

"You need to take a few more of those nut pills to calm your crazy ass down, and after you do, bring your ass back to the table with a different attitude. It's time for you to forget the shit that happened to you two years ago, because believe me, if you don't, you're going straight back to the looney bin. So, take off those grandma draws you're wearing, and put on a pair of sexy panties you're supposed to be wearing. In other words, sis, be a got damn woman."

Ashley left the ladies' room; slamming the door behind her. A stunned Lynn stood motionless, unable to process what happened. Ashley had never talked to her in that manner before, and though hurtful, Lynn understood why. Ashley was correct in what she said, Lynn was reacting like a spoiled brat. She was holding on to something she should have buried two-years ago. Perhaps it was time for her to exchange her grandma panties, for a sexier pair. Ashley's shot at her was more of a reality check than a jab. It was meant to motivate her to retake control of her life.

Wiping the tears from her eyes, Lynn removed her compact from her purse and began reapplying her makeup. Staring into the mirror, she tried convincing herself she would get through the evening, without difficulties. Once satisfied with her appearance, Lynn returned to join the Lathan's at the table. It wasn't long before her patience was again tested. It came after being asked about marriage. Like any good politician, Lynn dodged the questions, without giving a clear and concise answer, but knew sooner or later she was going to have to address the issue.

Unfortunately for Lynn, sooner came before later. Mrs. Lathan's interrogation intensified, with questions involving her working, and having children. At first, Lynn tried avoiding the questions, but it was becoming apparent she couldn't do so any longer. She was going to have to answer, whether she wanted to or not.

Regrettably for Marshall, Mrs. Lathan had gathered enough information to form an unfavorable opinion of Lynn becoming her potential daughter-in-law. Lynn had failed in every category, but what was most concerning, was Lynn's unusual behavior. It was a behavior Mother Lathan wished her son would separate from. In her opinion, Lynn shared no interest in wanting to marry him, and it was her job to convince him to walk away, while he still had a chance.

Chapter: 23

Finding herself standing alone on the rear deck of the beach house, Lynn looked across the sandy beach, into the darkness of the night. She was alone, and wouldn't have had it any other way. Her thoughts were of Drew, but her heart beat with excitement for Marshall. She wanted to escape the hold Marshall had on her, and felt Drew was the person to help her, but Drew wasn't here. She'd resisted Marshall's force for most of the day, but found herself wanting to relent to his charm.

Lynn felt uneasy being in Marshall's presence. As strange as it may have seemed, she still had strong feelings for him. Somehow, he maintained a hold on her heart that she couldn't break. Even after his attack on her that nearly killed her, she couldn't forget him. Like most abused women, Lynn made excuses for Marshall's actions, and as time passed, Lynn found herself hating him less. She'd accepted his immoral behavior for years, after being presented with many avenues of escape.

She should have told Ashley the truth about what Marshall did to her, and if she had, Ashley would've probably cancelled his party, but self-consciously, she didn't want to damage Marshall's image anymore. For some unexplained reason, Lynn found herself wanting to be with him. She was well aware of what could happen if she gave in to her desires, but Lynn felt herself wanting to be held. Allowing Marshall back into her life, meant jeopardizing her happiness. If she chose to engage in a temporary affair with Marshall, she would destroy what she shared with Drew, but the risk was proving to be too tempting to ignore. Lynn was strongly considering allowing Marshall back into her heart.

Drew had come into her life when she was lost, and afraid to step out on faith. He taught her how to love and trust again, and she was about to throw it away for the memories she shared with Marshall. How in God's name could she be so stupid to even consider giving Marshall another chance? God knew she wasn't thinking, and she needed his help to get through this weekend.

Minutes later, Marshall opened the sliding door to join Lynn on the rear deck. He brought with him, two glasses, and a bottle of wine. Tonight, he wanted to celebrate their future, and he started with pouring them a glass of wine. Marshall toasted to a well-deserved future, and with it came a kiss upon Lynn's lips. It was a bold move indeed, but it was receptive. Feeling the need to divert Marshall's attention, Lynn looked towards the sounds of the ocean. She was aware of what she was doing, but found herself wanting more. Marshall was imposing his will on her, and Lynn was finding it nearly impossible to resist him. After his passionate kiss, she turned to him, and melted in his arms.

Being in Marshall's arms, felt like the days of old, and her feelings helped erase all thoughts of Drew. Lynn understood that what she was doing was wrong, and to her defense, she tried fighting her emotions by pushing away, but her attraction to Marshall was too much to ignore. She was confused by what she wanted, opposed to what she needed. Her love for Marshall went far and deep, but her love, respect and admiration for Drew went even further.

Lynn took a second to think about what she was doing, and in doing so, she decided to follow her emotions rather than her heart. This week was supposed to be a celebration in honor of Marshall, and she didn't want to disappoint him.

"What's wrong?" Marshall asked.

"This isn't right." Lynn replied.

Confident he had the upper hand, Marshall began playing upon Lynn's emotions, by sharing his story about the moment he considered suicide. It was touching to think that Marshall considered killing himself because of what he'd done to her, but failing to accept any responsibility for his actions was a turnoff. Instead of admitting his guilt, Marshall blamed the synthetic drug "Rush" for his behavior. Maybe he was right to hold the drug "Rush" accountable for his violent behavior, but he chose to ingest the illegal substance. His decision to do so, nearly caused not only her death, but his own.

Rush was a cocktail, consisting of Modafinil, an undetected form of an anabolic steroid, mixed with Viagra. The drugs were combined and manufactured in a pill form, by a fellow chemistry student, and it was proven to be a success, at least by those who were foolish enough to use it. Marshall, along with ten percent of the students on campus who used, made it their drug of choice. However, there was a dark side to over prescribing the drug, and those who did, found it difficult to control their emotions. The effects from it brought on days of insomnia, a high sex drive, and an uncontrollable rage. Like many, Lynn found herself a victim of Marshall's rage.

Lynn endured several attacks from Marshall, yet remained a loyal girlfriend. There were times she wanted to walk away, but didn't have the will power to do so; she loved Marshall that much. Telling his story was therapy for Marshall, he wanted Lynn to know how sorry he was for what he did, but Lynn didn't seem interested in what he was saying. Her mind was on Drew, and the consequences their relationship would sustain if she chose to go in the wrong direction. Seeing he lost Lynn's attention; Marshall used his hand to redirect her focus back to him. Lifting Lynn's chin towards him, Marshall again kissed her, and as he felt her body shiver, he embraced her tightly in his arms.

"Lynn, I love you, and I want you in my life again." Marshall pleaded.

His heart wrenching confession left Lynn even more confused. She loved Drew, but her heart still belonged to Marshall. They'd been together since high school, and the thought of him not being a part of her life was a picture she couldn't foresee. To make matters more complicated, Marshall fell to his knees and pleaded for Lynn to forgive him for what he'd done to her. He promised to never deceive her again, along with promising to be an open book, as they shared their lives together. Marshall went on to state how he wanted to give her everything she wanted out of life, but before doing so, he needed her help to get the media off his back. In detail, Marshall explained how the draft worked, and how his future would be affected financially, if he slipped out the draft.

Once getting a better understanding of the draft, Lynn agreed to help in any capacity she could. If it took lying to protect Marshall so he could get the financial rewards he'd worked hard to achieve; she was open to doing so. To show her loyalty, Lynn pledged to do whatever was necessary to help clear Marshall's name. She worried about what it would do to Drew and his family if they saw it, but ultimately decided it was in the best interest for Marshall to recoup whatever losses she caused.

Somehow, Lynn hoped Drew would understand and forgive her for acting in good faith. She wanted to believe he would do the same for Gloria, if need be. It was her way of convincing herself that what she was doing was morally correct, but deep inside, she knew it wasn't. It was all she could do to erase the guilt she was feeling, but she felt obligated.

Lynn's decision to help Marshall was indeed surprising, but unbeknownst to her, Marshall had more up his sleeve. His list of demands included more than the press conference; his demands would include a marriage proposal. By agreeing to a fake marriage proposal, Marshall not only would get the notoriety he needed, but it would jumpstart his image. To further gain Lynn's sympathy, Marshall admitted to his infidelities. It was no secret about what he'd done; Lynn was widely aware of his incapability to concentrate on one woman. Lord knows, she'd caught him several times with different women, but chose to stay with him. Lynn was in love, and being in love for the first time, meant doing any and everything to keep what she felt she couldn't live without. Losing Marshall was devastating, and the mere fact that he wanted to become a part of her life again, was exciting, yet frightening.

Marshall's premature exit from her life, left her broken. Though abandoned, and left to fend for herself, Lynn couldn't rule out giving them a second chance. After all, Marshall was her first love, and the only man she'd given her all to. Exposing his serious side, Marshall argued that only Lynn could fill the void within his heart. He'd made a mistake by venturing out, and after realizing his mistake, he wanted desperately to come back to the only woman he truly loved. By his own admission, he was reformed from being the oversexed, drug addict, into a man Lynn could be proud of. He reiterated his love for her, and went on to say she was the reason he wanted to change.

It was because of his love for Lynn, that Marshall decided to change his lifestyle; stressing he didn't give a damn about basketball, the money, or the lime light. It was his love for Lynn that prompted him to abandon his wicked ways. Yeah, Marshall was lying through his teeth. He didn't give a damn about Lynn, or her feelings for him. His only concern was getting drafted and signing a huge contract that would make him a rich man. He had to say what he thought Lynn wanted to hear, and as he predicted, she quickly fell for the game. Marshall's cunning ways had worked better than expected. Lynn had fallen for it, hook, line and sinker. By Thursday night, his life was going to change for the best.

Lying in the comfort of Marshall's arms, Lynn was willing to do whatever it took to help him. Without hesitation, Marshall gave her first instructions. Surprisingly, it involved her becoming his fiancé. He explained his reason, and pleaded for her help. To entice Lynn, Marshall left her with thoughts that their fake engagement could become factual. Marshall's proposal left Lynn at a loss for words, her first inclination was to say no, but the thought of becoming Mrs. Marshall Lathan was too tempting to ignore. Marshall had presented her with the opportunity of a lifetime, and though the possibilities of his dark side still existed, Lynn was willing to embrace his proposal and accept the consequences that came with it.

It was hard to believe that only a few months ago, her life was in shambles and now, she was about to become engaged to the man she'd been in love with all her life. Saying yes to his proposal, Lynn could only hope that Marshall was being truthful. She feared he only wanted to marry her to salvage his career, but quickly omitted the idea from her mind. Feeling a chill in the air, Marshall removed his jacket and placed it over Lynn's shoulders. He wrapped his arms around her and kissed her behind the neck.

Making his first sexual move, Marshall slipped his hands under Lynn's skirt and caressed her buttocks. Skittish from their turbulent past, Lynn became nervous, spilling her wine. Her body shook, as she placed her back against the outside shingles of the house to create space between them. Seeing the disturbance, Marshall quickly backed away. He apologized for his behavior, citing it was an overreaction, after being overwhelmed by her agreeing to become his wife.

Understanding what his uncalculated move had done to Lynn, Marshall attempted to reclaim her trust by apologizing for his aggressive approach. He asked that she not compare him to the person he once was, and asked for forgiveness for his unintentional move towards her.

"I'm sorry. I didn't mean to startle you," Marshall pleaded, as he stood at arm's length of Lynn. He was puzzled by her reaction, but embraced her difficulties. To cut down on the confusion, Lynn pretended that nothing was wrong. She stated she was only startled by his advancement, but Marshall knew better; she was afraid of him. Now it made sense why she shook each time he was near. The abuse she sustained by his hands, not only affected her physically, but mentally.

Standing inches from him, Lynn didn't utter a word. She remained quiet; focusing her attention on the sounds of the incoming waves. She wanted to accept Marshall's apology, but couldn't. The effects of what she endured was too great to overcome. Lynn knew in order to put this tragedy behind her, she had to bury the past. She loved Marshall and wanted to be with him, but to make it work, she had to believe that his intentions were honorable. To ease the tension, Marshall refilled their glasses before leading Lynn on a walk by the beach. It was time to discuss their engagement and their life together.

Suffering from the mixture of wine and prescription drugs, Lynn became more relaxed and playful. Not wanting to jump the gun before jumping her bones, Marshall was more reserved. He assured Lynn, his intentions were only to talk about working towards their future and nothing more. But like the liar he was, Marshall's plans to get Lynn under the influence had worked as expected. He was going to impose his will, and it wasn't going to be long before he did. But first, he needed to butter her up before moving in for the kill.

Walking more than a half-mile, they came upon the southern part of the beach. Upon doing so, they found the carnival was still open. Excited about the bright lights and hundreds of people out patrolling the grounds, Lynn led Marshall to the ticket booth, and bought tickets for the bumper cars. After riding the bumper cars, the roller coaster quickly caught her attention. Marshall wasn't at all thrilled with the idea of having to drop from unimaginable heights into the darkness of night. It wasn't a feeling he wanted to experience, but the night belonged to Lynn. Excited, Lynn pulled Marshall by his hand, and got on the line to ride.

Though Marshall was dead set against it, he suddenly changed his mind after Lynn promised to make his night well worth it. Winning her affections was his goal, but if she was serious about what she was saying, then dammit, he would be willing to do just about anything to satisfy her. Marshall hid his fears as the line became shorter. He thought about all the things that could go wrong, like if the ride malfunctioned, but the thought of having sex with Lynn was worth the risk. Sitting in front of the roller coaster, Lynn was overly excited for the ride to begin. Though intoxicated, she was ready for the rush that came with the sudden drop.

Horrified by what awaited him, Marshall momentarily closed his eyes, as the car suddenly dropped from the sky at speeds exceeding one-hundred miles per hour. It was too late to show his bravery, he screamed like a pussy. Was the ride worth risking his life, just to have sex with Lynn? Probably not, it wasn't like he had never had sex with Lynn before. In all honesty, she wasn't at all proficient with her craft, and chances were, she hadn't improved any since they'd last been together. However, having the opportunity to bang both sisters days apart was worth the risk.

Once the ride was completed, Marshall was prepared to leave the carnival, but soon learned Lynn had other ideas. She led him by the hand; taking him deeper into the mix of the crowd.

"Got dammit, not another fucking ride." Marshall thought to himself.

He wasn't thrilled about having to leave the ground again, but found solace in knowing he was going to be locked inside the Ferris Wheel with Lynn. Once secured inside the cart, Marshall took a deep breath before placing his arms around Lynn. He held her tightly, as the Ferris wheel slowly began turning, and lifting them high into the night skies. Soon, Marshall and Lynn were high enough to see the lights illuminating miles across the city. It was a perfect view and romantic night, for two people in love. To the left of them, was a clear picture of the ocean; seen only by the light of the moon. The Ferris wheel painted the ideal setting for Marshall, and he took advantage of it.

Feeling Lynn's head rest against his shoulder, Marshall instantly knew he was about to benefit from the trenches he'd dug earlier. Lynn was putty in his hands, and it was time to mold her the way he wanted. Marshall was overconfident, but he had every reason to be. There was no doubt that Lynn was still in love with him, and because she was, he could once again, control her to do as he willed. Lynn placed her face firmly against his chest, while melting in his arms. Marshall was giving her the feeling of security she desperately needed, and it temporarily, caused her to forget about her feelings for Drew. Not only had she forgotten about her commitment, she had also forgotten about her turbulent past with Marshall.

Discombobulated from over prescribing herself with Prozac, and mixing it with alcohol, Lynn was vulnerable. Seeing that she was struggling to decipher reality from fantasy, Marshall made his move, and imposed his will. Though he remained skeptical about his decision to pawn Lynn for his basketball future, he didn't feel any guilt for what he was about to do. He knew Lynn didn't deserve what he was going to do to her, but he couldn't allow his basketball career to slip through his fingers.

Looking down at Lynn, Marshall kissed her, and did so without any resistance. It was just as he had expected, Lynn was his, and she substantiated it, by allowing him to invade her restricted area. Marshall placed his hand between Lynn's thighs, as he kissed her. He continued to move his hand up Lynn's dress as his kisses became deeper. He waited for her to stop him, and when she didn't, he continued.

It was surprising, that Lynn hadn't stopped his advances, but then again, she was enjoying the satisfaction he was giving her. With his fingers resting just outside her panties, she relented to the pressure of wanting him to break through the barriers she had set forth. Automatically, her legs opened; almost daring him to enter, but fortunately for her, the ride had come to an end. Marshall had passed the first stage of winning back Lynn's heart, and from the looks of it, he was going to have a successful night. Capturing Lynn's mind was much easier than he imagined, and by tomorrow morning, he predicted that Lynn was going to be his bitch once more.

After the ride, the couple played a few games, before leaving for home. As he'd done in high school, Marshall hadn't fallen short at winning his sweetheart, a stuffed animal. He won Lynn a giant giraffe by shooting basketball hoops, and she was more than happy to receive it. Leaving for home, she struggled to carry the large stuffed animal under her arm, and dragged it in the sand, as she rested her head against Marshall's shoulder.

They walked slowly home, often taking breaks to kiss. Marshall had gone all out to impress Lynn, and impress her he did. Up to this point, Marshall had reverted back to being the romantic gentleman he once was, and Lynn could only hope that he would continue to be. It had been an enjoyable night, and for the first time in two years, Lynn was pleased being in his company. One could contribute her emotions to the mixture of alcohol and prescribed medication, but Lynn refused to believe it had anything to do with what she was feeling. Marshall was proving he wasn't the abusive, cold-hearted bastard he once was. Since getting the treatment he needed, he was a much gentler and fun-loving man. He was back to being himself, and she couldn't have been happier.

He'd proven his worth, and though she remained skeptical about giving him another chance, Lynn wasn't afraid to reach out. She promised Marshall that she would go through with the fraudulent engagement, as well as give a press conference to help clear him of any allegations of abuse, but Marshall wanted more. His desire to join forces with Ashley, would undoubtedly ruin Lynn's life, but it wasn't going to stop him from getting his revenge. By all accounts, he blamed Lynn for his situation, and felt justified in repaying her for the agony she brought into his life. Lynn not only ruined his relationship with his supporters, but broadcasted his treatment of her across campus. Her coming out party had cost him millions, and though she agreed to speak on his behalf, the damage had already been done. Lynn's rhetoric, not only brought light on his past, but inspired the women he was previously involved with to come forward with their story. Some told the truth while others lied, but regardless of the outcome of the draft, he was holding Lynn accountable for him not being drafted number one overall.

Marshall and Lynn were minutes away from the cottage, before Marshall decided to make his move. Stopping Lynn's forward motion, Marshall pulled her close to him. He wanted to see her eyes glitter from the moonlight as he poured out his heart to her. Before Lynn could respond, Marshall kissed her; setting the mood for what was to follow.

"Lynn, there's something I want to say." Marshall said.

Without interrupting, Lynn allowed him to talk. Marshall reiterated the positive changes she had brought into his life, and how he wished he had done things differently. He went on to talk about his undying love and admiration for her, and how she was the woman he was meant to be with. But more than that, Marshall divulged that she was the only woman he truly loved. Again, Marshall was lying, and his reason for doing so was to satisfy his own ego. It was about getting his way with Lynn. It was his intention to butter her up, before having his way with her. Unfortunately for Lynn, she was fully intoxicated, and ripe for the picking. Her mind was cloudy and she was buying the bullshit Marshall was feeding her.

After spending a successful evening together, Marshall was led to believe that Lynn's love for him was greater than what she felt for Drew. With that in mind, it was time to cash in his chips, and collect his prize.

"Baby, we've had an amazing night, a night which I won't ever forget. Since being with you, I realize how much I love you, and how much I want you back in my life. I know what I did to you was wrong, but together we can get through this and work towards having a wonderful life together."

It was a line Marshall had rehearsed repeatedly for hours, and still he became tongue twisted when saying it. Facing Lynn, he waited to hear her rebuttal, but his bold move had caught her by surprise. Standing at a loss for words, Lynn felt it was in her best interest to respond. Somehow, she'd inadvertently got caught up in the moment, wanting to relive the past.

Hurting Marshall was the last thing on her mind, but a lapse in judgement had gotten her weekend off to a difficult start. Lynn was now faced with the task of having to tell Marshall the truth, but didn't know where to start. She allowed him to enter her mind, as well as nearly inside her panties, and now she was going to have to tell him, what her plans were. Placing space between them, Lynn's demeanor left Marshall predicting what she was about to say. Her smile had him anticipating what he'd been waiting patiently to hear. It was unavoidable what Lynn was about to do. She was about to lower her barriers, and allow him to re-enter her heart. She'd seen his change and by all accounts, seemed happy with the results. Lynn's actions gave Marshall, the confidence he needed to believe he was on track to steal her heart. So much so, he envisioned himself sweeping her off her feet, and lowering her onto the warm sand, to make love to her.

Marshall wanted more than anything to celebrate their reunification, by making love to Lynn, and by her body movements, he had no doubt, it was going to happen. Yes, it was true, their reunification was going to be bogus, but Lynn didn't think so. From her actions tonight, it was obvious, she wanted it to be real. Captivated by Lynn's beauty, Marshall waited to hear what she had to say. He hadn't expected her to say anything different, but as she stalled, doubt begin to flood his wall of confidence. It was hard having to tell Marshall about her desire to be with Drew, but Lynn summoned the courage from within.

After hours of uncertainty, her mind had cleared enough to realize what was at stake. Drew had given her everything she ever wanted in a relationship, and for her to throw it away for a failed past, was absurd. It was a decision Marshall wasn't in favor of, and like most men, he tried deflecting the blow without showing any distress, but it hadn't worked. The darkness of the night couldn't hide the hurt he was displaying, but his will not to fail, kept him in the game. Lynn's decision to go in another direction was hurtful, but Marshall couldn't allow it to interfere with his mission.

In all honesty, he shouldn't have been shocked by Lynn's decision. He'd known about her relationship for weeks, but what he was most concerned about was reviving his image he so desperately needed. Lynn assured him she would stand by him, but he got the feeling she was about to renege and jump ship before it had the chance to sail. Lynn was about to screw him again, and there wasn't a damn thing he could do about it. Sure, she'd agree to be his girl for draft sake, but her fears of losing Drew was causing her to want to back out. If he was going to salvage whatever career he had remaining, he had to convince Lynn to become his girl for real.

Removing Lynn's hair from her face, Marshall pretended all was well. God knew, he was afraid his basketball career was about to end, but he had to keep fighting. He couldn't allow his future to spiral down the drain. He was becoming desperate, and knew he had to do something. In a last-ditch effort to confuse Lynn's already clouded mind, Marshall made his move. He was familiar with all of Lynn's weak spots, and used them in his effort to seduce her. Holding Lynn, Marshall began kissing her neck; anticipating the moment he would lay her in the sand to make love to her.

Lynn tried fighting him off, but Marshall's advancements were too powerful for her to resist. Lynn did her best to fight her urges, but found herself wanting more. Her voice was calm but shaky as she tried warding off Marshall's advancements, but knew she was fighting a losing battle. She wanted him, perhaps more than she was willing to admit, but she had Drew to think about; she had their future to protect. Lynn's receptiveness to Marshall's aggression, allowed him to slowly lower her to the ground. Seeing what was about to happen, Marshall nearly panicked from his excitement. He'd never made love on the beach before, and doubted if Lynn had either. This was going to be a special night indeed for the both of them, but only if he could get through it.

Things were going according to plan, until Marshall sensed Lynn's hesitation. Lifting her dress, Marshall made his way below her waist. Using his tongue, Marshall slithered around the outer edges of Lynn's panties, causing her to squirm. Taking a chance, Marshall removed Lynn's panties; lowering the final barrier of her wall. He hadn't expected to get this far, and was shocked to have gotten as far as he did. However, that soon changed after Lynn put a halt to his progress. Lynn allowed him to get close, only to stop him. Marshall was accustomed to getting his way, but Lynn had thrown a monkey wrench in his plans. Her indecisive ways not only pissed him off, it was testing his patience. In an effort to prevent his dark side from floating to the top, Marshall had to control his emotions before he sabotaged his own plans.

"Baby, what's wrong?" Marshall asked.

"I'm not on the pill." Lynn responded.

"Got dammit." Marshall thought to himself. He used his last condom on Ashley the night before, and now, he was about to pay dearly for doing so. How could he'd been so stupid to do something so tragic. Chances were, he didn't even need to use protection on Ashley; she'd probably been on the pill since she was twelve years old. Marshall hated the idea that he'd gotten himself worked up over nothing.

There wasn't going to be any drilling tonight, but he wasn't about to give up so easily, especially after coming so close. Taking advantage of the situation, he kissed his way past Lynn's waist, and as he did, he felt Lynn squirming from the touch of his moist lips, against her body. He was on his way south of the border, and once he got there, he wasn't going anywhere, until he was finished. Desperate to get Lynn in his stable, Marshall was willing to do anything. The way he looked at it, it was a small price to pay for what he was about to cash in for. With the knowledge that Lynn hadn't been with another man since him, Marshall knew that once he placed his stamp on her, she was his for the long haul.

As predicted, Lynn was all in for what magic his tongue would provide, and she showed it by spreading her legs, to give him full access to her. Like a deep-water sea diver, Marshall dove in head first, and from Lynn's body movements, she didn't want to be teased, only pleased, and Marshall was all too happy to oblige her wishes. Marshall was doing what he did best, and as he began making magic with his tongue, his actions brought screams of pleasure from Lynn, as her screams echoed in the night. It didn't take long for Lynn to reach her pinnacle under the night skies. Her body shook enthusiastically; stopping Marshall short of finding out how many licks it took to get to the center of her tootsie pop.

Frozen in time, Lynn looked towards the starry night, after whispering the words; "I love you." Kissing his way upwards, Marshall had accomplished what he set out to do. Now it was Lynn's turn to take care of his needs. He wasn't referring to a head job, Lord knows Lynn was as horrible as they came when it came to satisfying him orally. He wanted her to be sincere when it came to speaking on his behalf at tomorrow's press conference. Once taking care of that part of his business, he would be in position, to begin plan B. It was approaching midnight, and Marshall was still on the beach with Lynn. He wanted to get his point across; hoping it was enough to convince her that he was serious about having a future with her. Lynn listened carefully, as Marshall discussed his plans of sharing their life together. He painted a beautiful picture, and though he did an excellent job at presenting it, it wasn't enough for Lynn to change her mind. Yes, she had slept with him, but her heart remained with Drew. She had made a stupid decision by allowing herself to get caught up in the moment, but now more than ever, she understood what she was jeopardizing. Marshall was at one time, the only man she'd ever truly loved, and though his offer seemed genuine, it wasn't enough to convince her to change her mind. Without a doubt, Marshall was going to revert back into the big bad wolf once the novelty of her had worn off, and when that occurred, she was going to be left alone, with no one and nothing to live for.

Lynn knew it was in her best interest to walk away, while things were still favorable. She had done everything she didn't want to do, and after doing so, she was left feeling accountable for her mistake. Never in a million years, would she have ever believed she'd cheat on Drew; the thought of it sickened her. It would be easy for her to blame Marshall, or the drugs mixed with alcohol she had consumed, but she couldn't.

She'd committed an unfortunate act, one which led her to search for and recapture her past. Thank God she had enough wits about her to see the game Marshall was playing. When listening to him talk about the future, Lynn realized it hadn't included her. His description of what it would be like living in his world, didn't include the role she was going to play in his life.

Financially she was secure, and didn't need his money to survive. She only wanted his love, support and trust, and from the way Marshall was talking, it was a sure sign that she didn't fit into his life. It was in her best interest to pursue a future with Drew, and though her love for Marshall would never waiver, it made more sense to be with Drew. Drew had not only invested time in her, he invested his heart. He'd shown how much he loved her by giving up his relationship with Gloria.

Lynn wanted a stable environment, as well as a successful future, and didn't have to weigh her options to know that Drew was the right man for her. She was just sorry that she hadn't realized it before sleeping with Marshall. It was too late to second guess her decision, but to make things right, Lynn had to separate herself from Marshall. She was going to keep her word and do the press conference for Marshall tomorrow, but was leaning against the charade of being engaged.

"I can't do this?" Lynn said to Marshall. "I don't want to play this game anymore."

With his life in the balance, Marshall saw the scales tipping in the wrong direction. He was in position to lose everything, if he didn't act immediately.

"You're not going to do this to me now, after promising you would help?" Marshall asked.

"I'm sorry, I can't." Lynn repeated.

"I'm fucked, I'm so fucked." Marshall ranted.

Fuming at Lynn's decision to renege on their agreement, Marshall rolled on top of her; holding her shoulders against the ground. He wanted her to see how dire his situation was, and what it meant to have her support.

"Get off of me." Lynn screamed as she tried fighting off Marshall. "Get the fuck off of me, I said." Lynn again repeated.

Lynn's squeal snapped Marshall back to reality. A crack in his armor had occurred, and for a few seconds, he reverted back to his old ways of being forceful. Seeing what he had done, Marshall went into damage control mode.

"I'm so sorry." Marshall said, as he released his grip. "I wasn't trying to hurt you, I just wanted you to understand how delicate my situation is."

Trembling and naked, Lynn struggled to her feet. Grabbing her dress, she quickly began running away. Marshall had shown her he was still a wolf wearing sheep's clothing. Although he claimed he'd been redeemed, he was still the same self-centered, lying bastard, he'd always been. Catching up to Lynn, Marshall apologized again for his behavior. He had a lot of explaining to do, and pleaded for Lynn to hear him out.

"Lynn please, please forgive me. I know what you must think, but believe me, it's not what you're thinking. I mean, I only held you down because I wanted you to understand how important this draft is to me. There's a chance I won't be selected, and the thought kills me. Baby, I need this, and if I don't get it, I don't know what I'll do."

Marshall was begging for her help. He was desperate, and his actions displayed it. He needed Lynn more than he'd ever needed anyone, and without her help, he was doomed. Scared out of her wits, Lynn took the time to hear him out. She didn't know what to make of his outburst, but she could see what was happening inside of him. Marshall was desperate, and the thought of losing his dream may have sparked him to go overboard with his decision to intimidate her, but she wasn't going to give him a pass.

On the verge of tears, Lynn managed to hold them back. She couldn't have felt any worse for betraying Drew, and wanted to cry out, by asking herself, why. Why had she betrayed the man who stood by her during her tough times? How could she have done something so deceptive? Her mistake was too much for her to bear. Stepping into her dress, Lynn pulled the straps over her shoulders. She whisked the sand from her body, and began making her way home. Marshall could only watch, as Lynn ran towards the beach house. He wasn't sure what the outcome of this night would be, but his concern that Lynn's mental status had been compromised grew. He was pessimistic about his chances to keep Lynn on track, and to go along with his plan, but felt he had an ace in the hole with her sister; she'd help fight for his cause.

Following Lynn at a distance, Marshall found it hard to fathom what had just happened. Things were going according to plan, and within seconds, Lynn snapped. She'd shown she was the same whacked out bitch he'd known for years. He should've handled her with kid gloves; especially knowing how much he needed her to secure his future. Marshall waited a few minutes after Lynn entered the house, before following her, and as he opened the rear patio doors, Ashley was waiting for him. By her facial expression, it was obvious she wasn't happy. Closing the door behind him, Ashley led him into the adjoining room. She poured him a drink, and had him sit, to examine what went wrong. In questioning Marshall, Ashley found that he had deviated from the plan by telling Lynn of his intentions. He was supposed to make Lynn think their engagement was real, without admitting it was fake.

"You fucked up." Ashley explained. "You weren't supposed to tell her no bullshit like that. Hell, I'd be pissed at you too."

"This shit isn't going to work." Marshall responded. "Your sister is batshit crazy, not stupid."

"Let me be the judge of that." Ashley replied.

In an effort to get a handle on what had happened, Ashley had Marshall wait until she returned. Leaving the room, Ashley walked down the hallway to their bedroom, only to find it was locked. Knocking lightly, Ashley announced her presence.

"Hey sis it's me, open up." Ashley asked.

It took Lynn a few seconds to open the door, and when she did, she looked as if she'd been crying. She was wearing her robe and from the sound of the water running in the tub, it was obvious she was about to take a bath. Lynn's unusual behavior was a sure indication that something had happened between her and Marshall. What, Ashley didn't know exactly, but you could bet your last dollar, she was going to find out. Ashley was quick to ask if everything was alright, and Lynn assured her that she was. Lynn blamed her mood on being exhausted and wanting to soak in a hot tub of water, before going to bed.

There was no question Lynn was lying, but Ashley was uncertain as to why. Was she concealing something she didn't want her to know? Again, Ashley couldn't say for certain. Playing the concerned sister role, Ashley sat on the edge of the bed and observed Lynn, as she selected a gown to wear to bed.

"Are you sure you're ok?" Ashley again inquired. "Did everything go well between you and Marshall tonight?"

"Will you stop questioning me." Lynn responded out of frustration.

Unable to hold back her tears, Lynn began to cry. Guilt was killing her, and she was having a hard time hiding her true feelings inside.

"What happened? Did Marshall do anything to you?" Ashley questioned.

"No, he didn't do anything, I didn't want him to do." Lynn mumbled.

"What do you mean?" Ashley asked.

"I messed up real bad sis." Lynn cried out.

"What did you do?" Ashley questioned.

"I cheated on Drew by allowing Marshall to go down on me?"

"You did what?" Ashley responded; surprisingly displaying a smile.

Hearing what Lynn had done was an obvious win for Ashley. She hadn't expected Lynn to crack so quickly, but now that she had, she needed to take advantage of her screw up immediately. But first, she needed to continue playing the concerned sister role.

"Shit happens, don't beat yourself up over it." Ashley said, as she consoled Lynn.

Erupting into tears, Lynn's worries of losing Drew consumed her sense of reasoning. She knew she had to tell him, and when she did, the likelihood of him breaking up with her was evident. To combat her anxiety, Ashley suggested Lynn take another Prozac. Lynn needed to regain control of her emotions and though she had taken more than was recommended, she knew it was vital that she didn't have a meltdown. So, she decided to take Ashley's advice and took another pill.

Ashley stayed with Lynn, until she finished her bath and dressed for bed; then sat with her until she fell asleep. Once Lynn fell asleep, Ashley slipped out of the room and rejoined Marshall, who was sitting in the family room, sipping on his third glass of cognac. Puzzled by Ashley sly smile, he questioned her.

"Why are you smiling?" Marshall questioned.

"You slick motherfucker, you didn't tell me you licked the kitty." Ashley teased.

"Quit playing, she didn't tell you that?" Marshall responded.

Surprised that Lynn revealed their private moment with Ashley, Marshall worried if the news had affected what happened between them, but it hadn't bother her at all. What was so strange, Ashley didn't seem to care that he had slept with her sister after sleeping with her yesterday. Lynn may have had some mental instabilities, but Ashley was nuttier than Lynn could ever be. However, the biggest mystery of the night, was what Ashley proposed. She said Lynn had just confided in her that she was deeply in love with him and wanted another chance. As Ashley put it, Lynn had taken a bath and was in bed waiting for him.

"Why are you telling me this?" Marshall asked.

In a surprise change of events, Ashley suggested this was the perfect time for him to make his move; if he was interested in securing his financial future.

"Go and get your prize." Ashley encouraged.

"You crazy as fuck." Marshall responded.

Marshall couldn't believe Ashley was giving him permission to go sleep with her sister while she was sleeping, but her suggestion excited him. Pumped, Marshall swallowed the last of his cognac, and stood to make his way down the hallway to Lynn's bedroom. He was feeling the effects from the Hennessey, and was finding out that it was true what men say, when they describe getting a special rock-hard penis after drinking Hennessey. As he exited past Ashley, he felt her hand slap his ass.

"Go get her tiger." Ashley said, cementing her stamp of approval.

Ashley stood in the hallway and watched as Marshall made his way to Lynn's bedroom. Once at the door, Marshall hesitated. He turned to look at Ashley; hoping she had regained her senses and changed her mind, but found she hadn't. Instead of waving him off, Ashley continued to encourage him to go inside. She was not only fucking him, she was doing the same to her sister; just to gain the heart of some country motherfucker she was sure to dump, once she got bored. Marshall's first thought was to abort his plan, but the thought of sleeping with Lynn intrigued him. It had been two years since he'd fucked her, and he'd forgotten what it felt like being inside of her. Slowly turning the door knob, Marshall quietly entered the room; closing the door behind him. It didn't matter that his parents were sleeping a few steps down the hall, his mission was to secure a spot on an NBA roster, and to do that, he needed Lynn's support.

Standing over Lynn, Marshall watched in amazement, as she slept peacefully. She was as beautiful as the first time he saw her. Seeing Lynn asleep, reignited Marshall's feelings for her. It brought back so many memories of the times when they were deep in love, and Lynn played an important part in his life.

It seemed so long ago when his intentions were to spend the rest of his life with her, but that was before he became a collegiate superstar. To say he allowed fame to go to his head was an understatement, and in the process, he treated Lynn like shit. He slept with all races of women, sometimes two and three women at a time. But none of them made him feel the way Lynn did and tonight was a prime example. Lying in the sand and looking to the heavens gave him the feeling he'd been searching for since their breakup.

Being with Lynn tonight showed him what he had been missing for so long. Marshall tried blaming her for what happened between them, but couldn't, and no matter which direction he tried spinning it, it was clear; he was the fool who wrecked their relationship. Not only had he ruined things between them, he'd done the same with his draft status.

Needing to make a decision on whether he should take advantage of Lynn, Marshall again questioned Ashley's motives. It was crazy what she was expecting him to do, but unfortunately, he was feeling the moment, and felt it was in his best interest to do what he needed to do to secure his future. Slipping his hands under Lynn's gown, Marshall removed her panties. He undressed, turned off the light, and got into bed. He wrapped his arms around Lynn, while placing her head on his chest. Rubbing her hair, Marshall kissed the top of Lynn's head. He didn't know how the night was going to end, but he prayed it would be successful.

Under the influence of the prescription drugs and alcohol, Lynn believed she was dreaming. Tonight, wasn't any different than any other dream she'd had before. She often dreamed of making love with Marshall, but tonight, it felt more intense than ever, it felt real. It felt as if he had penetrated her, and her body was naturally responding. It was a dream she was enjoying too much. Rotating her hips, Lynn felt her legs elevate. It wasn't until she fully opened her eyes, that she realized she wasn't dreaming; Marshall was in position on top of her, and her legs were wrapped over his shoulders. His penis was inside of her, and with every stroke he made, he huffed.

Still under the heavy influence of her medication mixed with the alcohol she'd consumed; Lynn was unable to scream for help. She realized what was happening, and fought to push Marshall off of her, but she was locked in position and unable to move. She attempted to scream out for help, but her screams were muffled by Marshall kissing her. Within seconds, his body began to spasm, and Lynn felt his semen entering inside of her. Fearing the outcome, Lynn fought frantically to free herself, but it was too late, Marshall had come inside of her.

Finishing, Marshall's body went limp. Her legs remained in place over his shoulders, as he gently sucked on her ear lobe.

Marshall had committed the crime she feared the most; he'd raped her.

"Get the fuck off me." Lynn screamed; pushing Marshall from on top of her.

Needing to defend herself, Lynn began striking Marshall, first with her hand, then using her metal lamp on the night stand.

"Hey, hey, hey, what the fuck are you doing?" Marshall asked. "You invited me into your room."

"Bullshit, I did no such thing." Lynn responded.

Lynn couldn't say for certain if she had invited Marshall into her bed. The night had been a haze, and she barely remembered any of it. The last thing she remembered, was talking to Ashley, before getting into bed. Getting out of bed, Lynn tried wrapping her head around what happened. She doubted that she had invited Marshall in her bed, much less agreeing to have sex with him. She awoke, not only to find Marshall on top of her, but to be inseminated by him. Desperate to calm Lynn down, and knowing his parents were sleeping in the next room, Marshall tried explaining what happened.

"Shhh! Let me explain what happened." Marshall pleaded. "You sent for me to come join you. You wanted us to be together."

"Get the fuck out of my room." Lynn screamed; covering her body with her robe. "Get the fuck out of my room. Get out, get out!"

"Baby wait, we need to discuss this." Marshall pleaded, as he got out of bed and began dressing.

"Discuss my ass, get the fuck out of my room." Lynn demanded.

Hearing the confusion, Ashley quickly responded, and headed to the room. Seeing Lynn at her wits end prompted her to act quickly, before the Lathan's were disturbed. Ashley entered the room, to find Marshall partially naked, while frantically trying to get dressed. Hearing the water running, Ashley went into the bathroom to find Lynn in distress, frantically trying to wash away the semen inside of her.

"Hey, hey, what's going on?" Ashley asked in a calm voice, trying to calm Lynn.

"That motherfucker did it again." Lynn said, wiping herself.

"What are you talking about?" Ashley asked.

"Marshall raped me while I was sleeping."

Ashley knew she had to do some serious damage control, if she was going to repair Marshall's boneheaded decision to take advantage of Lynn while she was asleep. Once again, he had placed their plan in jeopardy, by allowing his dick to think for him. She hadn't expected his stupid ass to rape Lynn while she was sleeping. She expected him to wake Lynn, then seduce her. Now it was up to her to do the patch work to correct his fuck up, and save his dumb ass from going to jail.

Like a great prosecutor, Ashley began laying out the events that led to Marshall ending up in bed with Lynn. Ashley used Lynn's admission to sleeping with Marshall on the beach, as her strategy. She told Lynn that she admitted to wanting to sleep with Marshall when telling her about what happened between the two of them. Ashley conveyed to Lynn that she asked if she minded sleeping in Marshall's room, because she wanted to sleep with him tonight.

Ashley's story was similar to Marshall's, but Lynn found the story hard to believe. How could she be so careless to make an ill-advised decision so vital to her future, especially knowing she wasn't on birth control. Dropping her head in shame, Lynn was devastated by what she had done. She perhaps made the worst mistake in her life, and soon may have to pay for it. It was true that she wanted to make love to Marshall, while lying on the beach. However, luck came her way, when Marshall didn't have a condom.

Lynn continued questioning her decision, if she indeed had decided to sleep with Marshall. She had no reason to doubt Ashley, but something didn't feel right about what happened. It was too late to do anything about it tonight, but maybe tomorrow, when her head was clear, she could replay the events in her head as she remembered it.

Though convincing; Ashley's statements weren't convincing enough. It was a ploy that hadn't worked as Ashley had hoped, and it forced her to apply a thicker coat of bullshit on her lie. Ashley was quick to tell Lynn that she shouldn't feel guilty for sleeping with Marshall, especially because of their long history together. It was her opinion that Lynn and Marshall consensually explored their inner feelings that resulted in the two of them making love.

In a spin of events, Lynn began to believe what her sister was saying. Ashley was correct in her assumptions, but it remained a tough pill to swallow. Until Lynn could prove what happened, she felt an obligation to apologize to Marshall for accusing him of taking advantage of her. It was troublesome not to remember, but Lynn didn't want to accuse Marshall of something he hadn't done this time around.

Feeling the need to talk to Marshall alone, Lynn asked Ashley for privacy. Once Ashley left the room, Lynn admitted to Marshall of her desire to have sex with him. To further swell Marshall's ego, she admitted giving serious consideration to a second chance for them. But before Marshall could outright claim victory, Lynn dropped a bombshell; she wasn't in love with him. She admitted to loving him, and though she felt an obligation to help him, she couldn't return to the hell she once lived through while being with him.

Chapter: 24

Lynn spent the morning in her room getting ready for the press conference that was set to take place at noon. It was also the eve of the draft, and in spite of the consequences, she was looking forward to completing the promise she made to Marshall. Like a fool, she had allowed Ashley to talk her into flying with the Lathan's to New York, even though the chances of Drew watching were probable. It was impossible to conceal what she was about to do, and knew it was only a matter of time before Drew would learn the truth. To rectify her misdeeds, Lynn opted to go against Ashley's wishes, and call Drew to tell him the truth. Lynn believed if she didn't do something immediate, her relationship with Drew would end.

Maybe, just maybe, if she explained the true nature of why she was giving a press conference and attending the ceremony with Marshall, Drew would understand. But it was going to be a long shot for her, and a tough pill for Drew to swallow. After tonight, all that was left was the party. Then, and only then, could Lynn return to living a normal life. More than anything, she wanted to concentrate on her relationship with Drew, but being a realist, she knew the chances of that happening was slim to none. Still, she had to at least try to reach Drew and tell him what she was doing was only to help her ex-boyfriend and nothing more.

Seeing she had no other options, Lynn called Drew. To her dismay, he answered on the first ring. He had been waiting for her call, and rightfully so, because he hadn't heard from her since her arrival yesterday. It took a few minutes before Lynn could build up the nerve to tell him of her decision to support Marshall by accompanying him to the NBA draft later that evening. She assured Drew that she was only going to support

Marshall, and nothing more. Her promise to catch a red eye flight out of New York, back to Norfolk after the ceremony was supposed to be comforting, but it wasn't. Drew was stunned by her news, and his cheery disposition quickly gave way to silence. Needless to say, Drew was appalled by Lynn's decision to travel to New York with Marshall. Furthermore, he feared what her association with Marshall could lead to. He couldn't understand why Lynn would choose to be seen with a man that nearly destroyed her life.

"I don't know what to say." Drew responded, while choking on his words.

His heart ached, but his mind remained strong. He wanted to believe that Lynn would do the right thing, but questioned her lingering feelings towards Marshall. Somehow, Marshall had managed to maintain a hold on Lynn's heart, and though Drew didn't know him personally, he knew the damage Marshall was capable of imposing on her. Lynn's sanity was at stake, but against his better judgement, Drew decided to put his trust in her.

Getting Drew's approval was only half the job; Lynn hadn't been totally honest with him. She chose not to follow her heart, and informed Drew that she was also going to speak on Marshall's behalf at a press conference that was scheduled for noon. Hearing that she was going to lie to protect Marshall's basketball career would undoubtably infuriate Drew, but Lynn felt she had no other choice. She made a promise to both Marshall and Ashley, and she couldn't renege on it. It was baffling to think that Lynn could extend a lifeline to a man who caused her to be admitted into a mental facility. But as grotesque as it sounded, Lynn was doing it.

Drew chose not to speak on Lynn's decision to be Marshall's date at draft night. He was upset and couldn't argue about a decision that shouldn't have been considered. Drew instead kept his feelings to himself. Frustrated, Drew abruptly ended their conversation. It wasn't in his nature to react so spontaneously, but he had endured more than he could stand. It shouldn't have been surprising that Drew abruptly ended their conversation, and frankly, Lynn wasn't surprised at all. She immediately called back, but Drew's phone went to voicemail. It was over, Drew was done talking for the day, and possibly for good. But it was too late for Lynn to agonize over it now because Ashley was standing at her door; waiting to drive her and the Lathan's to the airport.

Having only minutes before leaving, Lynn rushed into the bathroom to reapply her makeup. Though Drew didn't say it, his actions indicated that it was most likely over between them. Lynn didn't have time to think about it right now. She was giving the press conference at the airport in less than an hour, then flying out to New York with the Lathan's. Lynn remained quiet for the entire ride to the airport. Her actions not only left Marshall concerned, Ashley was concerned too. They had no idea what Lynn was going to say, and truthfully speaking, they were afraid to ask. They could only hope that she was going to do the right thing, and be the strong woman she was expected to be.

After standing on pins and needles for more than thirty-minutes, it was over. The press conference had been a success and Lynn kept her word. Now Marshall could leave for New York with hopes that Lynn's admission that she falsely accused him of physical and mental abuse would revive his sinking draft status. Feeling confident, Marshall was ready to celebrate, and wanted to start by taking Lynn on a shopping spree. God knows, she had earned it, and it was because of her loyalty, that he was going to keep his word to Ashley. Ashley's bullshit plan for him to fall to one knee, and ask Lynn to marry him, was exactly that, but a deal was a deal. He was going to ask Lynn to marry him during some point of the party, but he didn't have any intentions of seeing it through.

For one, Lynn had made it known that she was in love with Drew, and in all honesty, it was no skin off his ass. He didn't want the crazy bitch anyway. He only pretended to want her, because he was following the plan he and Ashley had put into place. His job was only to string Lynn along, until he got what he wanted. Fortunately for him, he'd gotten a few surprises out of the deal. He hadn't expected to eat her out, or smash her, but it happened. After tonight, Marshall was willing to bet his last dollar that Lynn would be willing to do anything to be with a professional basketball superstar and multi-millionaire.

Thanks to Lynn's press conference, Marshall got the reprieve he needed to help maintain his basketball career. He was cleared to go forward with his life, as well as his career, and for retracting her story, Lynn was invited to attend the draft as his guest. She appeared in New York, at the Barclays Center on Marshall's arm, and though Lynn was nervous throughout the evening. She prayed Drew wasn't watching, but her prayers weren't answered.

As it turned out, Drew had tuned in to see some of the draft, and though he was aware that Lynn was going to be there with Marshall, the sight of having to see Marshall kiss Lynn after his name was called, took all the steam out of him. It wasn't just a kiss it was a deep penetrating kiss; one that only couples partake of. The blow was devastating, it landed below the belt and it was fair to say that the event ruined the remainder of his evening. Marshall was chosen as the sixth pick, in the first round, by the new expansion team, The Las Vegas Gamblers. He'd been bypassed by the Lakers, the Knicks, and the Rockets, but it hadn't dampened his night. He was now a member of a fraternity where only a rare few were selected. Marshall was going to be playing in the NBA.

Though the allegations damaged his draft status, it hadn't destroyed it as first predicted. Marshall had Lynn to thank for it. Because of her loyalty, he was going to give her the present she deserved. Marshall decided to show his gratitude by asking Lynn to marry him. It wasn't going to be the fake marriage that she originally agreed upon, but a real proposal. One that had him dropping to one knee, and asking her to be his wife.

Something had happened during the two days they were together. As funny as it sounded, he'd fallen in love with Lynn again. His inspiration had nothing to do with her beauty, but her loyalty and dedication to him and his career. Lynn didn't need to be with him because of financial benefits. Her father was wealthy beyond what he was going to make with his first contract. But as crazy as it sounded, Marshall had fallen for the woman he was planning to use. Now, for the first time in his adult life, he was sure of what he wanted. He wanted Lynn, and was also hoping she had been impregnated during their sexual encounter. Although it wasn't the way he envisioned becoming a father, he welcomed the idea all the same.

After being drafted, Marshall joined the list of young men ready to celebrate being drafted into the NBA. He introduced Lynn as his fiancé; hoping it was enough to convince her to stay the night with him. But Lynn had other ideas. She planned to catch the last flight from JFK to Norfolk VA, and hoped Marshall wouldn't be joining her. She needed time alone to think about the mistakes she'd made, and how to correct them. She was sure Drew had watched the draft, and saw her kiss Marshall because minutes after it happened, he texted her and abruptly ended their relationship. Though Lynn understood his anger, she hadn't agreed with his decision. Drew should have given her the chance to explain. Instead, he chose to react irrationally. If given a chance to explain, Lynn was sure they could patch things up, without fighting.

Lynn quietly left the party alone, and returned to the hotel to pack. It had been a long and entertaining evening, but it was time to go home. Before leaving her hotel room, Lynn poured her heart out into a letter, and left it on Marshall's pillow. Initially her plan was to spend the night with him, but knowing that Drew was furious at her, she felt it was in her best interest not to. Lynn wasn't in love with Marshall anymore, and she needed to go home and devise a way to get her man back.

Noticing Lynn had left the party, Marshall assumed she had returned to their room. He wasn't ready to leave, but felt he should, to satisfy Lynn. Leaving the party, Marshall returned to his hotel room and found that Lynn had left for home. It was disappointing that Lynn had left without so much as a goodbye. It was detrimental to him if he didn't repair whatever was wrong. He couldn't allow her to get away before telling her how much he loved her. Sitting on his bed, Marshall found the letter Lynn left on his pillow. Opening it, he began to read.

My Dearest Marshall,

This has to be the most difficult letter I've ever had to write. I'm so confused about what to do. One minute I know what I want, and the avenue I want to travel, but each time I try walking away, something stops me. I don't want to love you, but I can't stop myself. No matter how hard I try to forget you, there's always something that prevents me from doing so. I'm afraid that I'm holding on to a dream that's not going to come true. Sadly, this is a dream I don't want anymore.

Let's face it, we both know this isn't going to work. We're too far apart to mend our differences. I want to free myself from this hold you have on my heart, because it's confusing me. Without a doubt, Drew is what's best for me, and he has shown it so many times, but for some odd reason, I keep wanting to hold on to something that's never going to come true. I need a clean break from you, and the only way I can break free, is not to have any further contact with you. After tomorrow, I will avoid you and expect you to do the same. As promised, I will finish our agreement, even though you don't need the fake engagement to achieve your dream; you accomplished that tonight. However, I will honor my promise I made to you, and agree to your engagement.

In closing, I will admit that you'll forever be my first love, and I will always love you, but the man I want to share my life with is Drew. I do regret leading you on to think that we could be a couple, and for that I apologize sincerely. May God guide you, while wrapping his loving arms around you. Lynn

Lynn's letter explained her feelings for him, as well as her request for him to let go of her. Her letter was clear about what she wanted. She was honest about her feelings, and she was asking that he release her heart. After reading Lynn's heartfelt letter, Marshall placed his head in his hands. Although the letter wasn't what he wanted to read, he'd gotten the results he was hoping for; Lynn was still in love with him. The ball was now in his court, and he had the chance to spin the bottle to get the outcome he was hoping to receive. Seeing that he had time to catch the flight before it left. Marshall packed, and left for the airport.

Having taken another dosage of her medication, Lynn was overly relaxed. Her mind continued to be on edge; knowing she'd embarrassed Drew by being with Marshall on television. She hadn't responded to his text, but was willing to do so once she returned to Norfolk. She had a lot of explaining to do, but ultimately believed they could work through her mistakes.

There was one mistake Lynn was uncertain about them working through, and that was sleeping with Marshall. The magnitude from it would undoubtedly ruin whatever chances they had to go forward with their lives.

She'd shot herself in the foot, by allowing herself to fall for Marshall's bullshit, and for doing so, she was going to have to pay. It was three o'clock when Lynn's plane arrived in Norfolk airport, and like always, Ashley was there to welcome her home. Ashley was excited to hear the details of the evening, but Lynn wasn't in the mood to talk about it. She complained of a migraine, and remained quiet the entire ride home. Once arriving, Lynn went directly to her room without saying goodnight to anyone.

Marshall waited a few seconds after Lynn went to her bedroom, before sharing the contents of the letter with Ashley. Hearing the news, Ashley was more than happy to learn she was half way to Drew's heart, and after tomorrow afternoon, life as Lynn knew it was going to change forever. Concerned about Lynn, Marshall went to her room to check on her. He stood outside of her bedroom, with his face pressed firmly against the door before deciding to knock. He waited for a response, and after not getting one, he knocked again.

"Who is it?" Lynn asked.

"It's me. Do you have time for an old friend?" Marshall asked.

Disgusted at the thought of Marshall standing outside of her door, Lynn reluctantly got out of bed. Opening the door, Lynn stepped aside, allowing Marshall to enter. Marshall cautiously entered the room, and sat at the foot of her bed. Lynn instead, chose to stand, as she waited to hear what Marshall wanted to say. As far as she was concerned, she had heard enough of his bullshit, and frankly, didn't want to hear anymore. She had lost Drew because of him, and because of it, she wanted to be alone to center her attention around how she was going to regain Drew's trust again. Marshall didn't care about what she was going through, his only concern was for himself and how having Lynn on his arm would benefit him, and his future.

"I want to thank you for speaking on my behalf at the press conference, as well as being at the draft with me tonight. I realize the sacrifice you made, and the consequences it may have cost you, but I want you to know, if I can do anything to make up for it, just ask me." Marshall said.

Though an asshole, Marshall genuinely meant what he said; Lynn had indeed resuscitated his draft status. She had put millions of dollars back in his pocket, and he couldn't have been happier. In a way, Marshall hated to have ruined Lynn's relationship with Drew, but a deal was a deal. Ashley had kept her end, and unfortunately, he would have to do the same. He watched, as tears fell down Lynn's cheeks. She was hurting after losing the man she truly loved. There was no doubt about Lynn's love for him. He strongly believed that he would forever have a special place in her heart, but Lynn wasn't in love with him, she was in love with Drew.

God knows Lynn didn't deserve this, and Marshall didn't want to be held responsible for sending her back to a mental facility, but his hands were tied. He thought about ending the game of deceit, created by him and Ashley, but Ashley wanted no parts of it. It was about winning for her, even though the results could be devastating to Lynn's mental health. Ashley was playing Russian roulette with her sister's mental health, and he didn't want to take part in it again. After careful consideration, Marshall decided to put an end to the charade they were playing with Lynn, and the surprise Ashley had in store for her tomorrow afternoon. He saw it as putting an end to a plan that was doomed from the start.

"Lynn, I have something I need to tell you." Marshall said.

He hesitated, because what he was about to reveal was going to implicate him, but he ultimately knew it was the right thing to do. For the first time since realizing what was at stake, Marshall's guilt was getting the best of him. Throughout his life, he blamed everyone for his fuck ups, but after seeing Lynn in action today, he understood. It wasn't Lynn who screwed him, he'd screwed himself. Lynn had suffered enough by his hands, and the time had come for him to make things right, but before he confessed to his role in the scam, Marshall wanted to apologize first.

Sadly, before he was able to do so, Ashley entered the room.

"Hey, is everything alright in here?" Ashley asked.

"Yeah, everything is fine." Marshall replied.

He was guilt-ridden, and unable to look at Ashley. Marshall's earlier actions sounded an alarm in Ashley's mind, and he tipped his hand when he followed Lynn to her room. Thank God she acted when she did, because he was about to do something stupid by spilling his guts about what was going to happen.

"I thought you had a bad headache?" Ashley asked.

"I do." Lynn responded.

"Then we're going to leave you to rest, aren't we Marshall?" Ashley asked.

"Yes." Marshall said cowardly.

Grabbing hold of Marshall's hand, Ashley led him from the room. From her grip, Marshall knew he was about to be in for it, but he didn't give a damn, he got what he wanted; at least that's what he believed. Marshall instantly found out that Ashley meant business when they went outside to the rear deck to talk. He'd underestimated her and to remind him, Ashley presented him with a copy of the tape she made of him admitting to sleeping with Lynn, after she was out cold from the medication she'd taken.

"If I release this tape, the only basketball you're going to be playing, will be on the prison rec yard." Ashley threatened.

Shocked by the turn of events, Marshall stood dumbfounded. His first thought was to choke her out, but he thought better of it; knowing Lynn was in the house.

"You're a nasty bitch, Ashley Boldmont." Marshall responded. "If I didn't know any better, I'd swear you hate your sister."

Marshall's hands were tied. He was being forced to do something he no longer supported, but Ashley had him by the balls.

"God please forgive me." Marshall said to himself. He could only pray that Lynn was strong enough to withstand the hurt she was about to be faced with, but most importantly, he prayed that Ashley got hers at the end.

Chapter: 25

Drew's alarm clock sounded off at 3am. He didn't have to put it on snooze for an additional ten minutes of sleep because he'd been awake for most of the night. As he sat up in bed to begin his day, he reached for his phone and saw a text from Lynn. His first thought was to delete it, but after further consideration, he decided to read it instead. Lynn's text was so touching that Drew nearly called her, but then decided against it. Drew was stunned, seeing Lynn's press conference on Sports Center. Not only was he embarrassed and angry, he was disappointed at Lynn's decision to destroy her credibility to help a woman beater.

In Drew's opinion, there was more to Lynn's efforts to help resurrect Marshall's professional career than she was admitting. Perhaps he promised Lynn something for lying for him. Then again, she could have done it because they'd gotten back together. Drew couldn't say for sure, but suspected he would find out soon enough. In her text, Lynn explained why she chose to help Marshall, but didn't explain why she chose not to share her plans with him.

Drew wanted to believe Lynn was acting in good faith, but couldn't help suspecting there was a motive. It was fair to say that Drew was jealous of Marshall, and the hold he had on Lynn. He wanted to be able to trust Lynn, but the surprises seemed to mount on a daily basis, and it was becoming too much for him to handle. Still, he didn't want to make a hasty decision he may regret later. So, until he was sure of how he was going to handle Lynn, he chose to wait.

Still in shock from his meeting with Ashley, Marshall decided to check on Lynn while on his way to his room. He knocked lightly on her door, before opening it enough to place his head inside. He saw Lynn sleeping peacefully on top of the sheets. She was wearing a large t-shirt and panties, and seemed so at peace. Closing the door, Marshall felt a tug on his shoulder; it was Ashley. Needless to say, she wasn't in a good mood, and her response confirmed it.

"I see you ain't got enough of my sister yet." Ashley said.

Marshall turned to her, and with a smirk, his response was unexpected, but truthful.

"You're right, I'll never get enough of her. I've been in love with her since she was fifteen." Marshall said, before going into his room and closing the door behind him.

Lynn awakened to a beautiful morning. She had a restful night, and was feeling positive about spending the last day with Marshall. To start the day off, Lynn met Marshall and Ashley for breakfast on the rear deck. Lynn wasn't hungry, but managed to eat a half raisin and cinnamon bagel; washing it down with a cup of coffee. She was excited to get the day started and knew that within a few hours, Marshall's party was going to begin. For two days, things had gone south for Lynn. She had made mistake after mistake, but after tonight, her plans were to rededicate herself to her relationship with Drew.

Unbeknownst to her, Marshall had other ideas. If he got his way, he was going to break down her guard, and reclaim his place in her heart. He started by inviting Lynn for a morning walk, by the ocean. Marshall wanted to talk about her letter to clear up any misunderstanding between the two of them. But the main reason he wanted to walk, was to apologize for putting her in a position that caused her to lose Drew. Against her better judgment, Lynn accepted Marshall's invitation. She refused to hold hands on their walk, but she did walk beside him; listening as Marshall began apologizing for ruining her life. He was politely interrupted by Lynn, as she put his mind at ease that he had nothing to apologize for. She made the decision to help him, and she accepted the consequences that came with it. Lynn believed in time, she would iron out her problems with Drew, and would do so after his party.

Still confused as to what happened between them in bed, Lynn wanted to clear the air. She wanted to believe what Ashley said, but wanted to hear it from Marshall. As much as Marshall wanted to be honest, he couldn't. Admitting what actually happened meant he would be admitting to being a rapist. It was something he was going to have to take to his grave, unless Ashley decided to release the tape. The ball was in Ashley's court and unless he followed the blueprint she set in play, he was going to be toast. So, Marshall did what he'd always done when it came to being honest with Lynn, he lied.

In the beginning, it was about him achieving his dream of playing in the NBA, but as time passed, he began seeing Lynn in a different light. Lynn wasn't the crazy bitch he once believed; she was actually the same caring, and loving woman she'd always been. She sacrificed, not only her reputation, but her relationship with her new boyfriend to save his professional career. He owed her, but now wasn't the time he could repay her. Somehow, he would have to make it up to her another way.

He didn't want today to be a bullshit fake engagement, but a real engagement between two people who belonged together. It's true that he'd been a jackass throughout his entire stay. He'd taken advantage of an innocent woman who was confused about her feelings, and for what? He was conspiring with Ashley to screw Lynn royally, and though he didn't agree with it, and Lynn didn't deserve it, there wasn't a damn thing he could do about it. The only thing he could do, was to be there to love Lynn the best way he knew how, once the surprise came her way. Stopping in the middle of their walk, Marshall reached in his front pocket and removed his ring. He fell to one knee, and grabbed hold of Lynn's hand. Looking up at her, he asked her what she hadn't expected.

"Will you marry me?" Marshall asked.

Lynn laughed, believing Marshall was conducting a dry rehearsal of what he was going to do later this afternoon.

"You sound like you really mean it," Lynn joked.

"I mean every word of it," Marshall responded. "I love you, and I know you love me. You told me as much in your letter."

Lynn should've been taken by surprise by Marshall's untimely confession, but she expected as much. She had seen the change in him. He was becoming a different person, but she wasn't the woman for him. She didn't love him enough to want to spend her life with him. That honor went to Drew Harrison, but only if he wanted her. It was going to be tough having to explain to Marshall why she didn't want to marry him. Yes, they slept together, but she was confused, and high on prescribed medication.

Lynn searched for words to let Marshall down easy. She would always love him, but she wasn't in love with him, nor did she have any interest in becoming his wife. Looking down at Marshall, Lynn gave him one of her incredible smiles before responding. There were a lot of things she'd learned about him after their breakup, and though most of them were horrifying, he had redeemed himself with the change he'd made. Still, she couldn't get over him sleeping with her best friend Mia.

Marshall once told her, he was in love with Mia, and they were planning to have a future together. What happened to their plans? Not once had he mentioned Mia's name since making contact with her a year ago. Each time she tried bringing up the subject, Marshall refused to discuss it. It was as if Mia had disappeared from the face of the earth. No one had seen her since she pressed charges against them. Though it was an inappropriate time to bring her up Mia's name, Lynn felt she had all rights to do so, because Marshall had asked her to marry him.

"What happened to Mia? You once told me, you were planning a future with her," Lynn questioned.

Marshall was stunned that Lynn had brought up his ex-lover, and her former best friend. Struggling to answer her question, he began stuttering, as he tried answering her question.

"I-I-I-I haven't seen her since you dropped the charges." Marshall stuttered.

Marshall went on to say he hadn't heard from Mia after she transferred to another university. He was quick to say he didn't know where she transferred to, and how he never tried finding her after she left.

"But you said you loved her, and she was who you wanted to be with," Lynn reminded.

Still on one knee, Marshall attempted to respond, but couldn't. Once again, he had been faced with a part of his past that he didn't want repeated. He was ashamed of what he'd done, and having to relive it again was heartbreaking. He'd made the biggest mistake of his life, and repairing it seemed impossible.

"About that, I don't remember half the mess I did back then. The steroids had me living in another world."

Marshall was lying, and remembered vividly; he just didn't give a damn back then. Now he was embarrassed, and less of a man to accept the truth, but what was more embarrassing, was Lynn neglecting to answer his marriage proposal.

"Now isn't a good time to discuss marriage. For one, I'm not in love with you, and two, I'm in love with another man." Lynn explained.

"I don't understand, we made love," Marshall questioned.

"What we made was a mistake. We both were living in the past; trying to rekindle a fire that had long burned out. I used you because I thought you were using me, but something good did come out of this," Lynn said.

"What?" Marshall responded.

"We both earned a new respect for each other."

It was a harsh reality for Marshall, but Lynn needed to be honest with him. It was true that her feelings were mixed before being intimate, but now Lynn realized how much she loved Drew.

Standing, Marshall brushed the sand from his pants, placed the ring back into his front pocket, and slowly made his way back towards the cottage. Never in a million years, would he have ever imagined Lynn falling out of love with him. It hurt like a motherfucker to be rejected, to the point that Marshall didn't even want to walk beside Lynn. As far as he was concerned, his fight to win Lynn's heart was over. He was going to fall back into being the dirty son-of-a-bitch he'd always been; Lynn had made sure of that. Returning to the cottage, Marshall went to his room and closed the door behind him. He needed a moment alone in order to pull himself together, especially if he was going to successfully complete the final leg of his plan.

It's funny how a person with good intentions, could transform into a mean-spirited cocksucker in the blink of an eye. It had been only a few hours ago that Marshall considered telling Lynn what he and Ashley were planning to do to her. But after being rejected, Marshall wanted revenge, and he didn't give a damn how he got it. Before he could put his plan in motion, Marshall had to know if Lynn was still going through with their fraudulent marriage proposal. He left his room and walked across the hall to her door. Hearing a knock on her door, left no doubt who it was. It was becoming frustrating for Lynn to have to keep repeating her intentions to Marshall. She made it known she had no intentions of giving him a second chance because she was in love with someone else. But for some unknown reason, it wasn't sinking into that thick head of his.

Opening her door, Lynn stood firmly in the threshold; preventing Marshall from entering. Surprisingly, Marshall made no attempts to enter. Instead, he asked if their agreement was still on. Not wanting to engage in further conversation about something they'd already discussed, Lynn quickly said yes, before closing and locking her door behind her. Marshall stood outside Lynn's door with a smile, before turning and walking away. Lynn was enjoying the pain she was inflicting on him, but before the end of the day, he was going to get the last laugh.

Waiting for a briefing on what happened during Marshall's walk with Lynn, Ashley quietly made her way down the hallway to his bedroom. She quickly entered, closing and locking the door behind her. She was anxious to know what happened, but the news wasn't what she had expected. Marshall's attempts to convince Lynn to fall in love with him had turned out to be a failure.

"I failed to convince her to marry me." Marshall admitted, hanging his head in shame.

Ashley suspected it was a tall order for him to fill, especially with such a short time frame to work with. But like any good planner, she had already put operation plan B in motion. It wasn't that she didn't trust Marshall, but figured if she was going to have success, she could only trust herself to get it done.

Although the news wasn't what she wanted to hear, Ashley was still excited about what was about to happen. To celebrate, she did something that was even uncharacteristic for her. In a surprise move, she pushed Marshall into his bed and on his back. She mounted him, pressing her body tightly against his, before straddling and kissing him passionately. Thoughts of their sexual affair was embedded inside of her mind, and she wanted his touch, one final time, before she committed herself to Drew. It didn't matter that Lynn was in the next room, Ashley's desire to feel Marshall's tongue work its magic inside of her, overpowered any thoughts of being caught.

Aggressive with her approach, Ashley began kissing, licking and biting on Marshall's neck. She used her teeth to tease him, and to slightly pull on his chest hairs, as she created a feeling too good to resist.

Ashley's approach, gave Marshall the excitement he'd lacked for months. The thought of getting caught lingered inside of his mind, and the rush of the excitement overshadowed any consequences that could come from being caught. Marshall hated the man he had become, and wanted more than anything to escape that life, but his sexual urges were too strong to resist. Lifting Ashley's skirt, he buried his face in her panties to savor her vaginal fragrance. Marshall was a freak by nature, which led him to take an unorthodox stance, and Ashley was his type of woman. She was a woman who loved exploring her sexual desires, and she excited him.

"Smell my pussy." Ashley commanded. "It smells good, doesn't it?"

Ashley was right, her pussy did smell good, and Marshall could hardly wait to taste it. Straddling his face, Ashley lowered her vagina over his mouth.

"Go ahead, eat it." Ashley teased. "I know you want to."

She didn't have to tell Marshall twice. He was willing and ready to do what it took to give Ashley the pleasure she was craving. Using his hands to pull her panties to the side, Marshall began giving Ashley what she wanted, and being a master at his craft, it only took seconds to give Ashley the high she was seeking. Feeling the urge to scream, Ashley clamped her teeth tightly together. She knew any sounds from Marshall's room would expose them, so to muffle the sound of her screams, Ashley placed the tip of a pillow into her mouth; biting down on it as hard as she could. Marshall was doing things to her she never knew was possible. His method of oral sex was unlike any she'd ever experienced, and she welcomed it.

Marshall's oral skills quickly sent her body into convulsions, nearly causing her to fall out of bed. Her body shook uncontrollably, as she tried clawing the wall to keep from collapsing, but it was too late. Ashley's orgasm became so intense, she released a deep moan before collapsing and falling to the floor. Marshall had done it again. He'd given her the ultimate feeling she had been craving, since Lynn arrived.

Dismounting Marshall's face, Ashley reminded him of their arrangement, while encouraging him to proceed with their plan to woo Lynn back into his life. She understood his concern regarding Lynn's indecisiveness, but assured him, Lynn would eventually fall back into his arms. Ashley remained clueless as to what occurred between Marshall and Lynn, but believed him when he said he'd never physically touched her. Marshall's claim of still being in love with Lynn was gladly received by Ashley, and it was welcoming news to know that her sister was in safe hands.

In Ashley's heart, she felt she was doing the right thing by reuniting the two. As she saw it, it was a win win situation for the both of them. Lynn was going to be with the man she'd always been in love with, and she of course, would get the man she wanted.

With time becoming of essence, and the increasing chance of being caught in Marshall's room; Ashley conducted a double take of herself in the mirror, before slipping out, unnoticed. After leaving Marshall's room, Ashley stood outside the bedroom door, she shared with Lynn. She took a second to reflect upon her sexual encounter with Marshall, as well as getting her legs back under her, because they were still shaking from the triple orgasms, she received from Marshall. As strange as it was, Ashley found herself, attracted to Marshall. She was sure about her feelings for Drew, but it was the way Marshall made her feel that had her wanting more of him. Ashley knew she couldn't allow herself to become another victim of Marshall's hypnotizing abilities, and she needed to maintain her focus on the large prize.

Drew was the goal she wanted to achieve, and though she was going to miss Marshall's hot fiery tongue, it wasn't a substitute for his childlike penis. Confident that her legs were under her, Ashley entered the room to catch Lynn attempting to call Drew. Seeing what Lynn was about to do, Ashley moved in quickly to stop her.

"What are you doing?" Ashley asked.

Going into action, Ashley swiftly suggested that Lynn give Drew time to settle down before calling to patch things up. What Ashley was saying made sense, but a guilt-ridden Lynn found it hard not to call Drew. She wanted to lay everything on the line by confessing her infidelities, and plead for mercy.

After talking to Lynn, Ashley was able to convince her to hold off on her secret a while longer, until she found a better way to tell Drew. Ashley reminded Lynn that it was beneficial for her to withhold the truth from Drew in order to save their relationship. She made Lynn promise never to tell Drew about her affair with Marshall, and assured her that her secret was safe. Ashley passed Lynn a glass of water and a pill out of her purse.

"What is this?" Lynn asked.

"It's the Plan B pill. I got it from the drug store this morning." Ashley responded.

Lynn took the pill without hesitation, chasing it with water. By taking the pill, Lynn had at least a ninety-five percent chance of not getting pregnant. Like always, Ashley had her back. She was the epitome of what a sister was. She constantly went out on a limb for her, and not once had she wanted anything in return. It was a belief that Lynn strongly believed, but unbeknownst to her, the pill she'd taken wasn't a Plan B pill at all. The pill she swallowed was a sugar pill. It was Ashley's intention that Lynn became pregnant, and if by chance it happened, Lynn wouldn't have a snowball's chance in hell to hold on to Drew.

Playing hardball with Lynn wasn't something Ashley wanted to do, but Lynn's ambivalence towards Marshall, had brought on unforeseen problems, she hadn't expected. She'd hoped Marshall's magic tongue would have shocked Lynn's heart back into loving him, and for a moment, it looked as if it had, but it was only a temporary heartbeat. Lynn reverted back to loving Drew, and the thought of it brought out the worst in Ashley.

Chapter: 26

There was still much to do before the party was to begin, and as expected, Lynn had taken over as the host. The caterers were due to arrive in less than an hour, and so were the Boldmont's.

Harold and Constance Boldmont, were the parents of the twins, and they were driving down to join in on the festivities. It was fair to say Constance wasn't on board with the sister's decision to host a party for the bastard that abused her youngest, but her will to support her daughters outweighed her personal feelings. Constance was aware of Marshall's intentions, along with his reasons for wanting Lynn back into his life. If she had her way, he wasn't going to get the opportunity to inject his infected fangs into Lynn again. Constance was willing to do whatever it took to prevent Marshall from poisoning her daughter's mind again, but feared she may have been too late.

Needing to take a seat after setting up for Marshall's party, Lynn took a moment to reflect upon everything that occurred during her visit. She never expected to sleep with Marshall, no less consider his marriage proposal. Yes, he had fallen to his knees and asked her to marry him, and though she knew he didn't mean it, it was flattering.

Marshall wanted her to believe that she was the only woman he wanted in his life, but that too was a lie. But what if Marshall had changed, and meant everything he said? What if, he actually wanted to make her his wife, and be the best husband he could be? Sadly, she would never know if he was sincere, or was doing what he did best, lie. Maybe if it had been a month ago, just maybe she would have given him another chance, but it was too late. Now, more than ever, she was sure of what she wanted, and no one could convince her otherwise.

Seeing that Lynn was busy setting up for the party, Marshall took the opportunity to compare notes with Ashley. Though Lynn had agreed to the fake marriage proposal, she had made it clear that she was in love with Drew, and wanted nothing to do with sharing a life with him. Marshall grabbed hold of Ashley's arm, and led her down the hallway to his bedroom; closing the door behind them.

"Are you crazy; pulling me inside of your bedroom like this," Ashley asked.

"We need to talk," Marshall said.

"About what? I told you I have everything under control," Ashley responded.

"I don't feel right about this," Marshall replied.

Marshall's intuition was telling him, not to follow through with their plan, but Ashley had the last word. Marshall warned Ashley, to abandon whatever plan she had in place, and accept the inevitable. Instead of giving up, Ashley dug her heels deeper into the ground; assuring Marshall that what was about to happen would send Lynn running back into his arms. Ashley was well aware of Lynn's romantic side, and was sure in time, she would succumb to Marshall's persistence. All he had to do, was drop to one knee and ask Lynn to marry him, and leave the rest to her. Marshall remained skeptical about Ashley's plan, but no matter what he thought, he couldn't convince Ashley to change her mind. She wouldn't listen to reason, and instead of accepting that her plan wouldn't work, Ashley was still determined to see it through.

Having had enough, Marshall threatened to tell Lynn about everything and needless to say, Ashley wasn't having it. She reminded him of the evidence she had that would send him down the river for years; not to mention disgracing his family. Ashley had him by the balls, and was twisting them to the point where he had no other choice, but to relent. Marshall's first thought was to choke her out, but knew he could never get away with it. He had no other option, but to follow her lead.

Marshall listened carefully, as Ashley hashed out her plan. She was excited to share the ace she'd been holding up her sleeve. She went on to surprise him by sharing that she had invited Drew to the party, and he unknowingly, had accepted. To ensure their plan would be a success, Ashley stressed the importance of timing, and how vital it was for them to work together in order for their plan to work.

On board after hearing Ashley's plan, Marshall was eager to get the ball rolling. It didn't matter how nasty the bitch Ashley was, she knew what she wanted, and she knew how to play dirty to get it. Ashley was as poisonous as a pit viper, but that's what excited him. No matter how dangerous and exciting Ashley was, he still wanted her to get what was coming to her.

Chapter: 27

Dressed in all white, the man of the hour was looking for his leading lady. It was time for Lynn to change out of the sweat pants and t-shirt, and into the white dress Marshall bought for her during their trip to New York. Making his way through the crowd, Marshall found Lynn discussing a problem with the servers under one of the tents set up for guests. Placing his hands around her waist, he whispered in her ear.

"It's time for you to get dressed." Marshall instructed.

Holding Lynn's hand, he led her through the crowd; entering the rear entrance of the cottage. Inside were pledgees from his fraternity, who quickly formed a line, and saluted them as they walked by. Making their way down the crowded hallway, Lynn stood outside of her bedroom door, before stopping Marshall from entering the room.

"Nice try buddy, but this is as far as you go." Lynn said, as she entered her room; closing the door behind her. She left Marshall wondering what her reaction would be once she saw the gift he had placed on her bed. He waited a few minutes, and after getting no response; Marshall returned to entertain his guest.

Feeling secure by knowing the door was locked, Lynn undressed to shower. She noticed a vinyl garment bag spread across her bed, toppled with a card. She smiled as she read the card. She was amazed at the idea that Marshall was thoughtful enough to purchase her a gift. Opening the bag, Lynn was floored by what she saw. Marshall had paid close attention to her when she window shopped at Saks, before the draft. The white Bellitude Strapless Bustier Mini Dress was perfect for the occasion. Not only had Marshall surprised her with a dress, he brought shoes to match.

Arriving just minutes earlier, Constance watched from a distance, as a confident Marshall waited for Lynn. His impatience displayed the characteristic of a vulture, who was waiting for the right moment to swoop down and feast. Little did he know, Constance was willing to go to any lengths to protect Lynn from his grips. In her opinion, Marshall was the predator that got away, and she blamed herself for not insisting that Lynn pursue charges against him. It was a mistake she'd regret for the rest of her life; a mistake that nearly cost her baby's life. As a mother, it was her job to protect Lynn and she failed to do so, but lucky for Lynn, she got a second chance at life.

Like the egotistical asshole he was, Marshall continued standing by the door; waiting for Lynn to come out. Lynn was seemingly taking forever, but it didn't deter Marshall from leaving. He knew it would be worth it at the end, and he was correct with his assumption. After what seemed like forever, Lynn emerged, wearing the white sleeveless dress he'd purchased for her. She also wore the diamond necklace and earrings her mother had given her for her birthday. Lynn was stunning to say the least, and mesmerized Marshall with her beauty. Her long slender legs seemed to go on forever, and with each stride she made, heads turned. The sight of her was more than Marshall could take. Lynn was everything he had imagined. She'd grown into her own, and it made him want her even more. Gone was the timid and depressed young woman of a year ago. The new and much improved Ashlynn Renee' Boldmont had taken a giant leap, and all eyes were on her.

If Marshall had his way, he would drop to one knee, and ask Lynn to marry him, right at that second, but now wasn't the time. Although he promised Ashley he would wait until she gave the signal, which was a logical one; he didn't agree with it. However, he understood that Drew had to be present for everything to work accordingly.

Ashley stood at the front door; trying to hide her jealousy. Throughout their life she had always been the center of attention, but now, her sister had taken center stage. Looking at her watch, Ashley laughed to herself, knowing that within minutes, Drew was scheduled to arrive. He would be shocked to see his precious little Lynn accept the proposal of her ex-boyfriend, and after seeing it, he would undoubtedly be crushed. But not for long, because she was going to be there to pick up the pieces of his broken heart. Swallowing her pride and hiding her envy, Ashley approached Lynn and complimented her on her appearance.

Although they were identical twins, today you wouldn't recognize it. Ashley was as beautiful as ever, but Lynn had the look of a fairytale princess, and Marshall was more than happy to be in her presence. He held Lynn's hand, as he introduced her to his agent and marketing consultant. Marshall wanted everyone to know, Lynn was with him. They may not have been an official couple yet, but within the next hour, she was going to be.

Leaning with her back against the wall, Ashley's smile was as wide as the state of Texas. She had received a call from Drew, informing her he was minutes away. Time was becoming of the essence, and Ashley made her move. Signaling to Marshall to put their plan into motion, Ashley proceeded outside to meet Drew in front of the house. She greeted Drew at the base of the steps, and welcomed him with a closed mouth kiss to his lips. It wasn't unusual for Ashley to greet him in that manner, she'd done so many times before, and often in the presence of her sister.

"Am I late?" Drew asked; seeing the multitude of people standing around associating with each other.

Assuring him the party hadn't begun, Ashley escorted Drew inside. As she led him through the crowd of people towards the doors where Marshall and Lynn were standing on the patio deck together, she couldn't wait to see the shock on Lynn's face, once she saw Drew. Stopping short of the patio doors, Ashley introduced Drew to several people, including her mother, who was standing near the doors. Drew was caught off guard by Ashley's introduction.

Instead of being introduced as Lynn's boyfriend; he was introduced as her friend from WFU. Ashley's introduction left Drew with an uncomfortable feeling. He was excited about meeting the twin's mother, but was greeted with the cold shoulder from Constance.

It wasn't that Constance had anything against him personally; her attention was clearly focused on what was happening outside. However, she had paid enough attention to see why Ashley was so smitten with the tall and handsome young man. Drew's congenial appearance made it easy for Constance to form a favorable opinion towards him, but now wasn't the time. Her focus was on what was occurring outside.

Hearing the request for everyone to gather around for a special announcement, Ashley made her way to the doors leading to the rear patio, with Drew trailing close behind her. From a short distance, Drew saw Lynn surrounded by three men, and as he got closer, he clearly saw who. Lynn was surrounded by an onslaught of invited guest, and displayed a look of shyness, as she waved to the crowd after being announced as the host of the party.

A concerned Drew, watched on, as the ocean breeze gently blew Lynn's hair into her face. Seeing something devastating about to happen, Drew braced for the worse. It was disheartening to have to see Lynn hold the hand of the man who broke her heart so many times, and even more discouraging to witness what was about to happen.

Feeling his worst nightmare was about to come true, Drew squeezed Ashley's hand, as if to brace for the inevitable. It was a sure guess, they were about to announce they were back together, and as Marshall began to talk, Drew could feel his throat close. He could barely hear what Marshall was saying from the noise of the crowd, but knew Lynn was his guest of honor.

Drew's legs had become so weak, that Ashley had to place her arms around his waist to support him. Seeing what was about to happen was too much for Drew to bear. He attempted to intervene, but was pulled back by Ashley. She wasn't going to allow him to ruin the big surprise, so she asked him to remain calm, and see what was about to happen.

"It's time you learn the truth." Ashley whispered to Drew.

Ashley was right, it was time he knew the truth. But damn, it hurt having to see the woman he loved, looking into the eyes of a weasel. Drew stood with his head hung, he didn't believe his heart could take what was about to happen. But for his peace of mind, he had to know what Lynn hadn't revealed to him. Seeing what was about to happen, reminded Drew of what he felt when he caught Gloria in bed with Mason. But unlike Gloria, he felt he was in love with Lynn.

"May I have your attention please," Marshall asked the crowd of invited guests. He waited for the crowd to settle down to make his announcement. By Marshall's excitement, Drew sensed, it was going to be bad news. Marshall held Lynn close to him, as he invited her father, as well as his own, to join them. The crowd's reaction halted the speech for a few more seconds, by loudly applauding, but Marshall managed to quiet them before resuming.

"First of all, I want to thank Mr. Boldmont and his family for honoring me with such a gala. This week has been one of the happiest times in my life. I've been blessed with things in life that I didn't deserve but I'm thankful to have. Mr. Boldmont, this includes your daughter. She's been my rock, and my main supporter. She has stuck by my side through some of the most turbulent times of my life. She believed in me, when I didn't believe in myself, and for that, I thank you." Marshall said to Lynn, looking down at her.

Marshall's gentle kiss to Lynn's lips sent a rage through Drew's body, like never before, but if he was to know the truth, he had to remain calm. Seeing Lynn kiss Marshall, made him sick to his stomach. He'd had enough, and was ready to leave, but Ashley refused to let go of his hand. She asked that he stay to witness what was about to happen. She wanted Drew to see how Lynn had been two-timing him, and as awful as it was, Drew needed to know the truth.

"Secondly, I want to say to Lynn, I know I was by no means the perfect boyfriend to you. I did things to you that I shouldn't have. I did so many things wrong, when it came to being with you, and I'm ashamed of that. But through it all, you never gave up on me. You fought diligently to get me back on track, and thank God you accomplished that. I thank God every day for you, because if it wasn't for you, I wouldn't be standing here right now. I couldn't handle the pressures of becoming a superstar, and by not handling it properly, I forgot about loving you.

I hurt you, and I apologize a million times over, in the deepest part of my heart. It wasn't until I understood what you meant to me, that I knew how much I loved you. I knew I had to make changes, if I was to get you back into my life, and now that I have, I've learned to appreciate you. Not only that, I've learned to respect you, but most importantly, I've learned how to love you."

Once completing his speech, Marshall reached inside of his jacket pocket, and removed a small blue velvet box. He knelt to one knee to the oooh's and aahh's from the crowd, as he opened the box.

"Ashlynn Renee' Boldmont, it is because of you that I am who I am, and by all rights, I want you to take your rightful place on top of the mountain with me. God knows, I may not have been the perfect boyfriend, but if you give me the chance, I promise I'll be the perfect husband. With that being said, Ashlynn Renee' Boldmont, will you marry me."

Shocked at the way Marshall proposed to her, it was hard to say no. The engagement wasn't supposed to be real, but for a split second, Lynn found herself wanting it to be real. It was the way he presented it that made it feel so real. He was sincere, as he expressed how deeply his love was for her. Hearing the crowd cheering for her to say "Yes", Lynn turned to look for Ashley. Marshall's proposal was supposed to be a sham, but you wouldn't have known it from the way Lynn was reacting. Marshall's promises of love and dedication was convincing enough for Lynn to reply by saying yes, without hesitation.

Scanning the crowd in search of Ashley, Lynn was unable to locate her. She wanted Ashley to feel her excitement, as Marshall slipped his ring on her finger. The crowd's applause went even higher, when Marshall stood to lift Lynn into his arms. Things were happening fast, and comprehending what was occurring became difficult for Lynn. She was in need of her sister's help, and called out for Ashley to join her in celebration. It wasn't until Marshall placed her back on the deck, that she saw Ashley standing a short distance away. She didn't see Drew standing beside Ashley, until she motioned a second time for Ashley to join her.

Stunned at the sight of seeing Drew, Lynn froze. She couldn't believe her eyes. She was busted, and there was nothing she could do about it. Struggling to make sense of it, she reached for Drew, but it was too late, he turned and disappeared into the crowd. Breaking from Marshall's grip, Lynn ran through the crowd after Drew. She nearly hyper-ventilated, as tears streamed from her eyes. She screamed for him to stop, but her screams were disregarded. Drew wanted nothing more to do with her, but Lynn wasn't going to allow him to leave without an explanation.

Taking all he could stomach, Drew wanted to get away from Lynn and the Boldmont family as fast as he could. Twice in the same week, he'd been duped; by two women he loved. But having to see Lynn accept a ring from the man that nearly drove her to suicide was more than he could handle. Pushing her way through the crowd, Lynn ran out the front door, and down the stairs behind Drew. He was about to get away, and she was determined to catch him before he did. It felt as if she was in a dream, but each time she pinched herself, she remained in the same scenario. Removing her heels to cover more ground, Lynn sprinted to catch up with Drew. Not sure how she was going to explain her engagement, she knew she had to, if she was going to save whatever was left of their relationship.

Seeing that Drew was just a few yards ahead of her, Lynn ran as fast as her legs would carry her. He was about to get into his car, and if he did, she wouldn't be able to stop him. Lucky for her, he was blocked between several vehicles, and was having difficulty maneuvering around them.

Lynn banged on Drew's driver's side window, to get his attention. Drew refused to acknowledge her presence, choosing to look straight instead. Lynn continued banging on his driver side window. She pleaded for him to allow her to explain, but her pleas went unanswered. Drew was done, he'd given up. Without a second to spare, Lynn had to make a decision that would stop Drew, and chose to jump on the hood of Drew's car. She was determined to get her point across, and she wasn't going to get down, until he heard her out. Not wanting to cause a scene, Drew put his car in park, and got out to confront Lynn. He saw a crowd of people gathering, and knew he had to take a softer approach. Lynn on the other hand, didn't give a damn who was looking, she couldn't allow Drew to get away without an explanation.

"What! What is so important you need to say?" Drew asked. He was frustrated by the scene Lynn was making. It wasn't the tears she was shedding, but the way she chose to handle the situation. If he wasn't her choice, then why wasn't she woman enough to tell him?

"What you saw, isn't what you think you saw. I mean, it's not what you think." Lynn said confusingly. She wasn't making any sense, nor could she explain herself. Maybe if she had stopped crying long enough, she could paint a much clearer picture of what she wanted to say. It was evident that she had lost Drew, and it was a devastating blow. He had been the only man who truly loved her, and she'd blown it, all in the name of chasing a dream that was never going to happen.

"You know, I'm glad Ashley invited me here to see this. Accepting Marshall's ring, proves you're still in love with him." Drew said.

"Noooo" Lynn cried out. "Please don't do this. It's not that, I was only trying to help Marshall."

"I'm done, I'm done with this obsession you have of Marshall, and I'm done with you." Drew said, as he turned to leave.

Lynn couldn't bear hearing the news that Drew was breaking up with her. In a desperate attempt to prevent him from leaving, she jumped on his back; locking her arms tightly around his neck. She cried out, saying how much she loved him, but Drew didn't want to hear what she had to say. As far as he was concerned, it was over between them. As gently as he could, Drew removed Lynn's arms from around his neck. He didn't want to make a scene so he respectfully unlocked her hands from around his neck. Though it was over between them, Lynn's unwillingness to concede, was making things difficult. It wasn't until Drew returned to his car that it struck her.

Falling to her knees, Lynn screamed out loudly; pleading for Drew not to leave. She didn't care who saw what was happening, she wanted Drew to know how much she loved him, and though she continued to say she loved him, it wasn't enough to sway him into staying. Unfortunately for Lynn, Drew wanted nothing else to do with her. His only concern was getting away from her. Having to see Drew drive away brought on more tears from Lynn. She had not only lost the man she was in love with, she'd lost her best friend.

Surrounded by onlookers, Lynn stood and brushed the dirt from her knees and dress. She carried her shoes by the straps, as she began her walk of shame back to the cottage. Her walk seemed longer than usual; prompting her to think that she was only having a nightmare. But when pinching herself, she realized she wasn't waking up, because she was already awake.

As she continued her walk back, Lynn continued to replay Drew's last words pertaining to Ashley inviting him to see her engagement. Something wasn't right, the air was reeking with the smell of rot, and her intuition was telling her, Ashley and Marshall were the culprits behind it. It was all making sense now; Ashley and Marshall were working together to break her and Drew up. Sadly, they had pulled off the perfect crime. Together, they'd sabotaged her destiny, just to satisfy their own selfish wants. She should have expected that dirty, no-good son-of-a-bitch wasn't sincere when he pleaded for another chance for them to be together. And to think that she slept with him made it even worse. Once again, she allowed Marshall to make a fool out of her in front of the world, but this time, he wasn't going to get away with it.

Lynn never imagined Ashley would sacrifice her to the devil, just to have a chance to be with Drew. It wasn't hard to figure out that she had feelings for Drew, and if Drew would've felt the same for her, she would've never agreed to have a relationship with him. But instead of being a sister, who talked to her about her feelings, Ashley teamed up with Marshall to cut her throat. Limping from running bare foot, Lynn arrived back to the cottage, carrying her heels in one hand, while wiping her tears with the other. A million thoughts entered her mind, while she made her way back.

She'd lost Drew over a silly game to deceive the world that she and Marshall were getting married. For hurting Drew, Lynn was looking to unleash her frustration on the first person to approach her disrespectfully, and from a distance, she saw her first victim. Standing on the front porch, waiting for her arrival, Ashley displayed the look of concern. Her arms were extended to console Lynn, as she walked up the steps. Lynn could barely see, from the tears streaming from her eyes, but her quest to reach her sister's comforting arms, kept her moving forward. Her mind was running twice the speed of sound, yet she tried remaining in control of her emotions. She limped from the cuts and bruises she sustained to her feet, while running after Drew, but resisted any assistance from the guests, who tried helping.

Dirty from being on the ground, Lynn held her head high to maintain her dignity. She ignored the snickering in the background, while holding the rail to climb the steps. It had only been a few minutes earlier that she was full of smiles, after receiving the proposal of a lifetime, but now she was eating crow, and wishing things were different. Grimacing, from the pain of her bruised and lacerated feet, Lynn slowly made her way up the stairs; bypassing a crowd of people watching on. Ashley had always been the loving, and understanding sister, who was often over protective. But today, she did the unthinkable, by humiliating her in front of her friends and invited guest. Today she became the villain who had destroyed her life.

Ashley expected Lynn to climb the stairs and run into her comforting arms, but as Lynn reached the top of the porch, she saw a change in Ashley's face. Ashley's show of concern was only a cover for what she was feeling inside. Her undisguised smirk was hidden behind a fake look of concern. Seeing Ashley's reaction to her tragedy, only solidified Lynn's suspicions that Ashley had played a major role in Drew's unexpected visit. Today shouldn't have been the day for Lynn to show her bad side, but Ashley's lack of respect towards her relationship with Drew brought out the worst in her. Ashley had opened pandora's box; releasing the rage of an unhinged woman who was looking for payback. It was a side of Lynn that she didn't want exposed, but she'd been provoked.

Reaching the top of the stairs, Lynn suddenly transformed from being a timid and broken little girl, into the hood rat of all hood rats. Without so much as a warning, Lynn sucker punched Ashley; striking her on the bridge of her nose, rendering her instantly unconscious.

Ashley fell like a sack of potatoes, striking the back of her head against the wooden porch. She laid motionless, with glassy eyes; like a boxer who had been knocked the fuck out. Physically knocking your sister unconscious was as cold blooded as one could get, but Lynn didn't stop there. She had one other bill to pay, and pushed her way through the crowd in search of Marshall.

Standing from a distance, Constance witnessed the commotion, but was unable to react in time. She screamed for Lynn to stop, but lost sight of her, as she disappeared in the crowd. Obligated to render assistance to Ashley, Constance rushed to her daughter's motionless body. Constance had no idea as to what happened, but was sure it had something to do with Marshall.

Pushing her way through the crowd, Lynn found Marshall still celebrating on the rear deck. Seeing that he was with his parents, she began having second thoughts of getting even, but changed her mind.

"That cock-sucker deserves to get his." Lynn said to herself, as she made her way over to where Marshall was standing.

Displaying a cool and calm demeanor, Lynn walked over to take her rightful place beside Marshall. In doing so, Marshall noticed her dress was torn, and full of sand. She had been crying, and her eyes were noticeably swollen. He was sure it had to do with Drew, and the fact that she had returned meant Drew had ended it with her. Although Ashley's idea seemed crazy, she was right, it worked just as she predicted and now Lynn was his again. Everything had gone just as they had planned, and tonight, he was going to celebrate like never before.

Pretending to have no knowledge of Drew ever coming, Marshall whispered into Lynn's ear, inquiring about her appearance.

"What the hell happened to you?"

"I tripped and fell outside, but I'm fine." Lynn said.

"Just as soon as we are finished here, I want you to go change, Ok?"

"Sure," Lynn responded.

Marshall passed her a glass of champagne, as his father prepared a toast to their future. Lynn didn't question Marshall, she did as she was instructed. She listened as Mr. Lathan went forward with his toast.

"To my son and his beautiful fiancé, I wish the two of you a life full of happiness. Lynn, you have been a part of this family since you were a teenage girl. You're now a beautiful woman, who is about to marry my son. I love you, and Joyce and I can't be any happier to have you as a part of our family."

Lynn raised her glass, and watched as Marshall unsuspectingly tilted his glass to drink. She remained patient, and waited until his chin was exposed. Once Marshall tilted his glass of champagne to drink, Lynn saw her opportunity. Marshall was vulnerable, and Lynn took advantage of her opportunity.

She unleashed her anger and frustration by using the heel of her shoe as a weapon; striking Marshall as hard as she could. The shoe shattered the champagne glass against Marshall's face, slashing him across the face, in several areas. The force from the blow, caused Marshall to stumble towards the railing of the deck. In an effort to regain his senses, Marshall tried escaping the line of fire, but was dealt two more blows to his face.

Staggering across the deck, Marshall fell recklessly over the rail, ten feet down onto the sandy ground that awaited him. The softness of the sand cushioned his fall, but Marshall landed on his shoulder, as well as the side of his face. Dazed and confused, he struggled to stand, but stumbled like a drunken bum and fell to the ground once more; striking his head against the wooden support beams that supported the deck. Again, Marshall tried standing, and again he fell.

Seeing his son struggling, Mr. Lathan frantically ran down the stairs to assist him, before further damage was imposed upon him. Marshall was bleeding profusely from the bridge of his nose, and by the way he was holding his arm, it was a sure sign that he had sustained an injury. Still not finished, Lynn leaned over the rail, and began releasing his dirty laundry, for the world to hear.

"You motherfucker, I went to bat for you, and lied to God and the world to help you get drafted. I told the world that you never physically hurt me, when we both know, you kicked my ass for more than two years. I was too ashamed to tell my parents what you were doing to me, because I was too afraid to lose you. So, instead, I allowed it to continue. I was a stupid young kid, who didn't know any better. I made bad decisions then, and I made another, by allowing my sister to talk me into helping you.

I never wanted to marry you, I only agreed to it, to help you get drafted and sign a lucrative contract. In spite of me sacrificing my reputation, and my relationship with the man I love, I opted to help you, and for what? You, and my backstabbing sister set me up by inviting my boyfriend to this bullshit party. So, fuck you Marshall Lathan and take your got damn ring." Lynn removed Marshall's ring from her finger, and threw it at him, striking him in his chest. "I refuse to accept anything from a fucking rapist."

Turning to walk away, Lynn's father attempted to calm her, but it was too late; she'd said all she wanted to say. It was time to leave, and Lynn didn't waste any time in doing so. She pushed her way through the crowd, running to her room to grab her purse. From there she left the house, only to find her car blocked in. There was no escape, and seeing her mother running towards her, Lynn abandoned her plan to drive away. Instead, she ran across the street, and flagged down an oncoming taxi to escape the scene. It was over, she'd gotten her revenge, but in doing so, she'd lost the man she loved.

Chapter: 28

The party had long ended and Ashley laid helplessly on the couch, crying, and denying any involvement in taking part of Marshall's plan to wreck Lynn's life. Constance placed a second Ziplock sandwich bag of ice across Ashley's face. Just as any concerned mother would have done, Constance fluffed Ashley's pillow to make her as comfortable as possible. It was certain her nose was broken; the discoloration surrounding both eyes substantiated it. Still, it hadn't deterred Harry's determination to get to the bottom of what happened. Missing was his youngest daughter, and he wanted information to help find her.

Denying everything, Ashley temporarily put a halt to her father's interrogation, by complaining of pain. No one could deny her pain, her nose was broken without a doubt, but her father's questions were bringing him closer to the truth. It went without saying that Ashley needed to go to the emergency room, but she couldn't risk coming into contact with Marshall. Doing so could unearth the truth, and Ashley couldn't allow her parents to know she was the main culprit behind it all.

Throwing her sister under the bus to get a man, was not only idiotic, but an injudicious decision that could sway her father from ever considering her as head of the company. Ashley was already playing second fiddle to Lynn, but if it ever came to light that she tried offsetting her sister's mindset, her father would likely disown her, so Ashley placed the blame on Lynn for everything that happened. She needed to save her own ass, and to do so, Ashley was telling everything, that hadn't involved her. It wasn't something Harry wanted to hear, but from it, he was beginning to get an overall picture of what was happening, and Ashley was drawn all over it.

Marshall left the ER in time to catch the last flight out of the airport, bound for Las Vegas. He'd spent more than four and a half hours being seen, and for his wait, he received sixteen stitches over the bridge of his nose and eye. Chances were that he would need surgery to eliminate the scarring left by the cut, but now wasn't the time to talk about it. Arriving at the airport, he was mobbed by reporters fighting to get the inside story on what happened. Marshall gave a short interview before catching his flight. He adamantly denied Lynn's allegations; categorizing it as being outlandishly false. He contributed her accusations to her mental illness; explaining Lynn had experienced another manic episode after learning he'd invited an ex-girlfriend to his party. Marshall's attempts to have the media zero in on Lynn's mental breakdown hadn't altogether worked, but for a hot second, it diverted the attention from him.

Completing his statement, Marshall quietly exited through the crowd to catch his flight. Once more his skeletons had resurfaced; leaving him to face more scrutiny. Lynn's verbal and physical attack on him could've possibly erased any leverage he'd have in negotiating a big contract, but he didn't want to think about it right now. His focus was on his future, and career. The chance of him receiving a long term multi-million-dollar contract was blown to shit, thanks to Lynn, but he still could earn a decent living, while playing the game he loved.

The punch seen around the world had gone viral; erasing Marshall's persona as being invincible. Not since the great Vincent Edward "Bo" Jackson, had anyone been regarded as the greatest athlete to have ever lived. Being a superstar All-American in football, basketball and baseball, Marshall was arguably the greatest collegiate athlete of all time, but like a fool, he allowed his life to spin out of control?

Although his ego had taken a beating, his shoulder wasn't as seriously damaged as once believed. He suffered perhaps, the worst embarrassment of his life, and in a four-hour span, more than 250,000 YouTube viewers had seen a one hundred fifteen-pound young woman, physically knock him over the railing, onto the ground below. For kicking his ass, Lynn was celebrated as the hero to woman across the nation who decided to stand up to a big brut who beat her. After years of abuse, she finally had the nerve to stand up to the bully, and demolish him.

"Ashlynn Boldmont" for president," one comment read. "The perfect way to get pay back," another said. Lynn was a hero, and a model for all who were afraid to stand up for themselves. Mrs. Lathan tried convincing Marshall to pursue charges, but he was totally against it. He knew filing assault charges would unearth the rest of his skeletons that he wanted to stay buried. His face, and bruised shoulder would heal. Even his badly damaged ego would heal, but his reputation and career wouldn't survive it. Marshall knew, his best option was to lay low, and wait patiently for everything to blow over.

****

Pacing the floor, Harry tried to make sense of what happened to cause Lynn to go berserk. He was stunned by the rape allegations and demanded to know what happened during her attendance at Penn State. Constance failed at her attempt to convince Harry that it was Lynn's anger that caused her to make the rape allegations. Harry believed his wife was hiding something from him, and demanded to know the truth. Faced with reality, Constance continued to deny knowing anything. She feared what would happen, if her husband ever found out what Marshall had done to Lynn.

Yes, she was lying, but it was to protect the family and the company from any further scandal that may arise. Constance wanted badly to tell the truth, but knew Harry's weak heart couldn't take what Lynn experienced. Lynn was his favorite, and to find out how she was abused, and what she endured would kill him. Frustrated by the sketchy details, Harry grabbed his keys to leave. He was desperate to find his baby girl, but he had no idea where to begin looking. Harry couldn't imagine what Lynn must have been going through, and more than anything, he wanted to be there for her.

He drove to every hotel and motel in the vicinity, but she wasn't at any of them. On a hunch, he checked his credit card transactions, and saw Lynn had used it to rent a room at a Super 8 Motel, just outside of town. Arriving, Harry convinced the receptionist to reveal to him the room Lynn was staying. Escorted to her room, Harry knocked on Lynn's door, and announced himself. He pleaded for Lynn to open the door, promising her that he was there to listen, and not judge. He wanted to know what happened, and why she reacted the way she did.

Harry felt he hadn't been the father he should have been. The company had become strenuous, during Lynn's sophomore year of college, which caused him to spend many long nights in the office. He had concentrated more on his business then he had his daughters. He apologized for not being there and promised he was willing to do whatever it took to help her get through whatever she was dealing with. Hearing what her father said made Lynn open the door and fall into his arms. Her father was always her knight in shining armor. He had arrived to save her from doing anything she would regret later.

Now, more than ever, she needed him and as tightly as he held her in his arms, it was obvious, he needed her too. Harry noticed an open bottle of vodka sitting on the table. From the looks of it, Lynn had only taken a shot or two. Lucky for him, he had gotten there in the nick of time to prevent her from possibly harming herself.

"I wanted to get drunk and pass out, but I can't stand the taste of liquor." Lynn said, as she picked up the bottle, and dropped it in the trash can sitting beside the couch. She knew her father wanted answers, and she was willing to tell him everything he wanted to know, and then some.

Before starting her story, Lynn first apologized for embarrassing the family. Harry didn't mind the embarrassment, but wanted to know what happened. He asked that she hold no punches, and tell what caused her to result to violence. Feeling the time had come to tell her story, Lynn began recapping the year she was hoping to block from her memory. It was time to clear the air as to what transpired in her life with Marshall. It was going to be a near impossible story to tell to her father, but Lynn felt obligated to do so. In telling the truth about what happened, Lynn could only pray that her father wouldn't look at her any differently than his little girl. Lynn hesitated out of fear before starting, but ultimately decided to go forward with her story.

"It was during my final semester that things between Marshall and me went from worse to worst. It was hard for us to spend time together, especially during basketball season. I tried adjusting my schedule to find time to be with him, but it was hard, because I didn't want my grades to suffer. Then came the rumors that he was seeing other women; lots of them. Like a fool, I refused to believe he would do that to me, so I approached him about it, and each time I did, he would lie, and say it was because people was hating on him. Like a fool, I believed him. I wouldn't see Marshall for days at a time, then he'd show up at my dorm room. Then, a friend and I caught him at a restaurant with another girl. He lied again, saying she was his tutor, and that they were having dinner while studying. The girl also admitted she was his tutor, so I let it go, even though I didn't believe him.

To substantiate my curiosity, I did the unthinkable and started casing his apartment. One night, I saw that same girl come to his apartment, wearing next to nothing. That's when I decided to take action. The cheating bastard opened the door, and scanned the immediate area before inviting her inside. I waited a few minutes before knocking on his door. It took him a minute to answer, but when he did, he was shocked to see my smiling face. Like the coward he was, he closed the door in my face. I stood outside of his door, banging on it for ten minutes or more before he opened it. He swore there wasn't a woman inside, and even allowed me to come in to search. I don't know if she jumped out the window, or hid in his attic, but all traces of her was gone. He tried explaining why he closed the door in my face, but his explanation was bogus. At the time, I didn't care, I was just happy to be spending the night with him.

I used to pray that one day, Marshall would realize how good I was for him. I did everything to show him how much I loved him, and he didn't seem to care. He'd know that I'd be waiting on him after one of his home games and would send one of his teammates to tell me to go home and he'll be by later. People used to tell me he would leave with other girls, but instead of seeing the red flag, I chose to stay with him. You see, I loved him and didn't want to lose him. I guess you can say, I loved him more than I loved myself, and I was willing to belittle myself, just to say he was my boyfriend.

I remembered falling to my knees and asking God to give me the strength to walk away from him. I could see that he was destroying my life, and I wanted it stopped, before it was too late. I must have prayed for hours and afterwards, I stood as a new woman. God had granted me the strength I asked for. I called Marshall and abruptly ended things with him. Well, as you can imagine, Marshall was livid by my decision to break it off with him. I remember it just like it was yesterday. Marshall came to my dorm room to argue his case. He even admitted to having one affair, but said it meant nothing. I told him he must be crazy to think I was going to take him back after he cheated on me.

After refusing to give him another chance, Marshall lost his temper and struck me across the face. It was the first time he slapped me, but it wasn't the last. I tried standing my ground, and fought back. I sported a shiner for a couple of days, but Marshall wasn't left unscathed either. I split his lip with a metal stapler, I had sitting on my desk. It should have been the excuse I needed to stay the hell away from him, but like a fool, crazy in love; I relented, and opted to give him another chance. Over time, I learned to accept his affairs with other women. I continued catching him with women, and each time I did, I forgave him. I did so, because I loved him, and though I continued to love him, I stopped being intimate with him.

Marshall changed after that, he promised to be faithful, and for a while it seemed as if he was. That was until I returned to my dorm room, and nearly caught him in what I thought was an uncompromising position with my roommate and best friend Mia. I didn't see them per say doing anything wrong, but it was their reaction to my arrival, that sparked my attention. I had no evidence to support my suspicions, so I let it go. I had two rules, they were that Marshall stay clear of my sister and my closest friends, but he couldn't do that.

It all came to a head one afternoon, when he invited me to spend the weekend with him. We hadn't seen much of each other in weeks leading up to March Madness, because the coach required them to stay in the gym during their free time. I hadn't expected to see him then out of the blue, Marshall called and invited me to spend the weekend with him at his apartment. It seemed appropriate, because they didn't have any scheduled games. I learned later that he needed my help to complete two term papers that were due the next week. I knew it was the reason he was inviting me over; but I didn't care. My self-esteem was so low, I was willing to do anything just to be with him. We decided that I would come by that Friday afternoon, after my two o'clock class was over. I have to admit, I was looking forward to it. My plan was to pack enough clothes for the weekend and drive to his apartment. However, my plans quickly changed, after an unexpected snow storm slammed us. The forecast predicted only a dusting, but the dusting instantly changed into a blizzard. It totally caught the entire community by surprise; leaving us baffled as to what to do.

Learning about the intensity of the storm, Marshall called to cancel our weekend together. As he put it, he didn't have any food at his house, and he didn't want me there without food. He thought it would be best if I stayed on campus for my safety. Maybe it was the way he said it that raised my suspicion, but nonetheless, I'd made up my mind that I was going, even if he'd made plans with another woman. I left class early and drove to the market to pick up a few items, and after doing so, the car got stuck in the parking lot. Luckily, I didn't have but two bags of groceries, and my clothes were in my backpack, so instead of driving, I left the car in the parking lot, and caught the bus to his apartment.

The driver announced it was the last bus running for the day, and I remembered thinking to myself, how lucky I was to catch the last bus. I was looking forward to spending the weekend with Marshall. It was something I felt we both needed, because the season had been a stressful one. I really missed him, and wanted to make the weekend a successful one; hoping it was enough to salvage our relationship. It was a slow ride to

Marshall's apartment, and by the time the bus arrived, the snow was nearly at my knees. I could barely see the entry to the complex because the hard-blowing snow had nearly blinded me. The wind was so intense, I slipped and fell twice before reaching the complex. Finally, I made it to his front door. I was covered in snow from head to toe, and took time to brush as much snow as I could off me, before entering.

I used my key to open the door to a dark apartment. I wasn't sure if Marshall was home, and waited by the door until my eyes adjusted. Carrying the bags of groceries, I placed them on the counter. As I proceeded through the kitchen, I saw what I believed to be a male figure standing at the kitchen table. I wasn't sure at first what he was doing, but as I got closer, I could see Marshall standing naked over a woman, who was stretched across his table. He was surprised to see me, and rightfully so, because he hadn't expected me. He tried shielding her, and screamed for me to go into the next room, so he could get his "Fuck Ho" out of his apartment, but I refused to leave the room, and turned on the light.

It was for my peace of mind that I had to see the type of woman he was sleeping with, and regrettably I got my answer. Lying under him was my best friend and confidant, Mia. She knew everything about us. She knew how much I loved Marshall and knew the embarrassment I endured with him flaunting women in front of me. So many countless nights, I cried on her shoulder after finding out he was sleeping with different women. Now, she was one of those women, she was doing the same thing to me. My best friend was screwing my man. Dad, I lost it, kind of like today. I began throwing the food I had brought at them, I wasn't going to allow her to sleep with my man, and get away with it. Marshall tried restraining me, but I kicked him in his groin; temporarily rendering him helpless.

273

I caught her trying to get dressed so she could get away and went ballistic on her. I threw her to the floor, and got on top of her. I began punching her in her face; trying to disfigure it. I remembered her screaming for help, as her blood spattered against my face. It was a rush like I'd never felt before, until today, and like today; I felt justified in doing it. I wanted more than anything to disfigure her pale white face, and tried pulling out every strand of her bleached blond hair out of her head, but before doing so, Marshall grabbed me around my waist and pulled me off of her.

He threw me over his shoulder and carried me to the front door. I couldn't believe it; Marshall was throwing me out in the blizzard instead of that bitch. I thought to myself, if this was going to happen, I was going out in a blaze. I screamed, kicked and grabbed onto any and everything I could grip; hoping to make enough noise for the neighbors to see and hear what he was doing to me. Opening the door, Marshall carried me out of his apartment to the front of the parking lot, and like a rag doll, he threw me across the hedges onto the hood of a car. Bam! I hit that car hood so hard, the impact of it knocked me temporarily silly. I remembered sliding from the hood of that car like a sliding board, before landing into a foot of snow that waited for me. I remained submerged in the snow for more than a minute or so, before regaining my senses. I got up to check the car I was thrown on for any damages, but in doing so, I realized it belonged to Mia. It had a visitor's pass hanging on the rearview mirror, indicating that she was going to be spending the weekend with Marshall.

Maybe it was from the shock of knowing what they had done to me, but I wanted more than anything to get even with them. As I stood in that blizzard, and watched them looking at me from his apartment window, I became enraged with anger. I'd never felt so disrespected in my life. I had no idea of how I was going to get back to campus, and by the way I was feeling, I didn't really care. My only concern was getting even. The thought of how cozy they were going to be, infuriated me. It was supposed to be me who was spending the weekend with him, not Mia.

So, I raided someone's trash can, removed three beer bottles, and threw them through his living room windows; shattering them. I didn't stop there, I removed three more bottles, ran to the outside of his bedroom, and broke his windows there also. Then, like a felon on the run, under the cover of the white out condition of the blizzard, I ran. I wasn't afraid of Marshall coming after me. In a way, I wanted him to, but like the coward he was, he stayed locked up in his apartment.

Having no way back to campus, I called the University Police, and told them I was stranded and needed a ride home. I told them that my boyfriend and I had got into a fight, and he kicked me out, and that I needed transportation back to my dorm. An officer arrived within minutes and transported me back to my dorm. He stayed with me until he felt it was safe enough for me to be left alone. I must have cried on that man's shoulder for nearly an hour before he left. He was kind, and he gave me the strength I needed to make it through the night.

Immediately after the officer left, I gathered all of Mia's belongings and threw them in a dumpster outside the dorm. I waited, hoping she would return so I could finish what I started, but as expected, she never returned. For the entire weekend, I sat in the room with the lights out; waiting for her to come back to the room. When she didn't, I gave up and decided to meet her outside her classroom. Unfortunately for me, she had contacted campus police, and they had an officer to escort her to and from class. I gave up after that; making the conscious decision to walk away. I even tried going on with my life, but Marshall wouldn't allow me to. That egotistical bastard was determined to return into my life, and he wouldn't take no for an answer."

Having told her father more than she had confided in with her therapist; Lynn was releasing unwanted pressure she had been carrying for two years. It was difficult to read her father's feelings because he hadn't shown his emotions, but Lynn knew it must have been killing him to know the cruelty she had experienced by the hands of Marshall, but her father needed to know the truth. After taking a needed breath, Lynn held her father's hand tightly, and went forward with her story.

"Marshall called three weeks later; begging me to take him back. He said he realized his mistake, and again, promised to never deceive me again. He wanted us to patch things up one last time, and like a fool in love, I agreed. We decided to talk over dinner and discuss what led him to sleeping with Mia; like I didn't know. On the day we were scheduled to meet, he conveniently changed his plans. He said something had come up, and asked if we could have dinner at his apartment instead. Silly me, I didn't know any better, and agreed without questioning it. I even agreed to purchase the dinner.

Calling a local Japanese restaurant that delivered, I ordered two complete dinners, including his favorite; Kobe beef steaks, imported from Japan. Nothing but the best for my man, I said to myself. God, I was so stupid to think he had changed, because he hadn't. His talk of love, devotion and commitment was bullshit, that bastard was still the snake in the grass he'd always been, and I refused to see it.

When my cell phone rang, I remembered thinking to myself; here comes another excuse. But this time he didn't have an excuse, he was calling to tell me he was going to be thirty minutes late, and to set an extra plate, because we were having a dinner guest. Assuming it was either a reporter or his training partner, I didn't think anything of it. I didn't expect a guest, and hadn't ordered any extras, but remembered seeing a pack of steaks in his refrigerator while putting away the groceries I'd brought for him earlier in the day. I got one from his refrigerator, and asked the neighbor across the hallway, to prepare it for me.

To compliment the dinners, I took vegetables from our plates to give them a completed meal, and for what? Marshall arrived, without his guest, which led me to believe he wasn't coming. When inquiring about his guest, his response was that she was on her way. She, I thought to myself. It was alarming that his guest was a girl, but I tried to keep an open mind without reading anything into it. While Marshall showered, I tidied up the apartment; ensuring everything was in order when our guest arrived. I was still uncertain who this mystery woman was, but assumed it was a reporter, or an agent of some kind.

Wearing a pair of shorts and a t-shirt, Marshall returned to the kitchen. I had straightened up the apartment, and the table was set perfectly for dinner; at least that's what I thought. As expected, Marshall wasn't happy with what I had done, and complained about the way I arranged the table. He said I had placed the guest too far in the corner, and he wanted her to be on the opposite side of him.

It was a weird request, but as always, I obliged his wishes. I sensed that something was wrong, and feared the worse. I was on pins and needles until I heard that dreaded knock. I was scared to death, not knowing who was standing outside of his door. My heart sank at the sound, but for Marshall's sake I wanted to keep an open mind.

Holding my breath, I watched him, as he went to answer the door. He opened it, and stepped outside; closing the door behind him.

Seconds later, he re-emerged, but did so with Mia following him. My heart nearly fell to the pit of my stomach. I didn't know whether to finish whipping her butt or leave. But before I could respond, Marshall spoke. His excuse was that he wanted us to have dinner together, and talk to correct the wrongs they had done to me. Like a fool, I reluctantly agreed and allowed the woman who had sex with my boyfriend to sit at the table and have dinner with us. In my mind I wanted to go ballistic, but I was too shocked to move. I just sat there, too stunned to utter a word. I knew I had to get out of that house, before I did something I would regret later, but I didn't have the strength to do it. So, I sat; too shocked to move a muscle.

Once gathering my thoughts, and courage to leave, I got up to leave. I made it as far as the front door, before Marshall stopped me. He talked me into staying, and escorted me back to the table. Returning to my seat, I sat and watched them eat, as if everything was ok. I tried eating but couldn't. Seeing them together made me sick to my stomach, because it was obvious, they were very much in love. It was at that moment I knew it was over between us. I couldn't stay and watch them make eyes at each other; I had to go. My dreams of spending a life with Marshall were over.

After dinner, we retired to the living room to talk. Still numb from the shock, I followed them and sat in a chair across the room. The two of them sat on his loveseat holding each other, kissing and caressing as if they were going to make love in front of me. I couldn't take the humiliation anymore, nor did I want an apology from them. I decided to step aside and allow them to be the couple they wanted to be. So, I got my purse to leave, but once again, Marshall intervened. But unlike the last time, I refused to return to the room. I didn't want anything to do with them, or their unnatural behavior.

That's when it happened, Marshall muscled me back into the room. He sat me in his lap and held my arms to keep me from fighting back. I fought to get away, but I was no match for him. I couldn't understand what they were about to do to me, but seeing Mia get undressed left me with no doubts as to what was about to happen. They were going to rape me. Marshall dragged me down the hallway into his bedroom. I couldn't believe the man I loved since ninth grade was doing this to me. Not only that, he was doing it with my ex-best friend since grade school. Once inside the room, he threw me across his bed and Mia began ripping my clothes off. I felt so helpless, I wanted to die."

Tears fell from Lynn's eyes as she began reliving her horrific ordeal. Her father squeezed her hand; knowing what she was about to tell him, would change his life forever. He could see what it was doing to his baby girl, but she was determined to tell her story, and after taking a deep breath, Lynn resumed her story, while trying to hold up.

"Determined not to be violated, I fought harder but again, I was no match for them. After feeling a pinch in my arm, everything went hazy. I don't remember much after that. I do remember them stripping my clothes off me."

Intervening, Harry spoke, "You don't have to tell me anymore, we can finish this when you're strong enough."

Harry didn't want Lynn to have to relive her nightmare without professional help on hand. He didn't want a setback in her recovery, but Lynn was determined to tell her story. She wanted her father to know what she had gone through, so she continued.

"After being drugged, I continued to fight to free myself, as my body began shutting down. I remember drifting in and out of consciousness, before everything went blank."

Pausing to maintain her composure, Lynn wiped her tears as if she fought to tell her story. Harry also felt himself breaking down, but knew he had to remain strong for his daughter. He couldn't allow her to see him lose it, but it was becoming difficult. His first thought was to catch a plane to Las Vegas and blow Marshall's head off, but it would only add to his daughter's burden. Marshall had violated his precious child, and he was still running free to continue his reign of havoc, on other unsuspecting young souls. Marshall had stayed in his home, ate at his dinner table, and disgustedly, called him dad. He had looked upon him as part of his family, and to learn he had betrayed him was devastating.

Seeing her father's frustration building, Lynn felt a sense of urgency to keep him calm. His heart was weak, and the last thing she wanted to do was to cause another setback in his recovery, but Harry was demanding the truth, and it was up to her to give him what he was asking. Erring on the side of caution, Lynn made her father promise not to retaliate against Marshall, or his family, for what she was sharing with him, and before going any further, she made her father promise he wouldn't.

Needing a break, Harry went to the bathroom and closed the door behind him. He splashed water on his face to hide his tears. Using a hand towel to dry his face, he stared at himself in the mirror, as he tried to imagine what his daughter had gone through. He blamed himself for not being there; promising that he would never again fail her. He had always been her protector, and prided himself, as being the ideal father that every child fantasized of having. But like most fathers, he became preoccupied with work, leaving his daughter to fend for herself, against the Marshall's of the world. If he'd only known, he could have protected her, but he couldn't be in two places at the same time.

Leaving the bathroom, Harry returned to his rightful place beside his daughter. Once back, he found Lynn waiting to resume her story.

"I awoke the following morning to find Marshall standing by his tripod, changing the tape in his camera. I knew my nightmare hadn't ended. My hands, feet and mouth were bound with duct tape, and I couldn't move. I wasn't sure what they were going to do next, but I knew it was going to be sexual. Marshall stroked my hair, as he removed the tape from my mouth. He unbound my hands, but left my ankles tied. He promised, he would remove the tape if I acted accordingly. He even gave me a couple sips of water, to rinse my mouth. The weird thing about it was, the damn fool thought he was doing me justice by giving me water.

I could barely open my mouth to drink, because I had been bound so tightly, my face was numb. Marshall reached down and gently massaged my face, helping the blood to flow again. He sat me up in bed and explained how he wasn't ready for me to leave. It was at that moment I began feeling the need to escape because I believed I was going to die. It was as if Mia also knew what was about to happen, because she abruptly left the room. After she left, Marshall told me he'd made tapes of the entire incident, and if I went to the police, he was going to release them to the public. I didn't know what to do. If I went to the police, my life would be ruined, and if I kept it to myself, my life was going to be ruined. I had the family to think of, so I promised Marshall, I wouldn't say anything.

I remembered lying on my stomach and sobbing, while asking Marshall why was he doing this to me? He never gave a definitive answer, but insinuated that it was something he thought I wanted. I'm ashamed to say this, but we had at one time, discussed a threesome with a girl of his choice, but I changed my mind, after further consideration.

As you may have imagined, Marshall wasn't too happy with my decision, and in all likelihood, this was his way of getting revenge. He laid down beside me, and removed the tape from my ankles. He admitted it wasn't his idea to drug me, or tie me up, and that it was something Mia wanted to do. You see, she was the woman he wanted to join us in a threesome. With the tape running, Marshall attempted to rape me again, but he underestimated me, and like today, he relaxed. I waited for him to make his move, and when he did, I grabbed hold of his genitals, and squeezed them as hard as I could. I wanted to inflict as much pain on him as he had done to me. The more he screamed, the harder I squeezed. My goal was to rupture him.

Desperate to get relief from his pain, Marshall struck me with several blows to my face to break my grip. It wasn't until he gave up that I saw my opportunity to escape. I knew, I had to get away now, if I was going to live. I didn't have time to reflect upon my injuries, or to get my clothes. My main objective was to get out of that apartment, as fast as I could. Running out of the room, all I could see was the front door, and I ran as fast as I could to get there. Before doing so, Mia was coming out of the bathroom. I didn't know what her intentions were, but I shoved her back into the bathroom, without breaking stride.

Fortunately for me, my keys were still on the kitchen counter, along with my purse. I opened the door, and ran as fast as I could to my car. While I was running, I was praying to God, to help me escape. It was freezing cold outside, and some snow was still on the ground. I was naked, but didn't care because I was free. I didn't think of screaming for help, my only thoughts were to get away.

I got into the car, and locked all the doors, and as soon as mom's car started, I sped off. I could barely see a anything from the frost on the windshield, but I didn't care, I had to get away. It was a miracle I didn't hit anything, and once I made it out of the parking lot, I used the washer fluid to clear my windshield. Too afraid to go to the dorm to get dressed, for fear of Marshall and Mia coming to finish the job; I drove directly to the city police station to report the incident. An officer came to answer the door and was startled to see me naked. He removed his jacket and wrapped it around me, taking me inside.

After giving a statement, the incident was reported to the university police department. They explained, they were required by policy to do so, being that I was a student. I knew, I would be in deep shit, if I reported who it was, because Marshall was the star basketball player at the university. Despite his popularity, I was convinced by a city police officer to pursue charges. She transported me to the Emergency Room, where I was humiliated even more with questions, and being probed. I found comfort with the female officer who stayed by my side, while holding my hand and crying with me. I knew I was doing the right thing, by reporting Marshall and Mia, but I had no idea of the consequences I would face by doing so.

Because of Marshall, word got out about what I had done, and all hell broke loose. As promised, Marshall posted the video of him and Mia, having sex with me. The bastard even posted my phone number for everyone to call me if they wanted to have a good time. Most students who knew me, believed I was telling the truth, but those who didn't, formed an unfavorable opinion of me.

Some went as far as vandalizing mom's car, and some went to the extreme by threatening bodily harm to me, but I tried not to allow it to interfere with my grades. I continued to walk with my head high; knowing that the truth would someday be revealed, but I felt so alone. My life at the university, had become a nightmare, and each day, brought on a new low.

My integrity was questioned, and my reputation had been destroyed. All that remained was my pride, and that began to erode with each day that passed. Days went by, and still the University and city police hadn't made an arrest. Each phone call was full of promises, assuring the investigation was ongoing, and arrests were in the works. I was told that the investigation was tight lipped, with every officer instructed to stay clear of the media. As the semester ended, and the spring flowers were in bloom, so was Marshall and Mia's relationship. They made sure I saw them each day, holding hands while intentionally kissing in front of me.

They convinced most of the students that I lied about being raped, and it was mainly because of the leaked tape. Little did they know, the tape was what got them arrested. I remember the day the news broke about their arrests. I was packing for home, when one of my friends began banging on my door and screaming for me to turn on my television.

Turning on the TV, I saw Marshall and Mia cuffed and being escorted by university and city police to the city lock-up. It was reported that Mia had confessed to what had happened, and was planning to cooperate fully with the police. Like me, she had fallen in love, and believed Marshall was the answer to her dreams, but like me, she found him in bed with another woman."

Chapter: 29

Harry remained curious as to why Marshall and Mia were never prosecuted, but it was obvious from Lynn's story that she didn't have the strength to go through with it. By her own admission the fear of testifying in court, contributed to her breakdown.

Feeling the comfort of her father's embrace, Lynn placed her head on his shoulder. It was at that moment, she felt comfortable enough to admit she had attempted suicide, by ingesting a bottle of sleeping pills. She told her father that she needed an escape from all the hurt and pain she was experiencing. Hearing the news for the first time, Harry became convinced that his wife deliberately kept Lynn's problems from him. How could his wife of twenty-six years, keep this from him? He needed answers, and after convincing Lynn to come back to the cottage with him, he was going to get them.

Acting as a buffer, Lynn quickly intervened by informing her father as to why he hadn't been told about her attempted suicide. She reminded him, that he was out of town on business, after recovering from a recent heart attack. Her mother's decision to keep the incident from him was based on her wanting to protect him. Like a good wife, Constance took on the burden of keeping the family safe and together, while moving the company forward.

Short of completing her story, Lynn chose not to talk anymore. She knew doing so would implicate her mother, as one of the sources that contributed to her near demise. Harry knew there was so much more to her story, but chose not to pursue it any further. Sitting with his head resting against the wall, Harry closed his eyes and thanked God for putting his arms around his precious daughter. At that moment, he promised himself to never overlook his family ever again. It was a commitment he made to himself and to God. From this moment, he would oversee their growth, as well as their happiness.

Harry spent the remainder of the night struggling to get comfortable on the hotel's couch, while Lynn slept peacefully in her bed. He thought of many ways to get even with Marshall; going as far as hiring someone to put the beatdown on him, but ultimately decided against it. There was no doubt in his mind that Marshall was going to get what was coming to him; it was just a matter of time.

Lying in bed with her eyes closed, Lynn pretended to be asleep. She resumed reminiscing about her past, and revisited the moment when Marshall and Mia were arrested. It was a jubilant feeling to finally see justice, after weeks of pressuring the police departments to make an arrest. But instead of feeling vindicated, Lynn was left feeling secluded.

Marshall and Mia's arrest had changed her life in the worst kind of way. She instantly became vulnerable to attacks by students attending the university who believed her allegations against Marshall and Mia were fabricated. It motivated them to get revenge against her for bringing down an athlete who was admired by the entire state.

For bringing down Marshall, students stopped at nothing to make Lynn pay for her allegations against Marshall and Mia. Lynn was a target, and was often verbally assaulted throughout her travels within the campus grounds. Her car was vandalized so many times that she was forced to store it off campus, and use public transportation to get around. The community made her life a living hell, but nothing could compare to what she encountered after Marshall's release from jail.

Online videos of her in uncompromising positions were posted for everyone to see. They were videos that was supposed to be for private use, but Marshall used them against her. Marshall's antics had turned her life upside down, and by using social media to spread lies, he rallied up a large number of followers, who vowed to fight for his cause. Information was uncovered that a retaliation against her was planned at the conclusion of exams. In an attempt to protect her from physical harm, the university granted her permission to take her finals a week early.

A week before exams were scheduled to begin, Lynn left Penn State under the cover of darkness for the final time; never to return as a student. Lucky for her, her father was temporarily living in Spokane Washington, while overseeing a new telecommunications system that was being installed during the construction of a private prison their company was heavily invested in. Her mother was home running the family's telecommunications company, and was the sole caretaker for her daughters. Talking to her mother was like talking to a brick wall. She was as cold as a Canadian winter's night, especially when it was something she wasn't interested in.

Building the nerves to tell Constance what happened, was the hardest thing Lynn had to do. Unfortunately for her, Constance had already been informed of what happened; at least from Marshall's mother's point of view. Mrs. Lathan had beaten her to the punch; fabricating a story that was as far from the truth as one could imagine. Before Lynn was able to speak to her mother, Constance had already formed an opinion about her, as well as the facts. The biased version she received from Mrs. Lathan, easily exasperated her opinion immensely, and due to their close friendship, Mrs. Lathan's lies challenged the validity of the truth Lynn was going to tell.

To say Constance was outraged at what happened was an understatement. She questioned Lynn, challenging her as to what happened, and why she chose to embarrass the family as well as herself. It was a moment Lynn hadn't expected. It hadn't occurred to Constance what Lynn had gone through, or what she was going through at that moment. All that mattered to Constance was that Lynn had brought a dark cloud over the family. It was shocking to know that Constance had reacted so prematurely, without having heard her side of the story. But what was most shocking was that Constance had chosen to believe what Mrs. Lathan had told her.

To avoid any confrontation, Lynn didn't respond further to her mother's allegations. Instead, she ran upstairs and locked herself in her room. This infuriated Constance, who followed Lynn to her room while demanding to know the truth. Constance was furious by Lynn's decision to disturb a hornet's nest. Constance knew Lynn's decision would not only damage their company's reputation, but impose more stress on her father's already weakened heart. Constance had her husband and his company to protect, and she was going to do any and every thing to protect them, even if it meant making Lynn drop all charges against Marshall and Mia.

Lynn spent the remainder of the evening in her room crying, as she continued to replay what happened in her mind. She hated herself for what she had done to Marshall, as well as her family. Her mother had stopped short of telling her she wished she hadn't been born. Obviously, she was ashamed of her. Disgusted at herself, Lynn stripped and got into the shower; hoping it would clean the filth from her soul. She was ashamed of herself and the embarrassment she brought to the family. Never in her life did she ever want to disappoint her parents and after years of making them proud, she had done the unthinkable.

Plagued with nightmares since the rape, Lynn took the final step to erase her pain. Getting out of the shower, Lynn rubbed her best body oils on her body, before dressing herself in her favorite gown. Opening her purse, Lynn removed the bottle of Tylenol PM she had brought on her drive home. She carried the bottle to the bathroom with her, and began taking one pill at a time. Lynn took the entire bottle of twenty-four pills, and got into bed. Finally, she was going to get the much-needed rest she had been after for months. Once she fell asleep tonight, it was going to be forever.

Opening her eyes, Lynn saw Constance leaning over her. She expected her to be upset, as well as disappointed in her failed attempt to kill herself, but Lynn found Constance to be more forgiving, and merciful. Constance showed the human side of herself, while expressing a warmer receptance to her. She wiped Lynn's forehead with a damp cloth, and apologized for her behavior. Constance asked for forgiveness; promising to listen to her and to hear her side of the story.

Lying on her back in the hospital wasn't the most ideal place to tell her mother what happened, but Lynn found herself faced with a much larger problem. It started when a psychiatrist entered her room. She was a kind woman, and when she revealed why she was there, Lynn felt it wasn't going to be a good visit. The psychiatrist had come at the request of the hospital to evaluate Lynn. Needless to say, Lynn wasn't happy with her visit, and refused to speak to her regarding her overdose.

Things quickly transpired from quiet, to chaotic within seconds, once it was made known that Lynn was being admitted to the psychiatric floor for a psych evaluation. Lynn became irate, her behavior became more than what the hospital had anticipated, and the decision was made to medicate her. Her fight against being medicated wasn't a successful one. Lynn was restrained by four hospital personnel, and given a shot of Haldol.

It was hard for Constance to have to witness her daughter being restrained and medicated. She was in agreement with the hospital's decision, but to see Lynn being manhandled and forced to take a drug to calm herself was more than she could handle. Lynn was admitted to the fifth-floor mental health unit, where she stayed for three weeks, before being released.

To prevent any ridicule or embarrassment to Lynn and the Boldmont Company, Constance strongly urged Lynn to drop all charges against Marshall and Mia. In Constance's opinion, it was the best way to avoid the hardships that surely would come their way. She believed a trial would set back Lynn's progress, and as a mother, it was her job to protect the family and the company.

Convincing Lynn to drop the charges wasn't as hard as Constance first predicted. It was an idea Lynn had considered, after believing she couldn't face her accusers in a court of law. In more ways than one, Lynn was ready to put her ordeal behind her. She had completed the semester at Penn State and had been accepted to begin classes at Whiteman/Fitzgerald School of Business, in the fall. Lynn's decision inspired Constance to surprise her, by treating her to a girl's day of shopping.

Her suggestion for Lynn to drop the charges, wasn't out of support for the Lathan family, but for her own. Constance's concern for her husband's health, and the stability of his company, depended on Lynn's decision to do the right thing. Her mental state was in question and it wasn't a wise decision for her to testify.

To butter Lynn up, Constance took her on a girl's day out. They began by visiting a beauty salon, followed by shopping at all the nearby boutiques. For the grand surprise, Constance drove Lynn to a Mercedes Benz dealership. Anyone would have thought that Lynn would jump out of her shoes at the opportunity to own her very own Benz, but she didn't. She was more interested in owning an old muscle car of the seventies. She did however, entertain the idea of owning a Benz, but ultimately decided not to. Constance obliged Lynn's wishes, and purchased her the 1967 Pontiac GTO she wanted. It wasn't a surprise that Constance was willing to do what it took to sway Lynn into doing what she wanted, nor was it a big surprise that she was willing to spare no expense to do so. Constance's mission was to cover up anything she believed could potentially hurt the family's business, and from the smile on Lynn's face, she had.

Reluctantly, Lynn agreed to travel to Happy Valley the following morning to drop the charges against Marshall and Mia. It was a decision she wasn't in total agreement with, but felt obligated to do. Unfortunately for Lynn, her mother's love and respect, had come at a price. By obliging her wishes to forget everything that had happened to her, Lynn was going against her desire to prosecute Marshall and Mia, for what they did to her; she was doing it to satisfy her mother. She found solace in knowing that her mother was a lawyer who was intelligent enough to look out for her best interest.

Sitting around the round table, Lynn was forced to face her accusers who had tortured her. It was by far the hardest thing she had to do, but she did it for her family. Under the guidance of her mother, Lynn went through with the meeting; dropping all charges against Marshall and Mia. She left Happy Valley with prayers of leaving her past behind her, but unfortunately her prayers weren't answered. Though her ordeal was over, there was too much for Lynn to overcome. Days after returning home, her mental health began to decline.

Chapter: 30

Rushing to answer what seemed like an endless knock, Drew opened the front door to find Gloria waiting to greet him. Wearing a pale-yellow sundress, and a pair of white sandals, Gloria stood proudly with a smile. Her hair was down, and her hazel eyes sparkled against the reflection of the morning sun. To set the tone, she greeted Drew with a kiss, before stepping back across the threshold. She was as beautiful as ever, and for a split-second, Drew nearly forgot she wasn't his girl anymore.

"You have a minute for an old friend?" Gloria asked, enlarging her eyes in a provocative way.

Not knowing how to react, Drew invited her inside, but Gloria declined. Instead, she asked if they could take a ride to the lake. Her excuse was that she wanted to talk, without any interruptions. Agreeing to her request, Drew left the house; closing the door behind him. He escorted Gloria to the back of his residence and retrieved his Gator ATV to drive the one-mile distance to the lake. Because it was such a hot morning, Drew stopped by the office to get a few bottles of water for their trip. He wasn't sure if Karyme was at the office working, but hoped she had elected to take the morning off to spend with her mother.

Climbing the stairs, Drew entered the office and to his relief, Karyme had indeed taken the day off. He didn't want to have to explain why he was spending the morning with Gloria, nor did he want to risk quarreling about him backsliding into Gloria's arms. Drew grabbed a few items, including water from the office refrigerator, and a blanket off the office couch. He placed the bottles of water in a small cooler, and filled it with ice; then tucked the blanket under his arm, and left the office to rejoin Gloria.

It was a soothing feeling to be in the company of a friend, after suffering through one of his most humiliating moments of his life. Drew was miserable because of Lynn's unexpected decision to be with Marshall. It was a sight he never thought he would ever see, though he should have expected it. All the signs were there like the letters Ashley had shown him and the daily phone calls from Marshall.

Lynn's inability to move on from Marshall was a sure sign that she was still in love with him. Sadly, he was too head over heels in love to see it. But thank God, Gloria had come by to see him. Even though the sight of her reminded him of what happened between them, the thought of being around a friendly face was enough to help ease his pain.

The drive to the lake was quiet; neither Drew or Gloria spoke a word, as each waited for the other to begin the conversation. They had traveled halfway to the lake before anything was said between them. Gloria was the first to break the ice. She apologized for the way she handled their breakup; along with the lies she told him. She was afraid to tell him the truth, because she was confused about who she wanted to be with. Gloria admitted to being lonely, and with him concentrating on his studies, she began to feel that she didn't have a place in his heart anymore. Gloria also admitted that Drew's mother had played a role in her decision to be with Mason. She explained, Nancy had never fully embraced her as his girlfriend, and often made her feel less of a person because of her family's social status.

As Gloria began to explain what led her on the path to Mason. Drew could only listen to and agree with what she said. Gloria spoke about being uncomfortable in Nancy's presence, and how inferior she made her feel. In a lot of ways, Gloria was correct in her assumptions; Nancy hadn't given her the respect she deserved. In all honesty, Nancy never thought she was the girl for him, and often expressed her feelings about how she felt about Gloria. Although she refused to give Gloria a chance to be a part of the family, Gloria hadn't helped herself in winning her over either. Gloria constantly did things that caused an unfavorable opinion of her from his family. Especially when she caused him to lose his scholarship to play football at the University of North Carolina, after involving him in a fight she created.

It was the last football game of the year and the Jefferson County High School Jaguars had just captured the state championship. It should have been a night for partying, but Gloria found a way to ruin it for everyone. While cheering on the football field, she had gotten into an argument with a group of students in the crowd and when the game ended, all hell broke loose. Seeing what was happening, Drew rushed to the side lines to protect Gloria from getting hurt, and in the process of doing so, he was mobbed by the onslaught of students rushing the field. Drew suffered a mild concussion, a bloody nose, a broken wrist, and a black eye, and for his heroism, he lost his football scholarship to play for the University of North Carolina.

He had lost his scholarship, all in the name of love, but lucky for him, his grades were good enough to get into one of the best business schools in the nation. Getting into Whiteman Fitzgerald University hadn't come as a shock, but it came with stipulations. He was not to have any disciplinary problems while being a student at the university; whether on or off campus. In other words, he had to stay squeaky clean during his four years there.

After the football fiasco, many argued that Nancy had reason to dislike Gloria. Gloria had robbed Drew of the chance to play football for his favorite university, but that wasn't the reason Nancy disliked Gloria. It was Gloria's self-centered ways that Nancy hated most about her. She hated the way Gloria would place demands on Drew, just because she knew he would do everything in his power to make her happy. Drew understood Gloria, and accepted the consequences that came with her. He knew their relationship wasn't a healthy one, but he loved her, and letting go was one of the hardest things he had to do.

Knowing Gloria was with Mason hurt, but he had to accept what he couldn't change. After years of being together, having to accept the idea of Gloria being with Mason was a hard pill to swallow, but Mason had stolen Gloria's heart, and she was in love with him. Nearing the lake, Drew found himself unable to look Gloria in her eyes. He couldn't say for certain if he was feeling love, or lust, but each time he looked into Gloria's hazel eyes; his heart skipped a beat.

They arrived at the lake minutes later and like always, Gloria was quick to run to the pedalboat. She loved peddling across the lake, and today was no exception. It was the perfect morning to be out on the lake, and being out there together presented them with the perfect opportunity to talk, and to put closure to their relationship.

Once reaching the far end of the lake, Drew and Gloria secured their pedalboat against the dock and took cover under one of three huge magnolia trees in the pasture. Drew spread the blanket on the ground for he and Gloria to sit and to continue their talk. They had a lot to discuss, with little time to do so. Gloria was quick to ask about Drew's association with Lynn. Drew was surprised to know that she and Mason had helped Lynn with a flat. Drew chuckled, before adding that he and Lynn weren't a couple, but had discussed the possibility.

It was uncharacteristic of Drew to be timid about discussing his relationship, because Gloria had been the only girl he'd ever been with and was once considered to become his wife. In a turn of events, Drew admitted to Gloria that he still had feelings for her. It was something Gloria hadn't expected, but welcomed. She too, had mixed emotions when it came to Drew. In a lot of ways, she still loved him, but his inconsistency in making her feel wanted, caused her to turn to Mason.

It seemed strange talking to Drew about being with another man, but Gloria was doing just that. She boasted about how she reached her goals without help from Drew. She even blamed him for his lackluster effort to solicit his mother's help to finance her education, but stated she ultimately forgave him. Gloria went on to talk about her accomplishments, and the bright future she was about to have. She did admit, she didn't know the role Mason was going to play in her life, or how he would fit into her future plans, but gave him credit for helping her reach her goals.

Gloria was making the point that she was only with Mason out of obligation. The likelihood of her being in love with him was slim to none, which meant the future Mason was hoping to have was only a fantasy. Gloria was still in love with him, and her admission only heightened Drew's hopes of them resolving their differences and becoming a couple again. Gloria went on to talk about how Mason stepped up, during the days leading up to her near dismissal from school. Mason's generosity not only helped her continue that semester; his generosity continued until she reached her goal of becoming an RN. It was just another example of the many things Mason had done for her. His dedication to look out for her best interest was what made him the man she wanted to share her future with.

Gloria stressed to Drew that her decision to be with Mason had nothing to do with her love for him. It was complicated for her because she felt obligated to Mason, but said Drew was the only man she had ever truly loved. Gloria had gotten herself into a mess by taking advantage of Mason and his undying love for her. By persuading him to help her financially, she hadn't taken into consideration the price she would have to pay for accepting his money. Lord knows, Mason never did anything out of gratitude, and you could bet there were going to be consequences for her to pay.

After listening to Gloria lay out her reasons for doing what she did, Drew felt the need to respond. It wasn't that he didn't want to assist her financially, he couldn't afford to do so. He, himself was a student, and was being supported by his mother. Though considered wealthy, most of their finances were invested back into the company, to strengthen its stability. It was no secret how his mother felt about Karyme. To Nancy, Karyme was just like her daughter, but her financial support had nothing to do with paying Karyme's tuition.

 Karyme received a full academic scholarship from the University of Virginia, and while studying for her degree, she continued working for the company as a part-time employee. It was because of her dedication to the company that she was given a car. It was something Gloria never understood. Unlike her, he and Karyme had concentrated on their academics. But Gloria chose a different path, she chose to concentrate on having fun and hanging out with friends.

The morning continued, with Gloria ranting on about herself, while putting others down. It was an act that Drew should've been accustomed to, but he continued to find it irritating. Like everything else, the world revolved around Gloria, and no one else. Perhaps, it was what attracted Drew to her, but today a funny thing happened. Gloria began speaking candidly about her future and where she wanted to be in five years. My God, this wasn't the Gloria Drew was accustomed to being around.

Had she finally grown up, and was ready to build a foundation for a successful future? Drew couldn't say for certain, but she was on the right track to doing so.

Gloria went on to briefly discuss her future with Mason. She complained about his resistance to pick up the pace to better himself for a better future. It was no secret that Mason wasn't the sharpest tool in the tool box, but what he lacked in book knowledge, he made up for in common sense. He had the ability to do whatever he set his mind to doing. His only problem was that he was too lazy to do so.

In retrospect, Drew believed Gloria was just as confused as him, and was looking to find her way out of the maze she was trapped in. She had no idea what she was going to be faced with if she pursued a future with Mason. They were opposites in every sense of the word. Gloria was a professional, and was in the beginning stages of her career. Mason didn't have a career, nor did he give a damn about one. He was all about having fun and enjoying life. To be frank, he had only one goal, and that was to steal Gloria from him. After doing that, Mason had settled himself with the idea that he and Gloria would be sharing the rest of their lives together.

Opening a bottle of water for Gloria, Drew made the mistake of looking into her eyes. His body shivered; forcing him to look away. Gloria always had the ability to break him down, and today was no exception. Drew found himself wanting her, but he couldn't have her because she had chosen another man. In an effort to divert his attention back to her, Gloria used her hands to cup Drew's face, before resting her forehead against his. Her eyes were giving Drew permission to kiss her, but he didn't want to take advantage of the situation. It did however, present Gloria the opportunity she was hoping to receive.

"Drew Harrison, you are such an amazing man." Gloria said, before kissing him. Knowing he still had feelings for her, excited Gloria, and though she was Mason's girl, she felt no guilt with her plans to seduce Drew. Drew wanted to think better about his urges, but he overwhelmingly allowed his feelings to take control of his thoughts. He pulled Gloria close to him, kissing her passionately. It was no surprise that he wanted more, Gloria had been his girl since middle school, and a part of his heart still belonged to her.

There was no one to blame, they both had fallen in love with someone else, but their hearts kept them linked. Time had somehow run out on them; leaving this moment as their swan song. Drew was going to miss those fiery hazel eyes, and her broad smile that lit up the darkest of nights, but life had thrown them a curve; leaving them with only their memories to reflect upon.

"I know I shouldn't have done that, but I wanted to?" Gloria said, and after Drew didn't object, she followed with another.

She hadn't expected Drew to show any affection but welcomed it. He was putty in her hands, and from his actions, he was willing to go wherever she wanted to take him. It was wrong what they were about to do, but it felt so right. The feelings of excitement had resurfaced, after being vacant for years.

Gazing into each other's eyes, they tried hiding their feelings, but their urges were too strong. Without uttering a word, they were in each other's arms, kissing passionately. It had been less than a week since Gloria ended their relationship and they were now undressing each other. Knowing what was about to happen, Drew wanted to slow the process, but it was too late. His mind had shut down, and his penis was urging him to continue.

He wanted Gloria, and his aggression towards her exhibited it. Having the same thoughts, Gloria hesitated too, but like Drew, she wanted it. There was no mistake about her being Mason's girl, but today she was loaning herself to Drew. She reached for Drew's crotch, and began massaging his penis.

Next, Gloria unzipped Drew's denims, removed his fully erect penis, and began performing oral sex on him. It was the feeling of relief that Drew was in need of after experiencing the worst day of his life. Releasing a low moan, Drew raised to a crunching position, only to fall helpless back to the ground. Gloria was working her magic, and was doing it well. Making love to Gloria was only a temporary fix to his problems. Drew was devastated over what happened with Lynn, but this moment was temporarily numbing his pain. Gloria had his dick in her mouth, and she was polishing it like she had never done before.

Removing the straps from Gloria's shoulders, Drew stopped to admire her perfectly rounded breast. He placed both of her nipples in his mouth, applying the right amount of pressure to stimulate them, sending Gloria into a near frenzy. Drew's foreplay had always made her overly wet, and today was no exception. Gloria's low moans quickly escalated as she aggressively pushed Drew to the ground.

Gloria was determined not to be a disappointment, and climbed on top of Drew. Gripping his penis, she placed it inside of her. Her moans of pleasure became even louder, as she slowly rode him cowgirl style. She looked to the sky for guidance as she fought to accept every inch of him inside of her. She couldn't understand why making love to Drew felt so good, even though she was in love with another man.

It was mind boggling the way Drew knew her hot spots. He instantly drove her to an orgasm, followed by another, then another. Her body trembled from the intensity of the orgasms, and at one time it became so intense, she fell off of him. Gloria wanted their last time together to be an unforgettable one, and rode Drew like a wild stallion. Her mission was to satisfy Drew to the fullest, and from his reactions, she was doing what was expected.

It was the way they made love that kept Gloria wanting more. It was incredible the way their bodies reacted to each other. Their screams of pleasure were more than the proof she needed to answer any questions she may have had regarding their feelings for each other. Gloria had never stopped loving Drew, and though she couldn't understand why she did the things she did to him, the fact remained; she had a choice to make before it was too late to turn back.

Chapter: 31

As promised, Lynn returned to the beach house and into the welcoming arms of her mother, who eagerly awaited her return. As expected, Ashley wasn't there to greet her. Instead, she remained tucked away in her room, after visiting the Emergency Room to treat her injuries. It was official, Ashley had suffered a broken nose, created from a punch to the face from Lynn. Doctors were optimistic that she wouldn't need surgery, but would evaluate her further after the swelling subsided. Ashley was in extreme pain, and cried for most of the night. Though the pain pills helped some, it couldn't erase her embarrassment of being knocked out.

How was she going to face everyone, after being K.O.'d in the presence of her friends, who happened to be standing on the front porch. What were they saying behind her back, and how much teasing were they doing behind her back? Inside the house, Lynn hoped Ashley would be there to meet her. She wanted to apologize for what happened, but after not seeing her, she wondered if Ashley would ever forgive her for what she did to her. Unaware of the damage Ashley sustained by her hands, Lynn asked if she had left for home. Lynn was very remorseful for her actions, even though she believed Ashley was in cahoots with Marshall to destroy her relationship with Drew.

Regardless, if Ashley had played a critical role in her breakup, she was still her sister and shouldn't hold it against her. Learning of Ashley's injuries, Lynn slowly made her way down the hallway to Ashley's bedroom. Standing outside her door, Lynn placed her forehead against the door, building enough nerves to knock. After doing so, she lightly tapped on the door, and waited for permission to enter.

"Come in," Ashley responded.

Reluctantly, Lynn opened the door. She found her sister lying in bed on her back with a large ice pack pressed firmly across her face. Lynn was ashamed for what she had done, and wanted to do something to help. She walked to Ashley's bedside, and grabbed hold of her hand.

"Does it hurt?" Lynn asked, not knowing what else to say. She gently lifted the ice pack from Ashley's face and was frightened by what she saw. Both of Ashley's eyes were black, and her face was nearly unrecognizable from the swelling. Seeing the damage she'd caused, Lynn pleaded for forgiveness. She was remorseful for breaking Ashley's nose, and as a show of good faith, she wrapped her arms around her. Lynn rested her head against Ashley's shoulder, and told her how much she loved her, and how devastated she was for taking such drastic means.

There was no excuse for her behavior, and Lynn clarified it by saying, she was willing to do anything to rectify it. She had allowed her emotions to get the best of her, and the results were regrettable. Feeling the need to eliminate Lynn's guilt, Ashley promised not to hold what happened against her. It was the first step in forgiving her, even though it was by her own doing. Still, it was Ashley's way of calling a truce. She had allowed her envy of Lynn to cloud her judgment, and now saw how much in love Lynn was with Drew.

Ashley's strong emotional attraction to Drew would have to take a back seat to her love for her sister. Maybe sometime in the near future, she would plan another run after him, but as of now, her sister's mental stability was more important than going after the man she wanted.

"You didn't ask anything about what happened to Marshall?" Ashley said, while sitting up in bed.

"I don't even want to hear his name." Lynn replied.

"You probably don't remember, but when you punched him, the wine glass he was holding, nearly cut his nose off. I heard he needed nearly eighty stitches to attach it back on his face."

"Are you fucking kidding me?" Lynn responded nervously. She felt horrible for what she had done to Marshall, but at the same time felt vindicated.

Ashley went on to tell the story about his visit to the ER.

"I also heard, he stayed in the ER for nearly four hours and his nose was swollen beyond recognition."

Laughing, Ashley began poking fun at Marshall, making the comparison of his nose being bigger than his dick. Lynn instantly picked up on Ashley's comparison. How could she have known about Marshall's small penis? She never revealed his secret, and Marshall was too embarrassed to talk about it. Suddenly, the guilt Lynn felt for breaking Ashley's nose had disappeared. She was glad she had dusted the both of them. They were two of a kind, and they both got what they deserved. Lynn didn't care if they slept together or not, her only worry was Drew, and how she was going to convince him of the truth, about what actually happened.

The sisters remained in their room for the remainder of the evening being civil to each other, while pretending they'd buried the hatchet between themselves. Ashley continued to deny her role in setting up Lynn, by inviting Drew to the party. Even though her story was inconsistent with the events that occurred, Lynn chose to believe her. Lynn was hopeful they could rebuild their relationship, but was doubtful it would happen anytime soon.

With Ashley sleeping soundly, Lynn had time to think. Second guessing herself, she now believed she may had overstepped her boundaries by accusing Ashley of conspiring with Marshall. She wanted to trust her sister, but she couldn't shake what happened, and how it happened. The jury was still out on her suspicions that Ashley conspired with Marshall to end her relationship with Drew, but she didn't have the proof to substantiate her claim.

Lynn's heart was broken over the loss of the love of her life, and only his love could heal the void she had inside of her heart. Even though she had the feeling that it was useless to call Drew; Lynn had to try again. She remained optimistic that he wouldn't answer; accepting the fact that he needed time to get over what happened. Thinking she would have to leave another of the many messages, she'd already left, Lynn waited for Drew's voice mail. Much to her surprise, Drew answered. He was ready to talk, as well as listen to what she had to say. He was hurting too, and like her, he wanted to alleviate the pain in his heart. He needed answers, and in order to get them, he had to talk to her.

Lynn was given the time to explain what happened, but before doing so, she first had to apologize for not being honest about everything. She accepted full responsibilities for her actions, and assured Drew her love for Marshall no longer existed. She explained, she only agreed to help as a favor to Ashley, as well as to Marshall. Lynn understood her story was going to be a hard pill to sell, but by the grace of God, Drew listened. He pointed out the facts surrounding Ashley and Marshall's motive, and agreed they had concocted an elaborated scheme to break them up.

Drew was well aware of what Ashley wanted, but chose not to confide in Lynn. Although it was his opportunity to confess his affair with Ashley, he chose not to do so. His reason was that he didn't want to impose further distance between them. Instead of bringing up something that happened before they became a couple, Drew opted to bury the past and start over. He felt good about their chances as being a couple, and didn't want anything to interfere with their opportunity of being happy.

There was still much to discuss, but as of now, Drew's wish was for them to start over slow, and slowly rebuild their relationship to make it whole again. Drew and Lynn talked well into the early morning hours, before ending their conversation by exchanging "I love you's." They shared their innermost feelings, and made promises to never hold secrets from each other again.

In an effort to get their relationship back on track, Lynn invited Drew to the family's beach house to meet her parents. It was an invitation Drew was looking forward to accepting, but felt it was too early, especially after what had transpired between her and Ashley, but Lynn was determined to have Drew drive down. Lynn assured Drew that things were settled, and he would be what the family needed to move forward.

Chapter: 32

Lying in bed, listening to the soft ballads over the radio, Gloria fantasized about Drew and their perfect morning together. Not surprised by how her body reacted to his, she could feel his body moving against hers, as if they were making love. Drew had given her feelings, she had forgotten existed, and the thought of walking away from him scared her.

After being with Drew, Gloria wasn't sure if Mason was who she wanted, but he was someone she felt she needed. Her sexual experience with Mason wasn't anything remotely close to what she felt with Drew. Being with Mason left her feeling as if she had been violated. He was forceful; giving her a feeling no young lady should ever want to experience, but with Drew it was different. He was gentle, patient, and willing to do what it took to give her the feeling she desired.

There was no comparing the cousins when it came to making love. Drew won hands down, but he wasn't the man she wanted him to be. He wasn't a go and get it type of guy. He was willing to accept what came his way, without fighting for what he believed in. Mason won hands down, when it came to going after what he wanted. He proved it, time and time again, by doing what it took to get her. Mason was a safe bet, at least until she could find a man she wanted to spend the rest of her life with.

God knows, Mason wasn't by any means an attractive man by anyone's standards. His mannerisms sucked, his future was bleak, and he barely had enough money to pay for a cheap dinner and a movie, but he made her happy. His qualities consisted of his sexiness, confidence and his unpredictability, which reigned supreme. Never had Gloria found such a man so intriguing, a man that made her feel like the queen she wanted to be. Damn, if only he had the wealth of his cousin and shared some of his qualities, he would be the ideal man.

Aware of Drew's new relationship with the "Rich Bitch," Gloria didn't feel threatened by it at all. She controlled her own destiny when it came to Drew, and sleeping with him gave her the comfort of knowing that she could get him back, anytime she chose to do so. To be frank, Gloria knew she had many options to choose from. There were several young interns who wanted a piece of her, as well as a number of old ass doctors, who salivated, and would give anything to sleep with her. But it was something about Drew, that kept her coming back.

Perhaps, it was because she had the chance to live the rich life, or maybe it was because she knew, she could get away with cheating and Drew would forgive her and take her back. God knows, Drew was as boring as they came, but he was what she needed in bed. No one had made her feel as fulfilled as Drew, but unfortunately for him, she needed excitement in her life; something he was incapable of providing.

It was funny to think they were voted the couple to most likely marry, while in high school. It was a prediction that nearly came true, and it would have, if it wasn't for his little Mexican Aztec Princess. Karyme became a thorn in her side, the moment she and Drew became a couple. She had an influence on Drew that no friend should have, and because of it, she became the third wheel. Whether it was the movies, or an afterschool event, the little "WetBack" always found a way to worm her way into Drew's car with them.

It was true that Drew had given her a ring for Christmas, but by then, the significance of it had worn off. Before the ring, Drew hadn't done anything to certify his intentions, or show her how much he appreciated her; not like Mason had. Unlike Drew,

Mason was eager to pay for having her nails, and hair done, while giving her money to spend.

Drew on the other hand was cheap, and unwilling to do anything that included spending money. He always had an excuse, unless it included his little Mexican Aztec Princess. When it came to Karyme, Drew and his mother went outside the box. Maybe it was her fault for allowing it to happen for so long, without doing anything about it, but she didn't have to stress about it anymore. She was with a man who was willing, but not able, to give her everything her heart desired.

Chapter: 33

By ten o'clock, Drew was on the road headed to Virginia Beach. Today was the day he was going to finally meet the Boldmont's, and the thought scared him. He was skeptical about fitting in, or if he could operate on their level, but he was going to give it his best shot. For Drew, this trip meant everything. It was all about being accepted for who he was, and he wanted more than anything for that to happen. His mother by no means considered herself high class. She was a hard worker, who fought for everything she had. Hopefully Mr. and Mrs. Boldmont accepted him for who he was, but Drew knew that depended upon their first impression of him.

Still, there was his affair with Ashley he had to consider. The chances of it getting out could increase, now that he'd been invited to join the family. There was no doubt in his mind that Ashley and Marshall were behind the plot to breakup he and Lynn, and only God knows what else Ashley had up her sexy little sleeve.

The damage she could cause would be irreparable if she ever revealed what happened between them, but Drew was willing to take the risk. He realized he should have told Lynn, but his cowardly ways wouldn't allow him to. He had placed himself between a rock and a hard place, and he could only hope his visit would be a successful one.

Lynn sat nervously at the table for breakfast. She tried building the courage to announce that she had invited Drew to come down for the afternoon, but thought of the consequences it would cause. Her suspicion of Ashley's crush on Drew could present a problem, but she wanted her parents to meet the man she wanted to share a future with.

Lynn couldn't help but feel she had made a mistake by inviting Drew. Their family was healing from the disaster that occurred two days prior, and though they planned to spend a day together as a family, Lynn wanted Drew to be a part of it. Drew was too important for her not to include him, and Ashley had to see how much he meant to her, as well as his feelings for her.

Ashley had played a role in ruining her relationships with every boyfriend she'd ever had; including Marshall. For months, Lynn suspected that Ashley slept with Marshall, and it wasn't until last night that she could say for certain, her suspicions were correct. This time, Ashley was going to see the love she and Drew had for each other. Lynn remained in deep thought, as her father blessed the table. Not having realized it was time to eat, she continued to hold her head down in prayer. Seeing that Lynn was in another world, Ashley nudged her.

"Are you ok?" Ashley asked.

Lynn smiled and nodded yes.

She put her head down to eat her first bite of food. She also saw that everyone was looking at their phones and removed hers. It was time to check if there were any messages from Drew.

Excited that Drew had texted, Lynn knew she would soon have to announce his arrival. By Drew's estimation, he was scheduled to arrive by noon, giving her only two hours to prepare, but first she had to figure out a way to tell everyone of his pending arrival. With time dwindling, Lynn made the decision to announce it to her family.

"Mom, Dad, I need to talk to you guys about something?" Lynn said. She realized her announcement would most likely offend Ashley; especially after suffering from a broken nose, but time was becoming of essence.

"What is it dear." Constance responded.

"I invited my friend Drew for dinner tonight. I hope it's okay." Lynn asked.

She was nervous that she had made the decision without consulting the family, and was prepared to accept the backlash that was sure to follow. Well, as expected Lynn's announcement caught Ashley totally off guard. She was unprepared by her sister's sudden reconciliation with Drew, and quickly opposed the idea.

"Why did you invite Drew for dinner, without consulting us first?" Ashley screamed out.

Her cry, caused concern for everyone sitting at the table, including Lynn. She knew Ashley had the hots for Drew, but had no idea, how far it had gone.

"I didn't mean it, in that sense, I'm just asking, why would you invite someone to dinner, without asking if it was ok with us. My God, look at my face." Ashley explained.

Ashley nearly lost her composure, and as everyone looked at her, she tried back peddling to repair the damage she may have caused. Ashley displayed a fake smile, while voicing her support. It was going to be embarrassing for her, after introducing Drew to her mother as her friend without acknowledging he was actually Lynn's boyfriend. Drew's pending arrival left Ashley searching for answers. It was as if Lynn was rubbing salt in her wounds, and the way she was overly excited gave Ashley the impression that Lynn was retaliating for what she had done.

Lynn's sudden, and unexpected announcement, left Ashley at the mercy of their parents. It was up to their parents to agree to what Lynn had done, and she was hoping they wouldn't. Their parents' decision wasn't going to be popular with either daughter, but it was a decision that had to be made. If they decided not to allow Drew to spend the evening with them, Lynn would be devastated, and if they chose to allow it, so would Ashley.

Ashley listened, as their father was the first to speak. Looking across the table at his daughters and his wife, Harry began to express his feelings. He spoke about wanting to spend the remaining week together as a family to bond. It was important to him, that as a family, they repair the damage that nearly ripped them apart. From the position their father was taking, it was apparent that he was going to vote against Drew coming to dinner. But instead of standing up for what he believed, their father lost his nerve because he was fearful of what it would do to Lynn. As he put it, it was the least he could do, after what she had gone through. Ashley felt it was a bullshit excuse for her father to make. He wasn't going to say no to Lynn, regardless if she hadn't been ambushed or not. Lynn was his favorite, and he would do anything to please her.

As for their mother, well, she didn't give a holy shit about what Lynn wanted. She was all about doing the right thing, and the right thing was for the family to spend the evening together as one; without allowing an outsider to worm his way into it. Ashley believed her mother wasn't going for the old okie doke Lynn was trying to present. Constance wasn't going to allow an outsider to set foot in their cottage. Yep, her mother was surely going to put her foot down, and over rule Lynn and their father. Everyone knew Constance wore the pants in the family, which meant, whatever she said went.

Ashley listened, with a positive frame of mind, as Constance began to talk. Ashley leaned back in her chair, and crossed her legs, while expecting to hear her mother lay down the law. It didn't take long for Ashley to realize that Constance was about to follow suit. Like her father, Constance was siding with Lynn.

"What the hell was going on. How in the fuck was Lynn able to sway the both of them to side with her?" Ashley questioned herself.

Her mother was all about the rules and had no problem saying no to them, but all of a sudden, she had turned soft. Ashley hated the idea of having to see Drew with her sister, but her objection would only cause more controversy. So, she smiled and showed support. Needless to say, there was no breakfast conversation afterwards. Harry attempted to jump start it, by suggesting they visit some of Virginia's historic sights before the week was completed, but Ashley objected to going anywhere, with a broken nose. She was comfortable at home, where she could hide out from the public. She discussed staying the summer there, until she was fully healed, and even though her parents weren't keen with the idea, they eventually agreed.

Drew arrived later that afternoon, and found Lynn waiting on the front porch for him. Overwhelmed by his arrival, she ran down the stairs, and jumped into his arms, interlocking her legs around his waist. In doing so, she greeted him with the kiss of all kisses. She wasn't shy at showing her emotions, it was no secret how she felt about him. She was in love, and didn't care who knew it. Then again, it was a demonstration for Ashley to display her feelings for Drew.

It's fair to say, Drew's arrival was a positive sign. Drew and Lynn were putting their differences behind them, and working towards their plans of being together. From the way they interacted, it was obvious their feelings for each other were strong. Ashley stood at a distance, and watched her kid sister kissing the man she was in love with. She wished it was her, and would've given anything to make it possible, but it wasn't to be. To salvage what was left of their closeness, Ashley would have to forget the idea of having Drew for herself. Outside, were two people deeply in love, and ruining it by her obsessive ways would be devastating to her sister.

If there was such a thing as a flip side, then seeing Lynn happy after months of being depressed, brought some comfort to easing Ashley's misery. Maybe she deserved some happiness in her life, but damn, why did it have to be the man she wanted? After seeing more than her stomach could take, Ashley turned and walked away. This moment belonged to Lynn and her beau. It was their time, and though accepting it was tough, Ashley didn't want to be perceived as a sore loser. This was only a momentary set back, because sooner or later she was going to get another chance, and when she did, she promised herself she wasn't going to blow it. Lynn was happy for now, but her secret affair with Marshall was going to be revealed soon, and once it did, Drew would dump her, like a bag of trash.

Entering the house, Drew was greeted by Harry and Constance, who eagerly awaited his arrival. Harry was first to welcome him. From his first impression, Drew was everything Lynn had made him out to be. Mr. Boldmont was serious, but gentle, as he welcomed Drew into his home with a smile, and a stern handshake, but Constance on the other hand, well, she presented another story. Constance was cordial, yet distant, and just as Lynn had done to him when he first met her; Constance extended her hand far enough for him to touch the tips of her fingers.

Drew's first impression of Constance was an unfavorable one. For one, Constance seemed snooty, and she more less spoke down to him; treating him as if he was a second-class citizen. Still, Drew refused to allow Constance to hinder his visit. He understood they were meeting for the first time, and perhaps she would warm up to him later, but as of now, his attention was on Lynn.

Searching for Ashley, Drew glimpsed down the hallway, hoping she was nearby. He remained skeptical about her promise to keep their affair a secret; believing she was desperate enough to reveal what happened between them without any remorse. But now wasn't the time to think about the possibilities of what Ashley could do, Drew's focus was on Lynn.

Lynn was excited, and overly hyperactive. There were a million things she wanted to do, and sitting on the living room couch wasn't one of them. She quickly pulled Drew from the couch; whisking him away through the rear door that led to the beach. Her dream was to walk along the shores of the beach, while holding his hand, and she was anxious to do so. After their walk on the beach, the couple spent most of the afternoon on the strip, window shopping, and buying cheap trinkets to remember their day together.

On their way home, they stopped to sit on a bench that faced the ocean. They discussed their future together and shared dreams of traveling the world. Lynn couldn't have asked for anything better, because after being with Drew, it couldn't get any better.

Chapter: 34

Isolating herself, Ashley attempted to relax under her umbrella by the shores on the beach. The cool breezes temporarily soothed her throbbing face, but it couldn't soothe the pain in her heart. Her plans to have Drew in her life had gone south, but she regained the trust of her sister as a consolation prize. There were many men out there who were far better than Drew, and her chances of getting one was high, but she didn't want another man, she wanted Drew!

Constance soon joined Ashley and brought her favorite cup of raspberry tea, filled with crushed ice. She could tell Ashley had been crying, and felt an obligation to spend time with her. It hadn't taken a rocket scientist to know Drew was the reason Ashley was feeling depressed. To what extent, she wasn't sure, but she would soon find out, even if it took until dinner to do so. Feeling there was more to the story, Constance began pressing Ashley for answers. In the beginning, Ashley pretended nothing was wrong, and denied that seeing Drew with her sister had affected her. It didn't take Constance long to put two and two together to realize both sisters were in love with the same man.

Relenting under pressure, Ashley confessed to having feelings for Drew, and told her story as to why. She began by telling her mother how she introduced Lynn to Drew. Not wanting to leave any holes in her story, Ashley was meticulous about telling her story. She didn't admit to pawning Lynn off to Drew because she didn't want the responsibility of taking care of her. Instead, she took advantage of the moment, to take pot shots at Lynn. She told her mother that Lynn was aware of her feelings for Drew, and after being warned to stay away, Lynn went forward with her plans to steal Drew's heart.

"He was only supposed to show her the ropes, and nothing more." Ashley stated. "Before I knew what was happening, they were spending weekends together by the river."

Acting on a hunch, Constance inquired if Ashley was intimate with Drew? Reticent of her suspicions, Constance's inquiry presented Ashley with the perfect opportunity to butt fuck Lynn with a hot poker, and she didn't disappoint. Ashley not only admitted to sleeping with Drew, she left the false impression that she was still sleeping with him. It hadn't come as a surprise to Constance, she'd suspected as much. Thankfully, she had the ability to read Ashley like a book.

Armed with the knowledge of knowing Drew had slept with Ashley, Constance couldn't accept Lynn's relationship with him. As a mother, it was her responsibility to intervene in her daughter's life, especially if it wasn't going according to her expectation. The fate of Lynn's future was at stake, and Constance believed it was her obligation to do something about it. There was no way she could allow Lynn to open her heart to another dead-end relationship; only to have it thrown away.

Though concerned by the news of her daughter's unstable relationship, Constance became even more concerned after being informed that Lynn had slept with Marshall. Lynn's choices left Constance questioning her mental state. It was uncharacteristic of her to be so reckless. It was all making sense now; the outburst, the temper tantrum, and her unpredictable behavior. Maybe it was time she returned to the hospital for additional treatment. Lord knows, Lynn couldn't afford to suffer through another emotional rollercoaster.

Clueless on what to do to protect Lynn, Constance had to find a way to do what was best for her family. She needed to know more about Drew and decided to stay with Ashley to learn more. Wearing a bikini, Constance removed her mini crochet cover, and joined Ashley to enjoy a mother daughter moment. While soaking in the sun's rays, Constance and Ashley pondered on ways to interrupt Lynn's relationship with Drew, without having to cause a hardship, of course.

While discussing their plans, Constance found it strange that Ashley was willing to spill her guts without hesitation. It was unlike her not to protect her sister, and for that reason, Constance was left to theorize her daughter's intention to reconnect with Drew once the breakup took place. Her intentions weren't to break Drew and Lynn up in order for Ashley to close in on him, but wanted Drew out of both of their lives. The only problem was, how to do it without hurting both girls. The two women continued to lay by the ocean, listening to the water splash against the shore. Constance continued to contemplate on what to do, but ultimately knew whatever decision she made was going to affect Lynn.

After thinking more in depth, Constance began to have a change of heart. Lynn had been through enough, and shouldn't have to be subjected to further hurt and pain. Constance was appalled by the thought of Drew possibly sleeping with both sisters, but it wasn't enough to convince her to crush her daughter's spirit. Drew needed to be exposed for what he was allegedly doing, but it wouldn't be tonight.

Eventually, she was going to expose him for the dog he was, but tonight, she was going to be a gracious host. Suspecting a sure retaliation from her mother, Ashley smiled, and leaned back in her chair to sip on her raspberry ice tea. Her dream of having Drew back in her life resurfaced after getting the impression that her mother was going to expose him after dinner. With that in mind, the pain from her broken nose suddenly subsided. Ashley was about to receive the justice she felt she deserved, and she couldn't wait to receive it.

Drew and Lynn arrived back at the house three hours before dinner. On a whim, they made the decision to spend the rest of the evening on the beach. Dressed in swimwear, the couple snuggled together by the shore. Watching from the rear deck, Ashley gloated at the thought of what was about to happen, and wondered if she had enough time to recapture Drew's heart before his upcoming graduation. Ashley questioned whether she was doing the right thing by destroying her sister in her efforts to get the man she wanted, but she ultimately felt she had no other options. Playing dirty was the only way she knew, and after being successful at it for so long, she felt confident she would win her prize. Over the years Ashley learned that good guys always finished last, and finishing last wasn't something she was accustomed to doing. So, if being sneaky and underhanded meant winning, then she had no problem doing it.

Sitting at the dinner table, the family held hands in preparation of gracing the food. As the family bowed their heads and Harry began his prayer, Drew found himself looking across the table at Ashley. Maybe it was Ashley's swollen face, and badly bruised eyes that held his attention, but Drew found himself unable to take his eyes off of her. Seeing Drew staring at her, Ashley formed her mouth and sent him a gentle kiss. Drew quickly looked away to focus his attention back to Lynn; Ashley's quick glimpses and unnerving smirks were sending chills down his spine. She was reckless in her behavior, and it left him with the feeling that his train ride with Lynn was about to derail.

It was only a matter of time before the truth of their affair would come to light, and Drew was left feeling helpless. There was no doubt that he made a big mistake, by accepting Lynn's invitation to meet her parents, but it was too late now.

During dinner, Harry saw how nervous Drew had become, and tried to lighten the mood by introducing a conversation he felt

Drew was comfortable talking about. Harry began asking questions in regards to receiving his upcoming Master's Degree, as well as his long-term goals. His questions seemed to put Drew at ease, and placed him back on track after being visibly shaken. Looking on, Constance remained distant by not having much to say. It was as if she knew that he had slept with Ashley, and like Ashley, Constance made him feel uncomfortable with her unusual stares and quick smirks. It was as if she was analyzing him and waiting for him to lie, so she would have a reason to spill the beans.

Nervous, Drew felt Lynn's hand gently squeeze his leg, as if to tell him it was going to be alright. Her gesture gave him the confidence he needed to fight his fears. He took a deep breath to relax, then flashed his fake smile. It looked genuine, but hiding his fears was a hard task to accomplish. There was something about the evening that scared him. Maybe it was the way Ashley and her mother's conspicuous stare left him feeling. It was as if they were conspiring to expose him.

Thinking the worst, Drew believed his night was over before it had begun. His decision to drive down could potentially ruin his chances of reuniting with Lynn. After dinner, the family retired to the den to wind down over a fresh cup of Jamaican coffee. It was time to discuss current events, and bring to the table any problems that needed to be clarified. It was something Drew was familiar with, because it was what his family often did on a daily basis.

Discussing the daily events relaxed Drew enough to temporarily overshadow his paranoia. All was seemingly going well, now that dinner was over. Constance and Ashley had warmed up to him, and had begun engaging in conversation with him. Constance even smiled when he told the heartwarming story of how his family took in their housekeeper and her daughter when they were homeless. Drew hoped his story was enough to give the Boldmonts, a clear picture of what kind of family he came from. He also hoped his story opened the way for their trust in him to always protect their daughter from harm. In talking to Constance, Drew felt a sense of confidence in knowing that he was winning her over, but he still had Ashley to think of.

Ashley held the perfect hand of cards, and she was playing it like a champion poker player would. Seeing the way she played her hand, reminded Drew of the mistake he made by sleeping with her. In an anticipated move, Ashley zeroed in on Drew; bombarding him with questions pertaining to his overnight camping trip with Lynn by the river. Like Drew, Lynn was utterly dumbfounded at the idea that her sister would go as far as to mention their trip. There was undoubtedly a motive behind her madness, and before the night concluded, it was highly likely that Ashley was going to reveal her darkest secret.

Harry showed concern after learning about Lynn's overnight trip with Drew, and objected to the idea of Lynn moving so quickly to begin another relationship. She was still recovering from her ordeal that nearly rendered her helpless. By Harry's analysis, Lynn had prematurely made an unconscious decision to do something against their wishes. After that, it didn't take long for Harry to form an unfavorable impression of Drew. He was left with many questions regarding Drew taking advantage of his daughter's emotions. However, Harry wasn't one to jump to conclusions, and chose to play it by ear as the night progressed.

Constance on the other hand, wasn't as reasonable as Harry. She suspected Drew's plan was to woo Lynn into bed, if he hadn't already. She knew for certain, he had slept with Ashley, but did Lynn know? The thought alone was repulsive enough to scream bloody murder, but Constance couldn't; not until she was sure that she was doing the right thing. Although Drew and Lynn tried to clear up any misconceptions regarding their overnight trip, the Boldmont's had already formed their opinion. Ashley had thrown a monkey wrench into their evening, and from the looks of it, she was loving every second of it. To her credit, Ashley had kept her promise to keep her affair with Drew a secret, at least to Lynn. But then again, the night was still young.

As the evening progressed, Constance's negative impression of Drew transitioned into more of a neutral opinion. It wasn't enough to call him out, but it was enough for her to keep a close eye on him. Looking at him, she understood how it was possible for both girls to fall in love with him. He was charming, good looking, and though he was only managing a farm, his future was bright. But even with all of his qualifications, to Constance, Drew was still a wolf dressed in sheep's clothing. However, she couldn't expose him now because it would definitely create a rift within the family. Unsure as to what to do, Constance got up to refresh her husband's glass of cognac, and did the same for herself; leaving Harry to wonder if everything was alright with her. You see, Constance didn't like the taste of cognac, she preferred a glass of red, or white wine after dinner. Like Lynn, Harry had no idea of what Constance was about to do, nor did Constance for that matter, but out of respect for her husband, and her daughters, she chose to carry on as if everything was fine. She didn't have to think about what she was going to do; she knew the right thing to do was to stand down.

Refilling Harry's glass, Constance returned to take her seat beside him. Watching on, she saw how deeply in love Lynn had fallen with Drew, and knew she had made the right choice not to expose him. She couldn't say for certain if Drew was the predator Marshall was, but from her observation, he seemed to feel the same for Lynn as she did him. Though it was her job to unearth the truth, breaking her daughter's heart was something she couldn't do. If by chance Ashley was being truthful, and it was revealed she had slept with Drew, Lynn could be affected permanently.

Constance strongly believed, it was her responsibility to protect her last born, and for self-assurance, she needed to know more about Drew. She continued to inquire about his family life, and was impressed by his intelligence, as well as his vision for his family's company. Still, it hadn't excused his behavior. Constance's interrogation of Drew, led Lynn to become suspicious. It was apparent she had an agenda, and for some unexplained reason, it seemed personal. Seeing that something was about to unfold in front of her, Lynn felt the urgency to intervene. She joined Drew at the mantle, and placed her arms around his waist. She rested her head against his chest, as if to show her solidarity towards the unseen force that was trying to impose their will.

Lynn had no idea of the point her mother was trying to make, but from her past history alone, it wasn't good. Constance was on a mission, and Lynn was uncertain as to why. To redirect her mother, Lynn used several facial expressions to stop her from going further, but Lynn's efforts were disregarded. Constance continued to press forward with her interrogation of Drew. Out of respect, Drew remained calm, and carefully listened to each question before answering. It was apparent that Constance was attempting to intimidate him, but it hadn't worked. Her failed attempt hadn't deterred her effort, it only encouraged her to take another angle. Constance was disappointed that things hadn't gone as well as she'd hoped, but it hadn't stopped her from searching for any signs of weakness to capitalize on.

Showing no signs of weakness, Drew maintained a calm demeaner, without caving into the pressure Constance was applying. He remained jovial with Lynn at his side, and remained determined; nothing was going to ruin his night.

Yes, it was true that Ashley's presence was somewhat intimidating, but Drew had gone on with his life, and wanted Ashley to do the same. He couldn't change the events of what happened, but he'd chosen to put the past behind him. Although Constance relented on some of the pressure she was applying, it hadn't stopped her from prying into his personal life. She wasn't ashamed to ask questions pertaining to his love life, or his history of girlfriends. After all, as a mother it was her obligation to know the guy her daughter was involved with, and as a mother, she had the right to protect her daughter's fragile heart, no matter what she had to do to accomplish it.

"Drew, you're a very handsome young man. I bet you get propositioned all the time?" Constance asked.

Drew smiled; he wasn't sure how to answer Constance's question. Unsure if it was a trick question, he answered carefully.

"Yes ma'am, I do get propositioned sometimes. However, since being with Lynn, it is well known that I'm in a relationship."

"How many girlfriends have you had?" Constance followed.

"Mom, what's with the fifty questions?" Lynn asked, nervously. Her mother was up to no good, and it was up to her to nip it in the bud before all hell broke loose.

Though Constance's questions were unexpected, it didn't hinder Drew from answering.

"I've only had one girlfriend." Drew responded.

That was a damn good answer, Drew said to himself, as he looked down at Lynn. He kissed her forehead and smiled, before silently whispering; "I love you," to her. Seeing how comfortable Drew seemed, Ashley chimed into the conversation. Things weren't moving as smoothly as she wanted, and from her prospective, her mother was getting cold feet. If she was going to expose Drew for the liar he was, she had to get things cooking, and she did so, by uncovering more of Lynn's secrets.

"How long have you guys been together?" Ashley asked; directing her question to Drew.

She smiled to herself, as she waited for his answer. By answering, Drew would unconsciously reveal that Lynn had spent the night at his family's home before arriving at the cottage. Seeing the unorthodox question from Ashley made Lynn nervous. She worried that Ashley was about to reveal that she spent the week with Marshall. More than that, she feared Ashley was about to retaliate for being sucker punched, by telling Drew that she slept with Marshall. It was terrifying to know that Ashley held the power to destroy her relationship with Drew for good. Lynn felt helpless, and held her breath, as she waited for Drew to answer Ashley's question.

To Drew's credit, he was evasive with his answers, and never directly answered any of them fully. Instead, he hinted that they made their decision official at the end of the spring semester. For Ashley, it was the information she needed to get things started. Her eyes luminated by the information Drew had given her; she dove in head first. She wasn't directly interrogating Drew for the sake of exposing him, but getting enough information to implicate Lynn as a fraud in their father's eyes.

For the past year and a half, Lynn had been made a victim after her relationship with Marshall ended. She was the so-called angel, who was gullible and taken advantage of when it came to love, and for getting her heart broken, she was pampered. Lynn was given everything, from the car, to her dream of being appointed a position on the Board of Directors. It wasn't that Ashley didn't admire Lynn for fighting to regain her sanity. She just hated the way their father wooed over Lynn and gave her things she hadn't rightfully earned. His actions showed that Lynn was his favorite, and because of it, she could do no wrong in his eyes. But that was about to change, their father was about to learn just how much of a slut his little angel was.

It was shocking that Ashley would go to such lengths to throw her sister under a bus, but Lynn wasn't surprised. By all accounts, Ashley had shown her hand. She was not only making a case for herself with their father; she was placing her bid for Drew. Seeing what was about to happen, it was up to Lynn to fight and maintain the progress she made with Drew, as well as to protect her privacy from their father.

Ashley's dirty tactics continued when she revealed that Lynn had spent the night with Drew and his family, before arriving at the cottage the following afternoon. It was a despicable thing for her to do, but she had thrown her cards on the table; hoping it was enough to win the approval of their father.

Again, Ashley forced Drew to revert back into damage control mode. His explanation was heard and accepted by both parents, when he announced it was his mother's decision for Lynn to stay, only because it had gotten late and she didn't want Lynn to drive at night. Even though Drew's story was believable, it left questions, pertaining to his intention. It's fair to say that his stock fell faster than the February 2020 crash. Harry considered asking him to leave his home, but then thought better of it.

Though Drew's intentions may not have been as honorable as he would have liked, Harry couldn't overlook the positive effect Drew had on Lynn. It had been months since he'd seen her this happy; yet he still had reservations about Drew and his motivations regarding Lynn.

Constance was also enraged by Lynn staying the night with Drew. Like Harry, she believed Drew had taken advantage of Lynn's fragile heart.

Lynn was quick to fall in love, and eager to do anything to please the man she fell for; even if it meant lowering her standards to satisfy his needs. If Constance was going to attempt to help Lynn, she needed to do it now, but she couldn't. Lynn was too important to her to force her to choose between the man she loved, and the family that loved her.

Rather than use tonight to crack Drew's egg; Constance decided to wait. Tonight, she was going to entertain Drew, and evaluate him, as all parents do. She was going to learn his ways, and what made him tick. If by chance he wasn't suitable for Lynn, she would intervene at the appropriate time. So, after careful consideration, Constance made an executive decision to end Drew's interrogation, in spite of Ashley's willingness to continue. Ashley hadn't taken her mother's decision to end questioning Drew too kindly, and opted to go rogue. There was a lot more that needed to be said; one being to expose the truth between Lynn and Marshall.

In spite of the consequences that was sure to follow, Ashley was willing to lay down her hand, and expose her sister's secrets. Maybe, it was having to see that fucking smile on Lynn's face, that sent Ashley over the edge. Seeing Lynn hold Drew's hand was already enough to make Ashley puke. Unbeknownst to Lynn, their little love connection was about to end. In all honesty, Ashley didn't give a damn what her mother expected of her; she was taking the lead in deciding Drew's fate. After all, she had to get even with Lynn for punching her in her fucking face, and breaking her got damn nose.

Not to get it twisted, Ashley loved her baby sister, but that skinny bitch knocked her out in front of all of their friends. Not only that, she stole everything that belonged to her, and for that, she was going to have to pay. Ashley couldn't believe it, her mother wanted to scrap their well thought out plan and wondered why she would foil a sure thing?

Constance had gotten cold feet, just like that baby dick, snatch eating, asshole Marshall, who failed to pull off the plan of a lifetime. Still, all wasn't lost because by some miracle, that dumb fuck managed to sleep with Lynn, and by doing so, he had made her job easier. Taking on full responsibility, Ashley decided to move in for the kill, by intensifying her questioning, regarding Drew's relationship with Lynn. It was important to know when their relationship began, because Lynn had slept with Marshall, only three days ago. Yep, the shit was about to hit the fan, and everyone in the room was going to get splattered in it.

"Lynn told me you guys made it official about a week ago?" Ashley asked.

Ashley laughed to herself, as she waited for Drew's answer. It was highly unlikely that they made it official at the end of Spring Break, and if they had, she would have known about it. Even if they had made it official the night Lynn spent with Drew and his family, their relationship would have become null and void after the little slut slept with her ex-boyfriend. Drew thought carefully, before answering. He knew what Ashley was doing, but wasn't concerned about her revealing any information regarding their affair. Drew knew Ashley would never implicate herself in front of her parents while scheming to undermine Lynn.

Lynn questioned the validity of her sister's intentions to deliberately destroy her relationship with Drew. Never would she have ever imagined that Ashley would go so far to backstab her, while smiling in her face. Holding a glass of wine, Lynn gulped the remaining contents; hoping it was enough to numb the pain of Ashley ripping out her heart. Ashley was her sister, but you wouldn't have known it by the determination she was showing to undermine her. Ashley was on a mission and that mission was to destroy her relationship with Drew, and from the blank stare on Drew's face, she had successfully accomplished her goal.

Before Ashley could make her move, Lynn took matters into her own hands by stepping up to answer for her mistakes. She asked Drew if they could talk privately, and suggested they could go outside on the front porch. It was hard for her to believe that her sister was willing to rat her out, in front of Drew, and their parents. Outside, Lynn searched to find the words to tell Drew, that she had cheated on him with Marshall. She would have given anything not to break Drew's heart, but if she didn't tell him tonight, Ashley sure as hell was going to.

Drew became alarmed, when Lynn invited him to sit. As a man, he wanted to accept the news like one, but was reminded to sit to avoid tumbling like a house of cards. Had Ashley gone against their agreement, and told Lynn about their affair, Drew thought to himself. He couldn't say for certain if she had, but something bad was coming down the pike, and it left him fearing the worst.

Reading Lynn's facial expression, Drew saw that she was more scared than angry. It was at that moment he realized what Lynn was about to tell him had nothing to do with him and Ashley, but most likely involved Marshall. Taking a deep breath, Lynn regrettably began telling her story.

"Drew, there's something we need to talk about. I should have told you this before you drove down, but I was selfish, because I wanted you to meet my parents. But regardless of how you may think of me, after I tell you this, you must never forget how much I love you. I never meant to hold anything from you, but I didn't want to lose you."

Unsettled by the thoughts of what Lynn was going to say, Drew prepared himself to hear the worst. He was certain the controversy surrounded Marshall, but was unsure of its depths.

Nervously, he rocked back and forth in preparation of what was to come. Refusing to cry, Lynn stood strong. Though she was about to lose the love of her life, she felt obligated to tell the truth.

Forgetting about his own fears, Drew held Lynn in his arms. It didn't matter what she was about to say, his instincts were to comfort her. Lynn was probably going to break his heart, and seeing her struggle not to do so, was more than enough to make him want to help ease her pain. But before Lynn could confess her indiscretion, Ashley abruptly interrupted her.

"Excuse me, I didn't interrupt anything did I?" Ashley asked; giving Lynn a wink.

"We were kind of in the middle of something," Lynn responded.

"Well, save it for later. Mom and Dad want you to come in the house," Ashley said.

"For what?" Lynn questioned.

"They want to speak to Drew about joining us on our upcoming family vacation," Ashley said.

Ashley was lying her ass off, but that was all she could think of to get Lynn back inside the cottage.

Though her intentions were to destroy her sister's relationship with Drew, Constance had put enough fear in Ashley to think twice about any attempt to sabotage her sister's relationship. She decided against it because after Lynn had escorted Drew outside to confess her indiscretion, Constance got involved. She ordered Ashley to end what she started, and if she refused, she was going to strip her of all her privileges.

Her mother's threats were enough to change Ashley's mind, so she quickly ran outside to stop Lynn from confessing.

Ashley hated having to fold her hand without seeing her plan through, but her back was against the wall. She wasn't going to lose her lifestyle for a man, or anything for that matter. Sooner or later Lynn was going to screw up, because she always did, and when that time came, Ashley strongly believed that she would be victorious. She would have to come up with another scheme and a more detailed web of deception to get what she wanted.

Made in the USA
Middletown, DE
13 February 2023

24576175R00186